ROBIN
COOK

CURE

PAN BOOKS

First published 2010 by G. P. Putnam's Sons,
a member of Penguin Group (USA) Inc. New York

First published in the UK 2010 by Macmillan
This edition published 2011 by Pan Books
an imprint of Pan Macmillan, a division of Macmillan Publishers Limited
Pan Macmillan, 20 New Wharf Road, London N1 9RR
Basingstoke and Oxford
Associated companies throughout the world
www.panmacmillan.com

ISBN 978-0-330-52382-0

1 3 5 7 9 8 6 4 2

A CIP catalogue record for this book is available from
the British Library.

Typeset by Ellipsis Digital Limited, Glasgow
Printed in the UK by CPI Mackays, Chatham ME5 8TD

To Jean and Cameron,
my partners in life

Oh what a tangled web we weave,
When first we practise to deceive!

—Sir Walter Scott, *Marmion*,
canto vi, stanza 17

ACKNOWLEDGMENTS

ACKNOWLEDGMENTS

As per usual, the writing of *Cure* required the help of many friends, colleagues, and even strangers who were willing to take a phone call out of the blue and field a question. I am truly lucky to have access to a wide variety of experts who are graciously willing to give of their time. I thank you all. Those whom I would especially like to acknowledge for having demonstrated exceptional patience are (in alphabetical order):

Jean E. R. Cook, MSW, CAGS, psychologist

Joe Cox, J.D., LLM, tax, estate-planning, and corporate law

Rose A. Doherty, A.M., academician

Mark Flomenbaum, M.D., Ph.D., forensic pathologist

Tom Janow, detective, NYPD

Carole Meyers, research assistant, OCME, NYC

Marina Stajic, Ph.D., director of toxicology, OCME, NYC

KEY PLAYERS

Aizukotetsu-Kai: Yakuza organization centered in Kyoto, Japan

Vinnie Amendola: mortuary technician at OCME

Louie Barbera: temporary capo for Vaccarro crime family

Dr. Harold Bingham: chief medical examiner, NYC

Clair Bourse: receptionist at iPS USA

Michael Calabrese: private placement agent

Paulie Cerino: capo for Vaccarro crime family, currently in prison

Grover Collins: a kidnap expert and one of the founders of CRT Risk Management

Dr. Benjamin (Ben) Corey: founder and CEO of iPS USA LLC

CRT Risk Management: stands for Collins, Rupert, and Thomas, a team of mostly previous Special Forces agents who have teamed up to help victims of kidnapping in particular

Tommaso Deluca: young enforcer for Vaccarro crime family, hired by Louie Barbera

John Devries: head of toxicology at OCME

Vinnie Dominick: capo for the Lucia crime family

Yoshiaki Eto: enforcer for Aizukotetsu-kai in New York City

Kenichi Fujiwara: senior vice minister of Economy, Trade, and Industry for the Japanese government

Hiroshi Fukazawa: *oyabun,* or head, of Yamaguchi-gumi

Saboru Fukuda: *saiko-komon* of Yamaguchi-gumi in New York City

Kaniji Goto: Yamaguchi-gumi enforcer in Japan

Carl Harris: chief financial officer of iPS USA LLC

Inagawa-kai: Yakuza organization centered in Tokyo, Japan

iPS Patent Japan: fictitious Japanese corporation dealing specifically with Japanese patents

iPS USA: fictitious U.S. corporation dealing with induced pluripotent stem cell patents and associated intellectual property

Hisayuki Ishii: *oyabun,* or head, of Aizukotetsu-kai

Tom Janow: detective lieutenant of the Bergen County police

Kenji: name Laurie gave to Satoshi Machita's corpse before it was identified

Tokutaro Kudo: *saiko-komon* of Yamaguchi-gumi in Japan

Lucia Crime Family: Long Island Mafia family run by capo Vinnie Dominick

Arthur MacEwan: enforcer for Vaccarro crime family

Satoshi Machita: researcher with wife, Yunie-chan, and son, Shigeru

Duane Mackenzie: young enforcer for Vaccarro crime family, hired by Louie Barbera

Rebecca Marshall: identification clerk at OCME

MLI: medical legal investigator at OCME; they have forensic training but are not MDs; MLIs go out in the field to investigate deaths

Brennan Monaghan: enforcer for the Vaccarro Mafia family

Hank Monroe: director of identification at OCME

Mitsuhiro Narumi: *saiko-komon* of Inagawa-kai

OCME: Office of Chief Medical Examiner, New York City

Carlo Paparo: enforcer for the Vaccarro Mafia family

Maureen O'Connor: supervisor of histology laboratory at OCME

Oyabun: head of a Yakuza organization, or Mob boss

Ted Polowski: enforcer for the Vaccarro crime family

Twyla Robinson: chief of staff at OCME

Saiko-Komon: head adviser of Yakuza organization just below the *oyabun* in the particular Yakuza's hometown, or the boss of a splinter group in a different town

Hideki Shimoda: *saiko-komon* for Aizukotetsu-kai in New York City

Lou Soldano: detective captain, NYPD

Jack Stapleton: medical examiner, OCME, NYC

Laurie Montgomery-Stapleton: medical examiner, OCME, NYC

Ron Steadman: NYPD detective at Midtown North Precinct

Jacqueline Rosteau: Ben Corey's assistant

Naoki Tajiri: manager of The Paradise club in Tokyo

Colt Thomas: a kidnap expert and one of the founders of CRT Risk Management

Tadamasa Tsuji: *saiko-komon* of Aizukotetsu-kai

Vaccarro Crime Family: Long Island Mafia family run by capo Louie Barbera

Dr. Calvin Washington: deputy chief medical examiner, NYC

Riki Watanabe: enforcer for Hisayuki Ishii

Letica Wilson: nanny for Laurie and Jack's son, JJ

Marlene Wilson: receptionist at OCME

Warren Wilson: basketball buddy of Jack's who is the neighborhood gang leader

Yakuza: organized crime organization in Japan

Yamaguchi-gumi: Yakuza organization centered in Kobe, Japan

Chong Yong: enforcer for Hisayuki Ishii

CURE

PROLOGUE

It happened in the blink of an eye. One instant everything was fine, considering the fact that Benjamin Corey was breaking into a foreign biological laboratory; the next instant it was a disaster in the making, and Ben Corey went from reasonably relaxed to simply terrified. Within seconds of the overhead lights flashing on, flooding the entire floor with raw fluorescent light, a cold sweat rose on his forehead, his heart began pounding in his chest, and, of all things, the tips of his fingers became numb, a fight-or-flight symptom he'd never experienced previously. What was supposed to be a walk in the park, as described the previous evening in Tokyo by his Japanese Yakuza contact, was now threatening to be anything but. An elderly uniformed guard approached down the lab's central corridor, his visored hat tipped back from his forehead, a flashlight held high in his right hand near the side of his head. As he advanced he swung both his head and the flashlight beam down the aisles between the rows of laboratory benches. He held a cell phone against his left ear and spoke in a hushed staccato voice, apparently keeping Kyoto University's central security office apprised of his progress investigating a lone light that had suddenly gone on in an office of the third floor in an otherwise completely dark and supposedly empty building. Each approaching step brought forth an ominous jangle from a large ring of keys clipped to his belt.

This was Ben Corey's first episode of breaking and entering, and he promised himself it would be his last. He shouldn't have been there, considering the fact that he was an M.D./Ph.D., a graduate of Harvard Business School, and the founding CEO of a promising start-up company called iPS USA LLC. He'd formed the company with the hopes of shepherding the commercialization of human induced pluripotent stem, or iPS, cells and, in the process, turning himself into a billionaire several times over.

The specific reason that Ben was there at that moment was under his arm: several lab workbooks owned by a former Kyoto University researcher, Satoshi Machita. In the books was proof that it was he, Satoshi Machita, who had been first to make iPS cells. Ben had found the books in the side office from which he'd just emerged. Satoshi had told Ben exactly where the books would be and essentially authorized Ben to get them, which Ben had used as the rationalization for his participation in the break-in. But there were other factors as well: Over the previous couple of years, Ben had struggled through a midlife crisis that still robbed him of age-appropriate maturity. He'd divorced his wife, with whom he'd had three children, now grown; quit his steady job at a highly successful biotech giant; married his former secretary, Stephanie Baker, and quickly fathered a new baby boy; lost forty pounds and took up triathlons and extreme skiing; and embarked on the risky venture of iPS USA at a time when raising capital was difficult at best, and to do so required significant compromises on his part, particularly regarding the source of the money.

In the wake of such significant life changes, Ben began to pride himself on being a "doer" rather than a "spectator." When he'd come in contact with Satoshi Machita and the researcher's story, he'd jumped at the chance to become involved. Soon Ben had come to consider Satoshi's lab books as potential manna from heaven. If what Satoshi had said about being the first person to make iPS cells from his own fibroblasts was even half true, Ben was confident the books' contents were going to shake up the biotechnology patent world by supplying the foundation of iPS USA's intellectual property.

From then on, over a period of many months, Ben had personally taken responsibility to recover them. Even so, he'd not considered participating in the actual theft from Kyoto University until the Yakuza mob boss he'd met in Tokyo, in a meeting set up by an equivalent Mafia mob boss in New York who was supplying Ben's seed capital, convinced him how easy it was going to be. "I doubt the door to the lab will even be locked," the nattily dressed man in his Brioni suit had said when he'd met him at the bar of The Peninsula in Tokyo. "At two o'clock in the morning there might even be students working at their benches. Just ignore them, get whatever belongs to your employee, and walk out. There will be no problem, according to my sources. I have you set up with one of our finest Yamaguchi-gumi enforcers, who will meet you at your Kyoto hotel. You don't even have to go into the lab yourself if you don't care to. Just describe what you want him to get and where you think they will be found."

At that point the new "doer" Ben had thought there was poetic justification for him to actually participate in the final step of what had been a months-long process.

As important as the books were, he wanted to be one hundred percent certain the right lab books were taken. And on top of that, the rightful owner had authorized their recovery, so in his mind he was not stealing. Instead, he was acting as a kind of modern-day Robin Hood.

"We've got to get the hell out of here," the panicked Ben squeaked to his co-conspirator, the so-called "real" professional, Kaniji Goto. The two men were crouched behind one of the lab benches. In addition to the jangling keys, they could hear the uniformed guard's sandals scuffing against the lab's tiled floor.

With obvious irritation, Kaniji motioned for Ben to shut up. Ben took the order in stride, but what he couldn't abide was that Kaniji had withdrawn a dagger from somewhere inside his outfit. The sudden light in the room glinted blindingly off the knife's stainless-steel blade. It was clear to Ben that Kaniji was intent on some kind of violent confrontation instead of getting them the hell out of the building.

As the seconds ticked away and the guard drew closer, Ben upbraided himself for not aborting the mission when the supposedly professional Kaniji had first appeared an hour earlier to pick Ben up at his *ryokan,* or traditional Japanese inn. To Ben's horror, Kaniji arrived dressed all in black, as though he was heading off to a masquerade ball. Over a black turtleneck and loose black pajama-like pants he wore a black martial-arts jacket cinched with a flat black belt. On his feet were black cross-trainers. Clutched in his hand was a black balaclava. To make matters worse, he spoke only limited English, making communication difficult.

But the combination of poor communication, the

foreign locale, and the excitement of getting hold of the lab books all contributed to Ben's willingness to let the raid go forward, despite the alarm bells going off in his head. And now, as Kaniji crept forward, brandishing the knife, Ben's anxiety ratcheted skyward.

Hoping to avoid any confrontation between Kaniji and the guard, Ben quickly duckwalked forward and caught up with Kaniji. In desperation he grabbed Kaniji's belt and yanked him backward.

Losing his balance, Kaniji fell over onto his buttocks but was up in a flash, spinning in the process like the martial arts professional he reputedly was. Momentarily flummoxed about having been unexpectedly upended by his partner in crime, he still managed to restrain his reflex attack. Instead he confronted Ben with an aggressively defensive stance. The knife tip quivered inches from Ben's nose.

Ben froze in place, trying desperately to judge Kaniji's mind-set while fearing that any movement on his part might unleash the attack that Kaniji was actively suppressing. It wasn't easy. The balaclava Kaniji had donned before they had entered the laboratory completely masked his face, making it impossible to read his expression. Even the eye slits were featureless black holes. A second later both Ben and Kaniji were blinded by the guard's flashlight.

Kaniji reacted by pure reflex. Spinning away from Ben and letting loose with a scream, he charged at the shocked guard, lifting his knife above his head, holding it like a dagger. Ben also sprang forward and again grabbed Kaniji's belt. But rather than preventing Kaniji's forward momentum, Ben found himself yanked ahead. The moment Kaniji collided full tilt with the guard, Ben slammed into Kaniji's back, and all three plunged to the floor in a kind of writhing sandwich, with the guard on the bottom and Ben on top.

At the moment their bodies collided, Kaniji had brought the knife down suddenly, plunging its tip into the sulcus between the guard's collarbone and the top edge of his shoulder. When the group hit the floor the blade was driven home, piercing the man's carotid arch in the process.

Other than the whoosh of air expelled from Kaniji's and the guard's lungs as they all collided with the floor, the first thing Ben was aware of was intermittent jets of spouting fluid. It took him a moment in the confusion of the event to realize that it was blood. As Ben scrambled away he could see that the blood was coming in progressively smaller spurts as the guard's heart extruded the rest of his total of six quarts.

Although Kaniji was now covered with blood, Ben had been hit with only a few large drops, which ran down his forehead when he stood up. He'd feverishly brushed them off with the back of his free hand and then shook the hand.

For a second Ben stared down at the two intertwined bodies awash in red, one still struggling to catch his breath, the other motionless and pale. Without another thought, Ben took off. Clutching the laboratory books under his left arm like a football, he ran headlong back the route he and Kaniji had taken on their way to Satoshi's old office.

Bursting forth from the building's main entrance on the ground floor, Ben hesitated for a moment, not sure what to do. Without the ignition keys to Kaniji's aged Datsun, there was no need to retrace the route to where the car was parked in a small copse of trees. As his mind raced through various but not too auspicious possibilities, he was shocked into action by the distant sound of approaching sirens. Although lost in a foreign city, he was aware of the Kamo River off to the west, which knifed through Kyoto north to south, and was near to the *ryokan* where he was staying in the old city.

With the stamina of someone who participated in triathlons, Ben struck off using the stars as a guide to get to the river. He ran swiftly and smoothly, trying to be as silent as possible. After only three blocks he heard the police sirens trail off, suggesting that the authorities had already reached the lab. Clamping his jaw shut tightly, Ben upped his pace. The last thing he wanted was to be stopped. Anxious and trembling, he would have trouble answering the simplest of questions, let alone explaining why he was out running at that time of night carrying books taken from a Kyoto University lab. When he reached the river, he turned north and settled into a rapid but consistent stride, as if he was in a race.

THREE WEEKS LATER
MARCH 22, 2010 – MONDAY, 9:37 A.M.
TOKYO, JAPAN

Naoki Tajiri had been in the *mizu shōbai*, or "water trade," for longer than he cared to admit. Starting at the very bottom just after high school, washing sake cups, beer mugs, and *shōchū* glasses, he'd slowly moved up the ladder of responsibility. To add to his résumé, he'd made it a point to work in all manner of establishments, from the traditional *nomiya,* or drinking shop, to hard-core prostitution bar-lounges run by the Yakuza, the Japanese version of the Mafia. Naoki himself was not a member of any gang by choice, but he was tolerated and even in demand by the Yakuza for his experience, which was the reason he was the general manager of The Paradise, one of the most popular full-service night spots in the Akasaka district of Tokyo.

Although Naoki had begun his career in his small hometown, he'd moved to progressively larger towns over the years, finally reaching the big time in Kyoto, then Tokyo. Over the years Naoki had thought he'd seen just about everything associated with the water trade, including money, alcohol, gambling, sex, and murder. Until that morning.

It started with a phone call just before six a.m. Irritated at whoever was calling him just after he'd fallen asleep, he answered gruffly but soon changed his tune. The caller was Mitsuhiro Narumi, the *saiko komon,* or senior adviser, to the *oyabun,* or head of the Inagawa-kai, the Yakuza organization that owned The Paradise. For someone so senior to be calling him, a mere general manager of a nightclub, sent a shiver of fear down Naoki's spine.

Naoki feared that something horrendous had happened at The Paradise overnight and, as the general manager, it was his responsibility to be aware of everything. But it was something else entirely: something rather extraordinary. Narumi-san was calling to inform him that Hisayuki Ishii, the *oyabun,* or head of another Yakuza family, would be coming to The Paradise for an important meeting with Kenichi Fujiwara, senior vice minister of Economy, Trade, and Industry: a very high-level, politically connected bureaucrat. Narumi-san had gone on to say that Naoki would be personally responsible for the meeting to go well. "Give them whatever they need or desire," was his final order.

Relieved the call was not about a serious problem, Naoki then became curious why an *oyabun* of another Yakuza organization would be coming to an Inagawa-kai property, especially to talk with a government minister! But it was not his position to ask, and Narumi-san did not offer any explanations before abruptly terminating the conversation.

As the hour neared ten a.m., Naoki began to calm down. All was arranged. The regular furniture had been pushed aside and a special table had been placed in the center of the main cocktail lounge on the second floor. Naoki's best bartender had been hauled out of his bed in case there was a request for exotic drinks. Four hostesses had been summoned in case their services were required by his visitors. The final touch was an ashtray, along with an assortment of cigarette packages, both foreign and domestic, at each of the two seats.

The *oyabun* arrived first, along with a cohort of cookie-cutter minions, all outfitted in black sharkskin suits, dark sunglasses, and spiked, heavily pomaded hair. The *oyabun* was dressed more conservatively in an expertly tailored dark wool Italian suit, worn with highly polished, English wingtip shoes. His hair was short and carefully groomed, and his manicure was perfect. He was the epitome of the highly successful businessman who ran a number of legitimate businesses on top of his responsibilities as the head of the Aizukotetsu-kai crime family, operating in Kyoto. He passed the bowing Naoki as if Naoki was a mere fixture of the environment. Once ensconced upstairs at the table, he brusquely accepted a splash of whiskey while distractedly shuffling through the assorted cigarette packs. As an added distraction, Naoki had motioned for his shift manager to bring out the women.

Naoki went back downstairs to the open-air entrance to the street to await the arrival of his second important guest. Since The Paradise was open twenty-four hours a day, three hundred and sixty-five and a quarter days a year, there was no door, per se. Instead there was an invisible curtain of moving air that kept out the cold of winter or the heat and humidity of summer. The idea was to capitalize on public whim by making entering as easy as possible. It was rare for a passing Japanese man not to step inside, intending to stay just for a moment, and then to remain for an hour or two.

The ground floor of The Paradise was a large *pachinko* parlor. Even at that time in the morning there were more than a hundred seemingly comatose players sitting in front of noisy vertical pinball games. With one hand they caused ball bearings to shoot up vertically before cascading down beneath the glass of the machines' fronts. During the descent the stainless-steel balls smashed against various obstructions and byways. *Pachinko* inspired a near-fanatical devotion in many players, and though Naoki didn't understand it, he didn't care. The game was responsible for almost forty-five percent of the take of The Paradise.

Down the street, he could see the black sedans that had brought the *oyabun* and his retinue. Among the Toyota Crowns was the *oyabun*'s own vehicle, an impressive black Lexus LS 600h L, the new flagship of the Lexus brand and of the Japanese auto industry itself. The cars were all parked in an obvious no-parking zone, but Naoki wasn't concerned. The local police would recognize the vehicles and leave them be. Naoki was well aware of the unorthodox and fluid relationship between government authorities, including the police, and the Yakuza, as was certainly evidenced by the upcoming meeting he was hosting that morning.

Checking the time, Naoki felt his nervousness return. Despite the slight pleased smile Naoki had perceived on the *oyabun*'s face when the hostesses had appeared, Naoki understood that the *oyabun* might consider his being forced to wait as a sign of disrespect on the part of the vice minister. To Naoki's relief, however, the moment he turned his line of sight to the right, he was rewarded by the sight of the vice minister's cavalcade.

Bearing down on him half a block away were three black Toyota Crowns so close together as to be seemingly conjoined. The middle one stopped directly in front of Naoki. Although Naoki extended a hand to open the vehicle's rear door, a team of black-suited men with earpieces jumped from the two other cars and waved Naoki off. Naoki hastily complied.

Naoki bowed deeply when Kenichi Fujiwara stepped out onto the sidewalk. The man, who was dressed almost as sumptuously as the *oyabun*, hesitated briefly while glancing up to survey the ten-story façade of The Paradise. The five upper floors of the building were part of a love hotel, whose themed rooms could be rented by the hour or by the day. Kenichi's expression was of mild disdain, suggesting the location had not been his choice. Regardless, he proceeded to enter The Paradise through the curtain of air by bypassing the bowing Naoki with the same disregard that the *oyabun* had exhibited on his arrival fifteen minutes earlier.

As Naoki straightened up and rushed ahead to gain the lead, he called out to his arriving guests loudly enough to be heard over the racket of the *pachinko* balls: "The meeting is to be held on the second floor. Please follow me!"

Upstairs, the hostesses were giggling and shyly covering their mouths. A moment later they found themselves swept to the side as the *oyabun* abruptly stood up from the table as he caught sight of the vice minister. Without complaint, the girls quickly retreated to the bar.

Although the two entourages eyed each other with a mixture of disdain and a twinge of suppressed hostility, the greeting between the two principals was cordial and painstakingly equal, like that of two friendly businessmen.

"Kenichi Fujiwara Daijin!" the *oyabun* said in a clipped, forceful voice, giving equal emphasis to each syllable.

"Hisayuki Ishii Kunicho!" the vice minister said in a similar manner.

At the same time they spoke they both bowed to each other at precisely the same angle, respectfully lowering their eyes in the process. Then they exchanged business cards, the vice minister first, holding out his card clasped by both thumbs and both forefingers while repeating a shallower bow. The *oyabun* then followed suit, mimicking the minister with precision.

Completing the business-card ritual, the men briefly turned to their respective attendants, and with simple glances and slight nods of the head directed them to opposite sides of the room. At that point the *oyabun* and the vice minister sat down, facing each other across the expanse of the mahogany library table that had been found for the occasion. Each carefully placed the other's business card front and center, exactly parallel to the table's side.

Without specific instructions to the contrary, Naoki, who was obviously not to be acknowledged, remained within earshot in case either of his two distinguished guests had any requests. He stood silently off to the side and tried vainly not to hear what was said. In his business, knowledge could be dangerous.

After a series of pleasantries, reaffirming their mutual respect, Kenichi got down to business. "We haven't much time before my presence will be missed at the ministry. First let me express my sincere appreciation for your willingness to have made the tedious drive from Kyoto to Tokyo."

"It was no bother," Hisayuki said with a casual wave of his hand. "I had reason to come to Tokyo for one of my other business ventures."

"Second, the minister himself sends his regards and hopes you understand that he would have much preferred to have had this meeting with you instead of me. He was unfortunately called to an unexpected meeting with the prime minister."

Hisayuki didn't respond verbally. Instead he merely nodded his head to indicate he'd heard. In truth the sudden change early that morning had irked him, but for fear he might risk cutting off his nose to spite his face, he'd accepted the alteration. A high-level meeting with the government, whether it was with the minister or the vice minister, was too unique not to be taken advantage of. Besides, in many ways the vice minister was more powerful than the minister. He was not an appointee of the prime minister but rather an established civil servant. And Hisayuki was curious about what the government wanted, and even more curious about what they would offer. Everything between the Yakuza and the government was a negotiation.

"I also want you to know that we would have liked to have come to Kyoto, but with the world economy and national economy as they are, we are continuously hounded by the media and felt we couldn't take the risk. It is important that this meeting between us is strictly kept from the media. The government needs your help. You know as well as I, Japan does not have the equivalent of a CIA or an FBI."

With some effort Hisayuki suppressed a contented smile. As a born negotiator, he loved being approached for a favor by someone capable of helping him. With his interest piqued, Hisayuki leaned over the table to bring his face closer to Kenichi's. "Is it safe to assume in this particular circumstance that it is my reputed position as the *oyabun* of a Yakuza family that affords me the opportunity of being able to help the government?"

Kenichi leaned forward as well. "It is precisely the reason."

Despite Hisayuki's attempts to avoid it, a slight smile appeared on his face, forcing him to contradict his mantra of showing no emotion when negotiating. "Excuse me if I find this ironic," he said as he controlled his expression. "Isn't this the same government that passed the anti-gang laws of 1992 now asking for help? How can that be?"

"As you know, the government has always been ambivalent to the Yakuza, and those laws were passed for political reasons, not for law enforcement. On top of that, they haven't been particularly enforced. More to the point, an equivalent to the American RICO Act has not been passed, and without such a law our anti-gang laws could never be truly enforced."

Hisayuki tented his fingers. He liked where the conversation was going. "The irony is that the anti-gang laws have not had as much influence on vice operations as they have had on our legitimate businesses. Would you be averse to looking into some of these specific circumstances if I were to help you and the government?"

"That is specifically what we were planning to offer. The more legitimate the operation or company, and the freer it appears from Yakuza control, the more we can do. It will be our pleasure."

"One other question before telling me what it is you are requesting: Why me? Why the Aizukotetsu-kai? Compared to the Yamaguchi-gumi or even the Inagawa-kai, we are very small."

"We've come to you because you and Aizukotetsu-kai, as the ascendant Yakuza of Kyoto, are already involved."

The *oyabun*'s eyebrows rose slightly, reflecting as much surprise as confusion. "How do you know we are involved, and what exactly is the issue?"

"We know you are involved because of the strong position you have taken in the relatively new company called iPS Patent Japan through your equity company, RRTW Ventures. With that much stock involved, we assume you feel, as the government does, that induced pluripotent stem cell technology is going to dominate the biotech industry for the next century. Most of us believe that within a decade or so these iPS cells are going to be the source of cures, not mere treatments, for a multitude of degenerative diseases. And they will spawn a highly profitable industry in the process. Am I correct?"

Hisayuki did not move.

"I'm going to take your silence as a yes. I'll also assume, because of the size of your investment, that you believe Kyoto University was ill equipped to deal with the patent aspects of the breakthroughs emanating from their stem cell labs, because that's specifically what iPS Patent Japan was to rectify and manage."

Kenichi paused again, but Hisayuki remained as immobile as a statue, taken aback by the accuracy of what he was hearing. He had no idea that the position he had taken in iPS Patent Japan was something the government would know about, since the company was still private.

After clearing his throat and waiting a moment to see if the *oyabun* wanted to respond, the minister continued: "To say that the Ministry of Economy, Trade, and Industry is concerned that our nation is in peril of losing its ascendancy in this critically important field of commercializing iPS technology to the Americans would make a mockery of our true feelings. We are desperate, especially as the Japanese public has already accepted Japan's ascendancy in the field as a point of national pride. Even worse, we have recently come to learn that there has been a critical defection of a researcher from the Kyoto University stem cell lab."

As if waking from a trance, Hisayuki straightened and blurted: "A defection to where?" The old-school Yakuza, like the Japanese extreme political right wing, were passionately patriotic. To him such behavior of a Japanese researcher would be anathema.

"To America, of course, which is why we are so

concerned: New York, to be more specific. The defection has been engineered by a start-up company called iPS USA, which plans to take advantage of the patent chaos in the stem cell arena and with iPS technology in particular. Although the company is reported to be in the 'stealth mode,' it seems that their goal will be to corner all relevant intellectual property in this promising field."

"Meaning they could end up controlling what promises to be a trillion-dollar industry, an industry that Japan rightfully should control."

"Well said."

"How much of a threat is this defector?"

"Enormous. iPS USA teamed up with a Yamaguchi-gumi cohort here in Tokyo with help from some New York Mafia connections in order to carry out industrial espionage in Kyoto. There was a break-in at their facility—a university security agent was killed—and they were able to acquire the only hard copies of the defector's work. These highly valuable lab books were irresponsibly stored in an unlocked file cabinet in a Kyoto University lab. It's a complicated and potentially disastrous mess."

Hisayuki had heard vague rumblings about the Kyoto University break-in, even about the security guard's death, but nothing about it involving the rival Yamaguchi-gumi. He knew there had been other attempted inroads by the Yamaguchi-gumi into his territory. In contrast to the other Yakuza families, the Yamaguchi, centered in the city of Kobe, flaunted tradition by being an expansionistic organization across Japan. But the idea that they were aiding an American concern by conducting industrial espionage in Kyoto was an outrage of the highest order. As the *oyabun* of Aizukotetsu-kai, he had to protect the investment in iPS Patent Japan.

"Why is this researcher's work so important?"

"Because of what he did behind everybody's back. As I understand it, he was working on mice stem cells and mice iPS cells as directed by higher-ups. But on his own time, he was working on human cells. In fact, he was working on his own cells from self-done biopsies from his forearms. As it turned out, he was the first to produce human iPS cells—not his bosses, who have taken credit. When he tried to point this out to his superiors at the university, he was ignored, then terminated, and then denied entrance back into the lab to collect his personal effects. Those personal effects included hard copies of his work that backed up his claims and that had been purposefully deleted from the university's computer. The man was treated abominably, though by standing up for his rights, he has been ignoring Japanese custom. Competition in today's academia, with its close association with industry, can be brutal."

"What do you think is going to happen?"

"What is already happening!" Kenichi said indignantly. "In fact, how we originally became aware of this whole mess was internally, from the Japan patent office. With iPS USA's help, our defector has already initiated suit against Kyoto University and against the validity of their iPS patents by retaining one of the most prestigious patent lawyers in Tokyo. In contrast to his previous lab bosses, he had no contract with the university concerning ownership of his work, meaning he owns it and not the university. He now has a series of U.S. patents pending, which will clearly challenge Kyoto's patents at the WTO here in Japan, as well as those held by a university in Wisconsin, since the United States recognizes the time of the invention, not the time of filing. They're the only country in the world to do so."

"This is obviously an emergency," Hisayuki snapped, with his face flushing. Inwardly he was bemoaning his decision to invest so heavily in iPS Patent Japan. If this scenario the vice minister was portending actually came to pass, the market value of iPS Patent Japan would fall to near zero. Angrily he demanded, "What is the name of this traitorous defector?"

"Satoshi Machita."

"Is he from Kyoto?"

"Originally, yes. But now he and his immediate family, including both sets of grandparents, are now quasi-domiciled in the USA and are fast-tracked to become legal residents. This all happened thanks to the collusion between the Yamaguchi-gumi and iPS USA, but mostly the Yamaguchi-gumi, who were responsible for getting them out of Japan and into the States. We're not sure why the Yamaguchi would do such a thing, but it could be due to a financial association with iPS USA."

"Where in the States is Satoshi living?"

"We have no confirmed information. We have no address. We're assuming he is in New York, as that is where iPS USA is located and he is a member of the company's scientific advisory board."

"Does he have family remaining in Kyoto?"

"I'm afraid not. Not immediate family. The Yamaguchi moved everyone, including his wife, an unmarried sister, and all four grandparents."

"It seems that you are informing me of all this rather late."

"Most of what I am telling you has come to our attention only over the last few days after the patent office was alerted to the initiation of the legal action. And Kyoto University hasn't helped. They only informed us what was missing after the break-in when we asked them directly."

"What is it that you would have me advise the Aizukotetsu-kai to do if I had the power to make some suggestions, which I'm not about to admit to?"

The vice minister cleared his throat by coughing into his closed fist. He was not at all surprised by the *oyabun*'s ridiculous caginess, and responded in kind. "I'm not going to presume that I can tell the Aizukotetsu-kai how to run their organization. I felt it was important for me to tell someone what the current situation is and what the immediate dangers are to the Aizukotetsu-kai and its portfolio, but nothing more than that."

"But something has to be done and done soon!"

"I totally agree, as does the minister and even the prime minister, but for obvious reasons our hands are tied. Yours, however, are not. You do have branch offices in New York, do you not?"

"What branch offices are you referring to, Fugiwara-san?" the *oyabun* questioned innocently, raising his bushy eyebrows for effect. There was no way he was going to tacitly acquiesce to such a statement, despite its being relatively common knowledge on the street.

"With all due respect, Ishii-san," the vice minister said with a slight bow, "there is no time for posturing. The government is well aware of Yakuza operations in America, and their ties with local crime organizations. We know it is happening, and, to be honest, we are actually happy about your sending as much crystal meth to America as you do, since it means that it is much less of a problem here at home. Your other activities in terms of gun smuggling, gambling operations, and vice we are not so fond of, but it has been tolerated in case your connections could prove beneficial in some future circumstance, as in the current unfolding calamity."

"Perhaps there are some acquaintances to whom I can pass along this information you have graciously provided," Hisayuki said after a short pause. "Perhaps they can think of something that may aid both of our interests."

"That's the way it is supposed to work, and we at the ministry—in fact, the entire government—would be most appreciative."

"I cannot promise anything," Hisayuki quickly added as he weighed ideas. He knew they had to find the defector immediately, which he felt would not be a problem. But the perfidy of some Yamaguchi-gumi gang flouting established rules and operating in his city of Kyoto without his permission was a different problem. It could not be tolerated. He hoped it involved an isolated, renegade gang, and it was done without the knowledge of the Yamaguchi-gumi *oyabun*. Before he embarked on any course of action here at home, he vowed to find out that crucial bit of information. But he was limited by the reality that the Aizukotetsu-kai were dwarfed by the Yamaguchi-gumi like a developing nation facing a superpower.

"One thing that I would like to emphasize," the vice minister said. "Whatever is to be done, particularly in America, must be done with the utmost discretion. Any harm to the defector must appear to be natural, and the

Japanese government cannot be implicated in any way or form whatsoever."

"That is a given," the *oyabun* said distractedly.

TWO DAYS LATER
MARCH 24, 2010 – WEDNESDAY, 4:14 P.M.
NEW YORK CITY

Satoshi Machita signed his name boldly and applied his personal *inkan* seal on all five copies of the agreement giving iPS USA exclusive world licensing rights for his pending iPS patents.

The contract provided for a fair and highly lucrative rate, including liberal stock options that would be in effect for the next twenty years. With a final flourish Satoshi raised his pen to those people present and acknowledged their excited applause. The signing represented a new chapter in both Satoshi's life and the future of iPS USA, which was now positioned to control the worldwide commercial development of induced pluripotent stem cells, which most molecular biologists were convinced would provide a cure for human degenerative disease. It was to be a revolution in the history of medicine, a breakthrough that would dwarf all others.

As the president and CEO of iPS USA, Dr. Benjamin Corey was the first to step forward and shake Satoshi's hand. Flashes popped among the cheers, intermittently washing the two men with bursts of frosty blue light. The six-foot-four, flaxen-haired Corey dwarfed his dark-haired companion, but no one took notice. Both were equal in the eyes of the witnesses, the larger man in biotech venture capital, the smaller in the rapidly advancing field of cellular biology.

At that point other members of the iPS USA team approached to shake the hand of the world's newest multimillionaire-to-be. The team included Dr. Brad Lipson, COO; Carl Harris, CFO; Pauline Hargrave, chief counsel; Michael Calabrese, placement agent responsible for raising a significant amount of the company's start-up capital; and Marcus Graham, chairman of the scientific advisory board, of which Satoshi was a member. As the mutual congratulations continued, since everyone present was certain to become much, much richer, Jacqueline Rosteau, Ben's private secretary/assistant, popped the corks of several chilled bottles of 2000 Dom Pérignon, and everyone cheered anew at the festive sound.

Drawing to the side with full glasses of champagne, Ben and Carl contentedly glanced out the front windows of Ben's office onto Fifth Avenue. The building was close to the corner of 57th Street, a busy part of the city, especially as rush hour neared. With a slight spring rain falling, many pedestrians carried umbrellas, and from above they looked like scurrying, insect-like creatures with black carapaces.

"When we first started talking about iPS USA," Carl mused, "I never would have guessed in a million years we'd get this far this fast."

"Nor I," Ben admitted. "You can take a lot of credit for having found Michael with his boutique investment firm and his unique clients. You're one in a million, my friend. Thanks."

Ben and Carl had been friends during college but had gone their separate ways. While Ben went to medical school, Carl had gone on to get an advanced degree in accounting. From there he'd gone into the finance world, from which Ben had recruited him with the founding of iPS USA.

"Thank you, Ben," Carl said. "I try to earn my keep."

"And it certainly wouldn't have happened if we hadn't learned of Satoshi's existence, what he had accomplished, and how badly he'd been treated."

"In that regard the real breakthrough was getting physical possession of his lab books."

"You're right about that, but don't remind me," Ben said with a shudder. Despite the passage of more than three weeks, thinking about the experience and his harebrained decision to participate still gave him chills. It had been a miracle that he'd not been nabbed along with his accomplice that night.

"Has there been any fallout in Japan?"

"No, not that I know of, and Michael insists his contacts haven't heard anything, either. The Japanese government certainly has a strange, widely known but never acknowledged bedfellow-type relationship with their Yakuza, which is the antithesis of our government's dealings with our Mafia."

"Speaking of the Mafia," Carl said, lowering his voice. "Are you worried about their continued involvement?"

"Of course, I don't like it," Ben admitted. "But as our largest angel investor along with their Yakuza partners, and considering the role they have played in our obtaining the lab books and getting Satoshi and his family over here so quickly, you have to grant we wouldn't be where we are if it hadn't been for their input. But you're right. Continuing to allow their participation is like playing with fire, and it has to change. I spoke with Michael earlier about this very issue before Satoshi arrived, and he and I are going to meet in his office tomorrow mid-morning. He understands and agrees. I told him that as of today, his clients' role has to revert back to their being silent investors, nothing more. We can offer some stock options to make them fade away."

Carl raised his eyebrows, doubtful it would be so simple, but didn't respond. Satoshi had come over to say good-bye and excuse himself from the party. "I want to get home to my family and give them the good news," he said, bowing collectively to both Ben and Carl.

"We understand perfectly," Ben said, exchanging a high-five with the diminutive and youthful-appearing researcher. When Ben had first met him he thought he was in his teens instead of his middle thirties. "Did you get a chance to meet with Pauline about those wills and trust documents?"

"I did and signed them all."

"Terrific," Ben said, exchanging another high-five. Satoshi had gotten his Ph.D. at Harvard and was well versed in American customs. After another round of handshakes, mutual congratulations, and promises to get together socially, Satoshi turned to leave, only to return after just a few steps.

"One thing I wanted to ask," Satoshi said, looking directly at Ben. "Have you been able to make any progress on finding me lab access?" Still in its infancy, iPS USA was merely office space in the building on Fifth Avenue. It had no research facilities of its own and probably never would. Its business plan was to take advantage of the chaos associated with patents involving stem cells in general and induced pluripotent stem cells in particular. The idea was to corner the stem cell market by controlling the intellectual property associated with other people's discoveries, and to do it before others knew what iPS USA was up to: a kind of intellectual-property blitzkrieg.

"Not yet," Ben admitted. "But I believe I'm making progress up at Columbia Medical Center to rent some space in their new stem cell building. We should hear any day now. Stop in or give a call tomorrow! I'll phone up there first thing in the morning."

"Thank you," Satoshi said while bowing. "I am very happy."

"Keep in touch!" Ben said, giving the smaller man a friendly slap on the shoulder.

"Hai, hai," Satoshi replied, and continued out.

"Research space?" Carl questioned after Satoshi left the room.

"He's yearning for some bench time," Ben said. "He feels a little like a fish out of water when he's away from the lab."

"I have to say, you guys have hit it off."

"I suppose," Ben said vaguely. "Jacqueline and I have taken him and his wife out to dinner a couple of times here in the city. He's got a little boy, a year and a half old. I tell you, the kid doesn't even look real, and he's silent. Not a sound. He just looks around with these huge eyes as if he's taking it all in."

"What is he going to do in the laboratory?" Carl questioned, ever the bean counter. "Isn't that going to be expensive?"

"He wants to work on electroporation techniques for iPS generation," Ben said with a shrug. "I don't know exactly, nor do I particularly care. What I do care about is keeping him happy, which is why we rushed to get him and his family into the States ASAP, without waiting for formalities to be completed. He's a real researcher at heart and considers all the legal negotiations a waste of time. We don't want him straying and changing his mind until we get everything completely buttoned up, patentwise. He's going to be our golden goose, but only if we keep him contentedly in the nest."

"So, right now, he's an illegal alien."

"I suppose, but it will soon change. I'm not concerned. Thanks to the secretary of commerce, the American consulate in Tokyo is in the process of getting them all green cards."

"Where do he and his family live?" Carl questioned. Given Satoshi's importance to the success of iPS USA, Carl felt it would be wise to know where he was at all times.

"I don't know," Ben said. "Nor do I want to know, if someone from the authorities were to ask. I don't think Michael even knows. At least that was my impression the last time we spoke about it. I do have Satoshi's cell phone number."

Carl laughed quietly, more out of amazement than humor.

"What's so funny?"

"Oh, what a tangled web we weave when first we practice to deceive," Carl said.

"Very clever!" Ben said sarcastically. "Are you trying to say that we shouldn't have brought Satoshi into this when our efforts at industrial espionage turned up his name and history?"

"No, not necessarily. It's just that I'm uncomfortable with our involvement with the Lucia family."

"All the more reason for us to sever all contact. It might require a bit more stock options to make them go away than I'm hoping, but it will be more than worth it. I'll leave the negotiations in your and Michael's capable hands."

"Thanks a lot!" Carl murmured equally sarcastically. "Hey, what was that about Pauline and trust documents? What kind of trust?"

"Satoshi is a little paranoid about Kyoto University and having bailed out of Japan. He worries about his wife and child if something were to happen to him. I realized that it was a good idea for iPS USA to have some safeguards in place as well. So I asked Pauline to talk to him, and she set him up with a couple of wills for him and his wife and a trust for the kid. Of course we stuck a statement in it that will also preserve our license agreement."

"Who's the trustee for the kid?"

"I am. Not my idea, but we can consider it an extra layer of safety."

Satoshi Machita was elated. As he descended in the elaborately decorated, art deco elevator, he realized he'd never been quite so happy in all his life. He'd just moved to the United States, and he and his family were occupying a house just across the George Washington Bridge from Manhattan. Of course, there were a number of things he would eventually miss from his old life in Japan—the cherry blossoms blooming around the glorious temples of his home city of Kyoto, and the view of the rising sun from the peak of Mount Fuji—but those serene pleasures would always be trumped by the sense of freedom he felt about life here: a life that he had learned to love while at Harvard and living in Boston. What he was not going to miss about Japan was the smothering sense of duty he'd struggled with for as long as he could remember: duty to his grandparents, duty to his parents and teachers, duty to his lab bosses and to the university higher-ups—even duty to his community and ultimately his country. There had never been any relief.

He paused inside the building's entrance to look out through the fogged glass at the scurrying pedestrians and the snarled confusion of yellow taxis and city buses attempting to head downtown in the light rain and dense mist. For a moment Satoshi considered hailing a taxi but then changed his mind. Despite recognizing that the contract he'd just signed would make him a multi-millionaire in the not-too-distant future, he still felt like the poor boy he had been growing up. Though the salary iPS USA was paying him to be on the company's scientific advisory board was generous, given how little work he was doing, it wasn't much, considering he had eight mouths to feed and rent to pay. Fearing retribution for leaving Japan, Satoshi had come to America with both sets of grandparents, his unmarried sister, and his wife and child. With such thoughts in mind, he decided to walk the three blocks over to Columbus Circle to catch a subway uptown to the George Washington Bridge Bus Terminal. From there, as he'd learned to do over the past number of weeks, he'd take a bus across the bridge to Fort Lee, New Jersey, where temporary housing had been found for him and his family.

As Satoshi exited the revolving door, he switched his athletic bag containing the newly signed contract from

his right to his left hand so he could use his right to
gather the lapels of his jacket and hold them closed at
the base of his neck. The mist he'd noted from inside
was both colder and wetter than he had imagined. After
walking only a few steps he reconsidered taking a taxi,
but all the taxis appeared to be occupied.

Satoshi stood at the curb until the light turned red
for the vehicles on Fifth Avenue at the corner of 57th
Street. As he searched vainly for an empty cab, his eyes
strayed to a Japanese man standing on the opposite side
of the street. What caught his eye and made him start
were two things. First, the man was holding what
appeared to be a photograph in his left hand, which
he was intermittently looking at and then looking in
Satoshi's direction. It was as if he was comparing the
photo with Satoshi. And second, and perhaps more
disconcerting, Satoshi was reasonably sure from the
man's appearance that he was a Yakuza enforcer from
Japan! He was wearing the typical black sharkskin suit,
had spiked hair, and was wearing dark glasses despite
the total lack of sun. Even more distinguishing was the
fact that the man was missing the last joint of his little
finger of the hand holding up the photograph. Like
most Japanese, Satoshi was aware that members of the
Yakuza, if they needed to show penance to their mob
boss, or *oyabun*, were required to personally cut off the
tip of their left fifth finger.

In the next second, making matters worse, Satoshi
realized there were two such men, not one, and that
the first was now pointing in Satoshi's direction while
the second was nodding his head in apparent agreement.

Now fearing that the men were about to cross the

street and approach him, Satoshi gave up trying to hail a cab, spun on his heels, and immediately began to quickly walk north toward Central Park, weaving in and out of the sidewalk crowds. Even though the Yamaguchi-gumi Yakuza had recently helped him and his family flee Japan and had found housing for them at the behest of Ben Corey and iPS USA, he'd never seen these particular individuals and assumed that they probably were from another Yakuza family. He had no idea why another Yakuza organization might want to talk to him, but he had no interest in finding out. As far as he was concerned, it could only end badly.

As he reached 58th Street, the traffic light encouraged him to cross Fifth Avenue instead of waiting to cross at 59th. As he did, he allowed himself to glance to his left to see if he could see the men in question in the crowd. Although he did not stop to search, he didn't see them and began to hope the incident was just a figment of his overactive imagination. With a lighter step, he ducked under the skeletonized branches of the squat tree in the small park in front of the Plaza hotel and hurriedly passed beneath the gaze of the naked bronze sculpture of Pomona forever washing herself in her fountain.

As Satoshi was about to turn around the northeast corner of the Plaza hotel and head west on 59th Street, he ventured a glance over his shoulder. What he saw caused him to suck in a deep breath. The same two men he'd seen earlier were skirting the fountain and heading in his direction while carrying on a conversation with two men creeping along in a black SUV going in the wrong direction in the roadway in front of the hotel. The two Japanese men caught sight of Satoshi having spotted them and responded by upping their speed to a jog and breaking off all conversation.

Jogging himself, Satoshi was now convinced he was being followed and that the Yakuza types must have been waiting outside iPS USA for him to appear. He had no idea who they were and what they wanted. Ben had dealt with the Yamaguchi as far as his emigration and immigration were concerned. Yet his being followed had to have something to do with his relationship with iPS USA and his abrupt switch from Japan to the United States.

Still clutching his athletic bag in one hand and his lapels in the other, Satoshi sprinted ahead through the press of people, unsure of what to do. Columbus Circle's always crowded, complicated subway station with its convergence of multiple train lines was like a distant oasis that promised safety, but how to get there before being overtaken by the men following him? He was anxiously certain that Yakuza look-alikes would be appearing behind him at any moment.

Salvation materialized in the next instant when a taxi pulled to the curb and discharged a passenger. Without a second's hesitation, Satoshi veered off through the other pedestrians and leaped into the taxi before the disembarking passenger had even closed the door. Out of breath, Satoshi gasped, "Columbus Circle!"

Miffed at getting such a brief fare, the driver made an illegal U-turn that caused Satoshi to slide against the door he'd just managed to get closed. With his face briefly pressed against the glass, he held on, fighting against the centrifugal force that had him momentarily immobile. Once the cab straightened out, Satoshi pushed himself upright and glanced out the back window in time to see the two Japanese round the corner of the hotel and stumble to a halt. Whether they'd seen him jump into the cab, Satoshi didn't know, but he hoped they hadn't.

Satoshi made it to one of Columbus Circle's subway station entrances without seeing the two Japanese men or the SUV behind him. Relieved to descend into the crowded, labyrinthine underworld, he quickly passed through the turnstile.

On the opposite side of the turnstile he confronted two very large New York City policemen. Reflexively Satoshi turned his head away as he passed. As an illegal alien, he was probably as afraid of the police as he was of the shady-looking men who he believed were following him. It was an uncomfortable plight of being afraid of both extremes, and he looked forward to obtaining the green cards Ben had been promising.

Quickly making his way to the proper track for the uptown A express, Satoshi approached the edge of the platform and stared into the maw of the tunnel to look for his train. He was eager for its arrival. Although he felt reasonably confident he had avoided a confrontation with the two Japanese men, he did not know what he would do if they suddenly appeared.

Stepping back from the edge of the platform, Satoshi found himself staring suspiciously at the other passengers, all of whom avoided eye contact. The platform rapidly filled as he waited. Commuters read newspapers or played with their cell phones or stared blankly ahead into the middle distance. More people arrived, pressing everyone closer and closer together. Trains thundered into the station but always on other tracks.

It was then that Satoshi saw him. It was the same

man who'd eyed him across Fifth Avenue, holding the photograph. He was only five or six feet away and regarding Satoshi out of the corner of his piercingly back eyes. A chill descended Satoshi's spine. With a renewed sense of fear, Satoshi tried to move to the side, away from the stranger, but it was difficult, as more and more passengers were arriving every few seconds.

Having managed to move only a few yards, Satoshi looked ahead to see what was specifically impeding him. It was then that he saw the second man, who was pretending to read a paper but who was in reality watching Satoshi. He was as close to Satoshi ahead as the other man was behind, trapping Satoshi between the track and a tiled wall.

With Satoshi's fear now maxing out, the formidable A train made its startling entrance, roaring out of the mouth of its tunnel. There'd been only a meager premonition of its imminent appearance. One second there had been relative quiet, the next a crescendo of ferocious wind, earsplitting noise, and earth-shaking vibration. And it was during this minor maelstrom that Satoshi became aware that the two men were pushing through the waiting crowd, pressing in on him. He was prepared to scream if either touched him, but they didn't. All he was aware of was a concussive hiss that he felt more than heard, since the noise had been completely drowned out by the arriving train. Simultaneously he'd felt a sharp, burning pain on the back of his leg where his leg and buttock joined, followed quickly by a yawning darkness and silence.

Susumu Nomura and Yoshiaki Eto had worked together as enforcers since they'd come to America more than fiye years previously on direct orders from Hisayuki Ishii, the *oyabun* of their Yakuza family, Aizukotetsu-kai. It had been a good marriage of sorts, combining Susumu's fearlessness with Yoshiaki's cautious planning. When they'd gotten the order to take out Satoshi Machita, Susumu was so excited and eager to please Hideki Shimoda, the *saiko-komon* and boss of the NYC branch office of the Aizukotetsu-kai, he wanted to do the hit immediately. On top of that, he wanted to do the hit in broad daylight on Fifth Avenue! For Susumu it was a serendipitous opportunity to demonstrate to the boss their loyalty and daring, which were prized Yakuza personality traits.

But Yoshiaki had been adamant, insisting that they had to take a few days to figure out a plan to fulfill the second part of the order: to make the hit look like the natural death of an unidentifiable individual. As it had been explained to them, it was important to avoid investigation of the affair by the police and possibly the FBI.

Having followed Yoshiaki's plan, which involved tailing the man for a few days in Manhattan as he went from work to the A train, the hit had gone down perfectly, without anyone suspecting that it was even in process. At Yoshiaki's suggestion, Susumu had purposefully waited until the A train had swept into the station to shoot Satoshi with the air gun hidden in the shaft of the umbrella that had been provided by Hideki Shimoda. The moment the trigger had been pulled, Yoshiaki had grabbed the man to keep him upright as his legs gave out. As the impatient passengers surged ahead to board the train, no one had noticed anything unusual as Susumu quickly relieved Satoshi of his athletic bag, his wallet, and his cell phone. The only minor surprise had been the seizure, but even that did not mar the hit. Having been warned that a short seizure was a possibility, Yoshiaki had just held Satoshi upright until his body went slack. At that point, when the last passengers were rushing for the train as the doors attempted to close, Yoshiaki merely laid the flaccid body down onto the cement platform, and he and Susumu walked calmly away.

Five minutes later the two Yakuza hit men mounted the final flight of stairs and emerged at the corner of Columbus Circle where they'd descended only a quarter-hour earlier. Both were pleased and proud that the event had gone down as well as it had. While Yoshiaki used his cell phone to call the men in the black SUV, Susumu unzipped the athletic bag and pulled out the thick licensing contract. After checking that there was nothing else of interest in the bag, he turned his attention to the document and quickly leafed through it, unsure what it was. His ability to read English was limited.

"No lab books?" Yoshiaki questioned as he waited for his call to go through. With his forefinger, he pulled open the athletic bag Susumu was still holding and looked into its depths. He was clearly disappointed that it was empty, save for a few magazines. What he was hoping to see were a couple of lab books, as their mission was both to assassinate Satoshi and to obtain the books. Yoshiaki, in particular, had become convinced the valuable lab books would be in the athletic bag because during the days they had been following Satoshi to plan the hit, Satoshi had been faithfully carrying the bag. "Just this bunch of papers," Susumu said, holding up the multipage contract.

Yoshiaki put the phone in the crook of his neck and took the contract from Susumu. While he was scanning the first page his call went through. "We're out," he said simply in English. "We're at the same subway entrance where you dropped us off."

"We're just across the circle. We'll be there in a moment."

"This is a legal contract," Yoshiaki said, hanging up and switching back to Japanese. Even though both men had been in New York City for more than five years, their English was hardly fluent.

"Is it important?" Susumu questioned hopefully. If they weren't going to be able to provide the lab books, Susumu wanted to supply something in their place. He was a man eager to please.

A black GMC Denali pulled over to the curb. Quickly Yoshiaki and Susumu piled into the rear seat, and as soon as the door was slammed, the vehicle angled out into the rush-hour traffic.

The man in the front passenger seat turned partially around. His name was Carlo Paparo. He was a big, muscular man with a shiny bald pate, large ears, and a pug nose. He was dressed in a black turtleneck, gray silk sport jacket, and black slacks. "Where is your researcher? Did you miss him?"

Susumu smiled. "We didn't miss him." Turning to Yoshiaki, he repeated his question in Japanese about the contract, but Yoshiaki shrugged his shoulders, indicating he didn't know, as he stuffed it back into the athletic bag.

"What happened?" Carlo questioned. "It couldn't have been much of a shakedown, as fast as you guys were." Carlo's orders had not been too specific. After having been reminded how important the business relationship was between the Vaccarros and the Aizukotetsu-kai, all he had been told was to help two guys who worked for the Aizukotetsu-kai to make contact with a Japanese guy who'd recently fled Japan. The help was to drive them around the city wherever they wanted to go.

"He had a heart attack," Yoshiaki said, wanting to end the conversation.

"Heart attack?" Carlo questioned with dubious surprise.

"That would be our guess," Yoshiaki said as he tried to restrain Susumu's burst of laughter. Susumu got the message and brought himself quickly under control.

Carlo glared at the two men in turn. "What the hell's going on here? Are you guys pulling my chain or what?"

"What is 'pulling my chain'?" Yoshiaki asked. He'd never heard the expression.

Carlo waved the two men off and turned back around in his seat. As he did so he shared a quick glance with his partner, Brennan Monaghan. Both Brennan and Carlo were assistants to Louie Barbera and frequently operated as a team. Louie Barbera was running the Vaccarro family operation in Queens while Paulie Cerino was still doing time at Rikers Island. Brennan was driving Carlo's car because Carlo hated to drive in traffic. He was too impatient and always ended up in some degree of road rage to the peril of everyone, including himself.

After having picked up the two Japanese men, Brennan had turned right onto Central Park West, heading north with the intent of getting to the East Side by cutting across the park. But it wasn't going to be fast, because the driving was stop-and-go, and more stop than go.

"All right, you two," Carlo said suddenly, while turning back around. It was clear he had become frustrated with the situation even though he wasn't driving. "Are we finished with your doings or what?"

Yoshiaki held up his hand: "We're trying to decide. Give us a moment!"

"Oh, for shit's sake!" Carlo murmured, and turned back around. He actually thought about getting the hell out of the car and walking, letting Brennan pick him up when he caught up to him. He again turned back to his two wards. "You bozos are going to have to make up your minds. Otherwise I'm just going to dump your asses here and let you find a taxi. I got things to do myself."

"Where is Fort Lee, New Jersey?" Susumu asked. He was holding a card. On his lap was Satoshi's open wallet.

"It's across the river," Carlo responded with some hesitation. With the traffic as bad as it was, one of the last places he wanted to go was Fort Lee, New Jersey, which required crossing the George Washington Bridge. At that time of day, what would normally take twenty minutes or so would probably take well over an hour, maybe as much as two, and only if they were lucky and there were no accidents.

Susumu looked at his partner and said in Japanese, "Since we have the address, we should go and see if we can find the books. The *saiko-komon* said he wanted the lab books for sure. After we take the books we can take all identification. No one will know."

"We don't know if the books will be there."

"We don't know if they'll not be there."

For a moment Yoshiaki stared ahead, pondering the pluses and minuses. "Okay," he finally said in English. "We go to Fort Lee!"

Carlo exhaled loudly and spun back around to look out the windshield. Ahead all he could see was a sea of stationary cars in both directions, even though there was a string of green lights stretched out into the distance. "I guess we go to New Jersey," he said in a tired voice.

As Carlo had feared, it did take two hours to get to Fort Lee, and then another twenty minutes to find the appropriate street. It was short and alley-like, with several deserted redbrick one-story commercial buildings covered with graffiti, as well as a number of tiny run-down houses clad in old-fashioned off-white asbestos shingles. The sun had nearly set, and with the cloudy sky, Brennan had to turn on his headlights. The lights in the small house that matched the address in Satoshi's wallet were also on, in contrast to those of the immediate neighbors', which were dark and looked deserted.

"Here it is," Brennan said. "What a palace! What's the plan?" He was looking out his window at the over-grown yard filled with all manner of rubbish, including a rusting tricycle, a broken swing set, several bald tires, and a collection of empty beer cans. "What do you want us to do?"

Susumu opened one of the rear doors, and he and Yoshiaki slid out. Yoshiaki leaned back in. "We'll be quick. Maybe it would be best if you turn off the head-lights."

Brennan did as he was told. The scene retreated into a misty gloom, which at least eliminated most of the trash and junk strewn about all the yards. At the same time it emphasized the dead-looking, skeletonized trees silhouetted against the pale, turbulent sky. "This place gives me the creeps," he said.

"Ditto," Carlo said.

The two hoodlums watched as the Japanese men hastily mounted the rickety steps leading up to a small covered porch. At that point they were mere dark silhouettes against the muted incandescent light emanating through the glazed front door. Pausing, both pulled out handguns from shoulder holsters.

"Holy shit!" Brennan voiced. "What the hell are they going to do?"

The next instant one of the intruders used the butt of his gun to smash the glass in the front door, reached in, and then opened the door. In a blink of the eye, both disappeared inside with the door left swinging silently on its hinges. Brennan turned to Carlo. "I don't like this! This is potentially turning into something that's a lot more than I expected. Worst case, I thought these clowns were going to beat someone up."

"I don't like it either," Carlo admitted. "I don't like being any part of this." He glanced at his watch. "Five minutes, then we're outta here. They can find their own way back to the city."

Both men fidgeted, keeping their eyes on the ostensibly peaceful little house. A few minutes later there was the muted sound of a gunshot followed quickly by several others. Both men jumped at each of the reports, guessing what each meant: a person was being killed in cold blood, and they, Brennan and Carlo, were accomplices.

During the next minute there were three more shots, for a total of six, causing Brennan and Carlo's fears and anxieties to skyrocket. The problem was that neither knew what they should do, meaning exactly what would their boss, Louie Barbera, want them to do. Would he want them to stay and risk getting caught and charged as accomplices, or should they get the hell away from there to avoid putting the whole Vaccarro organization in jeopardy? Since there was no way of knowing the answer to this question, they stayed frozen in place until Carlo suddenly had the idea of putting in an emergency call to Barbera.

With the sudden movement of getting out his phone, Carlo caused Brennan to start anew. "Jesus!" Brennan complained. "Give me some warning!"

"Sorry," Carlo said. "I've got to talk to Louie. He has to know what's going down here. This is crazy." Intent on dialing, Carlo didn't even feel Brennan tapping on his shoulder until Brennan increased the force to a near punch.

"They're coming out!" Brennan said anxiously, pointing out his side window.

Carlo looked. Both Susumu and Yoshiaki were charging down the porch steps and running toward the idling Denali, carrying loaded pillowcases over their shoulders. Carlo flipped his phone shut just as the men reached the vehicle and piled into the backseat. Without anyone speaking, Brennan put the SUV into gear and pulled away. He waited almost a block to turn on the headlights.

Brennan and Carlo didn't speak for about ten minutes, whereas the two Japanese men had been carrying on a progressively animated conversation in Japanese. It was obvious they were not pleased with their accomplishments inside the house. By the time they reached the George Washington Bridge, Carlo had relaxed enough to talk.

"Did something go wrong?" Carlo questioned. He made it a point to sound disinterested.

"We were looking for some lab books, which we didn't find," Yoshiaki said.

"I'm sorry," Carlo responded. "We heard what sounded like a number of gunshots. Were they?"

"Yes. There were six people in the house, more than we expected."

Carlo and Brennan exchanged worried glances. Their intuitions told them that Louie was going to be surprised, and it wasn't going to be in a good way.

CHAPTER ONE

Laurie Montgomery rolled over onto her side to look at her alarm clock. It wasn't quite five-thirty in the morning, and the alarm wouldn't go off for almost another half-hour. Under normal circumstances she would have been pleased to be able to roll over and go back to sleep. All her life she'd been an incurable night person who couldn't fall asleep and had even more difficulty waking up in the morning. But this was not going to be a normal day. It was going to be the first day back to work after an unexpectedly long maternity leave of nearly twenty months.

After glancing briefly at her husband, Jack Stapleton, who was sound asleep, Laurie gently slid her legs out from beneath the down comforter and placed her bare feet on the ice-cold wood floor. She thought briefly about changing her mind and climbing back under the warm covers. But she resisted and instead clutched Jack's T-shirt more tightly around her midsection and ran silently into the bathroom. The problem was that there was no way she'd be able to go back to sleep, as her mind was already going a mile a minute. She felt great turmoil stemming from her ambivalence about going back to work. Her main worry was for her just-over-one-and-a-half-year-old son, John Junior, and whether it was appropriate to leave him with a nanny for what would often be long days. But there was also a personal issue concerning a real fear of competence after such an unexpectedly long break: Would she still be able to handle her job as a medical examiner at what she thought was the most prestigious ME office in the country, if not the world?

Laurie had been working at OCME, or Office of the Chief Medical Examiner, in the city of New York for almost two decades. Self-confidence had always been an issue with her, going back to her teenage years. When she'd first started work at OCME, she'd worried about her competence at such an extremely challenging and demanding position, and she'd not overcome the concern for years, far past the time that her colleagues had dealt with similar fears. Forensic pathology was a field where book learning was not enough. Intuition played a major role in being good at practicing it, and intuition came from constant experience. Every day a good forensic pathologist was confronted with something he or she had never seen before.

Laurie studied herself in the mirror and groaned. From her perspective she looked terrible, with dark circles under her eyes and a pallor that was more suited to one of her patients. Motherhood had been more difficult and exhausting physically and mentally than she had ever imagined, particularly having had to deal with a serious, often fatal illness. At the same time, it had also been more rewarding.

Taking her robe from its hook on the back of the door and pulling it on, she slipped her feet into her mules with the pink puffs over the toes. She smiled at the slippers. They were the sole reminder of the time when she could feel sexy with lingerie and enjoy the feeling. Vaguely she wondered if that feeling would ever come

back. Becoming a mother had changed her sense of self
in a number of domains.

Back out in the hall, Laurie padded down to JJ's
room. The door was ajar, and she walked into the room,
which was bright enough for her to see. Dawn was
approaching, but more important there were a number of night-lights conveniently spaced along the base-
boards. Thanks to her mother, the room was decorated
with riotous blue wallpaper and matching curtains
covered with images of airplanes and trucks.

The furniture consisted only of a rocking chair, which
Laurie had used for breast-feeding, a bassinet swathed
in eyelet, and a crib. The bassinet was still there for
sentimental reasons, as was the rocking chair, although
she used the rocker occasionally when JJ was fussy and
needed her presence to fall asleep.

Moving over to the crib, Laurie gazed in at her son,
thankful for his healthy complexion. With a shudder
she could remember distinctly when it hadn't been so.
At the age of two months JJ had been diagnosed
with high-risk neuroblastoma, a very serious and often
deadly childhood cancer. But Laurie had been able to
thank the lucky stars, or God, or whomever or whatever,
that the cancer had disappeared. Whether it had been
through the divine intervention of a faith healer in
Jerusalem, the dedication of the doctors at Sloan-
Kettering, or the fact that neuroblastoma can, on
occasion, spontaneously resolve, Laurie would never
know—nor care, if truth be told. The only thing that
mattered to her was that JJ was now a normal one-and-
a-half-year-old boy whose growth and development,
despite chemotherapy and what was called monoclonal
antibody therapy, had reached normal percentiles in all

aspects, enough for Laurie to consider returning to work.

Glancing in at the peacefully sleeping child, a smile spread across Laurie's face despite the concerns and ambivalence she was suffering about going to work. JJ's angelic face reminded her of a conversation she'd had with Jack just the previous evening. It had started when they had both gone into JJ's bedroom to check on the baby before going to bed themselves. As they gazed at the boy, she admitted something she'd never mentioned before to anyone: She was so certain that JJ was the most beautiful child in the world that whenever she chatted with the other neighborhood mothers at the playground across the street, she couldn't help but wonder why someone had never remarked about it. "It's so obvious," she'd said to Jack.

To her surprise, Jack's response had been to break out in a guffaw so loud she had to caution him not to wake the baby. It wasn't until they had ducked out into the hall that Jack explained his reaction. By then Laurie was indignant, feeling as if Jack was making fun of her.

"I'm sorry," he said. "Your comment tickles my funny bone. Don't you realize that all the mothers feel exactly the same?"

Laurie's indignation faded rapidly, as did her frown.

"A mother's love must be somewhere in our genome," Jack had continued. "Otherwise we as a species would never have made it through the ice age."

Snapping herself back to the present, Laurie became aware that she wasn't alone in JJ's room. Turning her head, she found herself staring into Jack's shadowed face. All she could really see were the whites of his eyes, although there was enough light to appreciate that he was buck naked.

"You're up early," Jack said. He knew Laurie liked to sleep late, and it was part of the Stapleton routine for him to get up first, shower, and then nudge Laurie out of bed. "Are you all right?"

"Nervous," Laurie admitted. "Very nervous!"

"What on earth about?" Jack questioned. "Leaving JJ with Leticia Wilson?" Leticia Wilson was a cousin of Warren Wilson, one of the local men with whom Jack regularly played basketball. Warren had suggested her to Jack one recent afternoon when Jack had mentioned they were looking for a nanny so that Laurie could go back to work.

"That's part of it," Laurie admitted.

"But you said these last few days that you've had your so-called dry run and that things had gone terrifically."

Laurie had asked Leticia to come for two days, take JJ, feed him, take him out to the park, both the local playground and Central Park, and keep him until the time Laurie guessed she'd generally be getting home from OCME. There had been no problems, and best of all, both JJ and Leticia had taken to each other and had demonstrably enjoyed themselves.

"Everything went well," Laurie admitted, "but that doesn't mean I don't still feel guilty about the situation. I know I'm going to suffer the maternal quandary, meaning that when I'm here with JJ, I feel guilty about not working, but today, while I'll be working, I'm going to feel guilty about not being home. JJ is going to miss his mommy just like Mommy is going to miss JJ. Also, even though he's been symptom-free for over a year, I'm continually worried he's going to relapse. I guess I'm always going to be a little superstitious that the continuance of his recovery has something to do mystically with my presence."

"I suppose that is understandable," Jack said. "What's the other part of your nervousness? It's not anything about OCME personnel, is it? I mean, everyone is looking forward to your return, and I do mean everyone, from Bingham all the way down to the security personnel. Everyone I run into has said something about looking forward to your return today."

"Really?" Laurie questioned with disbelief. She thought it had to be a gross exaggeration, especially including Bingham, whom she was aware she addled on occasion with her independence and doggedness.

"Really!" Jack echoed spiritedly. "You are one of the most popular people at OCME. If you are nervous, it can't be about fitting back into the team. It has to be about something else."

"Well, maybe you are right," Laurie admitted reluctantly. She had a good idea about what he was going to say if she admitted to her worries about competency and wasn't sure she wanted to hear it, as nothing he said would make her feel differently.

"Let's continue this discussion," Jack said, his voice quavering. "But can we do it in the warm bathroom? I'm freezing in here wearing nothing but my pride."

"Good idea!" Laurie responded. "Let's go! I'm cold even with my robe." After pulling JJ's blanket up around his shoulders and tucking it in gently, she hurried after Jack, who'd made a beeline into the bathroom. When she got there he already had the hot-water tap going full blast, filling the room with warm, billowing steam.

"So what else has you nervous?" Jack asked, raising his voice over the sound of the shower as he reached in to adjust the temperature before climbing in. "And don't talk to me about worries concerning your competence, because I don't want to hear it." He'd heard her talk about her fears of competence back when she'd first started at OCME and was intuitive enough to guess it was bothering her again.

"Then I'm not going to say anything," Laurie shouted back.

Jack stuck his face out from the stream of water, wiped his eyes, and cracked open the shower door: "So it is fear of your abilities! Well, I'm not going to try to change your mind, because I know nothing I'd say would have any effect whatsoever, so you go on and worry. But you know something, the fact that you do worry is probably what makes you such a good medical examiner. You're a better forensic pathologist, in my mind, than anyone else in the whole place, because you're always willing to question and learn."

"I'm flattered to hear you say that, even though I don't believe it. I was okay before this maternity leave, but it's been almost two years since I've done an autopsy or looked at a microscopic slide."

"That might be, but over the last month you've been burning the midnight oil reading several standard forensic-path books. You're probably up to speed more than any of the rest of us who haven't looked at a text-book for years. You could probably even pass your board exams again today, which none of the rest of us could do."

"Thank you for your support," Laurie said. "But reading and actually doing are two vastly different things. I'm truly worried I'm going to mess up big-time in some form or fashion, maybe even on my first case."

"Could never happen!" Jack stated with surety. "Not to you with your experience. But look, let's make a point of doing our cases on adjoining tables and sorta maintain an ongoing conversation about what we are doing. Then, after the autopsies, we go over them together just to make sure we've both hit all the appropriate buttons. What do you think of that idea?"

"I like it," Laurie admitted. "I like it a lot." The idea didn't absolve her of all her anxieties, but it did lessen them. Most important, by relieving some of her nervousness, she knew she'd be able to turn her attention to what she had to do to get ready to leave for OCME. Leticia was due to arrive in less than an hour, and Laurie had a lot to do before she got there.

CHAPTER TWO

Hisayuki Ishii's driver, Akira, pulled into the roundabout facing the Hotel Okura Kobe and halted in front of the main entrance. Stopped ahead of them was the first car of the three-car motorcade that had driven the *oyabun* of the Aizukotetsu-kai Yakuza organization and his *saiko komon*, Tadamasa Tsuji, the forty-six miles from Kyoto to Kobe. The bodyguards climbed out of the first vehicle, all with their hands stuck inside their jackets, clutching the butts of concealed handguns so that they could be drawn out in an emergency. No one was comfortable visiting Kobe, the traditional home of the rival Yamaguchi-gumi Yakuza family, especially for an impromptu meeting with the organization's *oyabun*. If the Yamaguchi-gumi were inclined, there was too much opportunity to plan an ambush.

Akira leaped out and rounded Hisayuki's armored LS 600h L sedan and waved away the hotel doorman. Hisayuki preferred to have his own driver open his door to avoid any unwanted surprises. Behind came the third car with its additional host of bodyguards.

The move from vehicle to inside the hotel happened in seconds. Inside, Hisayuki was formally greeted by the general manager and guided to a private elevator, whisking him, his *saiko-komon,* and two of his most trusted lieutenants up to the penthouse floor, where they were escorted into a private dining room. There Hisayuki was greeted by his Yamaguchi-gumi equivalent, *Oyabun* Hiroshi Fukazawa. He too was accompanied by his *saiko-komon,* a slight bespectacled man by the name of Tokutaro Kudo, who, by his diminutive size, made his boss appear to be a giant.

Actually, Hiroshi was big. Although not a giant, he was almost a head taller than Hisayuki, with a broad, serious face. He was dressed as nattily as his guest, in elegant European business attire.

Besides the two principles and their respectful *saiko-komon*s and two personal bodyguards, the other people in the room included a hotel manager, a waiter, and a chef. The chef, outfitted in spotless white with a tall, highly starched toque, was standing patiently in the middle of a U-shaped dining table with a built-in grill. The table was at the far end of the narrow room near the window. Out the window stretched a dramatic sweeping view of Osaka Bay with the Port of Kobe in the foreground.

After the typical, ritualized greeting and exchange of business cards, Hiroshi gestured for his two guests to take seats in the seating area near the room's entrance, just beyond the private lavatory. As Hisayuki stepped over to one of the chairs, he could not help but take note that Hiroshi did not make a point of bowing slightly lower than he, which was traditional, since Hisayuki was clearly the more senior in age. Hisayuki wondered if the slight was deliberate or accidental, and if deliberate, if it was a sign of disrespect or merely a subtle statement that Hiroshi did not consider himself bound by the same old Yakuza cultural rules.

"This is a most pleasant surprise, Ishii-san," Hiroshi

said once the four men were seated and had ordered their personal favorite brand of Scotch whiskey. The four bodyguards faded to opposite sides of the room, glaring at one another.

"Thank you for agreeing to see us under such short notice, Fukazawa-san," Hisayuki said with yet another slight bow.

"It is good to see you looking so well. It has been too long since we were together, my friend."

"It was more than a year. We should not be so lax. It is, after all, less than fifty miles that separates us."

The pleasantries continued until the waiter brought out their respective scotches. When the waiter withdrew, the tone changed. It wasn't marked, but it was real. "What is it that we can do for the *oyabun* of the Aizukotetsu-kai?" Hiroshi asked with a more clipped style and impatient tone than he had used earlier.

Hisayuki cleared his throat and hesitated as if he'd waited until that very moment to decide what it was he wanted to say. "Several days ago—three, to be exact—I was called to Tokyo to meet with Daijin Kenichi Fujiwara-san."

"The vice minister Fujiwara?" Hiroshi questioned with muted surprise. He shot a quick glance toward his *saiko-komon* and got a slight shrug of the man's shoulders in return, suggesting that he was equally surprised. A government meeting at the ministerial level with a Yakuza *oyabun* was something akin to a blue moon.

"Exactly! The vice minister of Economy, Trade, and Industry," Hisayuki said. He leaned forward and made direct eye contact with his host. He knew he had the man's full attention. "The vice minister told me a number of surprising and disturbing things that we need to talk about. First, he told me that the Yamaguchi-gumi had been behind the break-in of a laboratory at Kyoto University, where there had been a death. I'm sure you have heard about it. At the same incident, some important laboratory books had been stolen, an issue you might not have heard about, since it was not reported to the media. The government is concerned about these laboratory books, as they have put in jeopardy the legitimacy of Kyoto University's patents on iPS technology."

Hiroshi sat back and took a sip of his scotch while returning Hisayuki's stare. It was obvious he was taken aback by the candor of Hisayuki's remarks even more than the content, although the content surprised him, too. The media had not named the Yamaguchi-gumi specifically, just that the break-in had been a Yakuza event.

"My concern is whether you personally were aware of this break-in. Perhaps it was the doings of one of the Yamaguchi splinter groups? We all know that the Yamaguchi is expanding quickly, which might mean that there is not the same internal cohesion as with the rest of us." Hisayuki wanted to provide an out for his rival, but the effort was ineffectual. Hiroshi's expression clouded.

"We subscribe to the same *oyabun-kobun* sworn brotherhood structure as everyone else," Hiroshi stated with some indignation. "I am the *oyabun* of the Yamaguchi-gumi. I know what my brotherhood is doing in all respects."

"My comments are not intended to disparage the Yamaguchi-gumi in any way. We all have great respect for the Yamaguchi-gumi, perhaps even a bit of envy for your recent successes. But I take your response to mean that you, personally, were aware of the break-in. If that is the case, I must formally complain that you did not inform me of what you were doing nor ask me to help. We Yakuza have, over the years, adhered to this policy of cooperation to avoid turf wars, and I would like to be assured that in the future you will contact me if you have needs in the Kyoto area. I don't mean this to be a serious confrontation, and I hope it isn't. We just need to maintain respect between our organizations, as has been the case over the years among all the Yakuza."

"We Yamaguchi have the utmost respect for the Aizukotetsu-kai," Hiroshi said without changing his expression.

As a realist, Hisayuki knew that Hiroshi's response skirted rather than faced the issue. There was no apology implied, but Hisayuki was content to take the response as the first step toward a solution. As close as Kobe and Kyoto were physically, it was imperative that the problem be recognized, and at least now it had been formally broached.

Moving on to the next issue—namely, the very real threat to the Aizukotetsu-kai portfolio from the Yamaguchi-gumi action—Hisayuki said, "If I may ask, why did you, as the *oyabun* of the Yamaguchi-gumi, want the lab books from the Kyoto University laboratory, and why did you help their owner and his family defect to America? Didn't you realize it was against our government's interests, meaning all our interests as Japanese citizens, and especially those citizens who have invested in the Japanese start-up company iPS Patent Japan?"

"Perhaps as Japanese citizens it could seem to be against our interests, but not as a Yakuza businessman struggling in a global economy. Money and effort should be directed where it will make the most money, not where a selfish, bureaucratic government like ours suggests. Our government is not for the Japanese people, despite what they say. It is for themselves, like most governments in today's world. Look what happened here in Kobe in the earthquake in '95. Who rescued the people and maintained order in the first terrible days? Was it the government? Hell, no. It was us, the Yamaguchi-gumi. The government only came in later when they suddenly realized it was a public-relations nightmare in the making.

"Why I gave the order to aid this Satoshi was because it had been a direct request from our New York City *saiko-komon,* Saboru Fukuda. Perhaps you know him. He was originally from Kyoto but moved here to Kobe to work the docks as a mere laborer but ended up joining the Yamaguchi family. We recognized his skills early in his career. He's a very smart businessman, a good administrator, and an intuitive investor."

"I don't know him," Hisayuki said with a shake of his head, hardly listening. He was taken aback by Hiroshi's statement suggesting that as a Yakuza businessman, he was not patriotic. The Yakuza had always been patriotic. It was part of the unwritten contract the Yakuza had with the government.

"Not only has Fukuda-san tripled our take with our gambling operations in New York, he's also been laundering the money on-site through shrewd investments with a clever New York placement agent. This placement agent is slick and has no fear of dirty money, which he most willingly uses as venture capital to fund medical and biotech start-up companies, which is his specialty.

Usually it costs money to launder money, as you well know, but with him we've been seeing up to a forty percent increase in original value. So the revenue Fukuda-san returns here to Kobe is already clean. With such a track record I have come to support him one hundred percent. Whatever he asks for, I give him and do so with confidence, no questions asked. Perhaps as sister organizations we could introduce you to this placement agent."

"As I said, I don't know him," Hisayuki said distractedly.

"Kyoto's loss and Kobe's gain," Hiroshi said, as if a proud father. "Since I appointed him more than five years ago, he has been running the Yamaguchi-gumi operation in New York. He's turned New York into our most profitable foreign branch. How is your New York branch doing, if I may ask?"

"Reasonably well," Hisayuki said. Normally he would not have even acknowledged there was a New York City branch of his operation, much less tell how it was doing, but he was asking Hiroshi similarly confidential questions, and Hiroshi was answering. Hisayuki needed Hiroshi to keep talking, because he needed to find out if Hiroshi had any idea why his *saiko-komon* wanted Satoshi aided. As Hisayuki was trying to come up with the next question without giving away why he wanted to know, it all suddenly hit him, and once it did, he was amazed it had taken him so long to figure it out. The vice minister had to have been correct. The Yamaguchi, through their *saiko-komon* in New York, Saboru Fukuda, were investing in iPS USA, the start-up company the vice minister had spoken of. It had to be the explanation.

"If your operation in New York is only doing reasonably well," Hiroshi continued, unaware of Hisayuki's epiphany, "then why don't we team up, merge our New York operations and share proceeds in proportion to our respective personnel roster. There should be more co-operation in these tough times between all Yakuza organizations, even here in Japan."

Glancing briefly at his *saiko-komon*, Hisayuki wondered if he'd come to the same conclusion, and was eager to ask him once they got back into the car. Looking back at Hiroshi, who was still going on about the idea of their two organizations colluding, Hisayuki wondered if he dared to ask Hiroshi some direct question, like whether or not the Yamaguchi had any stock in iPS USA. He was worried that Hiroshi might come to a similar conclusion, that the Aizukotetsu-kai had a serious financial involvement with iPS Patent Japan, meaning that their respective Yakuza organizations were in direct financial conflict. Of course, Hisayuki didn't know if the sizes of the investments were anywhere equivalent, but he didn't think it would make that much difference. It was an awkward situation, since the two companies' market values were inversely connected like a zero-sum game: If one were to go up, the other would invariably have to go down. Internecine Yakuza wars had been fought over circumstances even less definitively connected, and Hisayuki had the sudden fear that this was going to be a war as well. The Aizukotetsu-kai simply could not afford to lose what they had invested in iPS Patent Japan, nor could they simply pull out, since the company's cash reserves were nil. "It will be a war," Hisayuki found himself prophesying and already planning how to limit the collateral damage, and even possibly how to outsource the whole mess to New York City.

"So what do you think?" Hiroshi questioned. He had been continuing to talk up his suggestion of some kind of partnership between the Yamaguchi-gumi and the Aizukotetsu-kai, an idea Hisayuki dismissed out of hand since he knew that if that were to happen, Aizukotetsu-kai would be swallowed up by the Yamaguchi. The concept of partnership was one of the Yamaguchi-gumi's main methods of expansion. "I tell you, Ishii-san," Hiroshi went on when Hisayuki failed to respond immediately, "we all have to accept that the world as we knew it in our lifetime is rapidly changing, and we Yakuza have to change, too. The government is not going to leave us alone, like in the past, as evidenced by the anti-gang laws passed in '92. It's only going to get worse."

"When I met with the vice minister just the other day, this issue came up."

"And what did he say?"

"He said the laws that have been passed had been done so merely for political reasons, and that there was no intention of truly enforcing them."

"And you believed him?"

"He said that if the government was serious about enforcement, they would have to pass something similar to the United States' RICO Act, and they haven't, and I know for certain that there isn't anything in the works. So, yes, I believed him."

"With all due respect, Ishii-san, I believe you are being much too trusting and even a bit naïve," Hiroshi said, beginning a long monologue about his vision of the future with the Japanese government. "Soon the benign neglect that has characterized our relationship is

going to change to become progressively more antag-
onistic. It stands to reason. Even today the government
is envious of the money they believe that we, the Yakuza,
are, from their perspective, sucking from the economy
and paying little or no taxes on."

As Hiroshi talked, Hisayuki became progressively
more uncomfortable as a guest, and realized how easy
it would be for the Yamaguchi-gumi to overwhelm the
Aizukotetsu-kai, which he worried they might feel was
appropriate if Hiroshi were to make the association
between their conflicting investments in what was going
to be a trillion-dollar industry.

Hisayuki allowed Hiroshi to continue his ranting
about the government without offering any contradic-
tions, such as the fact that the government needed the
Yakuza. It was his sense and hope that if Hiroshi stayed
on the issue of the government vs. the Yakuza, he'd be
less likely to have any dangerous epiphanies.

"We Yakuza have to come together!" Hiroshi chimed
like a politician on a soapbox, going back to his original
issue of encouraging some sort of partnership between
their two organizations. Hisayuki let him continue, even
encouraging him a degree by nodding and smiling at
appropriate times to give the impression that he was
even considering the idea.

As Hiroshi droned on, Hisayuki thanked the gods
that he'd paused at the beginning of the meeting and
hadn't started as he had initially planned—namely,
to relate to Hiroshi what he had learned early that
morning from Hideki Shimoda, his New York City
saiko-komon. At nine-thirty he'd had a call from Hideki,
who reported that as ordered, the threat to Kyoto
University's iPS patents had been significantly reduced

because, as requested, Satoshi and his family had been eliminated. He'd been told that the hit on Satoshi had gone flawlessly and was certain to be interpreted as the natural death of an unidentified individual. The only problem, he'd been informed, was that the lab books had not been located.

Hisayuki breathed out with relief, thinking how close he'd come to disaster if he'd started the meeting with such a revelation. It surely would have had the opposite result of what he'd intended, as he never thought for a moment that Hiroshi was involved personally.

Suddenly Hiroshi stopped his soliloquy in mid-sentence. He'd seen Hisayuki's sigh and took it as a reminder of his responsibilities as a host. "I'm sorry for carrying on so," he said, rising to his feet and bowing slightly. "You must be hungry. I see that you have all finished your whiskey. It is time for our dinner and entertainment." He gestured toward the table and the chef in his blindingly white outfit. "Please, let us have some food and more alcohol to celebrate our friendship."

Hisayuki got to his feet with even more relief. He knew that once the sake, beer, and wine appeared and the dinner started, and whatever else Hiroshi had planned, there would be no more talk of business.

More than an hour later, as soon as it seemed socially appropriate, Hisayuki and Tadamasa excused themselves from what had become quite a party, citing that they were facing an hour-and-a-half drive back to Kyoto. Hiroshi had tried to talk them into staying the night at

the hotel, but they had graciously declined, claiming
that they needed to be in Kyoto for early-morning meetings.

Despite some concern, the departure was as smooth
as the arrival, with no untoward incidents, and soon the
three-car cavalcade was on the road north to Kyoto.
Hisayuki had not said a word for a number of miles,
going over everything Hiroshi has said. Tadamasa,
knowing his place, remained equally silent.

"Well?" Hisayuki questioned suddenly. "What was
your feeling about the meeting?"

"It went smoothly but does not bode well for the
future."

"My feelings exactly," Hisayuki said, holding on to
the strap above the rear window. He was gazing out at
the dark countryside as it flashed by. All he could see
were dim lights in the windows of farmers' cottages;
all he could hear was the muffled hum of his powerful sedan's engine. "Did you get the sense that the
Yamaguchi-gumi is invested in iPS USA?" He asked the
question casually so as not to influence his adviser's
opinion.

"Most definitely! I was trying to think of a way to
let you know, but then I was quite certain you already
did. I think they are significantly involved by the way
Fukazawa-san carried on about the placement agent his
saiko-komon has found."

"Tomorrow, have some of our analysts at the RRTW
office try to learn what they can about the Yamaguchi-
gumi involvement with iPS USA."

"The problem is that the market value of iPS USA
and iPS Patent Japan are inversely tied together."

"Don't I know," Hisayuki murmured regretfully.

"There is going to be trouble over this."

"I know that as well. We need time to prepare for the worst. The key thing in the short run is to keep Hiroshi in the dark as long as we can while we bolster the legitimacy of iPS Patent Japan's patents of iPS cells. Getting rid of Satoshi is good, but we need to get the missing lab books and destroy them."

"The question is, of course, where are the lab books? As Satoshi didn't have them on his person or at home, they must be in physical possession of iPS USA."

"Call Hideki and tell him he needs to get ahold of Satoshi's lab books if at all possible, but warn him that the Aizukotetsu-kai cannot appear to be involved."

Tadamasa got out his cell phone and started to dial Hideki Shimoda.

Hisayuki looked back out at the darkened landscape and wondered if there was anything else he should communicate to his New York *saiko-komon* while Tadamasa had him on the line. He thought back to the conversation he'd had with the man that morning, remembering he'd said that Satoshi's death had gone flawlessly and would be interpreted as a natural death of an unidentified individual. Hisayuki hoped that was going to be true, particularly the natural-death part, because if it were to be considered a murder and the Yamaguchi-gumi found out that the Aizukotetsu-kai were involved, there was a good chance a full-blown war would flare up almost immediately.

CHAPTER THREE

MARCH 25, 2010 – THURSDAY, 7:44 a.m.
NEW YORK CITY

Laurie was the first out of the taxi at the corner of First Avenue and 30th Street. The building was as unattractive as ever: a 1960s relic with its blue tile and aluminum windows. It was ugly then and ugly now. But it looked familiar to her, as though she was coming home after a long trip away. As for her earlier nervousness about her professional competence, seeing the building made it worse. The workday was about to begin.

Turning back to the taxi, she watched Jack climb out after having paid the fare. He'd graciously offered to ride with her instead of using his beloved bike, which had recently changed to a Cannondale after his Trek had been mortally injured by a city bus that had run over it. Luckily, Jack was not on the bike at the time, but he had had to watch the tragedy from a few feet away.

"Well, we're here," Jack said, glancing at his watch. It was later than he liked. Actually, later than they were supposed to arrive, which was early enough to start the first autopsies of the day at seven-thirty. But no one started their cases at seven-thirty except Jack on normal days. The seven-thirty rule had been made by the chief, Dr. Harold Bingham, but as he'd aged, his insistence of the hated early start had faltered. As a result, most of the senior staff began when they wanted to, sometime after eight. Jack stuck with the early rule because it gave him the chance to choose his cases rather than wait for what was assigned to him, by the on-call medical examiner, one of whose tasks was to arrive before the others to go over the cases that had came in during the night, to decide which needed to have postmortems and who would do them. The main part of the on-call medical examiner's job was to be available if one of the evening or night medical legal investigators, or MLIs, needed the backup of a forensic pathologist for a difficult case. It was a job Jack himself did for a week three or four times a year when his turn rolled around.

"I'm sorry we are late," Laurie said, noticing Jack checking his watch. "I'll do better in the future." They were behind schedule because the handoff of JJ to Leticia had not gone as smoothly as Laurie had hoped. Every time she'd descended the stairs to where Jack was waiting at the front door, she'd think of something else and dash back up to the kitchen, where JJ and Leticia were dealing with oatmeal and pears, most of which, but not all, was being swallowed.

"No problem," Jack said. "How do you feel?"

"As best as can be expected."

"You are going to be fine," Jack assured her.

Yeah, sure, Laurie said silently to herself. She followed him up the front steps and through the door. She entered the foyer with a sense of déjà vu. There was the same tired-looking sofa, with the same coffee table in front with a smattering of outdated magazines, some without covers. There were the same locked doors leading into the identification room and into the administrative offices of the chief medical examiner and the chief of staff.

Finally, there was the same reception counter guarded by Marlene Wilson, a kind African-American woman whose flawless complexion belied her years and whose attitude was always happy and welcoming.

"Dr. Montgomery!" Marlene exclaimed, catching sight of Laurie. "Welcome back," she cried with obvious glee. Without a second's hesitation, she slipped from her stool and came out from behind the desk to give Laurie a forceful hug. Laurie was initially taken aback by Marlene's enthusiasm, but she quickly relaxed and let herself enjoy the warm welcome. It was a good thing, because Marlene's reaction to seeing Laurie was to be repeated by just about everyone Laurie would encounter throughout the day.

Inside the ID room where relatives were confronted by photos of the dead or the body itself if they insisted, Laurie and Jack found Dr. Arnold Besserman, who'd been working at OCME for thirty-some-odd years. As it was his turn to be the on-call medical examiner, he was sitting at the old, dented metal ID desk, checking through the most recent arrivals. It was immediately obvious it had been a quiet night in the Big Apple, as there was only a short stack of case files for him to deal with.

Like Marlene, although not quite so ardent, Arnold got up as soon as Laurie appeared and gave her a welcoming hug.

Also in the room was Vinnie Amendola, one of the mortuary techs. He regularly came in a half-hour early to transition from the two night techs, but really what he did was make the communal coffee in an institution-size drip coffee machine. He had to wait for Arnold for his turn to greet Laurie, then retreated to one of the old leather club chairs and his copy of the *Daily News*. He and Jack were close, though it was sometimes hard to tell amid their verbal sparring. On most days Vinnie and Jack started autopsies as much as an hour before anyone else.

"What do we have today?" Jack asked as he followed Arnold back to the desk.

"Not much," Arnold said vaguely. He knew full well what Jack was up to—namely, cherry-picking cases—which had always rubbed him the wrong way in contrast to all the other medical examiners, who forgave Jack this habit since he always did more cases than anyone else. Animosity had simmered between the two because Jack saw Arnold as a slacker who was merely putting in his time, doing as little as possible, certainly not carrying his weight, to reach retirement age, affording maximum pension.

Despite a threatening look from Arnold, Jack started pawing through the case files, checking each one quickly for the circumstances of death, such as GSW (gunshot wound), hospital-based if unexpected, accident, suicide, murder, or somehow suspicious.

With his hands on his hips and a frustrated, impatient expression on his face, Arnold let the whistling Jack continue with no attempt of assistance, which he could have given, since he'd already gone through the cases himself.

Still absorbed in his rapid assessment of the day's autopsy workload, Jack became aware of another occupant in the room. In one of the club chairs facing the radiator was another male figure scrunched down so that just the top of his hat could be seen over the back of the chair. The only other parts of his body that were visible were his scuffed shoes, which were balanced on top of the radiator cover. Thinking the hat and shoes could belong only to one person, Jack dropped the case files, rounded the desk, and walked over to where he could glance down at the sleeping figure. As he'd suspected, it was a longtime friend, the recently promoted Detective Captain Lou Soldano.

"Look who's here!" Jack called out to Laurie, who was busy making herself a cup of coffee to her liking.

Laurie immediately walked over and, standing next to Jack, joined him in gazing down at Lou. Not much of Lou's face was visible, as he had his hat tipped down to cover most of it. His arms were crossed on his chest. Over them was an open newspaper. His coat was on but unbuttoned and trailing on the floor. He was breathing deeply but not snoring, and the open newspaper across his chest rose and fell rhythmically.

"He must be exhausted," Laurie remarked like the mother she now was.

"He's always exhausted," Jack said. He reached down to tip Lou's hat back to expose his face, but Laurie grabbed his arm and pulled it back.

"Let him sleep!"

"Why?"

"As I said, he must be exhausted."

"He's here for a reason," Jack remarked as he pulled his hand free from Laurie's grip and gently lifted Lou's hat off the sleeping policeman. "The sooner he gets into a real bed, the better."

With his face now visible, Lou appeared the picture of absolute repose, despite the surroundings. He also looked exhausted, with dark circles under his somewhat sunken eyes. The dark circles were even apparent with the man's deep complexion. He was handsome in a masculine, muscular fashion: a man's man, clearly Italian. His clothes were disheveled and rumpled, as if he'd been in them for days, and it appeared he'd not shaved for an equivalent amount of time.

"He's been here as long as I have," Arnold called from behind the desk.

"Hey, big guy!" Jack said, giving Lou's shoulder a light shove. "Time to get you home to beddy-bye."

Lou's breathing changed its rhythm briefly, but he didn't awaken.

"Let the poor man sleep, even for a short time."

"Come on, my man," Jack said, increasing the force on Lou's shoulder and ignoring Laurie.

Everyone jumped when Lou suddenly sat bolt upright, his feet hitting the floor with a solid thump. His eyes had gone from fully closed to fully open such that the whites could be seen all around his irises. Before anyone could respond, he caught sight of Laurie. "Hey, Laurie! What a surprise! I thought it was next week you were going to start work." With a slight wobble, he got to his feet and enveloped Laurie in a big hug. "How's the little one?"

Laurie recovered from having been startled and hugged Lou back despite his reeking of cigarette smoke. She had known Lou even longer than she'd known Jack, having met him the year she had started at OCME in the early nineties. They had even dated briefly before both realized they were more suited to be friends than lovers. Lou knew the whole difficult story of JJ better than anyone at OCME, as he was a regular visitor to the Stapleton home.

After a bit more personal talk, Jack asked Lou what

he was doing at OCME, which Lou insisted on calling "the morgue." Although Lou knew that OCME was a lot more than a morgue and that the actual morgue was only a small part of the operation, he still couldn't change, and Jack had given up getting him to do so.

"There's a case I want you to do for me," Lou began. "The incident happened in Queens, but I threw my weight around and got the body brought here instead of being taken to the Queens office. I hope you don't mind."

"Me mind?" Jack questioned humorously. "Not on your life. Now, Bingham may throw a fit as a stickler for rules, and our man in Queens might have his feelings hurt that you didn't think he could handle it, but I'm certain he'll be able to put it behind him before retirement."

Lou chuckled. "Will it be that bad?"

"I sincerely doubt it, at least not with Dick Katzenburg."

"Katzenburg won't mind in the slightest," Laurie threw in. She'd had lots of opportunity to work with the chief of the Queens office. The New York OCME had four physical locations, with 519 First Avenue serving Manhattan and the Bronx, and with separate offices in Queens, Brooklyn, and Staten Island serving their own boroughs.

"It was a GSW," Lou began.

"Hey, Arnold!" Jack called out. "Can I do the gunshot victim?" Ultimately, as the on-call ME, it was Arnold's choice which case was to be assigned to which pathologist. Some people had specific preferences, especially if they were doing a study on a specific forensic issue. Other people had specific dislikes, and no one liked unpleasant decomposed corpses, which were doled out on a semi-rotating basis.

"No skin off my nose," Arnold said gruffly as he passive-aggressively tossed the case file toward Jack as if he were throwing a Frisbee. Not unexpectedly, some of the contents flew out, forcing Jack to retrieve them. "Sorry," Arnold said, being anything but sincere.

Jack swore under his breath as he retrieved a partially filled-out death certificate, a completed identification sheet, and a lab slip for the required HIV antibody analysis. "Asshole," he mumbled when he rejoined Lou and Laurie. Laurie had her hand partially covering a smile. She always told Jack not to provoke Arnold by letting him know how he felt about him.

"So what's the story?" Jack said as he returned the missing papers to the case folder and withdrew the medical legal investigator's report. He was glad Janice Jaeger had been the MLI on the case; she was thorough and professional. Typical of Janice, she'd even drawn a map with actual distances and angles.

"The incident involved two off-duty police officers by the name of Don and Gloria Morano," Lou began. "They are husband and wife after meeting at the police academy. Good kids and good police officers. They've been on the beat for a little over two years and are still green, as expected. Last night, somewhere around three a.m., they heard the sound of breaking glass outside their bedroom window in Bayside and correctly surmised it had come from their new car, a Honda. Anyway, they leaped out of bed with Gloria grabbing her service automatic in the process. They ran outside into the driveway just in time to spot a couple of kids climbing into a van parked next to their vehicle. Later they learned the teenagers had stolen a Garmin GPS from their car's dash. At that point, things went down pretty fast. The driver pulled forward toward the Moranos, who were standing in the driveway, with Don in the middle of the drive directly in the path of the van and Gloria slightly ahead of Don and to his left, closer to the house, and standing in the grass. Do you get the picture?"

"Yeah, I get it," Jack said.

"Was the driver bent on running into Don?" Laurie asked.

"Nobody knows," Lou admitted. "Either that or it could have been a mistake on his part, putting the van in drive rather than reverse in the excitement. But that's something we'll never know. Anyway, with the van lurching forward toward Don, Gloria pulls off a single round through the windshield, hitting the driver in the chest. He doesn't die immediately; instead, he stops, then backs out into the street and dies a few yards down the road."

"So what's the problem?" Jack asked with a furrowed brow.

"The problem is the two other kids. They both insist the van never pulled forward. They say that the driver was looking back at them as they were climbing into the van via the open sliding door. They even insist he had his arm over the van's bench front seat."

"Okay, I got it," Jack said. "If the dead driver was backing up the whole time, the cops are in deep doo-doo, using unnecessary lethal force, whereas if he drove forward it would be justifiable homicide."

"Exactly," Lou said. "And to make it more interesting, the bullet's core jacket was on the front seat and the victim has a wound on his forearm."

"That makes things even more interesting," Jack said happily. "Vinnie, let's get a move on. We got work to do." Then, glancing at Laurie, he added, "Get a case and come on down. I'll save the neighboring table like we talked about."

"Great," Laurie responded, as Jack, Lou, and Vinnie disappeared back through the communications room, where operators sat waiting for death call-ins. She went over to Arnold. "Do you have a case for me yet? Perhaps it could be a straightforward case rather than something controversial. I'd like to get my feet wet rather than jumping into the deep end. I'm anxious about avoiding screwing up."

"No case for you today, Laurie," Arnold said. "Bingham's orders. He left word that unless there was an absolute flood today, I was to give you a free day to allow you some time to acclimatize after such a long absence. So you're free. Welcome back!"

Laurie let out an audible breath through pursed lips. She didn't know whether to be pleased or disappointed. On the one hand, there was something to be said about getting up to her office and getting things organized since she'd not been there for almost two years, but on the other hand it was putting off the inevitable, and now she'd have to go through the anxiety all over again tomorrow. "You sure he was insistent, or did he say anything about what my preference might be?"

"He was insistent as only Dr. Harold Bingham can be. You know the boss. He is never wishy-washy. He did say for you to come by his office first thing so he could welcome you back."

"Okay," Laurie said with resignation. She left Arnold to his charts and headed after Jack and the others. She thought she'd descend to the morgue and tell Jack she was not going to be in the pit for the day. When she got to the back elevator, she changed her mind. Knowing Jack and his strong penchant for interesting cases, which Lou's GSW certainly was, and how absorbed he'd be, she decided to tell him later. Instead, she turned around and headed for administration to see if Harold Bingham had arrived yet. As she walked she took out her mobile phone to make the first of many checks on JJ.

CHAPTER FOUR

MARCH 25, 2010 – THURSDAY, 9:05 a.m.

Ben Corey commuted into the city almost every week-
day in his prized 2010 Range Rover Autobiography from
his home in Englewood Cliffs, New Jersey. Despite the
usual traffic, he enjoyed the drive, especially across the
George Washington Bridge. He always made it a point
to be in the far-right lane on the upper deck so that he
could appreciate the view of the Manhattan skyline and
the expanse of the Hudson River. It didn't even bother
him when the rush-hour traffic occasionally stopped
dead, since it allowed him to appreciate the view even
longer. To enhance the experience, he always loaded his
CD player with classical music. It was the one time
during the day that he allowed himself to be alone, even
turning off his cell phone.

On that particular day, the commute had done its
job. By the time he drove into the parking garage just
west of 57th Street, he was feeling very rested and happy,
as well as wonderfully ignorant of what had occurred
the previous evening.

Ben walked less than a block to the office building
where iPS USA had rented space on the eighth floor
facing Fifth Avenue. The day was warm, in the high
fifties, and the sun was out, all in sharp contrast to the
misty, chilly, cloudy weather of the previous day. All in
all, it promised to be a glorious day in every respect.

Ben pulled off his coat as he passed the receptionist,

Clair Bourse, whom his assistant, Jacqueline, had recently hired. He said good morning, and she returned the greeting.

Entering his corner office, Ben hung up his coat and sat himself at his desk. Front and center was a fully signed and notarized copy of Satoshi's contract with a yellow Post-it note saying "for your files." There were also wills for Satoshi and his wife, and the trust documents Satoshi had signed concerning his infant son, Shigeru, with another Post-it note saying Satoshi had to get his wife's signature on both her will and the trust document. There was also a reminder for Ben to ask Satoshi if he wanted to take physical possession of them all or whether he'd like to have them put in iPS USA's safe-deposit box in the vault at JPMorgan Chase or in the safe there in the office. Finally, there was a current copy of an obscure biomolecular journal titled *Reprogramming Technologies*. On its glossy cover was a third yellow Post-it, also in Jacqueline's handwriting: *Check out the article on page 36. I think we'd better move on this*. The suggestion was followed by several exclamation points.

Ben put the papers for Satoshi on the corner of his desk, intending to give them to the researcher when he saw him, which he thought would be within the hour. Nine-thirty was Satoshi's usual time of arrival, and Ben had no reason to believe it wouldn't be as usual that morning. The only way he thought he might not see the man until afternoon would be if Satoshi had decided to indulge in some serious celebrating the previous night. From Ben's trip to Japan to rescue the now-famous lab books, Ben knew what sake could do.

"Did you read that article?" Jacqueline questioned.

She'd poked her head in from the neighboring office through the connecting door.

"I'm looking at it at the moment."

"I think you'd better," Jacqueline encouraged, "and before we sign the deal with Rapid Therapeutics up in Worcester, Massachusetts."

"Oh?" Ben questioned. He didn't like the sound of that. He and Carl Harris had been negotiating with Rapid Therapeutics over the course of many months to license their patents on increasing the efficiency of creating induced pluripotent stem cells. A deal was finally imminent, so there was no time to waste if something better was in the pipeline.

With his feet perched on the corner of the desk, Ben proceeded to read the article, realizing as he did so that Jacqueline was certainly correct. The article was about a small start-up company in California named iPS RAPID that had recently licensed a mechanism that dramatically raised by hundreds of times the efficiency of producing human induced pluripotent stem cells, a heretofore stumbling block in their use. The new technique involved what were termed *small molecules.*

Ben was shocked, not that the breakthrough was so astounding, although it was, but that it had gotten to the point of licensing without there even being a whisper of its discovery. Usually such an invention would first appear in *Nature* or *Science,* as its importance was obvious as a giant step in the direction of the commercialization of stem cells, but here it was showing up in an essentially unknown journal as a patented process already licensed, meaning that iPS USA was going to have to join the fray late and pay hundreds of times more to corner it. Although he was in a very real way adding to it, Ben recognized it was an unfortunate sign of the times. Universities now all had their own patent offices and considered filing for patents associated with the researchers' work more important than the research itself, and the behavior was definitely slowing the progress of science. Before the patent mania, it was the immediate publication of advances that kept the investigative pot boiling. Of course, adding to the problem was the fact that government patent offices, both in the United States and Europe, were also granting patents for life processes, which they weren't supposed to do by law, with Europe better than the United States in this regard. Ben could not believe some of the patents that he had recently seen emanating from the U.S. patent office. Often he marveled how anyone could justify a patent on a process that had developed by evolutionary forces over millions if not billions of years. The current patent mania would not only slow research but might also bring it to a halt. No one will be able to do anything without impinging on someone's patent, which will result in ever more lawsuits, of which there were already enough today. Ben saw it as being akin to throwing sand into the gears of progress in medical research, a consequence that iPS USA was trying to avoid, at least in the arena of induced pluripotent stem cells.

"Put in a call to this iPS RAPID!" Ben called out to Jacqueline through the open connecting door. "You're right about this article. Get the CEO's name and get him on the line!"

Jacqueline's head poked through the doorway, her red hair backlit from the sun streaming into her office.

"Didn't you notice that iPS RAPID is in San Diego,

where it's just after six in the morning?" Jacqueline said patiently.

For a moment Ben just stared at her without being able to make out her facial features in the glare. It took him a moment to comprehend that it was far too early on the West Coast to get anyone on the line. "Then get me Carl," he said. "And what do I have scheduled for this morning?" He was thinking of canceling everything to get right on the issue of iPS RAPID.

"Other than in-house meetings, you are supposed to meet with Michael Calabrese in his downtown office at ten-forty-five. Did you forget?"

"I forgot," Ben admitted. He thanked himself for having hired someone as good as Jacqueline to keep tabs on his schedule. He considered himself more of a concept guy. Although it was important to deal with the issue of this new company, in the long run it was more important to deal with Michael and break off the Mafia-Yakuza connection. Intuitively, he understood that the longer the association went on, the harder it was going to be to stop it. He also knew that if the connection were ever leaked he'd probably have to resign, or at the very least he'd have to kiss good-bye any chance of launching an IPO anytime soon. What he didn't let himself even consider was the possibility of an indictment.

With Jacqueline off to find Carl, Ben went back to the article, musing over what class of small molecules was involved. He guessed it was probably some kind of suppression of growth factor inhibitor, but that was only the obvious. As he read he marveled over the speed of biomedical discoveries, especially knowing that such discoveries invariably pointed to other possibilities, which spawned even more discoveries, in a quickening self-fulfilling process. He also knew there were discoveries and there were *discoveries,* meaning some were huge steps and others not so huge. He considered this present discovery to be one of the relatively big ones, at least in relation to the commercialization of iPS cells.

"You wanted to see me?" a voice called from the doorway to the hall a few minutes later.

Carl was standing there with his tie loosened, the top button unbuttoned on his shirt, and his sleeves rolled up to just above the elbows. He was the picture of the hard-working accountant rather than the CFO, which was why he was so good at what he did. There was nothing beneath him. He was involved in every aspect of the business's finances from the mundane to the conceptual, and Ben trusted him implicitly and relied on him completely.

"Come in! Sit down and take a look at this!" Ben said, handing Carl the article.

Ben watched his chief financial officer's expression as he read, noticing a frown develop. Then, in an apparent moment of frustration when he was finished, Carl slapped the journal down onto the surface of Ben's desk and lifted his face to him. "There's something I have to come clean about. It's a confession of sorts."

"What in the blazes are you talking about?" Ben asked, while in his mind he was concerned about being blindsided by some kind of major financial problem just when things were looking so rosy.

"This is something I should have admitted a year or two ago," Carl said so contritely that Ben's concerns soared.

What now? Ben thought silently, trying to prepare

himself for the worst, such as that the company had run out of money from having been embezzled or from some other disaster. With the contract signing yesterday, he'd been confident their financial situation was solid, especially with the contract certainly upping their market value.

"I hate to admit it, but I just don't know enough about stem cells," Carl said guiltily. "I understand up to a certain point, but when you hand me something really technical like this, it's just beyond me. I'm sorry. As the CFO of this company, I should be more knowledgeable with it, but the fact of the matter is that I'm better on the financial side than the scientific side. Remember! You recruited me from the financial world, not biotech."

For a moment Ben was stunned into a brief silence by a combination of relief and surprise. As a biomolecular scientist, he was so familiar with the material that he had trouble believing everyone else wasn't equally well informed. Quickly the relief and surprise turned to humor, and Ben found himself laughing. At that point it was Carl's turn to be confused. "Why are you laughing?" he questioned, genuinely bewildered. He had expected surprised irritation from Ben, not laughter.

"I can't help it," Ben admitted. "You've always convinced me you understood the field as much as anyone. Hell, I've asked you your opinion on a lot of issues, and I've always felt you gave me solid advice. How could that be?"

"Most of the advice I've given has been financial, and whether a company deals with stem cells or oranges, that advice is usually pretty similar. If it was outside of the financial arena, I suggested you ask Brad, Marcus, or Lesley. That was always good advice, and has worked pretty well. I've been trying to pick up more info as time's passed—there's so much to learn."

"How about a quick review," Ben said.

"It would be most welcome."

"Okay," Ben said, thinking about how to begin. "It all started in the early sixties, when a couple of Canadian researchers found the first stem cells in mouse blood. These were rather primitive cells that could divide and make progeny, of which, say, half became various blood cells and half would be merely self-renewing. Then there was about a thirty-five-year gap before a researcher in Wisconsin was able to isolate similar human stem cells from very early embryos and make them grow outside the body in glass dishes by a process called *in vitro*. At the same time other researchers learned to turn these stem cells into every different kind of cell in the body, such as heart cells, kidney cells, and the like, opening up the very real possibility for creating human replacement cells and parts to cure degenerative disease.

"Of course then disaster struck, involving the use of embryos originally created as part of the in vitro fertilization industry to get stem cells. Brushing up against the long-standing and very emotional abortion debate, the idea of getting stem cells from embryos caused Bush Two to restrict federal funding for stem cell research except from a narrow source of existing stem cell lines."

"I remember all this," Carl interrupted. "But what's all this about induced pluripotent stem cells? Are they the same as embryonic stem cells?"

"Amazingly enough, they do seem to be pretty much the same, and in ways their creation defies what science thought about development. For a long time scientists thought development of a cell from a primitive stage to a mature cell was a one-way street. But that turns out not to be the case. In studying the process of development, there appeared to be about thirty genes that are involved in varying amounts and timing in the maturation process. By packaging these genes in different amounts and mixtures, and putting them inside a fully developed mature cell with the help of viruses, reprogramming was shown to occur, taking the mature cell back to an embryonic state, seemingly the equivalent of an embryonic stem cell."

"So that's why these new stem cells are called 'induced'?" Carl questioned.

"Exactly!" Ben said. "And that's why they are also called pluripotent, meaning like embryonic stem cells, they are capable of forming any of the three hundred or so cells that make up the human body."

"It is surprising," Carl exclaimed.

"It's more than surprising, in my estimation," Ben said. "It's more like astounding. The science of induced pluripotent cells is racing ahead at breakneck speed. Four years ago it was the genes associated with development that were put into mature cells by viruses, and some of these genes were oncogenes, closely associated with cancer-causing capabilities. Even the virus vectors were known to be occasionally carcinogenic, or cancer-causing, so the resulting induced pluripotent stem cells could never be used in patients, as they would be far too dangerous. But since that early beginning just four years ago, genes have been placed as the agents to reprogram the cells to a more primitive state with the protein products of the genes, and the insertion by potentially dangerous viruses has been changed to using electric current called electroporation, or even more recently by certain chemicals that pull the development proteins in through the cell membranes without damaging them."

"Okay," Carl said. "*Astounding* is a better word than *surprising*."

"More important, does this give you a better understanding of the field?"

"Much better. I've finally got some context."

"I'm always happy to give you an explanation of the science. Don't feel embarrassed to ask."

"I will take you at your word," Carl said, putting his hand back on the reprint. "So if I understand correctly, this article is concerned with a process that speeds up the production of induced pluripotent stem cells, and it's another one of those key processes that we need to control?"

"Yes, and I believe, by the way, this iPS RAPID is behaving like it's for sale, an issue you know more about than I. My sense is that they would be better to control than the company in Massachusetts. It would be a coup to snap them up before they get a chance to test the market. Do we have significant equity on hand?"

"Probably not, but with the signing yesterday, we're in good shape market value–wise, and it won't take long to be able to estimate what we could raise in the short run."

"Do it," Ben ordered.

"It'll be done," Carl said, and got up from his chair. "Thanks again." A moment later he was gone.

Ben got up and poked his head into Jacqueline's office. He had to squint into the sun shining through her windows facing east. "Any sign of Satoshi?" he called out to her.

Since she was on the phone, Jacqueline merely waved and shook her head, voicelessly indicating that she'd not seen him.

Returning back to his desk, Ben half joked to himself that in regard to Satoshi he felt somewhat akin to the father of a teenage son, constantly concerned to a degree where the kid was and what he was doing. It was now going on ten, and Satoshi had yet to show up or call. Ben sighed, recognizing that he was always nervous until Satoshi appeared at the office, even though the man had nothing specific to do. Ben had asked him to at least call if he wasn't planning on coming in, but Satoshi never bothered. One time Satoshi didn't show up for a week and never bothered to call or even turn his cell phone on, causing Ben significant concern. When Satoshi did show up, he said he had taken his family to Niagara Falls. Although things were obviously better now with the licensing agreement signed and notarized, losing Satoshi would be more than inconvenient.

Thinking about Satoshi reminded Ben that he'd promised to call up to Columbia and check on the status of his request to lease laboratory space. As he put the call through, he mildly chided himself for not following up on it sooner. Knowing Satoshi as he now did, had he been more responsible, he wouldn't have to worry about Satoshi's whereabouts, because the man would spend all his time in the lab.

The conversation with the powers-that-be at Columbia was short and sweet, and very positive. The space was definitely available, the price was high but fair, and all Satoshi would have to do was provide a list of equipment and reagents, which the school would be happy to provide.

On a three-by-five card Ben scribbled the words *Columbia bench space available, can start immediately, need to know reagents and special equipment.*

Adding the index card to the already sizable stack of contracts, wills, and trusts, Ben reached for the phone. He'd waited long enough, and his impatience had taken over. He dialed Satoshi's cell phone number, which he'd committed to memory.

With an uncomfortable premonition building with each hollow ring, Ben impatiently drummed his fingers on the edge of the desk. When the prerecorded generic outgoing message came on, Ben's premonition was unhappily vindicated. When appropriate, he left a message for Satoshi to return the call, adding that he had some good news to report. It was Ben's hope that such a message was the best way to ensure a call back as soon as possible.

With that accomplished, Ben went into his closet and dragged out his coat. It was time to leave for his morning meeting with Michael.

CHAPTER FIVE

Laurie realized she was not concentrating as she went back once again to the beginning of the chapter of the book she was reading. With nothing else to do, she resigned herself to reviewing general forensics, reading up on gunshot wounds. She had chosen GSW after hearing Lou's story about the case that Jack was currently doing down in the pit. The trouble was that her mind was running all over creation, jumping from one thing to another. She'd already called Leticia so many times just to check in that she had detected a bit of frustration on Leticia's part. During her last call Laurie had even detected irritation. While Leticia said everything was fine, she suggested that perhaps she, Leticia, should be the next to call, and only if there was a problem of any sort. In her highly sensitive state, Laurie felt as if she was being told that she was not quite as important as she thought and that it was she who was having the problem of adapting, not JJ.

As for her general reception at OCME, Jack had been right. Everyone from the janitorial staff and building engineers all the way up to the chief and the deputy chief had been effusive in welcoming her back. The universality of the response had been warming, but it had done nothing for her professional anxieties. If anything, they'd hardened partially as a consequence of not having been assigned a case. She had found herself unreasonably interpreting the situation not as a favor to her to get acclimated but rather because they, meaning Bingham, didn't think she could do it to their expectations. The problem, however, was more because she had too much time on her hands with essentially nothing to do.

Laurie's eyes drifted around her office. There were no Post-its clinging to the tops, sides, or bottom of her computer screen, as there usually were. No stacks of case files on the corner of her desk waiting for information or laboratory results before they could be signed out. In fact, the entire room looked so clean as to be sterile. The microscope standing by itself without slide trays seemed the most lonely, with protective covers on its eyepieces.

Laurie was about to give up trying to read, thinking she would wander down to the autopsy room and at least participate with Jack and Lou on the GSW case. By doing so she hoped she would feel that she was participating, if not contributing. Instead her phone surprised her by filling the room with its persistent jangle. Laurie snapped it up as if it was a desperate emergency, thankful that someone wanted to talk with her.

"Laurie, I have a problem," a voice said. It took her a moment to recognize that it was Dr. Arnold Besserman, the on-call medical examiner who'd denied her a case that morning and who was thereby guilty of intensifying her anxieties, or so she irrationally and unfairly thought.

"Oh?" Laurie questioned with a glimmer of hope. Maybe a new case had just come in.

"Kevin's going home sick," Arnold continued. Kevin

was Dr. Kevin Southgate, one of Arnold's sidekicks. The two argued over everything, particularly religion and politics, despite being quite fond of each other. "I gave him only one post, from the looks of it an easy one at that: an apparently natural death following a collapse on the Fifty-ninth Street platform of the A train. It's just a routine case. Anyway, he claims he's coming down with H1N1, and he's heading home." Arnold laughed into the phone. "Have you seen Bingham yet, and if you have, could you come down and take over? I know I said I'd give you the day as a freebie, but I'm kinda stuck, and you're the only one available. What do you say?"

Laurie smiled. Of course she wanted the case, even if it turned out to be a natural death. In fact, she thought a natural death was probably a good way to start; it was hard to screw up a natural death. What made her smile was the fact that Arnold didn't mention whether he was busy or not. Often when he was the on-call medical examiner, he rarely assigned himself any cases.

"Who's the mortuary tech on the case?" Laurie asked, more out of curiosity than anything else.

"Marvin," Arnold said. "That's another reason I thought you might be willing to take over."

Arnold was speaking the truth. Marvin Fletcher was Laurie's favorite tech, and she worked with him as often as she could.

"I'll be happy to do it," Laurie said. "I'll be right down."

True to her word, Laurie left her office as soon as she'd replaced the receiver, and wasted no time pulling on a Tyvek suit, gloves, and her plastic face mask. So attired, she pushed into the autopsy room and glanced around. All eight tables were in use, and Marvin waved from where he was standing at the head of the fourth table. As luck would have it, Jack and Lou were at the neighboring fifth table. They were just finishing up by closing the autopsy incision, with Lou doing the stitching. He'd become such a frequent visitor that he enjoyed helping. Laurie made a brief stop to say hello.

"Hey, how's it going?" Jack said, catching sight of her. "I'd heard you were to have a free day, thanks to our fearless leader. What brings you down here?"

"That was before Kevin Southgate fell ill next to you guys."

Jack glanced at the table just behind him and nodded to Marvin, who was patiently waiting. "I had no idea," Jack said, returning his gaze to Laurie. "Of course, Arnold couldn't come down and stand in for his friend."

"Of course not," Laurie agreed. "But I'm pleased. I wanted a case, particularly a straightforward case." Since she didn't want to get into a discussion of Arnold's shirking tendencies, which was one of Jack's pet peeves, she changed the subject and asked how the GSW case had gone.

"I'd say very well," Jack responded.

"I agree wholeheartedly," Lou chimed in. "The path of the bullet into the driver's chest was definitely from the right to the left, meaning he was facing forward when he was shot and not straight on, as he would have been if he was twisted in his seat, backing up, as the accomplices contend. And the core jacket, which separated off as the bullet went through the windshield, did quite a number on the man's forearm, which couldn't have happened if he'd had his right arm over the back of the van's bench seat, as the accomplices also contend."

"Congratulations," Laurie remarked, and she meant it. It was a good case to demonstrate the power of forensics.

Moving on, Laurie greeted Marvin, who returned the greeting with great enthusiasm. Up until that moment, they'd not yet seen each other since Laurie's return to work. After a short discussion of the rigors of parenthood, since Marvin had three kids of his own, Laurie directed the conversation to the victim stretched out on the autopsy table.

"So what do we have here?" she asked.

Looking down at the corpse, which had been butterflied with the typical Y-shaped autopsy incision to expose the internal organs, Marvin said, "The victim is an Asian male, which Dr. Southgate estimated to be approximately thirty-five years old, weighing one hundred and forty-two pounds, who collapsed on the subway platform. There is no known medical history, and no prescription drugs were found on his person."

As Marvin continued his description, Laurie picked up the case file and extracted the MLI's report. It had been written by Cheryl Meyers. Still listening to Marvin, her eyes scanned the report and immediately picked up on the fact that there had been no identification found on the victim.

"Is this an unidentified individual?" Laurie asked, interrupting Marvin.

"Yup," Marvin said.

Laurie went back to the case file and pulled out the notice-of-death sheet and the identification-of-body form. The latter was blank and the former barely filled out with the facts that the body was picked up by emergency medical techs who'd responded to the scene after a call to 911. They'd found the victim unresponsive, with no heartbeat, no blood pressure, and without respiration. CPR was instituted and continued until the arrival at the Harlem Hospital Center emergency room, where he was declared dead.

Laurie looked up and locked eyes with Marvin. To her, an unidentified case was a complication, and she was disappointed to a degree. She knew it wasn't necessarily a rational response, because she could do her forensic work just the same whether the corpse's identity was known or not known, but on her first case back from her leave, she wanted the case to be definitive, with no loose ends. For her, being unidentified was a loose end, and more important for her, it was a loose end that was largely beyond her control to influence. There would be no medical history to help her confirm her findings.

"Was there anything unique about the external exam?" Laurie questioned.

Marvin shook his head. "No scars or tattoos, if that's what you mean."

"How about jewelry?"

"There is a police custody voucher for a wedding band."

Laurie's eyes brightened. A wedding band meant a wife, and glancing at the victim's general appearance, she knew this was no derelict individual, as he was well groomed. "What were his clothes like?"

"Well dressed, with shirt, tie, and jacket under a long overcoat. The overcoat looked new, although it was soiled from the subway platform."

"Those are all good signs," Laurie said with relief. From experience she knew that identification of unidentified bodies depended largely on the victim being searched for, and in a situation like the one she was currently facing, a wife starting a search within twenty-four hours or less was the rule, not the exception. In contrast, identifying a body in a situation where there was no one looking for it was a very difficult task, even in this day and age, with tools such as DNA matching.

"Did Dr. Southgate mention if he had any suspicions about the cause of death?" Laurie asked.

"Not that he said," Marvin offered, "but I think he was leaning toward a stroke or something intracranial. One witness—actually, the man who made the nine-one-one call—said that he thought there had been a short seizure involved."

Laurie glanced back at Cheryl Meyers's note and saw that she had duly included the suggestion of a stroke, but she'd gotten that from the EMTs and had not spoken with the individual. "What about the X-rays? Anything interesting seen on them?"

"Dr. Southgate said they were negative. But they are still up on the view box, if you care to look at them."

"I care," Laurie said. Clasping her hands together, she went over and gave them a look, concentrating on the head and the chest. She saw no abnormalities. She then scanned the abdomen and finally the extremities. Nothing.

"Okay," Laurie said, returning to Marvin. "Let's get the show on the road, and we'll see what we find."

Since Laurie and Marvin often worked together, the autopsy itself went quickly. The slowest part was when they removed the lungs and the heart en bloc, as cardiac arrest was often involved with sudden death. But the heart was normal and no abnormalities of the vessels were noted, particularly the coronary arteries. The second time they slowed the pace was after Marvin had cut off the crown of the head and gently removed the skullcap. Both had expected to see blood if there had been a fatal event in the brain, but there had been no blood whatsoever, either in the coverings of the brain or within the brain itself.

"Well," Laurie said after finishing suturing the autopsy incision. "That's about as normal an autopsy that one can have. Usually there's some pathology that can be found, but with this unfortunate fellow, he seems to have been entirely healthy and normal."

"What's your guess, then?" Marvin asked.

"I suppose I'd have to guess that he suffered some sort of cardiac conduction abnormality despite the possibility of a seizure having been involved," Laurie suggested with a discouraged shake of her head. "After the heart and great vessels appeared normal, I was surprised when we didn't come across a solid tumor when we were slicing the brain. So now it will be up to histology—at least I hope histology will help. I don't want to have to sign this case out as an unknown cause of death of an unknown individual, and especially not as my first case back from my maternity leave. It's not going to be any help for my confidence."

"What about the extra fluid we found in the stomach and the beginning of the small intestine?" Marvin questioned. "That seemed to surprise you when you saw it at the time. Any significance you can think of now?"

"Not really," Laurie admitted. "As far as I know, that's not associated with any natural cause of sudden death. The man must have drunk and eaten not long before he died. It will be interesting to see what his blood alcohol will turn out to be."

"What about unnatural cause?"

Laurie paused. Marvin had reminded her that it was always important to keep an open mind, as one could be fooled, for example, by a homicide made to look like a suicide or an accident. Yet the possibility of this case fitting into that scenario seemed very unlikely, with the victim collapsing on a subway platform. At the same time, just to be complete, she had already decided on doing a toxicology screen as well as a BAL, or blood alcohol level test, and had taken the appropriate samples. OCME toxicology screen included some two to three hundred legal and illegal drugs, so she felt confident to be covered in a drug poisoning or overdose situation.

"I'm pretty sure, when all is said and done, this is going to be a natural death," Laurie predicted. "We just have to wait for histology and toxicology to help us out if there is something else involved."

"Are you booked for another case?" Marvin asked.

"I doubt it," Laurie answered. "I wasn't even booked for this one."

Laurie helped move the body onto a gurney, then gathered up the toxicology and the histology sample bottles and put them in two brown paper bags. "I'll carry these up myself," she told Marvin. "I want to make a personal plea that they get processed quickly. I've nothing else to do."

"Be my guest," Marvin responded.

On her way out, she stopped at Jack's table, where he was already starting another case. Lou had long since departed for home and some much-needed sleep.

"How'd it go?" Jack asked, referring to Laurie's case. When he'd returned to start his second case, he'd decided not to disturb Laurie, who'd appeared to be totally absorbed with the Asian. "What did you find?"

"Unfortunately, nothing," Laurie responded. "And to make matters worse, it's an unidentified body."

"Why the long face?" Jack questioned.

"Don't ask. I found no pathology whatsoever. And with no medical history, my chances of missing something important go up considerably."

"So?" Jack questioned. "That happens. Sometimes there's no pathology whatsoever. Not often, but it happens."

"Yeah, it happens, but I didn't want it to happen on my first case PMS."

"PMS? You have PMS?" Jack was incredulous. Laurie never complained of PMS.

"Post-maternity sojourn." Laurie said, trying to be funny to buoy her mood, but her would-be joke fell flat. "But I'm not going to give up. I'm going to find some pathology if it kills me. At least I have the time. It's my only case."

Jack merely shook his head, and without even smiling questioned, "You're not using a negative autopsy to fan your professional competency concerns, are you? Because if you are, you're being"—he paused, trying to find an appropriate word—"silly."

"I refuse to answer on grounds of incriminating myself," Laurie offered, and tried to smile.

"You're impossible!" Jack said with a wave of dismissal. "I'm not even going to respond, for fear of encouraging such nonsense."

"What's your second case?" Laurie asked, to change the subject. She was glancing at the body of a young, healthy woman with no obvious abnormalities or trauma. Vinnie was standing at the table, obviously impatient to get under way, nervously shifting his weight from one foot to the other.

"I guess similar to yours: sudden death. Boyfriend saw her walk out of the bathroom as you see her now, completely naked. He described her as looking surprised or confused, and then she just collapsed."

"Any health problems?"

"Nope, no health problems. She was a cabin attendant for Delta and completely healthy. She had just returned from a trip to Istanbul."

"You're right. Sounds like my case," Laurie suggested.

"Except for one thing," Jack said. "The boyfriend wasn't supposed to be there. There was a restraining order against him, as he'd supposedly tried to kill her a month earlier when she started dating a pilot colleague."

"Uh-oh!" Laurie voiced.

" 'Uh-oh' is right," Jack agreed.

"Keep me informed," Laurie said. It did sound like her case, except for the benefit of an identification and history.

Laurie left the autopsy room, carrying bags containing the histology and toxicology sample bottles. In the locker room, she got out of her Tyvek suit and dealt with her headgear. As she rode in the elevator to the fourth floor, she thought about Jack's case. She was jealous that he would undoubtedly find some nefarious cause of the woman's death. She wished her case could have been similar in that regard.

"Well, well, ladies!" Maureen O'Conner, the histology lab supervisor, cried out in her famous brogue as she took the brown bag from Laurie. Maureen had spent the first half of her life working at a hospital in Dublin,

Ireland, before coming to New York. Vivacity was her middle name, and no one was spared her sharp and humorous tongue, from the chief down to the janitors. Laurie was a favorite, as she was the only medical examiner who made it a point to visit Maureen's fiefdom regularly. Laurie was always eager to have the histology slides on her cases sooner rather than later.

"If it isn't Dr. Laurie Montgomery!" Maureen continued, causing all heads in the department to turn in Laurie's direction. "Welcome back! How is that little one of yours—well, I hope." Everyone at OCME had heard the story of JJ's neuroblastoma, as well as the good news of his miraculous cure.

Laurie took the added attention in stride, even the usual kidding about her frequent requests to have her slides back overnight. Maureen's usual teasing was to remind Laurie that her patients were all dead, so there was no need for speed, a comment that never ceased to put all employees of the histology lab into fits of laughter.

Next Laurie descended back to the first floor and visited Sergeant Murphy of the NYPD. His tiny cubicle office was situated off the communications room, where operators were on call for reports of deaths twenty-four hours a day. Besides the desk, there was barely enough room for two metal folding chairs and an upright file cabinet. The desktop and the top of the file cabinet were strewn with newspapers, soiled coffee cups, and crumpled Burger King wrappers.

"Did you get word on the unidentified Asian that came in late yesterday afternoon?" Laurie questioned. She'd run into the sergeant earlier, and they'd already gone through their welcome-back greetings.

"I did," Murphy said. "The transit patrolmen out of District One who responded to the nine-one-one call copied me on their report to the Missing Persons Squad as they were supposed to. Apparently, there was no billfold on the victim or other identification. In fact, there wasn't anything whatsoever except a wedding band. There wasn't even a watch."

"Do you know if there were any witnesses to his wallet being swiped? As well groomed and dressed as he was, it seems unlikely that he'd not been carrying one."

"None that I know of."

"What's the status of the case?"

"It's been assigned to a missing-persons case detective out of Midtown North Precinct as an unidentified body. It's being worked."

"Do you have the detective's name?"

"I do. It's right here someplace." Murphy pulled out the center drawer of the desk, requiring him to suck in his stomach. There was barely enough room to open the drawer. He fumbled through the contents for a moment before producing a crumpled single sheet. "Detective Ron Steadman, who also occasionally works out of Precinct Twenty." He jotted the numbers on a piece of scrap paper and gave it to her. "If you try to call him, use the Midtown North Precinct, because that's where he is ninety-nine percent of the time."

"I'll do that," Laurie said. "In the meantime, if you hear anything, please let me know."

"Will do!" Murphy said cheerfully.

Next Laurie climbed the stairs to the anthropology department, which had expanded significantly after 9/11, when identification had become an operational nightmare. She knocked on the closed glazed door of Hank Monroe, the director of identification. Originally, identification had been solely the purview of Sergeant Murphy as the liaison with NYPD Missing Persons Squad, but following 9/11 the job became much larger, and an in-house department had been created.

"Come in!" a voice called out. Hank Monroe was a medium-size individual with a face full of sharp angles.

"My name is Laurie Stapleton," Laurie said, introducing herself. Hank was relatively new to OCME staff, and he and Laurie had never met. After some pleasant chitchat, Laurie asked if he'd heard about the unidentified case that had come in late the previous afternoon.

"Not yet," Hank confessed. "There's usually a note from one of the night mortuary techs, but not this time. The body probably came in around shift change, but it's no problem. What's the story?"

Laurie gave a rapid synopsis of her John Doe case.

"Not much to go on," Hank said. He'd grabbed a pad and pencil to write down the critical details, which were limited to *Asian, well groomed,* and *had been wearing a wedding band.* "No scars or any other distinguishing characteristics?"

"Unfortunately not."

"Any help from Missing Persons?"

"Nothing—at least not yet."

"It's early. I guess you realize that?"

"I do, but this case is important to me for personal reasons."

Hank stared at Laurie, confused as to how the identification of an unidentified corpse could be a personal concern for a medical examiner, but he chose not to question. At the same time, he wanted his colleague to be realistic.

"I'll try to help," he said, "but cases like this are very difficult if someone like a wife, a coworker, a friend, or a child doesn't come forward. But the critical period is this first twenty-four hours. If someone doesn't appear, the chance of ever making an ID begins to fall precipitously. Most people don't realize this, not in this era of DNA technology, but it's the reality."

"That doesn't sound encouraging," Laurie said.

"Well, let's try to be positive. We're still within the first twenty-four-hour period."

Feeling progressively depressed, Laurie thanked Hank after he offered to keep his eyes and ears peeled, including calling his contacts with the Missing Persons Squad at the NYPD at One Police Plaza. Slowly she mounted the stairs, sensing that her first day back to work was going to end on a down note.

For a while she sat at her desk, staring with unseeing eyes at her computer screen, wondering if she should give up being a medical examiner and fully embrace motherhood, which she now knew was much more demanding than she'd ever considered. Of course, the first issue such thinking brought to mind was what Jack would think if she suggested such a thing, and could they live on one salary? As close as everything was every month financially, she knew it would not be easy without her salary, and they'd probably have to sell the newly renovated house that they so enjoyed.

Thinking in such a vein made her even more depressed, to the point that she suddenly shook her head, took a deep breath, and straightened up in her chair. She remembered some of what she'd thought were normal changes after giving birth, and wondered if she was still experiencing such effects now. The stress of leaving JJ in the hands of someone else, no matter how capable, combined with the stress of worrying about her job skills, was enough to depress her. At the same time, she thought she should give herself some slack and not give up so soon.

Laurie picked up her phone and called Detective Ron Steadman at the Midtown North Precinct. If anyone was going to learn anything about her corpse, it was going to be the detective, as it was his job as part of the police department's Missing Persons Squad to actually actively investigate the case. How that was specifically done, Laurie didn't know, as she'd never been inclined to look into the process. Now she felt differently and hoped to find out.

After ten rings, which she'd actually counted, Laurie began to become discouraged anew. Her experiences calling police precincts for information were always a difficult affair, where all too often the phone would ring interminably. Forcing herself to be patient, Laurie let it ring. Finally, on the twenty-third ring, and just when she was about to try the other number, some-one answered, and to her shock it was Ron Steadman. Usually with the NYPD she had to leave a name and hope for a callback, which she'd get about fifty percent of the time.

Any hope for a dynamic individual faded the moment she heard the man's voice. He sounded as if he was exhausted by merely breathing. Laurie explained who she was and why she was calling, and when she finished, there was a silence on the other end of the line that seemingly was to extend indefinitely.

"Hello!" Laurie said, thinking the connection had surely broken. Instead, it seemed the man had fallen asleep. At least, that was Laurie's guess.

"What was that again?" Ron said without apology.

Laurie told herself to take the situation in stride, and she took her own advice. Speaking more slowly and more clearly, she repeated the message.

"We have the case," Ron responded. His voice was flat.

"Good!" Laurie said. "What's happened so far?"

"What do you mean what's happened? I copied it to your guy, what's his name?"

"Sergeant Murphy."

"Yeah, that's the one. I copied it to him while I sent it down to One Police Plaza to Missing Persons, along with the responding officers' description."

"And what has Missing Persons done?"

"Not much would be my guess. I suppose they've added it to the list."

"The list of missing persons, I suppose?" Laurie responded sarcastically. Somehow she couldn't believe what she was hearing. The man sounded totally disinterested.

"No. We got a list of people wanting to be extras in TV cop shows. Of course the case was added to the missing-persons list."

"And as the assigned detective to the case," Laurie said with more sarcasm, "what have you done during this critical period?"

There was another short silence until Ron said, "Look, lady, I don't know why you are busting my balls. I send the info where I'm supposed to send it and then sit back and wait."

"Wait for what?"

"I wait for you to send us some prints, photos, and whatever you get from the autopsy, including DNA info, so that we can improve on the description. The prints we'll run locally. If no hits, we run on the state level on up to the federal. But I gotta warn you, we don't get many hits in this kind of case. It's up to the family to come to you guys or us. Now, if there had been criminality involved, things would be done differently."

"How do you know there was no criminality?"

There was another short period of silence. "Are you trying to tell me something by wandering all around the block or what? Did you find something at autopsy that suggests this was a homicide? If you are, please come right out with it."

"Nothing was found at autopsy that suggested criminality," Laurie admitted.

"Well, there you go. If anything changes let me know, and vice versa. Meanwhile, I'll let it sit here with my other hundred cases."

Laurie hung up the phone without responding to Ron's last statement. It was clear to her that he intended to do essentially nothing in this initial phase of trying to come up with the identity of her case. Although frustrated, Laurie could understand such rationality. There really wasn't much to be done at that juncture except hope that someone would come forward.

Rising up from her desk chair, Laurie picked up the collection of specimens for toxicological testing. The main test she was interested in was the BAL, or blood alcohol level test. There was something on the intuitive level that kept telling her it was going to be high. How high or the significance, Laurie didn't know. As for the screen for all sorts of other drugs, chemicals, or toxins, Laurie felt it was important just to be complete. She felt the same about electrolytes as indirect evidence of possible metabolic disease, such as diabetes, but she wasn't optimistic with the normal autopsy.

In years past Laurie had had a difficult relationship with the toxicology supervisor, John DeVries. John had been a cantankerous man permanently paranoid that the chief of OCME was forever denying him adequate funding yet demanding a first-rate lab. As it was often with such battles, there was right and wrong on both sides, so the problem was more a clash of personalities than anything else. The problem for Laurie was that, as with Maureen, she'd frequently come to the lab essentially asking that her cases get priority. She always wanted the results immediately, which always reminded John of his budget crisis, since he was always behind. He was so conscientious that on occasion he used his own money to buy needed reagents.

But 9/11 changed things. Not only did OCME budgets for all departments rise significantly with the challenge, but with the new building at 421 East 26th Street creating more space in the old, John's lab metamorphosed from being totally inadequate to occupying two complete floors of the old building, and from using outdated equipment liable to failure to using the newest and the best. Coinciding with such upgrading, John's personality went from grouchy and hotheaded to helpful and even genial. He'd also gone from wearing soiled and tattered lab coats reflecting what he thought of the financial state of his lab to new, clean, and pressed ones that he changed every day.

Laurie found him along with his assistant supervisor,

Peter Letterman, in his new corner office facing out south and east over the corner of First Avenue and 30th Street. The sunlight was dazzling even through partially closed miniblinds and hopelessly dirty windows.

As Laurie had yet to see the two men who now lorded over a bevy of lab technicians, she had to suffer through a warm greeting not only from John and Peter but also all the techs, who filed in at John's request. More than half had been hired during the course of Laurie's maternity leave, requiring formal introductions. It all took almost a half-hour.

"Well, what can we do for you?" John asked after all the techs departed. Laurie told her story about her John Doe and her plight of being unable to identify the man or provide a cause of death, much less a manner of death. She added that it had her quite upset.

John glanced at Peter, and both men raised their eyebrows questioningly.

"Why are you upset?" John questioned for the two of them.

"Because . . ." Laurie began while glancing back and forth between John and Peter. But she didn't finish. She suddenly felt embarrassed at why she'd made such an unprofessional admission.

"Well, it doesn't matter," John said, sensing Laurie's discomfort. "What can we do for you?"

Laurie felt a wave of inappropriate emotion spread through her, accompanied by the horror that tears were not far behind. Sudden unexpected displays of emotion had been a mild problem since her teen years. She hated the tendency and considered it to be a personality flaw. Over the years it had improved dramatically as she'd gained confidence. Unfortunately, JJ's diagnosis of neuroblastoma had brought it back with a vengeance. Just as it had been in her teenage years, she had little emotional control these days.

Both John and Peter were confused, watching Laurie struggle. Although they wanted to help, they didn't know quite what to do.

Finally Laurie was able to get control of herself by taking a deep breath and letting it out forcibly. "I'm so sorry," she said.

"No problem," the men echoed.

"It is a problem," Laurie admitted. "I'm sorry. I was so eager on this first day back to have everything go smoothly that now that it hasn't, I feel unreasonably emotional."

"Well, no harm done," John said, trying to reassure Laurie. "I assume you have some samples for us." He pointed to the brown specimen bag Laurie was clutching.

Laurie looked at the bag as if she'd forgotten she was holding it. "Oh, yes! I do have samples I'd like you to run. I need a toxicology screen and also a BAL." She handed the brown bag over to John's waiting hands.

"I suppose you want a rush on this like usual," John asked, trying to lighten the atmosphere.

"That would be terrific," Laurie said, wanting to get away. She was still embarrassed.

CHAPTER SIX

Ben climbed out of the cab in front of Michael Calabrese's building. It was a new spire of granite and reflective glass a stone's throw from Ground Zero. He signed in with security on the first floor, got a nametag that he stuck on the breast pocket of his jacket, and took the elevator up to the fifty-fourth floor.

Michael's office arrangement was rather unique. He and a group of other individual financial wheeler-dealers shared the entire floor, paying rent only for the proportion of the square footage they occupied as a private office. As for the office help and office equipment, including secretaries, receptionists, copy machines, computer monitors, computer servers, janitorial service, and common areas, such as conference rooms and restrooms, they all paid a common fee based on month-to-month occupancy. The relationship created an opportunity for the individual practitioners to enjoy far better quarters and services than they would have if they were all on their own. They even had a full-time computer wizard in-house.

Ben went directly to Michael's office. As the communal secretaries and receptionists were not close, Ben went to Michael's open door and knocked on the jamb. Michael was on the phone, as he always was, tipped back in his chair with his feet up on the corner of his desk. Looking up, he used his free hand to wave Ben inside and motioned for him to take a seat on a black leather couch.

Ben took in the surroundings as he sat. It was immediately evident by the furnishings that Michael's boutique placement firm was highly successful. The French polished mahogany walls gleamed with a finish that reminded Ben of his brand-new Range Rover. Various bronze knickknacks, including a large telescope on a tripod, shone like gold. On the coffee table was a black walnut humidor with a flush inset humidity gauge.

The office was a corner office with floor-to-ceiling walls of glass, not mere windows, as in Ben's office, and a stunning view out over the Hudson River. To the left was the elegant Statue of Liberty, standing stolidly on her tiny island.

A loud burst of laugher brought Ben's attention back to Michael. Although Ben tried not to listen to Michael's conversation out of courtesy, he now realized Michael was talking to someone about Angels Healthcare, a company that had proven how much money there was to be made in the hospital industry. Angels Healthcare had been an early entry into the boom associated with surgical specialty hospitals in such diverse fields as cardiology, orthopedics, ophthalmology, and plastic surgery. By having no emergency rooms and servicing only the insured or paying patents and ignoring the truly sick, the noninsured, and those on Medicaid, such hospitals were moneymakers, and Angels Healthcare's market value went through the roof. In fact, it was because of Michael Calabrese's pivotal role in the initial stages of raising capital for Angels Healthcare that Ben had heard of him and his boutique investment firm, Calabrese and Associates.

Ben's impression of Michael did not start out very well, as Ben had heard Michael had been indicted for a number of white-collar criminal activities and even one count of violent crime. But subsequently all charges had to be dropped because the evidence obtained by the police and the prosecutors turned out to have been tainted and had to be thrown out.

As soon as Michael had been absolved of any wrongdoing, Ben had scheduled a meeting with him to talk about iPS USA. From that very first tête-à-tête meeting, the two men had hit it off: Michael was enamored with biotech and had specialized in biotech start-ups, while Ben had extensive biotech experience and had come up with a terrific business plan of cornering the intellectual property associated with the commercialization of induced pluripotent stem cells. In many ways it was an ideal match, as they shared certain personality traits: Both were excessively vain in appearance and accomplishment, both were excessively competitive in work and play, both saw individual wealth as a crowning motivator, and both considered overly ethical behavior as a potential handicap in life's journey.

As soon as his phone call was concluded, Michael's feet dropped from the corner of his desk. He stood up, stepped over to Ben, and the two shook hands. "What's happening?" Michael asked with his strong New York accent. He reached for a straight-backed chair and turned it around to sit on it backward.

Although Michael's comment was more a figure of speech than a real question, Ben answered, "Not much," but then quickly corrected himself: "Actually, a lot is happening."

"Like what?"

Ben told Michael about the biotech journal and its article concerning the new method for increasing the formation of iPS cells by a hundred times.

"Is that significant?"

"Very significant. In fact, so significant I think I want to change what I came here to talk about."

"You mean about giving the Lucia people and the Yamaguchi their walking papers?"

"Exactly," Ben agreed. "I think we might want to buy this new company or at least exclusively sublicense the new process. We've been in negotiations with another company up in Worcester, Massachusetts, for their process to do the same thing, but their process is nowhere as efficient as this new one in San Diego."

"What kind of money are we talking about," Michael asked, "and how do you see doing it? As stock or as a bridge loan?"

"Stock if we decide to buy, and maybe as a bridge loan if we decide to exclusively sublicense."

"How about the money. What are we talking about, approximately?"

"I'd say in the neighborhood of half a million if we sublicense, which is what I think we should do. At first I thought about buying, but it would be much more if we buy, and buying is more risky with how fast the technology is advancing."

"After the signing yesterday," Michael said, "I'd recommend we use stock whether we buy or sublicense. I can make a good case that our market value has gone up considerably."

"You think our angels will go for it?"

"I don't see why not. I know for a fact their business

is booming, particularly in the gambling arena. They are virtually swimming in money."

"I've never asked," Ben said, "but something tweaks my curiosity about how their partnership works."

"You mean between the Mafia and the Yakuza? It's interesting you ask, because I had to ask as well. It's actually quite simple. It's the Lucia people who site, set up, and run the Italian restaurants that front the high-end gambling joints they have peppered around the Upper East Side. They're also the ones who arrange for the women or whatever. It's the Yakuza who find the clientele: mostly high-end businessmen from Japan, who, by the way, notoriously love to gamble. I mean really love to gamble. It's also the Lucia people who provide the credit when and if needed, and it's usually needed, as the Japanese clients more often than not run out of cash. As Japanese, they are encouraged to borrow as much as they want from the Mafia, with the understanding that they can pay back the loans on their next trip to New York. Of course, this affords the gamblers the opportunity to borrow much more than they ordinarily would, because they have the mistaken idea that, if needed, they can avoid ever repaying by never returning to NYC. But here's where the partnership really works. The grossly in-debt Japanese businessman then returns to Japan, where he believes he is immune from the Mafia. But he soon learns that that's not the case. It is the Yakuza who collect, and the Yakuza are very good at collecting, as they can be extraordinarily violent. The Yakuza then share the take with the Mafia, often in crystal meth, not cash. It is a very lucrative setup for both sides."

Ben shivered with the thought of what a nasty surprise that would be for an unsuspecting Japanese business-man.

"So, let's go over this again so there is no misunder-standing," Michael said. "You want me to go to the Lucias' capo, Vinnie Dominick, and Yamaguchi-gumi's *saiko-komon*, Saboru Fukuda, and talk about increasing their stake in iPS USA even though just yesterday after-noon you were talking about sidelining them. Are we on the same page here?"

"Yes, unless you have another potential angel invest-or?"

"I have a couple of people I could go to, but I think it's better to stay with what we got."

"You're the placement agent, not me!"

"I'm actually glad that you've changed your mind."

"How so?" Ben questioned.

"I was worried you were coming in here this morn-ing to insist on my going to them and telling them they were being demoted to garden-variety investors."

"It will have to happen, but just not now," Ben said. "But it will have to be before any IPO. Due diligence might bring it out in the open."

"I think you're being a bit naïve. You don't tell either one of these guys what to do and what not to do."

"I fully plan to reward them with extra stock for the role they've been playing."

"I think the only thing you will succeed in doing is pissing them off, which is not a good thing to do. But let's not argue and become distracted. Let's keep our eyes focused on when we want to go for the IPO, because that's when we all get our just rewards."

"Maintaining a working relationship makes me

nervous," Ben admitted. "As soon as we don't need them, I want to break it off."

"I was open with you when you first came calling. These are not people you can order around."

"I know you were open with me, and I appreciate that you were."

"I'll tell you what I'll do," Michael said. "I'll call our friends and find out if I can see them this afternoon. I'll tell them the good news concerning yesterday's contract signing, then hit them up for more equity, which I'm sure they'll like to hear. Then I'll bring up the issue that they'll have to fade into the background for the IPO. With the good news, maybe they'll take it all in stride. I'll see what I can do and get back to you."

"I appreciate it," Ben said, rising to his feet.

A few minutes later as he was on his way down in the elevator, Ben placed a call to Jacqueline and said he'd be back at the office soon and asked if she wanted to get lunch at Cipriani, located in the Sherry-Netherland up the street from the iPS USA office. What he really wanted was for her to tell him Satoshi had shown up, since he was superstitious about asking. When she didn't offer the information, he finally asked and was told he hadn't appeared. With similar superstition, Ben had avoided redialing Satoshi's cell phone but finally did. What he got was voicemail, and passive-aggressively he chose not to leave a message. Ben was now angry that the man didn't have the sense to call if he wasn't planning on showing up.

CHAPTER SEVEN

Carlo Paparo pulled into the strip mall on Elmhurst Avenue that housed the Venetian restaurant. The restaurant was situated between Gene's Liquors, which was more of a wineshop than a liquor store, and Fred's DVD Rental. Several years previously Fred's had gone out of business, but the old sign was still in place.

Sitting shotgun was Brennan Monaghan. They regularly commuted together from their homes in New Jersey to Elmhurst, Queens, on Tuesdays and Thursdays to play penny ante with their boss, Louie Barbera.

Several years previously Louie had been ordered by the don of the Vaccarro crime family to take Paulie Cerino's place in Queens while Paulie was in the slammer. Previously Louie had been head of the New Jersey operation, but the Queens branch was considerably bigger and much more important. Initially, the higher-ups thought Paulie would be paroled in five years or so, but the years had dragged on. Every time Paulie had come up before the parole board, he'd been turned down.

"Should we bring up about last evening and what went down with those crazy Yakuza guys right away or put it off until after lunch?" Brennan asked as he got out of the car. "I know Louie's going to be fucking fit to be tied."

"That's a good question," Carlo said. He slammed the Denali's door and started toward the Venetian's entrance. "I think we should tell him right off. I don't want him taking it out on us in any way or form, which he might do if we delay it."

"Yeah, but it's going to ruin his game, and he hates to have his game ruined."

"True. So in a way we're caught between a rock and a hard place. What do you say we flip for it?"

"Good idea."

The two men stopped in the middle of the parking area while both searched their pockets for a coin. Brennan was the first to come up with a quarter. "Heads, we tell him right away; tails, we wait until after lunch and after the game."

"Right on!" Carlo said.

Brennan used his thumb to flip the coin up over his head before snatching it out of the air on its way toward the ground. With a quick motion he slapped the coin onto the back of his left wrist. The two men leaned forward. It was heads.

"It's decided," Brennan said.

A car horn beeped, making the two men jump out of the way. When they glared at the offending vehicle, they saw the driver was Arthur MacEwan, one of their colleagues, who was laughing at having startled Brennan and Carlo. As he drove past, Brennan gave him the finger. Behind Arthur was a black Chevrolet Malibu driven by another colleague, Ted Polowski. Both cars found slots in the angled parking lot, and their drivers joined the others.

"What are you two losers doing out here in the middle of the parking lot?" Arthur asked, still chuckling about how much he'd scared Carlo and Brennan. He had a high-pitched voice that drove everyone nuts.

"Screw you," Carlo said.

"We were deciding when to tell Louie what happened last night," Brennan said, immune to Arthur's antics.

"What happened?" Arthur questioned.

"You'll know soon enough," Carlo said.

Together the group walked toward the restaurant, the façade of which was sheathed in fake stone. Beyond the door, they pushed through a heavy dark green curtain whose job it was to seal out the cold on frigid nights. Inside, the walls were full of paintings of Venice on black velvet. Most of the classic scenes were represented, such as the Ponte dei Sospiri, Saint Mark's Basilica, the Ponte di Rialto, and the Doge's Palace.

To the left was a small bar with a half-dozen barstools. Running along the right wall was a row of tufted red velvet–upholstered booths with white tablecloths, which were considered the coveted tables from dinner to the wee hours of the morning. The establishment was open for lunch only on Tuesdays and Thursdays, and then only for the owner, Louie Barbera, and his soldiers: Carlo, Brennan, Arthur, and Ted. The other tables in the room featured a newly added Chianti bottle nestled within a straw basket and covered with layers of candle drippings. In keeping with the rest of the décor, the tablecloths and napkins were red-and-white checkered fabric. The room was dimly lit from several hanging fixtures over the bar and over each booth.

"You guys are late," Louie snapped. He folded his newspaper and pushed it aside as he glanced at his watch. "When I say noon, I mean noon. You got it?" Louie was an overweight man in his mid-forties with dull features indistinctly indented into a full face the color and texture of dough. He was dressed accordingly in stretched-out corduroy with worn patches over the knees and elbows. The only thing exceptional about his appearance was his eyes. They were sharp and piercing between flaccid lids, reminding one of a sluggish, fat reptile.

The men didn't respond, knowing that no matter what was said, Louie would pounce on whoever had the nerve to speak. The one thing everyone learned over the years was that when Louie was in a bad mood, which seemed to be the case that day, it was better to say as little as possible. As they slid into the booth from both sides, since Louie was sitting in the very back, they were all silent.

Louie looked from one to the next to find a victim to appease his irritation, but no one was willing to lock eyes with him.

"Benito!" Louie finally called out, loud enough to be heard from the kitchen, making everyone at the table jump. Then he added, "You guys are pathetic," recognizing that no one was willing to stand up for the group.

Benito burst out of the double swinging doors and sprinted to the booth. He was a slight man with a pencil mustache and was dressed in a tired tuxedo. "Yes, Mr. Barbera?" he questioned with an Italian accent seemingly from central casting.

"What's for lunch?"

"Pasta con carciofi e pancetta."

Louie's eyes brightened. "Terrific! Let's also have some Barolo and San Pellegrino and arugula salad." He then glanced around at the group. "Everybody happy with that?"

Everyone nodded in turn. "That's it, then," Louie said to Benito with a wave of his hand. He then yelled after him, "And tell John Franco it's gotta be al dente or it's all coming back."

Louie turned his attention to his guests, looking directly at Carlo. "Well, did you bring the cards or not?"

Carlo pulled out a new box, broke the seal, and placed the deck in front of Louie, all the while continuing the debate with himself whether to bring up the issue of the two crazy Yakuza guys and what had gone down the previous evening then or later, despite the results of the coin toss. As Brennan had reminded him, Carlo was certain Louie was going to go through the roof, because he'd been making it a strict point over the last several years to tone down violence, meaning murder, with all of the local gangs, be they Asian, Hispanic, Russian, or American. His leadership in this regard had been paying off dramatically, and everybody was thriving, even in the depressed economic environment. His point was that by eschewing killings the police were leaving everybody alone, allowing the gambling and drug businesses to prosper, particularly on the drug end. Without police interference, Louie had actually spearheaded an association with the Japanese Yakuza group Aizukotetsu-kai, run by Hideki Shimoda, who called himself a *saiko-komon*, which Louie interpreted to be equivalent to capo, like himself. The association afforded Louie an inexhaustible supply of "ice," as well as access to high-stakes Japanese gamblers. The association had increased to an extent that it now comprised a very large portion of the Vaccarros' income. Of course, Louie's main rival, the Lucia family, got wind of the operation and found a rival Yakuza group, the Yamaguchi-gumi, to form an equivalent association. They were now competing directly, a situation that in the past would have resulted in some sort of turf war. But not under Louie's leadership. Instead, he saw the competitive situation as a plus rather than a minus in that it stimulated demand. Ice was becoming an extremely popular recreational drug in the city, a fact he used to convince Vinnie Dominick of the Lucia family that there was more than enough room for both their organizations.

As Louie dealt out the first hand, Carlo found himself focusing on a compelling reason to break the bad news right away. If he did, he was reasonably confident Louie could not blame him, as Louie had ordered Carlo to help the Yakuza guys. On the other hand, if Carlo waited, as he was tempted to do for convenience' sake, there was a good chance he would be blamed, at least to some degree, for the killings, making a bad situation even worse. Carlo understood that Louie was not fun to be around when he was angry, but it was also much worse when he was specifically angry at him.

"Yesterday afternoon when you sent us to help the Aizukotetsu-kai guys, things went . . ." Carlo paused, trying to think of the most soothing way to bring up the issue, but no words came to mind until he thought of the word *awry*. He'd probably never used the word in his life, and he questioned himself where it had come from when it came out of his mouth.

Louie stopped organizing his cards, and after slowly lowering them, he stared at Carlo. "'Awry'?" he questioned with true confusion. "What do you mean?"

"Sorta unexpected," Carlo explained.

"'Unexpected' is as confusing as 'awry.' Unexpectedly good or unexpectedly bad?"

"I'd have to say bad."

Louie glanced at Brennan, as if he expected Brennan

to explain Carlo's word choice. When Brennan refused to make eye contact, Louie said, "Okay, you guys, I think you'd better tell me what the hell happened."

"We're not a hundred percent sure about the first part, but we're totally sure about the second part."

"Come on, quit beating around the bush."

"You told us that we were supposed to help these two Yakuza guys shake down a Japanese named Satoshi who worked for a company called iPS USA."

"That was what Hideki Shimoda told me. There was some problem with this Satoshi back in Japan. I assumed it was probably a big gambling debt, since the man had recently fled Japan and showed up here in New York City."

"Well, it wasn't much of a shakedown. They followed the dude down into the Fifty-ninth Street subway station. But they weren't down there for more than ten or fifteen minutes. When they came back they were kinda jazzed up and had the man's athletic bag, the contents of which seemed to disappoint them. When I asked them what had happened they told me that Satoshi had had a heart attack, which caused one of the dudes to burst out laughing."

"I know about this supposed heart attack," Louie said. "Hideki Shimoda called me earlier to thank us for the help you guys gave his boys. Actually, what he really called about was that he'd heard from his boss in Japan. Anyway, the big boss asked him to ask me for your help again for tonight, which made me ask if everything had gone okay last night and if he'd gotten what he wanted. He then told me *no*, he hadn't gotten what he needed, which is why he needed help again tonight. He also told me Satoshi had had a heart attack, which he finally admitted was actually a hit. When I blew up at him, saying we American families have learned to avoid all killings to keep the authorities off our collective backs, he told me to calm down, that the hit was done in a way that would look like a heart attack, or at least natural, and that no one was going to figure out that the guy had been whacked. I mean, those weren't his exact words, but that's what he was saying."

"I knew it was a hit!" Carlo said with an air of self-congratulation. "It was over too quickly. It ticks me off they weren't square with us. They should have told us what they were up to. They were treating us as taxi drivers, which I guess we were. I tell you, I'm not excited about helping them again."

"I can understand," Louie said, "but the situation is a little more complicated. So what is this second part you're referring to?"

"When Susumu and Yoshiaki popped up out of the station, they had Satoshi's wallet as well as his athletic bag. From the wallet they found out where the guy was living with his family out in Fort Lee, New Jersey. Then they argued with each other in Japanese, which ended up with all of us driving to Fort Lee."

"I didn't tell you to drive them to New Jersey. What the hell did they do in New Jersey?"

"Yeah, well, you didn't specifically tell us not to drive to Jersey; you told us to drive them around wherever they wanted to go."

"So what happened in Jersey?" Louie asked while beginning to wonder if he did not want to know. He was already out of sorts concerning the hit.

"We found Satoshi's house, and the two guys went inside, but before they did, they pulled out handguns like in the movies, holding them with two hands. I mean, I never hold my gun with two hands."

"Don't tell me!" Louie raged. He knew what was coming.

"While we were sitting there, we heard six shots. Bam, bam, bam, bam, bam, bam! At that point I got my cell phone out to call you to ask you what the hell you thought we should do. I mean, now we're murder accomplices for just driving them around."

"I never got a call," Louie snapped.

"No, I didn't get a chance to make it. The next thing we saw was Susumu and Yoshiaki hightailing it out of the house, carrying pillowcases full of stuff and leaping into the back of my car. At that point all I wanted to do was hightail it myself—plus, I wanted to get rid of the two trigger-happy nuts. I mean, that was it! I'd had it. I didn't want to have anything more to do with those assholes. I wouldn't have taken them out there to Jersey if I knew they were going in with guns blazing."

"This is a disaster!" Louie growled. "A freaking hit on a subway platform and a massacre of the victim's entire family. It spells organized crime in capital letters. And to think of all the work I've done to keep violence down and the cops happy. It's outrageous. Why kill the family? What did they take from the house? Drugs?"

"We don't know what they took, but we know what they didn't take."

"What do you mean?"

"I mean that what they were looking for was a couple of lab books, whatever they are, because as we were heading back across the GW Bridge, they specifically told us that was what they had been seeking."

"Shit!" Louie shouted, causing his guests to flinch.

"That's what Hideki wants to get tonight. For a couple of lab books, which obviously weren't even found, we're going to have to deal with the fallout from a subway hit and the hit on the family," he raged while everyone else remained silent. "And if the so-called heart attack is proved to be homicide and not a natural death, the authorities are going to go nuts, because the public will demand it. For us around here it could become a war zone, forcing us to cut back on everything. Shit! Two years of effort down the drain. I have it in mind to break my own rule and whack Hideki Shimoda and let him feed the fish out in the Narrows. Actually, I'd do it in a second if we had an alternate source for crystal meth. Here we've built up the demand for ice, so we got to maintain a reliable source, so knocking off Hideki would be like shooting ourselves in the foot. The problem is that in these difficult times the ice has become a major source of our revenue, and the main source of ice is mainly Japan."

"So Susumu and Yoshiaki are not done," Carlo added. "Asking our help again tonight means they're still going to be out causing trouble. These are obviously two guys who don't think twice about pulling out their guns and blazing away."

"Unfortunately, I think you are entirely correct," Louie said, slapping his cards down on the table. "This is outrageous, all for a couple of lab books. This guy Hideki has some balls. First he tries to tell me Satoshi had a heart attack and then he doesn't even mention what you've just told me about the New Jersey side of this story. I can't believe all this."

"Whatever you believe," Carlo said, "I'm telling you up front, I don't want to have anything to do with those crazy-ass bastards."

"I'm the one who gives the orders!" Louie snapped. For a few moments no one spoke until Louie added, "What Hideki wants is help with a single attempt at burglarizing iPS USA, whatever that is."

"This iPS USA's office is on Fifth Avenue, for God's sake," Carlo said with heat. "To try something like that would take serious planning."

"You're probably right," Louie said, preoccupied with his own thoughts. "But there's still the problem of maintaining our source of crystal meth. When Hideki sensed my hesitation to supply help on the phone, he was quick to suggest the Lucia organization would love to help. Can you believe it? Along with everything else, he's threatening to switch allegiance to Vinnie Dominick if we don't help him get the lab books. How is it with this guy Vinnie Dominick? How is he so damn lucky? Talk about the Teflon don. First he beats the rap about being caught up in the Angels Healthcare affair, and now there's a chance that the entire lucrative association between the Yakuza and the Mafia may fall into his lap: all because of some lab books."

"Hideki can threaten, but I can't imagine it could happen," Carlo said. "There's no love lost between the Aizukotetsu-kai and the Yamaguchi-gumi, at least according to Susumu and Yoshiaki. The two organizations can't even be in the same room together, much less cooperate and work together.

"Would you like us to try to talk sense into Susumu and Yoshiaki?" Carlo continued. "We'll explain how suicidal it would be to try to break into iPS USA. Yoshiaki seems to be more reasonable and might take our advice. At least more reasonable than Susumu. Susumu is the one who scares me."

"One thing that we're forgetting," Brennan said, speaking up for the first time, "is that neither episode, the killing in the subway nor the slaughter in the home in New Jersey, has been in the papers. I think that tells us two things. The subway hit, at least so far, has been considered a natural death, and if Susumu and Yoshiaki got all his IDs, which I think they made a point to do, it's going to be a natural death of an unknown individual, which isn't the kind of case that causes a lot of attention. Now, the killings in Jersey are another thing entirely, and the only explanation for it not being in the tabloids is because it hasn't been discovered. And the fact that it hasn't been discovered is not surprising if you saw the locale. I mean, the house and the neighborhood were about as trashy as you can imagine and seemed deserted. I mean, we didn't see a soul or a light in any other building."

"That's right," Carlo chimed in.

Louie stared at Brennan and realized for about the tenth time he'd underestimated the kid. As usual what Brennan was saying made sense. Maybe the situation wasn't as bad as he initially thought.

"If everyone in the family was killed," Brennan continued, "and there's no one to go to the house and find the bodies, and if there's no one around outside to smell what it's going to smell like around there for a couple of weeks, then, hey, the massacre might not be discovered for weeks or even months or even years."

Silence reigned after Brennan's comments until Louie spoke up. "You know, I think you're right on both accounts, the hit and the house, but if we sit back and do nothing, we're leaving it all up to chance: chance that the cops continue to view the hit as a natural death and that the postman isn't going to lose his lunch delivering mail. My sense is that we have to be somehow proactive. Our relationship with Hideki and the Aizukotetsu-kai is in the balance."

"I hope you are not considering sending us out with Susumu and Yoshiaki to pull off a heist on Fifth Avenue, because it would be out-and-out suicide," Carlo said. "It would be turning a problem into a disaster."

"I don't know what the hell to do," Louie admitted. "I need some expert counsel. I need some perspective before I decide."

"Who are you going to ask?" Carlo questioned. He couldn't imagine Louie going to the don, Victorio Vaccarro. The man was in his nineties. For all intents and purposes, Louie was running the Vaccarro crime family.

"I'm going to pay Paulie Cerino a visit in the slammer," Louie said before shouting to Benito to bring out the freaking food!

CHAPTER EIGHT

MARCH 25, 2010 – THURSDAY, 12:45 p.m.

As he backed his new Mercedes SUV into a plum parking spot by the Neopolitan Restaurant, Michael Calabrese could not help but marvel how one's course though life could change. Just three years earlier he was making the same trip, but the situation had been entirely different. Back then he was scared to death and had reason to believe he might be killed. It was so bad that in the back of his mind he was beginning to plan on trying to disappear. At the time he was the placement agent for Angels Healthcare LLC, which was about to go public while not having revealed it was insolvent. That day he was visiting Vinnie Dominick with the unenviable task of having to tell Vinnie of the regrettable situation that was unfolding. The problem was that Michael had talked Vinnie into investing a huge portion of Mob money, more than fifteen million dollars, into the company.

Just thinking about the situation still brought a shiver of fear down Michael's spine, despite what ultimately happened. Angels Healthcare went on, as Michael had originally believed, to have a truly amazing IPO and was now a thriving company, returning to Vinnie and the Lucia organization hundreds of millions and to Michael himself millions. Instead of being considered a lackey, Michael was held up to be a genius and a favorite son of the Queens neighborhood of Rego Park, where he and Vinnie had grown up together.

Now out of the car, Michael had to wait to cross Corona Avenue, as it was a four-lane road with lots of traffic. When a spot opened up, Michael dashed across and then slowed to walk. This time, Michael was arriving as a welcome guest. After Ben's visit that morning, Michael had called Vinnie Dominick to request a lunch visit for himself and Saboru Fukuda, with the explanation that he had some good news about iPS USA.

As Michael approached the restaurant, he had to smile. Besides its name, Neapolitan, it was so obviously American Italian that it was like a joke. With vain hopes of being more elegant than it was, the façade was fake brick that came in fiberglass sheets, which didn't even come close to appearing real. Under its windows were fake window boxes sporting out-of-season plastic flowers. No customers were coming in or out as the restaurant was not open to the public for lunch. The noonday meal was open only to Vinnie, his dedicated minions, and guests. For the owner it was a small price to pay to do his evening business, which was quite a business. The restaurant had a mythic appeal due to its long history of association with the underworld, particularly in the thirties, during prohibition.

Inside, Michael pushed through the entrance drape and paused until his eyes adjusted. To the left was a newly constructed U-shaped bar with glasses hanging down from a wooden valance structure running around the area's ceiling. Off to the side, near a cluster of small cocktail tables, was a fake fireplace whose fire was a rotating drum covered with crinkled aluminum foil. The logs were made of concrete. The origin of the fake fire was a red bulb hidden behind one of the fake logs. Above the mantel was a large, dark painting of the Virgin

Mary holding the Christ child in a huge tarnished gilt frame.

To the right were the coveted booths extending down into the depths of the restaurant. The first two were occupied, one by Vinnie's close associates, several of whom Michael recognized as former schoolmates. There was Richie Herns, who had taken over Franco Ponti's position as head enforcer. Franco was in prison along with Angelo Facciolo, the two people who had always terrified Michael. Freddie Capuso, who'd been the class clown, was there as well. There were three other physically impressive guys Michael didn't know.

Vinnie Dominick was seated at the next table. He caught sight of Michael and waved him over. Sitting next to Vinnie was his girlfriend, Carol Cirone, who had lunch with Vinnie every day except Sunday, when Vinnie stayed home with his wife and family. Next to Carol was Saboru Fukuda, a slight, elegant man in a superbly tailored glen plaid suit. To Michael he looked more like a Fifth Avenue ophthalmologist than the head of a branch of the violent Yamaguchi-gumi Yakuza organization.

As Michael approached the table, Vinnie slid across the vinyl seat and stood.

"Hey, brother," Vinnie exuded, and enveloped Michael in a brotherly hug. He too was dressed to the nines, with even more panache than his Yamaguchi-gumi guest. Whereas Saboru had a carefully folded dark brown pocket square in his jacket's breast pocket, Vinnie had a wildly colorful Cartier silk that billowed out with an explosion of color.

With his arm still draped over Michael's shoulders, Vinnie tapped Saboru on the arm to get his attention.

"Hey, psycho! Mikey's here," Vinnie said. He and Saboru had spent significant time together as their business relationship had blossomed, and Vinnie had come to use the word *psycho* versus *saiko* from *saiko-komon,* as humorous wordplay. Saboru found it entertaining, once it had been explained to him.

Saboru stood, quickly bowed, and gave Michael a business card. Michael took the card after a quick, awkward bow and dispensed one of his own. Back at his desk in his office, he had a collection of Saboru's cards.

"Sit down, sit down!" Vinnie repeated to Michael but then remembered Carol. "Listen, sweetie, we have to talk business. How about you sit with the men for a little while." He gestured to the group at the next booth.

"I want to sit with you people," Carol whined.

"Carol, dear," Vinnie said slowly, without raising his voice, "I said how about you sit at the next table."

Michael felt the hackles on the back of his neck rise. Vinnie had a short-fuse temper and a penchant to be violent. For a few moments Vinnie and Carol stared each other down. The entire room was silent until Carol wisely relented and slid out from the table. With a pouty expression and a petulant air she changed tables. The moment she did so, conversation returned to the room.

"Please," Vinnie said, gesturing for both of his guests to sit. As if by magic, a waiter appeared and asked Michael what he preferred to drink, gesturing to an open bottle of Sassicaia, Vinnie's favorite, and then at an ice bucket containing a pinot grigio and a bottle of San Pellegrino.

"So what's the good news?" Vinnie questioned once Michael had his wine and water. When it came to business, Vinnie was impatient. He didn't mind small talk, but it was for after business, not before.

Leaning over toward Vinnie and in a voice that suggested importance, Michael said, "Yesterday an exclusive agreement was signed with Satoshi Machita for iPS cells."

For a moment there was silence. Vinnie and Michael merely stared at each other. The only sounds in the room were from those at the neighboring table, who were busily entertaining Carol. Back when Michael had first explained iPS USA to Vinnie, he'd gone into great detail about the unbelievable promise of stem cells and the regrettable entanglement that the promising science and fledgling industry had encountered with the highly emotional abortion issue. He then explained how induced stem cells skirted the issue. Aware of Vinnie's innate intelligence, Michael had also explained the patent issues involving stem cells and how important it would be to control the big patents. It was Vinnie who finally broke the silence.

"And it's this iPS cell patent that's going to be the mother of all patents?"

"That's what Ben Corey believes, and the guy's a genius who wants to control regenerative medicine."

"And we'll be right there with him," Vinnie proclaimed.

"Right there," Michael agreed.

Vinnie picked up his glass of wine and held it out to the others. He had a wry smile on his face. "I never knew that it was health care where all the real money was. First hospitals and now biotech. I love it."

They all clinked classes and drank.

Vinnie turned to Saboru. "I told you this guy was great," he said, nodding toward Michael.

"Thank you!" Saboru said several times, nodding first toward Michael and then toward Vinnie.

"Now I want to bring up another subject," Michael said, putting down his wineglass and moving forward on his seat as if he was about to tell a secret. "I met with Dr. Corey just this morning. With the new contract signed, the market value of the company will soar. There's no telling what its value will be. On top of that, this morning he confided in me that there is a new company that controls a patent for a process that will speed up the production efficiency of making induced stem cells. He's interested in either acquiring the company or, at the very least, exclusively licensing its intellectual property. The question is, do either of you want to acquire more equity before the IPO? If so, this would be the time."

There were questions from both Vinnie and Saboru, which Michael fielded, cleverly honing his client's interest so that if Ben wanted or needed more equity, it would be immediately available.

After an interruption with the waiter coming to take their lunch orders, Michael then broached the third, last, and most sensitive subject on his agenda—namely, Ben's interest in distancing iPS USA from their respective organizations. When he finished and fell silent, he could sense a change in mood. Clearly both Vinnie and Saboru were not pleased, feeling blindsided by the issue's even being broached.

"It's rather late for Dr. Corey to feel he's not interested in our help," Saboru said. It was Saboru who'd engineered the theft of the lab books from Kyoto University and getting Satoshi and his family from Japan through Honolulu to New York City, the same route he used for drugs and child porn.

"I agree," Vinnie said in that particularly calm voice that Michael feared and that all too often presaged a temper tantrum of one sort or another.

"There is no disrespect intended here," Michael quickly added. "It is only something that Dr. Corey feels will be in the best interest of the company if and when the company goes public. If such association were to suggest itself during any due diligence, the company would probably have to cancel the IPO to avoid a full SEC investigation."

"He knows that the Lucia holdings are held secure under a series of shell companies, does he not?" Vinnie questioned.

"Of course he does," Michael added quickly to defuse the situation, "and he's tremendously thankful for what you gentlemen have done for the company. He even mentioned that some significant additional equity would be involved to recognize your special contributions if it comes to that."

At that point Michael felt as if he'd been saved, as several waiters burst from the kitchen with a wide variety of steaming pastas for the first course. Relieved, Michael sat back and took in a deep breath. From his perspective the downside of dealing with criminal organizations is that one always felt as if he was standing on the edge of a precipice.

CHAPTER NINE

MARCH 25, 2010 – THURSDAY, 1:05 p.m.

Louie Barbera took the chair that had just been vacated at the very end of the visiting room at the Rikers Island visitors center. He'd been there about a half-dozen times over the years to visit Paulie Cerino, the capo he'd replaced when Paulie had been sent to prison more than a decade previously. Louie had visited mostly to ask specific questions about specific people or events, since it was difficult to take over someone else's operation, especially when that person was expected to return. Like in all businesses, even illegal ones, consistency was important.

Louie's visits to Paulie had grown less frequent over the years, as Louie became more familiar with Queens and its characters and specific challenges. But now Louie was at a loss. He had no idea what to do about the situation with Hideki Shimoda, and especially Vinnie Dominick, Paulie's old archrival. It was like a balancing game over a cauldron of molten lava. One slip and everybody might fall in.

Louie used a tissue and some Purell to wipe off the telephone handset, which was still warm from the previous user. Paulie had yet to arrive. Louie's plan was simple: give Paulie the details, get Paulie's response, then get the hell out. Although Rikers Island was the biggest and busiest penal institution in the world, the place was also notorious for its run-down condition. Louie shivered at the thought of staying in the place overnight, much less for more than a decade.

Glancing to his right, Louie looked at the long line of other visitors, most of whom appeared to be women talking to husbands. Many appeared as if they were barely making ends meet, though some tried to dress up. There were guards on both sides of the glass with glazed eyes and bored expressions. Louie looked at his watch. It was after two, and he already wanted to leave. He promised himself he'd never come back to this place.

At that moment he caught sight of Paulie and started. The last time he'd seen him, Paulie had looked much the same as always, plus the scars he'd suffered after someone had thrown acid in his face a year or so before he had been imprisoned. He'd always been heavy and unconcerned about his appearance. Now he was comparatively skinny, and his prison outfit hung on him like an oversized shirt on a metal hanger.

As Paulie took his seat on the other side of the glass, Louie had to briefly look away. He'd forgotten about Paulie's double corneal transplants, where the clear area of his eyes contrasted so sharply with the scarred area as to be startling.

Controlling himself, Louie picked up the telephone and raised his eyes to Paulie even though it was like looking down a couple of gun barrels. After a bit of chitchat, Louie said, "Paulie, you look different, like you lost some weight."

"I am different," Paulie agreed wistfully if not mystically. "I've found the Lord."

Good grief, Louie thought but didn't say. He lamented the fact that he'd made the effort to come all the way to Rikers Island to seek advice about a difficult underworld conundrum now that Paulie had found God. It made the whole situation so absurd that Louie thought about leaving, when Paulie suddenly refocused and said, "I know you probably came out here to get some advice about some problem, but I want to ask you a question first. How did that bastard Vinnie Dominick weasel his way out of all those indictments last year? I thought for sure he was going to end up in here with me. Nobody's told me nothing."

The question took Louie by surprise. Maybe Paulie wasn't quite as overwhelmed by his newfound Christianity. Maybe he could still offer some advice.

"Strange you should ask, because I was the problem with Vinnie Dominick and most of the others getting off, and it's related to how they were caught with their hands in the cookie jar."

"I don't follow," Paulie admitted with interest.

"I found out Vinnie had himself a yacht for all sorts of nasty work-related entertaining. I had my guys place a GPS on the boat. When I knew Vinnie and company were up to no good, I gave the password and user name to Lou Soldano so he could nab them, which he did."

"Lou!" Paulie exclaimed. "How is the old bastard?"

"As much of a bastard as always. Why do you ask?"

"We butted heads for so many years, we became sorta friends. He still sends my wife and kids a Christmas card every year. Can you believe it?"

As far as Louie was concerned, he saw Soldano as the embodiment of the enemy and refused to see him any other way, Christmas cards or not. "Do you want to hear how Dominick got off or what?"

"I want to hear," Paulie admitted.

"Dominick got some great lawyers who jumped on the role played by the GPS, and with one of New York's famously liberal judges, they were able to get thrown out all evidence obtained from the GPS device, since there was no warrant. Can you believe it? In one fell swoop the guts of the prosecutor's cases was unusable. I tell you, on occasion the whole justice system in this country is its own worst enemy."

"Thanks for clueing me in about Vinnie, the lucky bastard," Paulie said. "Now it's your turn. Tell me what you want. I can't imagine it's a sermon."

"No sermon, thank you," Louie began. "Just your advice. After more than a year of smooth sailing businesswise, we're in one of those no-win situations that could easily escalate into a disaster. Now, it's a bit on the complicated side, so let me fill you in about our partnership with one of the Yakuza families."

To be certain Paulie understood the whole situation, Louie went back and explained how their relationship had developed between himself and Hideki Shimoda, the head of the Aizukotetsu-kai Yakuza. "I set up a number of high-stakes gambling locations on the Upper East Side that looked and acted like restaurants to ensnare foolish visiting Japanese businessmen, which Hideki supplies. We offer unlimited credit and female companionship, and then Hideki's associates collect from the surprised deadbeats back in Japan. After the Yakuza back in Japan take their cut, they pay us off in either cash or crystal meth, but generally crystal meth, which we prefer, and they seem to have an endless supply. The setup has been working perfectly, providing a large percentage of our current working cash. In fact, it has been so profitable that the copycat Vinnie Dominick has created his own setup with another Yakuza organization called the Yamaguchi-gumi."

"We never teamed up with nobody," Paulie commented with disdain.

"I understand, and maybe I shouldn't have done it," Louie admitted, lowering his voice when a guard drifted near. "But Dominick is now doing as well as we are, and it's actually helping up the demand for crystal meth. The current problem I want to talk to you about came out of the blue. Hideki Shimoda called me up just a couple of days ago, asking me to help a couple of his guys shake down some Japanese researcher type and steal the man's laboratory books. I didn't necessarily like the idea about getting involved in someone else's business, but Hideki was insistent, and I went along because, as I said, it was supposed to be only a shakedown. But that wasn't what it turned out to be." At that point, Louie related what had happened the previous night, and the potential bomb that had been created.

"You're surprised that these Yakuza thugs are prone to violence?" Paulie asked with surprise of his own.

"I was surprised about the extent. There'd been no problem until last night. They seemed respectful of the way we were operating, keeping killings to a minimum. I mean, Vinnie Dominick and I are hardly friends, but we've just learned over the years that real violence is bad for business. Maybe it's more that I learned and Vinnie has been willing to follow suit. I've actually made it a personal crusade of sorts."

"Okay, so now what?"

"Hideki calls me up this morning, supposedly to thank me for sending the help, and he doesn't admit anything had gone wrong. I had to pull it out of him. And he didn't even mention the New Jersey part. Then he demands we help him again tonight to get the lab books he didn't get last night, with the same trigger-happy soldiers. The plan is to break into an office building on Fifth Avenue. When he senses my obvious hesitation about agreeing to such a harebrained idea, he threatens me with breaking up our comfy business relationship. He says that Dominick would surely help him with the robbery if he were offered to get the Aizukotetsu-kai business as well as the Yamaguchi-gumi's. You got the picture? The man is extorting me."

"I'm getting the picture, but I don't understand why you were willing to hook up with these Yakuza guys in the first place."

"They just didn't seem to be overly violent, at least not until last night. But let's get beyond that issue and focus on the current one. After all, this is your territory. As soon as you're out you'll be back in the driver's seat. When does it look like that might happen?"

"It's up to the parole board. I mean, I've been eligible for longer than I like to think about. I've been turned down so many times I'm starting to think Vinnie is involved, but that's another story. Back to your problem. My first instinct is to get rid of this Hideki. You can't let anyone get away with extorting you. Not in this business. Cut off the head and the beast won't bite."

"Can't do!" Louie said definitely and without hesitation. "He's too high-profile. The Aizukotetsu-kai would be over here and a real war would break out. Besides, you can't bite the hand that feeds you. As I mentioned, a good part of our current cash flow would halt."

"Then get rid of the two enforcers who did the dirty work," Paulie said. "You don't need guys like that around who take it on their own to shoot whoever the hell they please. You have to send a message that that kind of behavior is not okay."

"I'm listening," Louie said, "but whacking them is going to involve abandoning my antiviolence campaign. I've been really strict about it. I've even talked down the little stuff, like avoiding knocking around gambling deadbeats unless absolutely necessary. Dominick and I even had a meeting about it, and we agreed. So there's been no violence to speak of, and the cops have left us alone and business has been as good as can be expected, even in this down economy."

"You can't have it both ways," Paulie snapped. "You can encourage everyone to keep the violence down, that's all well and good. But this is different. This is serious, from the leader of a foreign gang. You have to react, and you have to react now. If you don't do something dramatic, word is going to get around that you've lost your touch. I mean, it's nice to have a nonviolent stance, because it can be useful with the police, but it can be counterproductive with all the competition. If you don't want to cut off the head, then you have to inflict some serious damage to the vital organs. You have to get rid of Hideki's two lead goons. Listen to me!" Paulie suddenly motioned with his eyes for Louie to look to his right. One of the bored guards was sauntering in their direction on Louie's side of the glass. As he approached, Louie and Paulie switched their conversation to small talk about how much better it was in the old days with Louie in Bayonne, New Jersey, and Paulie there in Queens.

Unfortunately, the guard went behind Louie to the window and stared out at the bay for a time, forcing

Louie and Paulie to think up things to talk about. They finally hit on the Yankees and what the 2010 season would be like. When the guard finally strolled away, Louie said, "We've got to speed this up. The clock is ticking on how long I'm allowed to be here."

"You have to do something dramatic or you are going to lose control," Paulie said. "What I'd do is call Hideki, pretend you've changed your mind and play up your willingness to help; tell him you want to have a meeting because the more you know about what's going on, the better you can help. And do it face-to-face. You learn a lot more at a meeting than with a phone call. Of course, have the meeting in your office. Come up with some plan about how you're going to break into the office where the lab books are to give yourself something real to talk about to make him believe you're definitely going to do something."

Louie nodded, knowing he could come up with something believable. Certainly the idea of finding out more about the lab books and Satoshi would be helpful.

"I mean, the plan doesn't have to be elaborate, since you're never going to do it—something like creating a major distraction, such as a fire or an explosion nearby so you can slip in and out of the office building with everyone concentrating on the distraction."

Louie was impressed. Apparently, Paulie hadn't lost any of his edge, especially coming up with a plan so quickly. Louie also started to believe the born-again Christianity might have more to do with the parole board than true religiosity.

"Make plans to meet up with the enforcers someplace in the city where there's always a crowd. Once you have them in the car, you're golden. Make sure to get rid of the bodies. Then after an hour or so, call Hideki back and be pissed off, asking where the fuck are his guys, as you've been waiting all this time, blah, blah, blah."

"You think he'd buy it and not smell a rat? I don't want to make this situation worse."

"I think there's a good chance he'll buy it outright," Paulie continued. "But here's the tricky part that will take some thought on your end. Drop some offhand comment about your guys hearing from his guys last night that they were somehow concerned about the rival gang. What was the name of the group hooked up with Vinnie?"

"Yamaguchi-gumi."

"That's it. I mean, don't overdo it. Just some trifle reference his guys were concerned about a couple of the Yamaguchi-gumi enforcers, or whatever they call their hit men. The Yakuza are paranoid about each other and do more harm to each other than the police. Am I making sense?"

"A lot of sense," Louie said.

"Are you going to take my advice?"

"I'll think about it," Louie answered.

"But it's key that you don't add to your violence problem by anybody finding a couple of bodies with a single bullet in their brains."

"Understood," Louie agreed.

"Now, about the current violence problem," Paulie continued, lowering his voice. "I haven't heard anything about a guy getting whacked on any subway platform, nor any mass murder in New Jersey. How come? What's the story? Here inside, we learn about such things sometimes even before they happen."

"When I got upset with Hideki telling me the truth

instead of the wacky story of a heart attack, he tried to calm me down by insisting that the death was done in a way that would be considered natural and would be undetectable to the police. Also, his guys took all the man's IDs, so it's going to be an unidentified corpse until someone comes out of the blue to identify him."

"What about the mass murder?"

"The only explanation for now is that no one has stumbled on the scene. If the whole family was home, except for Satoshi, who surely is not going home, it might be a while before it's discovered. My guys say it's not the best part of town, mostly empty buildings, trash, and graffiti. They didn't even see a single person, and it was evening, when you most often see people coming home from work."

"That's in our favor. Under such conditions it could be months, and it would never be associated with the hit on the subway platform, which is important, in my mind. As far as going over there and cleaning it out ourselves, I say definitely no. We shouldn't go near the place."

"I agree with that totally," Louie said.

"That leaves the victim who was whacked. Did Hideki tell you how he was killed?"

"No. All he said was that no one is going to figure it out, so it will be considered a natural death."

"That means it's important that it remains a natural death."

"I suppose you're right. But there's nothing we can do about that."

"That's not necessarily true," Paulie said. "I know a kid that works at the medical examiner's office named Vinnie Amendola. Well, he's no kid anymore. Hell, he's got to be in his forties. Nice kid. I literally saved his father way back when, so the kid owes me big-time. Of course, we used him once a number of years ago to sneak a body out of the morgue. He got into a bit of trouble over it, but I smoothed it over, since he's lived all his life out here in Queens. He could help you on this case."

"By doing what?" Louie questioned.

"He could tell you the status on the case, like if the cause of death has been signed out as natural. Vinnie loves his job, God knows why. He knows everything that goes on in the medical examiner's office."

Louie took a moment to look back at the visitors' desk. He was afraid they would soon be asking him to leave, yet he wanted to hear the rest of Paulie's suggestions. As Louie had envisioned, Paulie had some good ideas. When no one waved at him from the desk, Louie turned his attention back to Paulie.

"You waiting for someone?" Paulie asked.

"No. I'm afraid they're going to kick me out. So you think it's worth it to take the time to go to the morgue?"

"I definitely think you should go for one very important piece of information."

"Are you going to tell me or what?" Louie questioned. It seemed Paulie was stalling on purpose with time running out.

"The most important thing I want you to ask Vinnie Amendola is the name of the medical examiner on the case."

Louie knotted his brow in surprise. "Are you serious? What the hell for? Why does it matter?"

"If it's Laurie Montgomery, we are in trouble."

"Who the hell is Laurie Montgomery?"

"She's one of the MEs," Paulie said. "If I had to pick the single person most responsible for my being here in prison, it would be Laurie Montgomery. She's the smartest one at the morgue, and certainly the most dogged. She figured out stuff from the bodies I was responsible for sending in there in ways that still mystify me. We even tried to whack her and couldn't. We even had her nailed in a coffin at one time—you know, one of those simple pine boxes they use for the unidentified dead. She's like a cat with nine lives. Even Vinnie Dominick tried to kill her without luck."

"You must hate her guts."

"No, I've forgiven her, since she's also responsible for me finding God."

Louie didn't respond for a moment, instead staring into Paulie's scarred face again, trying to figure out if Paulie was seriously religious or seriously into character for the parole board's benefit. Paulie remained placid, a smile at the corners of his distorted lips.

"My point is," Paulie continued, "if you find Laurie Montgomery involved with your subway platform victim, you must, and I emphasize *must,* do something about it. Somehow she will figure out it was homicide. I'm telling you. From there she will figure out that it was an organized-crime event involving the Yakuza and you guys. You have to get her off the case if she's on it."

"What would I do, have her killed?"

"No. Absolutely not. I tried. Dominick tried. And merely by trying you will unleash from the police just what you are trying to avoid: probably a decade of harassment, because she's connected in high places in the police department. She used to date Lou Soldano.

And when they stopped dating, the relationship didn't change. In fact, it got better."

A piercing whistle got Louie's attention. Checking the desk, he saw the guard waving at him. Time was up. Louie looked back at Paulie. "If she's on the case, how do I get her off?"

"Can't help you there. You gotta figure that one out yourself. Ask Vinnie Amendola. He might have a suggestion."

Another whistle penetrated the general background hum of voices filling the room.

"See ya," Louie said, standing up.

"You know where to find me," Paulie said as they hung up their phones in unison.

CHAPTER TEN

Laurie took off her coat and hung it on the back of her office door, then pushed the door closed. At least for a while she wanted to be out of contact with the rest of the world. She'd just returned from a rather rowdy lunch in her honor at a nearby restaurant called the Waterfront Ale House. Feeling as she did, she would have preferred not to have gone, but she couldn't refuse, since the lunch was celebrating her return to work, and Jack had been the organizer. Most of the MEs had shown up, filled with good cheer and laughter. For Laurie it had been exhausting to act as happy as everyone else. The day was not going nearly as well as she'd hoped, with only one case with no identity and no cause or manner of death. And she couldn't stop thinking about JJ and Leticia. Laurie had stopped calling when Leticia asked, saying Laurie was interfering with her ability to pay adequate attention to JJ. "If there's the slightest problem, I'll call you," Leticia had insisted earlier. "Please relax and do your work. Everything is going to be fine."

Laurie sat down at her spotlessly clean desk. She stared at the phone for a moment. "Screw it!" she said abruptly, then angrily punched in Leticia's number. "Nobody's going to tell me I can't call about my child!"

The phone rang more times than Laurie expected and caused instant alarm, compounded by Leticia being out of breath when she finally answered. "Sorry," Leticia said. "I was pushing JJ up a steep hill when the phone began to ring. I wanted to make it to the top."

"Sounds like you two are in the park," Laurie said with a combination of guilt and relief.

"You got that right. He loves it, and it couldn't be a nicer day."

"Sorry to be a bother," Laurie said.

Leticia didn't respond.

"Everything okay?"

"Everything is just fine," Leticia answered.

"Did he have his lunch?"

"No, I'm denying him food and water," Leticia said, then laughed. "Just kidding. He ate a big lunch and now he's sleeping. He couldn't be better. Now get back to work."

"Aye, aye, madam," Laurie said.

After a few more parting comments, Laurie hung up the handset.

Then she looked at her desk and noted again the lack of reminders about pending cases. All there was was the single case file of her unidentified patient. She pondered how little she knew of the man and how sad it was that he was all alone in the cooler downstairs. She wondered where his wife was, and if she missed him. Laurie chewed her cheek and tried to think if there was some way to learn anything more, anything at all about her lonely, unidentified corpse.

Suddenly she snatched up the case folder and dumped out its contents to find Cheryl's note. What she was suddenly interested in was the time of the 911 call. After she found it, five-thirty-seven p.m., she turned on her monitor and searched through her address book for the 911 call center out in Brooklyn. With a mind-set of excitement, which she tried to suppress, she dialed and asked to be connected to her old contact, Cynthia Bellows.

When she got Cynthia's voicemail, she left a message, then gave Detective Ron Steadman another try. If he was still resistant, she'd go to Lou Soldano. She imagined that Lou, having recently made captain, could certainly light a fire under the man.

To Laurie's surprise, he answered after a couple of rings and sounded like a different man—maybe not much friendlier but significantly more awake. Laurie reintroduced herself and asked if he remembered her from her call that morning.

"Vaguely," Ron said. "What was it about?"

"An unidentified Asian corpse from the Fifty-ninth Street station that came in last evening."

"Now I remember! You were giving me a hard time about not rushing out and single-handedly solving the identity crisis. What's up? Did someone suddenly show up and make the ID?"

"I wish," Laurie said. "No ID yet, so I thought I'd view the tapes from the subway platform cameras."

Ron did not respond immediately. Then, with some exasperation, he said, "Why would you want me to have to call around for tapes on a natural-death case, especially one that's not yet twenty-four hours old? That's a lot of work for nothing if a family member shows up in the next couple of hours."

"How do I get copies of the tapes, or whatever form they come in?" Laurie persisted. She heard Ron take in a deep breath.

"You really want to go through with this?"

"I do. The nine-one-one caller said the victim might

have had a seizure, but he wasn't certain. It would be important to confirm it. It would point toward a neurological cause of death rather than a circulatory cause, meaning we'd look harder at the brain even though on gross there was nothing."

"Jesus, lady . . ." Ron began.

"The name is Laurie Stapleton," Laurie interrupted.

"I got a hundred-plus cases here on my desk that are all unsolved and that need my attention. This really isn't the best use of my time—the case isn't even a day old."

"How much work effort does it take?" Laurie questioned, hoping not to be denied.

"I got to get in touch with officers at the Brooklyn Special Investigation Unit and tell them what I need."

"Okay," Laurie said. "Is that it?"

"I suppose," Ron said, a bit embarrassed at how simple Laurie's request really was.

"How do you get the information?"

"As an e-mail. I'll burn a disk or two for you. It's a lot of data."

"Could you just forward it as an e-mail attachment to me?"

"I know it sounds funny, but I'm not permitted to do that. But I can give you a disk if you're who you say you are."

"When could you do it?"

"Now, if I reach the right people. What period of time at the subway station are you looking for?"

"I guess about a half-hour centered on the nine-one-one call at five-thirty-seven p.m., so let's say five-ten to five-fifty-five."

"Okay," Ron said. "All nine cameras?"

"Might as well be thorough."

"That's over six hours of watching time. Are you up to it?"

"Funny you should ask. I happen to have a lot of time on my hands. How soon would you have it in hand?"

"Let me make the call to the Transit Bureau Special Investigation Unit. I'll knock it right out as soon as they send it to me. Maybe within the hour."

"My goodness," Laurie commented. She'd found over the years that city servants were never quite so accommodating. Ron had gone from one extreme to the other.

"I'll call you right back. Is it a deal?"

"Absolutely," Laurie said, but before hanging up, she added, "I hope you don't take offense, but you're a different person than you were this morning, and it's meant as a compliment."

"This morning you caught me before coffee and my Red Bull."

No sooner had Laurie disconnected when the phone rang. Picking it back up, she found herself talking with Cynthia Bellows out at the 911 call center. After some small talk, Laurie described the details of the case and said she'd like to contact the 911 caller.

"Do you have the time of the call?" Cynthia asked. "That makes it a lot easier."

Laurie gave the time.

"Okay, I got it here on the screen," Cynthia said, "and let's see what we have. Actually, we have three calls, though I suppose you want only the first. The other two callers were told that the incident had already been reported and that police and the EMT had been dispatched."

"Sounds like a plan," Laurie said. As Laurie reached for a pen and paper, she heard the click of her call-waiting. Excusing herself and asking Cynthia to hold on for a moment, Laurie changed lines, and as she had expected, it was Ron.

"Good news, my friend," Ron said. "I got right through to the guys at the Special Investigation Unit. Apparently, there are two more cameras besides the nine of the new security system. For the old system, that includes the two nonrecording cameras used for the train's engineer and conductor to make sure all doors are clear, plus two more recording cameras at the fare booth and at the elevator."

Feeling anxious about Cynthia hanging on the other line, Laurie interrupted Ron and asked if she could call him right back.

"No need," Ron said. "I just wanted to let you know there'd be two additional feeds. I should have the material in a few minutes, and I'll have the disks burned so you can come get them any time you want."

"Terrific," Laurie said. "Your precinct is on West Fifty-fourth Street?"

"Three-oh-six West Fifty-fourth. I'll see you when I see you. I'll be here until five."

Laurie thanked Ron profusely, then switched back to Cynthia, feeling guilty. "I'm sorry," Laurie began.

"No problem," Cynthia said graciously. "Do you have something to write on?"

The caller's name was Robert Delacroix. After thanking Cynthia and disconnecting, Laurie dialed Robert Delacroix immediately. While waiting for the call to go through, she wrote the number on a three-by-five card and added it to the case file. When she got his outgoing message, she left her cell phone number with the request that he call her back as soon as possible. She explained that she was a medical examiner but was leaving her mobile number, not her office number, as she was on her way to the police station.

With that taken care of, Laurie headed outside to catch a cab for the Midtown North to meet up with Ron. While she sat in traffic, Laurie's mind turned to JJ and how well he was apparently doing in Leticia's care. Suddenly her mobile phone rang. It was Robert Delacroix.

Laurie thanked the man for calling and thanked him also for acting as a responsible citizen and making the 911 call in the first place. "Too many New Yorkers are capable of just walking past someone in distress," Laurie continued.

"At first I assumed someone had already called, like I guess a lot of people generally think. But then I said, Hell, there's no reason why not to call even if I'm not the first."

"As I mentioned on your voicemail, I'm a medical examiner," Laurie said.

"I guess the man on the subway platform died."

"I'm afraid so."

"That's too bad. He looked young."

"Can I ask you exactly what you saw?"

"Well, it wasn't much. I mean, it all happened so quickly. The train had been delayed, and the platform was really crowded. When the doors opened, there was a surge forward, making it difficult for the people trying to get off the train."

"So there was a little pushing and shoving."

"I'd say a lot of pushing and shoving. Anyway, out of the corner of my eye, no more than three or four feet away, I saw this Asian man, he was kinda bucking, like his head was going back and forth."

"You thought he was having a seizure or something—at least that's what you said."

"That's how I described it to the operator. I said to myself, It's so damn crowded the man is having a seizure and he can't even fall down. I mean, we were all packed together and pushing forward because everyone was afraid they weren't going to get on the train."

"I get the picture," Laurie said. "Did you try to help?"

"Not really. He was to my left at that point. I'm not even sure I could have gotten to him if I'd tried. I was being pushed ahead by the people behind me. And to be truthful, I thought the people right next to him were attempting to help. In fact, when I got to the train's door, I tried to look back. At first I couldn't even see him because he wasn't all that tall."

"We're here, lady," the cabdriver said, looking at Laurie in the rearview mirror.

"Can you hold on?" Laurie asked Robert, a little flustered at her predicament. "I'm in a taxi and have to pay and get out."

"I can wait," Robert assured her.

Laurie paid the driver and climbed from the cab to stand in front of the Midtown North Precinct, its flag snapping in the breeze and a bevy of cop cars parked every which way.

"I'm back," Laurie said. "You were saying . . ."

"I was saying that as I was boarding, I got a fleeting look at the man lying on the platform. Standing by him were two other Asians. But it was truly fleeting, because I was looking through a bunch of other riders pushing to get on the train, some of whom didn't make it. I was also getting my cell phone out."

"At that time, did it look like the man was still seizing?"

"It happened so fast, with such a limited view, but if I had to guess, I'd say no. I was also dialing the nine-one-one operator to get the call in before the doors closed, and I lost the little signal I had."

"Look," Laurie said. "I really appreciate your being willing to talk with me. You have my number if anything else comes to mind, anything at all."

"I will," Robert said. "Actually, now that you've made me relive the moment, I feel guilty at having boarded the train. Maybe I should have tried a little harder to see if I could have helped."

"Don't torture yourself," Laurie said. "You made a nine-one-one call so medical help could arrive."

"That's nice of you to say."

Laurie disconnected her call and then climbed the steps into the busy precinct.

CHAPTER ELEVEN

Louie felt energized as he neared his restaurant. He'd used the bus ride from Rikers Island to consider Paulie's advice, and by the time he got back to his car he'd decided to follow Paulie's suggestions. It was now clear in his mind that there was a time to avoid violence, and there was a time in which violence was the only solution. And this was one of those situations. At the same time, he was convinced he was right about not taking out Hideki. There were too many negatives, including the concern of losing the Japanese income stream and flow of crystal meth, even short-term. Instead, the disappearance of Susumu Nomura and Yoshiaki Eto was the perfect message to everyone, but most specifically to Hideki. The plan wasn't necessarily going to be easy, but it was doable. Accordingly, Louie had started by calling Hideki and requesting a meeting at the Venetian for three-thirty to go over the evening's plans, to which Hideki had immediately agreed.

Louie parked his car in his spot at the rear of the restaurant and walked in the back door. He knew all the guys would still be there, because after he'd made the call to Hideki to set up the meeting for that afternoon, he'd called Carlo.

"Did you get to see Paulie?" Carlo had asked. "And do we have a plan for tonight with the two crazy-ass Japs?"

"Yes to both questions," Louie had said. "We have a plan but with different rules of engagement."

"How so?" Carlo had asked, not trying to hide his disappointment.

"You'll know soon enough," Louie had snapped back. "Why I'm calling is to make sure you guys are still there when I return."

"We're here," Carlo had said.

After walking through a short hallway containing the restrooms, Louie pounded open the swinging door leading into the kitchen, catching Benito off guard as he sat on the countertop, shooting the breeze with the chef, John Franco. Guiltily, Benito dropped his feet to the floor and stood. Louie glared at him for a moment but quickly decided he was too busy to ream him out for behavior the health department would hardly condone. "Did the guys eat?"

"Yes, they did," Benito answered smartly.

"Is there any of the pasta left?"

"I have the sauce," John Franco said. "I'll have fresh pasta in ten minutes."

Without answering, Louie pushed through the swinging doors leading into the dining room. Carlo, Brennan, Arthur, and Ted were sitting around the table, poker chips and dollar bills piled up in the table's center. Empty espresso cups littered the table's periphery. Carlo slid out from the booth so Louie could slide into his usual spot.

"So how was Paulie?" Carlo asked after Louie had nodded a greeting to each of his henchmen.

"Weird," Louie said. "He's lost a lot of weight. Plus, he's found God."

"You mean he's become a Bible banger?" Carlo questioned.

"I don't really know," Louie admitted. "He said he'd found the Lord and then talked like the old Paulie Cerino. The issue didn't come up again until almost the end of our talk, and then only briefly. It might be an act for the parole board. I think he's getting desperate about not getting parole."

"So what's the plan for tonight?" Carlo asked.

Louie then told them about his conversation with Paulie, trying to remember all the details, such as the clever idea of the diversionary explosion concept to convince Hideki that Louie was serious about helping with the break-in. The only time he paused was when Benito brought out Louie's pasta and placed the steaming plate under his nose. Benito poured him a glass of Barolo and another of sparkling water.

"Will there be anything else?" Benito asked.

Louie waved the waiter off without responding, and as soon as Benito was out of earshot, he went back to his conversation with Paulie and Paulie's suggestions, most specifically about getting rid of both Susumu and Yoshiaki.

"So we're going on the offensive here?" Carlo asked. He was pleased and happy to show it.

"Most definitely," Louie responded. "In this business, sometimes you need to use violence to keep the peace. We can't have the likes of those two wandering around shooting whomever and wherever they please. It gives us all a bad name. At the same time, when you use violence you have to limit the fallout, which brings us to the morgue issue. You all understand that, don't you?"

No one spoke, causing Louie to repeat the question.

"I guess so," Carlo said. As the head enforcer, Carlo was expected to speak for the group.

"The point is that it is important Satoshi's death continues to be thought of as a natural death. We would be accomplices if it were considered a homicide, and we don't want that."

"Surely not," Carlo agreed.

"Paulie was also insistent about this medical examiner, Laurie Montgomery. We have to make sure she's not associated with the case. If she is, we have to do something to get her off the case. It's as simple as that."

"What exactly do we do if she is on the case?" Carlo asked.

"Paulie didn't have any suggestions. He was just insistent she not be involved. But we'll cross that bridge if and when we come to it."

"Now let's go back to Susumu Nomura and Yoshiaki Eto," Carlo said. "We're supposed to pick them up as if we are going to help them break into iPS USA but whack them instead."

"That's it," Louie said. "And I don't want their bodies found. Drive them way out to the tip of Brooklyn, way out near the Verrazano-Narrows Bridge. I want them in the ocean, not the bay."

Carlo looked at Brennan and shrugged, wondering if his partner had any questions.

"How are we going to pick them up?" Brennan asked. "Like last night, in front of their apartments on the Lower East Side?"

"No," Louie said. "There's always the chance someone will spot you hanging around their neighborhood. I want to arrange a pickup in a public place. Do you have any preference?

Carlo and Brennan exchanged a glance.

"Come on, guys, give me a location. Hideki's going

to be here at three-thirty, and I want to have this planned out."

"How about Union Square in front of the Barnes and Noble bookstore," Brennan said. "There are always enough people loitering around the area."

"That's settled," Louie said, taking another bite of his pasta. "What time should we say for them to be in Union Square?"

"Well," Brennan said. "If we're supposed to be breaking into a Midtown Fifth Avenue office building, it shouldn't be too early."

"I don't think the time matters," Carlo said. "I mean, we're not going to be actually doing the break-in."

"Well, then just pick, for chrissake," Louie snapped. "Where do you have in mind to do the hit?"

Again Carlo and Brennan looked at each other as if waiting for the other to decide.

Louie looked skyward in frustration. "This isn't rocket science," he complained. "What about at the pier." The Vaccarro organization in the past had had a fruit import company as a cover in Maspeth on the East River just south of the Queens-Midtown Tunnel. The warehouse and the pier were still there but in sad shape. They hadn't been able to sell them. They used the warehouse for storage.

"That's fine," Carlo said. Brennan nodded in agreement. The whole area was deserted, especially at night.

Louie looked at Arthur and Ted. "You guys in agreement? Because I want all of you in on it so there's no trouble, as wild as these Japs are supposed to be."

Arthur and Ted nodded.

"All right," Louie continued. "We got the pickup place, we got the location of the hit, but we still don't have the pickup time. What about eleven o'clock. What do you say?"

"That's fine," Carlo said, looking over at Brennan, who nodded.

"Jesus," Louie said. "Must I come along and be the band leader? You guys can be pathetic."

"How are we going to get them to come to the pier?" Carlo asked.

"Do I have to tell you everything?" Louie said, shaking his head in despair. "Tell them that's where the explosives are stored for the distraction during the break-in. I don't know. You figure it out." Louie paused. "Are we okay now? We have the pickup location and hour, and we have the hit location, and what you're going to do with the bodies. Of course you'll remove all identification. I mean, that's a given."

Everyone nodded.

"Now let's go back to the morgue issue. Carlo, you and Brennan head over there right now." Louie glanced at this watch. It was almost three-thirty. "Go in and ask for Vinnie Amendola. Say you're family. When you talk to him, say that you're working for Paulie and that you know what Paulie did for his father."

"What was it?"

"I'm not sure of all the details, but Paulie said it had to do with the father having embezzled a couple hundred bucks in union funds, nothing huge. For that Vinnie's father was supposedly going to be iced unless he came up with the money, plus fifty percent. Since he had done some work for Paulie, Paulie lent him the money, saving his life."

"What if he refuses to talk to me?"

Louie stared at Carlo with disbelief. "What is this, a

new Carlo? Usually when I tell you to do something, you do it, no questions asked. What should you do if he refuses to talk to you? Threaten to kill his dog. You're a professional. Plus, all you want is some information about Satoshi. Of course, you can't use Satoshi's name. Call him 'the body from the subway.' And don't threaten Vinnie right away. Be calm and reasonable. Don't let them know who you are. Tell him you heard Laurie Montgomery was good at what she does. Be creative."

"Okay," Carlo said. "I get the picture."

"If it turns out she has been assigned the case and she's still working on it, and if Vinnie seems favorably inclined, meaning he's not going to blab to the authorities about our questions, then ask if he has any suggestions as to how she might be encouraged to get off the case. Without being too obvious, suggest there might be money in it for him and for her. If that doesn't work, then have Vinnie convey some threat. Got it?"

"I got it," Carlo said.

"Then get your ass out of here!"

Carlo slid out from the table, tossed the cards that he'd been holding since Louie's arrival, picked through the cash to extract what he thought he'd contributed to the pot, and motioned for Brennan to follow suit. When the men were halfway to the door, in walked Hideki Shimoda, flanked by Susumu and Yoshiaki.

The *saiko-komon* was the size and shape of a sumo wrestler, with a bloated, florid face whose features seemed lost in folds of skin. As he walked he swayed from side to side.

Carlo and Brennan had to quickly move aside to avoid a collision. Susumu and Yoshiaki stuck by their *saiko-komon*'s side, slightly behind the immense man, causing the group to move like a wedge. As if detached from the world about them and with slight sneers on their faces, they didn't even acknowledge Carlo and Brennan, despite spending the previous afternoon and evening with them.

In contrast to the apparent camaraderie between Louie and his minions, the relationship between Hideki and his soldiers was impersonal, almost martial. Their attire was also strikingly different, with the Japanese wearing what they had had on the previous day: shark-skin suits, white dress shirts, black ties, and dark glasses, while the Americans, for the most part, wore casual sweaters and jeans. Only Carlo was smartly dressed, with his gray silk jacket, black silk turtleneck, and black gabardine pants.

As Louie got up from the table Hideki halted, bowed slightly. "Hello, Barbera-san."

"Welcome, Shimoda-san," Louie said, feeling awkward as he tried to imitate Hideki's bow. Louie stepped back and gestured for Hideki to sit at a clean booth, unclut-tered by coffee cups and pasta dishes.

Hideki and Louie settled into the booth while Susumu and Yoshiaki walked to the bar and sat stiffly on a pair of stools, their arms crossed. They did not speak but continued to stare at their boss.

"Thank you for coming out to visit my humble restaurant," Louie began. While he spoke he wished it was going to be Hideki who was going to be whacked, or better yet, all three instead of just the impudent soldiers sitting at the bar with their stupid dark glasses and their spiky hair.

"It is my pleasure," Hideki replied in passable English. "And it is my pleasure to thank you for your gracious help, especially for tonight. It would be hard for us to do it alone, as it is on such a famous avenue."

"It is my pleasure to help, and you are correct that the location makes the task more difficult. It would be the equivalent for us to rob an office on the busiest street in the Ginza district in Tokyo."

"Not easy."

"Not easy," Louie agreed. "Excuse me, Shimoda-san," Louie said before calling out to Carlo and Brennan, who had backed up against the wall opposite the bar to keep an eye on Susumu and Yoshiaki. "Why don't you two go ahead with what we discussed, and call me as soon as you finish?"

They nodded and quickly left the room.

"I'm very sorry to interrupt, Shimoda-san," Louie said. "I'm sending my two men to the city morgue to make sure that what you said about your hit was as you promised. I want to be certain it is being considered a natural death and not a professional homicide."

"You have contacts in the city morgue?" Hideki asked. He was clearly impressed.

"A resource we rarely tap," Louie answered.

"I would appreciate hearing what they learn."

"Getting back to what we were talking about," Louie said, "I want you to know it will not be easy to break into the offices of iPS USA. It can be done, but it will have to be done quickly. To be as safe as possible, we will have only minutes to be in the office. My under-standing is we will be looking for lab books. Is that correct?"

"It is entirely correct. We must get these lab books."

"What kind of lab books are they?"

"I am not authorized to say."

Louie was taken aback. He stared at Hideki. Here the guy was going to the extent of trying to extort Louie into helping him obtain lab books but wasn't willing to say anything about them. It was irritating to say the least. And what was more irritating was that after speaking with Paulie, Louie knew the basis of the extortion was, in Louie's vernacular, a crock of shit. There'd be no way that Hideki's Aizukotetsu-kai would be able to team up with Dominick, because it would mean teaming up with the hated Yamaguchi, which would never happen. Louie felt himself getting more angry but more curious, too. Why were these damn lab books so important?

"What do they look like? I mean, once inside the office, my guys and your guys are not going to have a lot of time. Everybody will have to look for the missing books."

"I was told they were dark blue, but the most important way to recognize them is that they say 'Satoshi Machita' in yellow letters on the front cover. They will be easy to recognize."

"What the hell?" Louie questioned. "You said they were stolen."

"They were stolen. They were stolen by the man who owns iPS USA."

Louie rubbed his forehead roughly. Nothing was making sense. He was beginning to believe Hideki was teasing him, making fun of him, but for what reason he had no idea.

"I think we should stop talking about the lab books and get on with the plans for tonight," Hideki said.

"Just a few more questions," Louie said. "I gotta have some sense of what we're after. I mean, we're taking a risk here for you."

"I'm not authorized to discuss the lab books."

"Look!" Louie said suddenly. "You're pissing me off. Up until these lab books, you and I have gotten along superbly. We've never had a disagreement, and we're making money together hand over fist, which means we're making a lot. Either you answer my questions or we're out, and you can get the lab books on your own. The trouble is, you didn't level with me about Satoshi right from the beginning. You said it was a shakedown, making me believe it was a gambling debt or something. But it turns out it's a lot more, and I want to know what it's about."

"You are going to make me turn to your competition," Hideki warned.

"Bullshit!" Louie scoffed.

Sensitive to a sudden change in atmosphere, Susumu and Yoshiaki slid off the barstools and stood. Simultaneously, Arthur and Ted slipped from their booth. Each twosome eyed the other.

"You're not about to go to Vinnie any more than I am," Louie rejoined. "I learned something today. You Aizukotetsu-kai and Yamaguchi-gumi get along like oil and water."

For a few tense minutes, no one in the room moved. It was like those charged moments just before a summer thunderstorm, when lightning was on its way but no one knew exactly when. Then suddenly the atmosphere lightened as Hideki audibly breathed out and said, "You are right."

"Right about what?" Louie demanded. He'd gotten himself worked up that Hideki had been playing him for a fool.

"Everything you said. I have not been truthful with

you. I had been given orders to kill Satoshi and get his lab books. I had hoped I could achieve both goals at the very same time, but it did not work out that way. I do not know all the details about the lab books myself, as it is a complicated story related to who will own the very important patents for the next kind of stem cells, the induced pluripotent stem cells."

"Slow down. What was that?"

"What do you know about stem cells?" Hideki asked.

"Nothing," Louie admitted.

"I'm no expert, but it's a topic covered constantly in the Japanese news media," Hideki said. "We're constantly reminded that it was a Japanese scientist named Shigeo Takayama who produced the first pluripotent stem cell. Kyoto University patented the process on his behalf. Then my *oyabun* learned that another researcher, Satoshi Machita, had actually beat Takayama in creating the special cells, which was proved by his lab books. Although during the day he'd been working on mice under Takayama's tutelage, during the night he was working by himself on his own mature fibroblasts, creating human iPS cells before anyone else."

"So the man your guys killed yesterday is considered the granddaddy of these special cells."

"That's correct."

"Which makes the lab books quite valuable."

"Yes. In Japan they are to be used to challenge Kyoto University patents, and here in America they are to be used to get the patents. Same with the European patent office and the WTO."

Louie pondered this revelation for several beats and thought about its money-earning potential, then tucked it into the back of his mind. There was no way he would consider actively going through with the planned break-in at iPS USA. Then Hideki told him something that totally shocked him.

"My *oyabun* learned these things from the government."

"The government?" Louie questioned with surprise. "Which government?"

"The Japanese government."

"Now, that's hard to believe."

"But it is true. A vice minister met with my *oyabun* and told him all of this, including the fact that Satoshi had fled the country illegally with the help of the Yamaguchi-gumi. They were the ones who engineered the theft of the lab books from Kyoto University. It was Kyoto University which had physical but not legal control of the lab books, as Satoshi had been an employee. It is the Japanese government who wants the lab books."

"Good grief!" Louie said. "I can't believe the Japanese government approached your leader for help. What's his name again?"

"Hisayuki Ishii-san."

"Our government would never come to me for anything," Louie said, laughing heartily.

"There has always been give-and-take between the Yakuza and our government. That's how we operate so openly in Japan. The Japanese government has found us useful on occasion, and we Yakuza are generally left alone by the authorities. It's the same with the Japanese people; they too find us useful as an out in an otherwise strict and stratified culture."

"If that's true, why did the Yamaguchi-gumi go against your government by helping Satoshi to flee the country and help iPS USA, presumably to get the lab books?"

"We are not sure," Hideki said, "but it is assumed by my boss that the Yamaguchi-gumi is financially associated with iPS USA as a way of laundering money."

"That's not working together."

"No, it's not," Hideki admitted. "You have to remember that the Yamaguchi-gumi is a younger organization than other Yakuza, and not bound as tightly by tradition. They are also much larger, almost double the size of the next smaller.

"Now that I have been fully open with you," Hideki continued, "how about we get back to discussing tonight's break-in?"

Before speaking, Louie silently questioned himself if there was anything else he wanted to know about the lab books and their backstory, but nothing came to mind. As up-front as Hideki had seemingly been, Louie was glad that there weren't plans to kill him after all. Killing the two out-of-control enforcers would be enough.

As concisely as possible, Louie then went on to describe that night's faux plans, including the pickup location and time, and the fact that the robbery was designed around a diversionary explosion to preoccupy the police, to be set off on Fifth Avenue, south of the break-in location, perhaps at the New York Public Library. When he was finished, he paused to give Hideki time for questions. He felt confident the plans sounded real.

"What if there are still police or general public around the iPS USA building after the explosion?"

Louie thought it was a good question, and gave it a

bit of thought before responding. "If there are people or cops in the immediate surroundings, then we abort. We don't do the break-in. We postpone it until another day. There's to be no civilian casualties whatsoever if we can possibly avoid it. This is to be a clean break-in with no violence to others, except possibly to an inside security guard if there is one. Have your guys wear masks, gloves, and nondescript dark clothing, not white shirts and sunglasses."

Louie looked at Hideki. There was a pause. Louie couldn't believe Hideki didn't have more questions. Hideki was clearly inexperienced at organizing such an event and was seemingly buying into the plan even though from Louie's perspective it was, as he would say, nuts.

"If you have no questions for me," Louie said finally, "I have one for you. When we spoke on the phone, you assured me that Satoshi's death would be considered natural. How was the hit done?"

"I have been open with you as you requested about the lab books," Hideki said. "But about this special technique, I can say nothing, as my *oyabun* has specifically ordered. We use it rarely, but it has always worked as designed."

"Why did you use it on this occasion?"

"Specifically, we did not want the hit to appear as a hit."

"I appreciate that you made the effort. If it is signed out as a natural death, it won't cause the police to become agitated. That's important to me, but why did you care?"

"Because of the Yamaguchi-gumi's involvement. They had made a big effort to bring Satoshi over to

America after they had helped iPS USA to acquire his lab books. If his death had been an obvious hit, we were fearful they might suspect us, the Aizukotetsu-kai, as the instigators. They are our rivals, and there has been tension between us because they stole the lab books from under our noses in our home city of Kyoto. In the past, such a situation could have resulted in violence. The problem is that they have grown too large. We would be overwhelmed even if we acted preemptively."

"My God!" Louie exclaimed. "Such intrigue."

"It is a time of change, I am afraid. The Yakuza used to be more respectful of tradition. The Yamaguchi-gumi are mere upstarts."

After confirming that Susumu and Yoshiaki would be waiting outside the Barnes & Noble store in Union Square at eleven p.m., the three Yakuza left, all bowing before slipping out the door.

"Weird people," Arthur said as soon as the sound of the outer door closing slipped back through the heavy draperies.

"This whole situation is weird," Louie responded.

CHAPTER TWELVE

I don't like this," Carlo said. "I've never been in a morgue. How can people work in such a place day in and day out?"

"I think it's kind of interesting," Brennan said. He liked the forensics shows on television.

They had pulled into a no-parking zone on First Avenue at the southeastern corner of 30th Street. OCME was ahead of them on the northeast corner.

"It doesn't bother you?" Carlo asked nervously. He was in the driver's seat of his Denali, unconsciously gripping the steering wheel with white knuckles.

Brennan shook his head. "Why? Come on, let's get this over with. Maybe we should call this Vinnie Amendola and see if he'll come out and meet us in a bar or something. Having worked here for so long, he undoubtedly knows the area."

"I think Louie was pretty clear that he wanted you to talk to him face-to-face in the morgue."

"He didn't say specifically me," Brennan said. "He said 'we.' And he didn't say we had to talk to him in the morgue. But you're in charge." There were times that Carlo irritated him, especially with the fact that he was officially in charge when the two of them were on assignment, as they were at that moment. Brennan was not impressed with Carlo's general intelligence and thought that his intelligence should trump Carlo's

CURE

175

seniority. Once he'd brought the issue up with Louie but had gotten reamed out for doing so, such that he'd never brought it up again. But the issue sat there in the back of his mind, like a mildly bothersome toothache.

"I am in charge," Carlo acknowledged. "So here's how we're going to handle this. You are going in the morgue, make contact with the guy face-to-face, and tell him I want to talk to him wherever he wants, but I want to talk now."

"And what are you going to do while I'm in the morgue?"

"Sit here and watch the car. It's a no-parking zone. I don't want to get a ticket. If I'm not here when you come out, I'll be driving around the block."

Brennan stared at Carlo for a beat, feeling Carlo was making him play gofer. "Suit yourself," Brennan grumbled as he climbed from the SUV.

"I could use a beer, so suggest a bar."

Brennan merely nodded before slamming the door harder than he needed to. He knew that it irked Carlo but didn't care since the slacker was taking advantage of him. By the time Brennan crossed 30th Street, he'd forgotten his peevishness and was curious about what, if anything, he was going to see. When he entered the building's foyer he recognized the reality that he probably wasn't going to see much. All the doors into the interior of the building were tightly closed. In front of him was a pleasant-looking, grandmotherly African-American woman with sparkling eyes and a warm, accepting smile. She was sitting behind a U-shaped reception counter in a high swivel chair. According to a nameplate, her name was Marlene Wilson.

"Can I help you?" Marlene questioned, as if she was the concierge at a fine hotel.

"I'm looking for a Vinnie Amendola," Brennan said, thrown off balance by Marlene's pleasant appearance and demeanor. He'd prepared himself for something more intimidating or even gothic.

Marlene used an OCME directory before dialing, making several calls before she got Vinnie on the line. She then handed the phone to Brennan.

After making certain he was talking to the correct person, Brennan said he'd just come from talking with Paulie Cerino and wanted to convey a message.

"The real Paulie Cerino?" Vinnie questioned with a hesitant voice. It was, perhaps, the last person he suspected he'd be hearing from that day.

"The Paulie Cerino from Queens," Brennan said. He knew that it was a name that used to strike terror in certain people, particularly deadbeats who had borrowed money or who had been unlucky at poker or picked the wrong horses or athletic teams.

"Is Paulie Cerino out of prison?" Vinnie questioned. Although Vinnie was not a gambler, he did not like to hear from Paulie Cerino.

"No, he is still in prison but expects an imminent parole. That's why he sent me. Is it possible for you to come to the front reception area? We need to talk."

"What are we going to talk about?" Vinnie said while frantically trying to figure out what to do. He intuitively knew that whoever this person was, he was not someone Vinnie should be associating with.

"Paulie has a few questions he wants me to ask."

"Can't he call me himself?" Vinnie questioned hesitantly. "I'll give you my cell phone number."

"Paulie has limited opportunity to call."

"I see."

"It's just some simple questions," Brennan explained.

"Okay, I'll be up," Vinnie said, and hung up.

"Are you family or just a friend of Vinnie's?" Marlene asked, to make conversation. She'd heard Brennan's side and wondered if something was amiss with talk about prison.

"Family," Brennan said. "Very distant family."

When Vinnie appeared, he purposefully took Brennan out of earshot of Marlene. The two men eyed each other. Although they were approximately the same age, any similarity ended there. Vinnie's dark hair and olive complexion was a sharp contrast to Brennan's transparent freckled skin and supposedly red hair, which was more a carrot orange.

After they introduced themselves, Vinnie said, "The last time Paulie sent a couple of his people to see me, it ended with me being forced to do something illegal, which got me in trouble, and I almost lost my job. I say this just to let you know I'm less than overjoyed to hear from Paulie Cerino."

"We're not going to try to get you to do anything," Brennan promised. "As I said, we're here just to ask you a few questions."

"What do you mean 'we'?"

"My partner is out in the car. We thought we could buy you a beer somewhere in the neighborhood."

"Can't do, not before I get off at four-thirty."

"What a shame," Brennan said sincerely. After Carlo had suggested a beer, Brennan had grown progressively fond of the idea.

"Well, nice meeting you."

"Hold on!" Brennan blurted. "How about right here? I'll call my buddy. We can sit here on the couch."

Vinnie looked from Brennan to the couch to Marlene and back. He didn't like the couch idea. In fact, he didn't even like standing there in the foyer with the likes of Brennan, understanding that Brennan was most likely a member of the Vaccarro crime family, perhaps even one of their enforcers or hit men. When Vinnie was young, he and his friends were in awe of Brennan's type, but that changed when one of Paulie Cerino's guys had shot a guy outside the local candy store. Vinnie and his friends had been down the street in the ice-cream parlor when they'd heard, and had challenged one another to run down to catch a glimpse before the police arrived. When Vinnie saw the body lying in the street, blood and pink brain matter coming out, he'd gotten sick instantly as blood drained from the victim's head. It had been one of those visual horrors of childhood that had been irrevocably stamped on Vinnie's visual cortex. From then on, Vinnie felt nothing but fear for the gang lifestyle.

"Not here!" Vinnie said, worried the chief might suddenly appear. The chief's office and the rest of administration was right off the reception area. Desperately he tried to think of what to do, as he was also reluctant to let them into the restricted interior of the building. "I know," he said suddenly. "Let's meet on Thirtieth Street. Go back out and walk down to OCME receiving area and the garage doors. I'll meet you there." Vinnie gestured toward the building's front entrance as if Brennan had forgotten. "I'll see you down there in two minutes."

Feeling like he'd been given the bum's rush, Brennan

left the building and walked back to Carlo's car. He opened the passenger door and leaned in.

"Well?" Carlo asked.

"He's nervous as hell, mentioning his last dealings with Paulie. He claims to have almost lost his job."

"He's not going to talk with us?"

"He claims he can't go out while he's on the clock, but he's willing to meet us out in the street," Brennan said while pointing down 30th Street.

"For the love of God," Carlo complained, climbing out of the car. He left the flashers on.

As they rounded the corner and started down 30th Street, they saw Vinnie appear from between a cluster of white vans. "At least we don't have to go inside," Carlo said while zipping up his coat.

Brennan introduced Carlo to an obviously anxious Vinnie, who kept looking back over his shoulder to see if anyone was paying them any heed.

Vinnie's intuitions about Brennan's occupation were confirmed when he saw Carlo's attire, particularly the gray silk jacket over the black mock turtleneck and the gold chains. That was how the wiseguys all dressed back in his youth.

"Listen!" Vinnie said. "We have to make this short, because I'm still on the clock. What is it you want to ask me?"

"You know we're here on Paulie Cerino's behalf," Carlo mentioned.

"So your friend said."

"He wanted me to remind you what he did for your father."

"You can tell Mr. Cerino that I will never forget what he did for my father. But you can also remind him what

I did for him the last time I heard from him, and that I hope he feels we are more or less even."

"I'll tell him," Carlo snapped, immediately taking mild offense at Vinnie's implied brazenness. "But it's the capo's decision when a debt is paid, not the debtor's."

Vinnie took a deep breath to calm down. The last thing he wanted was to get into an argument with these guys. "Please ask me whatever it is you want to ask."

Carlo glared at Vinnie for a beat, restraining himself from giving him a good slap. "You people here at the morgue got a body that came in sometime last evening. A Japanese man who'd collapsed on the subway platform at Columbus Circle."

"I know the case," Vinnie said. As one of the more senior mortuary technicians he prided himself that he knew just about everything that went on at OCME. "What do you want to know about it?"

"Who is the coroner that is involved?"

"We don't have coroners," Vinnie said with an air of superiority. "We have trained medical examiners who are medical doctors, not mere civil servants."

"Whatever," Carlo snapped back irritably. He was getting progressively tired of Vinnie's attitude, but again he let it go. "Who is assigned to the case?"

"Dr. Southgate was assigned," Vinnie began.

After hearing Southgate's name, Carlo immediately began to relax. It was always pleasurable to report back positive news, especially if it meant less work, which Carlo thought would be the case in this instance. Unfortunately, his relaxing didn't last as Vinnie continued, "But Dr. Southgate became ill, and Dr. Laurie Montgomery took over."

Carlo did a double take. "What was that?" He'd

heard, but his mind was not in a receptive mood for a change.

"Dr. Southgate started the case, but he became ill and Dr. Laurie Montgomery, or now it's Dr. Laurie Montgomery-Stapleton, took over. Why do you ask?"

"Why would they change?" Carlo demanded, ignoring Vinnie's question.

"I told you. Dr. Southgate became ill. He left OCME to go home."

"Shit!" Carlo voiced, trying to reboot his brain from the sudden reversal.

"What was the diagnosis?" Brennan asked, as Carlo seemed to have momentarily lost his voice.

"So far there is no diagnosis," Vinnie said. He found himself wondering why Paulie Cerino would be so interested.

"How about the manner of death?" Brennan continued, using lingo learned from TV forensics dramas.

"At the moment I'd have to say natural, but that could possibly change. It's Dr. Montgomery's first case since returning from an extended maternity leave, and I heard her say that she was determined to find some pathology if it kills her. She didn't find anything whatsoever during the autopsy, so she'll be reviewing the case with extra care."

"So it's your opinion Dr. Montgomery is still going to look into this case more than she already has."

"That's what she suggested," Vinnie agreed. "And she's persistent. I have to give her credit for that."

Brennan and Carlo exchanged an unhappy glance, then Brennan's eyes brightened. "I want to be sure you understand that we are here in strictest confidence. Paulie would be extremely unhappy if you were even tempted to mention the content of our discussion to anyone. You do understand, don't you?"

"I do," Vinnie said, and he was speaking the truth. "For sure," he added. Vinnie, more than most people, knew that the myths about the Mafia were mostly all true. If provoked, mobsters were capable of episodes of extreme nastiness.

"I mean, something might happen to you or to your family."

Although Vinnie's anxiety had lessened to a degree as the conversation had proceeded, it now came back in a flash. In response to the threat, he merely nodded. It was this type of intimidation he'd feared when he'd first heard Paulie Cerino's name.

"Paulie is very interested in the case of the mystery subway man. If you are interested, I can assure you that we did not kill the individual, but it is in the best interests of everyone that the case fades into the woodwork, so to speak. Paulie would prefer it stays as an unidentified individual who had a natural death. Do you understand?"

Vinnie nodded but wondered why he was being told what he was being told, as there was no way he could influence how the case was to be signed out.

"Let me hear you?" Brennan demanded.

"Yes," Vinnie squeaked. All brazenness had evaporated.

"We are interested in this Laurie Montgomery-Stapleton. In your estimation, do you think she will follow up on her threats of finding pathology until it, quote, 'kills her'? I believe that's what you said."

Afraid of contradicting himself, Vinnie was impelled to tell the truth rather than tell them what he sensed they wanted to hear. "She said she was going to find some pathology and that she was not going to give up."

Brennan looked at Carlo. "Paulie's not going to be happy."

"I was thinking the same thing. No one is going to be happy."

"What are we going to do?" Brennan asked, as if Vinnie was not standing there.

Carlo turned back to Vinnie, who was beginning to feel like an anxious mouse trapped by several cats. "Let me ask you something else. How do you think Dr. Montgomery would respond to a little grease on the order of several grand and maybe a grand for you?"

Nervous enough to be unsure of what was being asked of him, Vinnie said, "Are you talking about a bribe?"

"Some people call it that," Carlo admitted. "There are lots of names."

"I don't think she'd respond well at all," Vinnie said quickly. "I think offering her a bribe would make her certain there was something to be found. I mean, now she doesn't know. All she knows is that it is rare not to find some pathology when you do an autopsy, maybe not enough to kill someone, but something abnormal. The man I work with the most—actually, Laurie's husband— always finds something. It's a challenge for him as well."

"Anything else?' Carlo asked Brennan. "Anything else you think we should ask?"

"I can't think of anything," Brennan admitted.

Carlo turned back to Vinnie. "It might turn out we have some more questions. How about you give us your cell phone number?"

Impatient to get away, Vinnie recited his phone number even though he didn't want to do it.

"Thanks, buddy," Carlo said, writing the number down. "Now, let's see if there were any unintended mistakes made." It was a 917 number, and Carlo quickly punched the numbers into his own phone. A moment later Vinnie's personal ring sounded from his lab coat's pocket. "Perfect," Carlo said. He waited until Vinnie's phone had answered the call before stopping it.

Carlo then reached out to shake Vinnie's hand, and after doing so he squeezed tighter rather than letting go. "Remember about keeping quiet about our meeting," Carlo said while looking unwaveringly into Vinnie's dark pupils. "And if you can think of any way to dampen Laurie Montgomery-Stapleton's enthusiasm for following up on the case of the subway platform, give me a call. As for my cell number, you have it on your phone."

Finally, Carlo let go of Vinnie's hand. "We'll be around," he said simply, and walked away. Brennan locked eyes with Vinnie for the briefest of moments and hurried after.

"Louie's not going to be a happy camper when we tell him what we've learned about the case and Laurie Montgomery-Stapleton," Brennan said.

"You can say that again," Carlo responded.

Suddenly, Brennan stopped. "Wait a second! We forgot to ask Vinnie something else that Louie wanted us to ask."

"What?"

Brennan turned, but Vinnie had already disappeared back into OCME.

"We forgot to ask if he had any suggestions of how Laurie Montgomery might be encouraged to just give up on Satoshi and sign him out as a natural death."

"We asked him about whether she'd take a bribe."

"But that's not the same thing, you know what I'm saying? He might have another idea."

They walked in silence until they got to the corner of First and 30th. Carlo pulled Brennan to a stop. "You're right! We should have asked him."

"Let's call him. You wisely asked for his number—call him!"

"Good idea. Let's do it from the car." The car was where Carlo had left it, with its parking lights flashing. Unfortunately, there was already a parking ticket under the wiper, and a meter maid was standing next to it, waiting for a city tow truck. "Shit!"

"Sorry, ma'am," Carlo said as he jogged up to the vehicle. "I had city business here at OCME."

"Then you should have left the vehicle down the street with all OCME vans. We never bother tagging them."

"Maybe you could reconsider this ticket," Carlo said hopefully.

"Can't do!" the meter maid responded. "Now get your SUV out of here before the tow guys arrive."

Carlo mumbled some choice words for the meter maid but climbed into the SUV along with Brennan. Once settled behind the wheel, Carlo took out his cell phone and activated the redial button. Before the phone was answered, the meter maid was back rapping on his window.

"Okay, okay," Carlo called out through the glass. As he started the engine, Vinnie answered.

"Now you're going to get a ticket for being on your handheld while driving," Brennan said, attracting a dirty look from Carlo. Hanging up on Vinnie before speaking,

Carlo drove ahead on First Avenue until he could make a left onto a side street. Then he pulled over to the first fire hydrant and called Vinnie back.

"Let me get to a private spot," Vinnie said when he answered. A minute later he added, "Okay. What's up?"

"Listen," Carlo said. "We realized we forgot to ask your opinion about this situation. Do you have any suggestions about Dr. Laurie Montgomery-Stapleton? Is there any way you can think of getting her to forget the subway case and just sign it out?"

"No, not at all. If I tried to do anything it would be the same as a bribe. It would make her more committed than she is now. Now it's just an oddball challenge for her own personal reasons. If she thinks there is some criminality involved, it will turn her into a dog with a bone. I know because there already have been several cases in which she'd said A and everyone else said B, and after she'd looked into it, it turned out she was right. Besides, I don't want to be involved with you people. I'm sorry, but it is true. I mean, I'm not going to say anything to nobody, like the fact that you were here or anything like that."

Brennan, who could hear both sides of the conversation, motioned for Carlo to hand him the phone. With a shrug, Carlo handed it over.

"It's Brennan. Listen! What about you writing an anonymous note saying that there are some nasty people who want the subway natural death to be signed out immediately, as it is an insurance issue for the family."

"How can it be an insurance issue if the person hasn't been identified?"

"Good point!" Brennan admitted. "Well, forget the

insurance issue. Just write it so she knows that if she doesn't leave it be as she's already found it, being a natural death, she's in trouble, big trouble. Make sure she knows it's serious situation."

"Then she'd hand it to the police, and then the police will know something is amiss. I don't mean to tell you guys how to run your business, but my thought is that anything you do that calls attention to the victim will increase the odds that Dr. Montgomery-Stapleton will look at the case with more suspicion."

"What if you include in the note that if she talks to the police or anyone, she's going to suffer. I mean, if I were this doctor, and I got a note saying that I would somehow suffer if I didn't ease up on an autopsy case by signing it out as I saw it, meaning natural death, I would sign it out in the blink of an eye. Why would I take any risk in such a circumstance?"

"That's you and not Laurie Montgomery-Stapleton."

"Hang on," Brennan said. He looked at Carlo. "What should I say? It seems to me having a threatening note written is what Louie had in mind when he sent us over here. He practically said as much. I mean, how else is Vinnie going to 'convey a threat.'"

"I think you are right," Carlo said. "Plus, she just came back from a maternity leave. Isn't that what Vinnie said, or am I making it up?"

Brennan put the phone back to his ear and asked Vinnie.

"Yes," Vinnie said. "This is her first day back, and it has something to do with her continuing interest in this case."

"Women change after they have a child," Carlo said.

"I know. My wife has had two children. Being a mother takes over, and they'll do anything to protect their children."

"Did you hear that?" Brennan asked Vinnie.

"I heard it," Vinnie responded. He was getting progressively worried about having anything to do with these people.

"So compose a note for her that there's going to be serious consequences for her and her family unless she signs out the case. Be sure to emphasize family. And be sure to emphasize that there will be the same consequences if she tells anyone about the note, particularly the police. It doesn't have to be as long as *War and Peace*. In fact, clarity is more important than length."

"I thought you said earlier that I wasn't going to have to do anything, that all you wanted to do was ask a couple of questions."

"You're not going to give us any trouble, are you?" Brennan questioned, lowering his voice. "Actually, we are heading out to your house right this moment to watch your girls come home from school."

Carlo made a questioning expression. Brennan waved him off.

"No," Vinnie responded quickly. "No, thanks."

"Okay," Brennan said. "I tell you what. Compose the letter and then call back on this line. We might have some editorial input."

Brennan handed the phone back to Carlo. Carlo took it, abruptly disconnected, and dialed Louie. "I think we should give the bad news to Louie sooner rather than later," he said to Brennan as the call went through.

"Good idea," Brennan said. "Let's also run the idea

of the threatening letter by him to get his input. I mean, it is taking a chance if all it does is increase this lady doctor's curiosity rather than scare the pants off her."

"It's Carlo," Carlo said when Louie picked up. "I'm afraid we have bad news. . . ."

CHAPTER THIRTEEN

Laurie had the taxi drop her off directly in front of OCME so she didn't have to cross First Avenue, which was bumper-to-bumper with traffic. It was rush hour in full swing. It had taken her well over an hour to get from Midtown North Precinct back to OCME, which should have taken less than half that. New York City traffic was worse than ever.

She waved at Marlene as she entered, then headed for the third floor. Before reaching her office, she poked her head into Jack's open doorway.

"Where the hell have you been?" Jack asked, pretending to be irritated. "I've stopped into your office several times, and I knew you weren't in the pit."

Laurie's face assumed a mischievous smile as she dug in her shoulder bag and produced two computer disks. She held them up for Jack to see.

"What have you got?" Jack asked as he leaned back in his desk chair and stretched. In front of him was a mass of case files, books, journals, microscope slides, and lab reports, as well as a hair dryer with its cowling off, exposing its innards, suggesting he was doing twenty things at once. He was wearing latex surgical gloves.

"A couple of exciting movies," Laurie said.

Jack made a face of exaggerated disbelief.

"Really," Laurie persisted. "Thrillers, I'm sure."

"Come on," Jack said. He reached out and took one, which was labeled NYPD. "What in tarnation?"

"Video from each of the cameras at the A train platform at Columbus Circle."

Jack allowed his shoulders to slump as he let out a deep breath. "Don't tell me you are planning on watching all this. What's it, ten hours of people getting on and off the subway?"

"More like seven."

"And you're planning on watching it all."

"If I have to," Laurie said proudly. "I know it's going to lack something in plot and characterization, and it will probably be in grainy black and white, but I'm going to watch it just the same."

"Laurie, if you don't mind me saying this, I think you're going overboard on your one and only case. Why on earth would you be willing to subject yourself to such torture? Just because you found no pathology on the case isn't a healthy reason to beat yourself up. Tomorrow, when we come in, you can check the slides, as I'm sure you asked Maureen O'Conner to do them overnight, and you can check the toxicology screen, because I'm sure you asked John for a rush on that, too, and then be done with it. You don't need to watch seven hours of video."

"I'm counting on getting new cases in the morning."

"Then all the better. So that means you check the histology and the toxicology in the afternoon, and I'm sure it is going to be negative, case closed, death certificate signed and delivered."

"The security video might show me something I need to know."

"Like what?"

"Like whether the victim had a seizure or not. The nine-one-one caller wasn't certain. It was a fleeting image that he got while he was compressed in a surging crowd and being pushed onto the train."

"*Hmm,*" Jack said. "I suppose that could be significant information. Anyway, I commend you for your thoroughness. I doubt that anyone else here would have thought of getting security tapes. Tell me! Are you just getting back now or have you already been to your office?"

"I'm just getting back now," Laurie said. "Why do you ask?"

"Not for any particular reason," Jack said distractedly.

Laurie looked askance at Jack. It seemed to her that he had a kind of mischievous smile on his face where the corners of his mouth were slightly curved upward.

"Really?" she questioned. "Why did you ask me if I'd been to my office?"

"Oh, it's not a big thing," Jack said. "The last time I was in there looking for you, I noticed a note from John with a normal blood alcohol level on your case. I guessed that you had managed somehow to get him to do it stat. I was wondering if you'd had a chance to see it?" He chuckled.

"No, I haven't seen it yet," Laurie said, somewhat confused. Sometimes Jack could act slightly weird, and this was one of those times. When it did happen, she tended to attribute it to his tendency to be thinking about a dozen issues all at the same time, as the mess on his desk suggested he was doing at that moment.

"What time do you want to head home?" Laurie questioned to change the subject. She was anxious to leave. She'd made it a point, with effort, not to call Leticia for Leticia's benefit. And since Leticia had not called her, she'd been out of touch for longer than she felt comfortable with. She wanted to know when Jack was willing to leave so she could use it as an excuse to call to let Leticia know when they'd be home.

Jack shrugged. "How about after I write up what I've found here. It's pretty interesting—at least to me."

"Are you talking about the hair dryer?" Laurie asked.

"I am indeed," Jack said as he picked up the appliance. "Remember the case I was just beginning when you'd finished your case."

"The Delta cabin attendant. What did you find?"

"I found what you found: nothing. Well, it was nothing, if you discount the insignificant uterine fibroids. So I called down to Bart Arnold and asked if he could send one of the MLIs back to the woman's apartment and gather up all the handheld appliances from the bathroom, which he did. I got the hair dryer and that dental contraption. What's it called?"

"Waterpik."

"Anyway, the Waterpik was fine, but look at this hair dryer!" Jack picked up the apparatus and applied the contacts of a voltmeter to one of the prongs of the plug and the remaining casing. He then leaned back so Laurie could read the gauge.

"Zero ohms!" she said, reminding her that she'd had a similar case the first year at OCME. "Low-voltage electrocution."

"Which is why the boyfriend saw her walk out of the bathroom before collapsing and dying."

"But it looks like a new hair dryer!"

"I agree, which makes the case doubly interesting. Take a peek inside at that black wire." Jack pointed with a screwdriver.

"It looks like it's been stripped, going over that metallic edge of the dryer's chassis."

"My opinion exactly. When the young woman got out of the shower, maybe even standing on a damp floor, and turned on the hair dryer, she got zapped."

"It was a homicide, then, for certain," Laurie said. "Good pickup. Did she have any burns, like on the soles of her feet?"

"Nothing," Jack said. "But that's not too surprising, since one-third of low-voltage electrocutions don't have any burns."

"How did you remember that?"

"I didn't," Jack admitted. "I just read it before you popped in."

"Do you think the boyfriend did it, maybe while the victim was on her trip?"

"It would be my guess, but it might be hard to prove. One way would be to find the boyfriend's fingerprints somewhere inside the hair dryer, which is why I'm wearing gloves. Whose ever prints are in there is guilty of murder."

"Good pickup," Laurie repeated wistfully. It was just the kind of case she wished she'd come back to. It required experience, knowledge, and a certain creativity to put it all together, and in return it provided a true feeling of accomplishment that justice might be served.

"So how long will you need to write up the report about the hair dryer?"

"About a half-hour."

"Okay. As soon as you finish, come down to my office and we'll head home."

"Has everything been okay with Leticia and JJ?"

"Apparently I'm not quite as indispensable as I

thought. Everything's gone smoothly. Leticia even told me not to call so often."

"In so many words."

"In so many words."

"I have to say, such a comment seems mildly inappropriate."

"I have to agree with you."

"See you in thirty minutes."

Laurie pulled out her cell phone as she walked the quiet third-floor hallway. With Jack's comment as encouragement, she dialed Leticia. She waved as she passed the deputy chief's door, but Calvin Washington was too busy to notice. As she approached her office, Leticia still had not picked up. As she entered, she began to count the rings. By the time she'd put down her bag and the two computer disks, she'd reached ten. By the time she'd hung up her coat, she was nearing fifteen. Finally, on the seventeenth ring, the phone was picked up. By that time, Laurie's heart rate had reached approximately one hundred and fifty.

"Hello," Leticia said calmly, to the point of suggesting boredom.

"Is everything all right?" Laurie blurted, although she was already reassured that everything was fine by Leticia's forced serenity.

"We're doing just fine," Leticia said.

"The phone rang so long."

"Well, that was because we were having a little bath here after a particularly dirty diaper."

Once again Laurie felt mildly embarrassed at her overreaction. "I just wanted to let you know that we'll be home in an hour or so."

"We'll be here," Leticia said.

"How about dinner?"

"That's next on the agenda."

"Tell the little guy we miss him."

"I'll let him know," Leticia said apathetically.

Laurie hung up the phone feeling some ambivalence. It was obvious Leticia was annoyed at the call, but so was Laurie, at Leticia's inability to cut her a little slack on the first day. Laurie recognized that a dozen or so calls over the course of the day was over the top without there being any problems. At the same time, Laurie realized she should be giving Leticia a little slack as well, since calls could be distracting with the amount of attention a one-and-a-half-year-old child required.

Sitting down at her desk, Laurie picked up the lab slip that Jack had mentioned. It indicated the BAC, or blood alcohol level, was 0.03 percent, meaning it was well under the legal limit, but not zero, suggesting the man had had a drink or two within a couple of hours of his death, a fact that Laurie confidently felt had nothing to do with his demise.

Adding the lab slip to the victim's case file, Laurie caught sight of a plain white envelope on her keyboard with her complete name typed out: Dr. Laurie Montgomery-Stapleton. Stuck to the front was a Post-it note from Marlene saying the envelope had been found in the foyer, having been slipped under the front door. Taking out the single sheet of white paper it contained, Laurie unfolded it and saw it was a short typed message addressed to her simply as "Doctor."

Doctor,

   Excuse me for interfering, but I have been threatened if I do not do so. I happen to know that there

are some terribly nasty people who wish you to stop
your investigation into the natural death of an Asian
man on the A-train subway platform. If you do not
do this immediately, you and your family will suffer
serious consequences. Going to the police about this
warning will cause the same consequences. Be smart.
It is not worth your time.

Although having caught her breath on the first reading, as Laurie read it again a slight smile formed at the
corners of her mouth. When she read it a third time,
the smile turned into a suppressed giggle. When Laurie
asked herself who could have been responsible for writing such a note, she immediately thought it had to have
been Jack. Childishly inappropriate, it was his type of
humor, and he did want her to stop obsessing about
the case. In fact, the more she thought about it, the
more sure she was that it had been Jack. The strange
way he'd asked her if she'd been in her office before
visiting his was a dead giveaway. It was also an indication
that he expected her to run to him and be all out of
sorts, having gotten such a scary letter. She then read
it for the fourth time, and again laughed. It was so
improbable. If someone was concerned about her investigation and wanted her to stop, the last thing they'd
want to do was call attention to it, as it would undoubtedly solidify her interest in investigating it more in-
tensely.

As soon as Laurie realized who was responsible for
the note, she started to think how she could turn the
tables—namely, get back at Jack, as it was inappropriate
at best. Rather than overreact, she thought she'd play
it cool. It would be more fun to ignore it and see how

long Jack could tolerate her lack of response and not knowing whether she'd found it or not. Laurie slipped the refolded note back into its envelope and placed it in her center desk drawer. She was confident her total lack of response to this childish prank was going to drive Jack bananas.

She turned to her case file, a yellow pocket-like affair made of heavy, stiff paper. It contained all the paperwork associated with the case: a case worksheet, a partially filled-out death certificate, an inventory of medicolegal case records, two sheets for autopsy notes that she'd already filled out, a telephone notice of death as received by communications, an identification sheet, an investigative report by the MLI, a sheet for the autopsy report, and a sheet to show the body had been x-rayed, fingerprinted, and photographed. The photographs were also in the files, and these Laurie removed. There was a full frontal photo, and ones of the back and profile of the body. Laurie put them in her bag, as she planned to refer to them that evening when she got around to watching at least some of the subway disks. Then she had another idea. Since Jack was right about how long it would take to watch the whole thing, she thought she'd narrow down the footage, if possible. Also in the case file were the phone numbers for the 911 operator and the 911 caller, Robert Delacroix. Laurie dialed Delacroix's number, and this time the man answered. Laurie identified herself and apologized for bothering him again.

"No bother whatsoever," Robert responded. "Anything I can do that makes me feel less guilty is good."

"Can you tell me where you were on the platform when you saw the Asian man get into trouble?"

"Gosh," Robert said, pausing to think. "It was so crowded, I never got too far from the staircase."

"Could you see the end of the platform in either direction?"

"Not that I can remember."

"So you were somewhere in the middle? I guess that would be the only choice."

"I'd say that's a safe assumption."

She thanked Delacroix and hung up, then decided to wait for Jack to finish writing up the autopsy on the hair dryer in his office. It was her thought that lingering around him would spur him to wrap it up more quickly. Now that she was ready to leave, she wanted to get home as soon as possible.

CHAPTER FOURTEEN

Are you busy?" Carl Harris asked, poking his head in Ben Corey's open doorway.

Ben looked up from the biomedical journal he was scanning. His desk was stacked with others that arrived daily. It was important for iPS USA to be aware of all advances in stem cell science to make sure their expanding control of intellectual property was up-to-date. Scanning all the appropriate biomedical literature was almost a full-time job.

"Never too busy for you," Ben said. "What's up? Come on in and have a seat."

"I wanted to know how your meeting with Michael went this morning."

"I guess I'd have to say it was mixed."

"How so?"

"Our meeting this morning was fine, but as a result he went out to talk to Vinnie Dominick and the Yamaguchi-gumi head, Saboru Fukuda. Michael just called me a few minutes ago. He said that he discussed with them first about iPS RAPID, and that went well. Michael said that the two actually seemed happy to come up with more cash to increase their equity, especially after hearing about yesterday's signing with Satoshi. Moneywise, everything was very positive, so we just have to decide how we are going to proceed: purchase or license? Have you made any progress on that?"

"I've started due diligence. They haven't been in business long enough to have much of a track record, but I believe I will be advising purchase over licensing. If they get the patent they've applied for, it's going to be a big deal and lead us to litigation of their patent impinging on ours. I ran this by counsel, and Pauline agrees. I'm glad our two angels are standing with us."

"Me, too," Ben said. "But they're not too happy about changing our relationship with them."

"Well, we wouldn't be changing it in the short run if we're going back to them for a major second round."

"No, but it doesn't portend well for stepping away from them in the future."

"I think we can wait until we're ready for the IPO."

"That's a good point," Ben said. "At that juncture, we'll be able to show them how much they might profit from the IPO when we have the expected figures. We'll make sure they understand we can't do the IPO unless they step back."

"I think that sounds like a plan," Carl said, getting to his feet. "Are you going to stay much later? It's already after five."

Ben tapped the stack of journals. "I'll stay an hour or so longer. I've got to make this pile smaller. Besides, if I left now I'd hit so much traffic it would hardly be worth it."

"See you in the morning," Carl said, heading for the door.

"Wait!" Ben called out.

Carl stopped and turned around.

"Have you seen Satoshi or heard from him today? I got him the lab space up at Columbia and have these legal papers to be signed, but I don't think he's been in at all today."

Carl shook his head. "I haven't seen him. Did you call his cell?"

"Yeah, a half-dozen times. I think he has it switched off, because it goes directly to voicemail."

"Maybe he went on the trip he was going to take."

"What are you talking about?"

"He asked me a couple of days ago where to stay in Washington, D.C. He said he wanted to take his family there."

"Shit!" Ben groaned, shaking his head.

"What's the matter?"

"He did this once before to me. He disappeared for a week with his family on a visit to Niagara Falls."

"Well, you can't blame him. He's finally free for the first time in his life."

"Yeah, wonderful," Ben said sarcastically. "Now I have to worry about him like a wayward son."

"Let's think positively. Maybe he'll come in in the morning."

"That would be nice. Why do I have this feeling it's not going to happen?"

CHAPTER FIFTEEN

Sitting in the back of what looked to her like a brand-new yellow cab, Laurie found herself silently counting off the street numbers as she and Jack sped northward on Central Park West. Passing the Museum of Natural History and then 86th Street, her excitement took another quantum leap. She could feel her pulse quickening; she was that excited. Though Jack sat next to her, carrying on about how he and Lou had confirmed the findings of the autopsy on their gunshot victim, she couldn't concentrate on what he was saying; she was too excited about seeing JJ. She let Jack drone on, since he did not seem to mind that she'd stopped giving him any feedback whatsoever about a mile or so earlier.

"What was the number again on One hundred and sixth?" the driver inquired.

Laurie blurted out the number, interrupting Jack in midsentence.

"Are you listening to me?" Jack asked as Laurie strained forward to look through the plastic divider and the front windshield as their street rapidly approached. It wasn't until the cabbie turned left that she settled back.

"Did you hear me?" Jack questioned.

"No," Laurie admitted. To the right was the small playground that Jack had had renovated ten years earlier, adding outdoor lights to the basketball court, where there was currently a game in progress. He'd also restored the children's section, adding slides, swings, and a large sandbox.

"I asked you if you'd been listening to me."

"Should I lie or tell the truth?"

"Lie so I don't get my feelings hurt."

"Do you mind paying?" Laurie said as the taxi cruised to the curb in front of their renovated brownstone. Laurie had the door open before the vehicle was totally stopped. With bag in hand, she dashed up the stoop and inside. Without even removing her coat, she rushed up the stairs to the second-floor kitchen.

Leticia had heard the front door open, and picking up JJ, she met Laurie as Laurie topped the stairs. Leticia was an attractive, athletic African-American woman in her mid-twenties with a soft cloud of dark hair. She was rarely without a trace of a wry smile and refused, as a matter of principle, not to suffer fools. As a cousin of Warren Wilson, Jack's basketball buddy, she shared the family trait of a well-sculpted body, which was shown off to great effect with tight jeans and form-fitting tops. Unsure about pursuing her graduate studies after recently completing college, Warren had suggested she consider working as a nanny for Jack and Laurie.

"Hey, little guy," Laurie crooned as she reached out to take the infant. But as eager as she was, she caught the child unaware, and JJ responded by turning back to Leticia and grabbing on fiercely. He cried as Laurie and Leticia peeled his little fingers away from Leticia's neck.

Almost immediately JJ recognized his mother and quieted, but the damage had been done. Laurie felt rejected, at least for a few minutes until rationality prevailed. At that point, Laurie's response was more embarrassment than hurt feelings.

By the time Jack came up the stairs, the women were laughing about the incident. He listened while Leticia apologized for being put off by Laurie's multiple phone calls. "Every time you called it was somehow at the worst possible moment," she explained, "like when I had him in the bath. I had to rush to get him out, which he clearly did not want to do and resisted, then I had to get him dried and wrapped in a towel before getting to the phone."

"I'll be better tomorrow, I promise," Laurie said. "Clearly the separation has been worse for me than for him."

"I think that has been the case, I'm afraid," Leticia agreed. "He's been a true delight all day. He loved being in the park."

Jack tried to take JJ from Laurie, and JJ clutched Laurie this time. Both women found themselves laughing as Jack gave up, confused at the laughter. Jack raised his hands in surrender and said to the child, "Okay, you can have your mommy to yourself for now, but my turn's coming later." He said good-bye to Leticia, adding that he was heading out to play basketball with her cousin. With a squeeze of Laurie's shoulder, he climbed the stairs to get into his basketball gear.

"They play most every night," Laurie explained.

After talking about JJ's day a little more and agreeing on the time for Leticia to arrive in the morning, Leticia took her leave. "He's a doll," she said just before giving JJ a wave and departing.

With Jack outside, Laurie played with JJ for almost an hour before putting him in his bouncy chair while she put together a light supper for Jack and herself. With the time constraint it was just going to be a salad with cheese and bread. Then she put JJ down in his crib, sitting in the rocking chair next to him. She was happy he went to sleep more easily than usual, reinforcing what she now knew: The day had been easier for him than it had for her.

After their repast, Jack and Laurie retired to their combined study. Jack wanted to skim one of their general forensic texts to brush up on gunshot wounds, while Laurie booted up her computer and put in one of the subway security tapes. She had no idea what to expect. Next to the computer she put the John Doe's three photographs.

"I still don't think you should waste your time on that," Jack said.

"Of course you don't," Laurie responded, thinking of the threatening note for the first time since she'd stuck it into the center drawer of her desk. "Why? Do you think it's too dangerous?" She turned to face Jack.

"'Dangerous'?" Jack questioned with confusion. "Why dangerous? My point is that nothing you can find in there would change how you finish the case. You're still going to look carefully at the brain, even if you don't confirm whether there was a seizure or not."

"Oh, really?" Laurie questioned superciliously, clicking on the DVD drive.

"Suit yourself," Jack said, turning back to his own business. If she wanted to waste her time, so be it, he thought.

The first screen Laurie encountered was a menu with

the recording cameras arranged in numerical order, one through nine. Clicking on number one, the action came on immediately. The quality of the video wasn't great; the wide angle created definite distortion, and the image was as grainy as she feared. On top of that, it ran at double speed. When she slowed it down, it was better but still hardly optimum. "I'm going into the family room," Laurie said. "I'm going to try the HDTV and see it if helps."

"Good luck," Jack said distractedly.

In the family room, Laurie inserted the disk into the DVD player. With the TV, she was pleased that the quality seemed better. With the photos on the couch next to her, she lifted her feet onto the coffee table and watched for twenty minutes. It was as boring as expected, people silently boarding the train or getting off. Then she caught something interesting. She watched as a teen dressed in oversized clothing, his pants' crotch between his knees, purposefully bump into a middle-aged man reading a newspaper. At the same time the man's wallet came out of his pocket with such speed Laurie had to stop the tape, back it up, and run it forward frame by frame.

"My goodness," Laurie said, and called Jack to watch the sequence. He was as impressed as she had been.

"What should I do?" Laurie asked.

"I don't want to sound like a cynic, but even if you report it, I don't think anything will come of it. The NYPD is swamped with much more serious issues."

Laurie noted the time indicated on the screen and wrote it and the camera number on the back of one of her case's photos. She thought she'd give it to Murphy in the morning and let him decide.

Finishing up on camera number one, Laurie decided to skip to camera number four, hoping that the numbering of the cameras was sequential on the platform, meaning number four would be near the platform's center, where Robert Delacroix thought he'd been. Camera number one had shown the northern tunnel entrance.

Only a few minutes into camera number four, Jack appeared at the door to the family room and got her attention. "I'm going to read in bed."

"Okay, dear," Laurie said, stopping her tape. She knew full well that Jack's idea of reading in bed was to fall asleep within a page or two. "I'll see you in the morning."

Jack smiled at her, knowing she was right. In response, he came to the couch, bent over, and gave her a kiss on the lips. "Don't stay up to all hours watching this stuff," he said. "I'll never get you out of bed in the morning."

"I'll just watch a little more," Laurie promised, with good intentions.

When she finished camera four she clicked on camera five. She watched for several minutes until she realized with a start that she'd been asleep. The silent stream of people in and out of the trains was mesmerizing. Since she had no idea when she'd fallen asleep, she reversed the video back to the beginning, recognizing that if she didn't she might risk missing what she hoped to find.

Struggling to stay awake at least until the end of camera five, she suddenly did a double take. Not quite in the middle of the screen was the man she was looking for. At least she thought so. Quickly she pressed pause on the remote to freeze the scene. At that moment the man was looking back over his shoulder and up the stairs that he'd apparently just descended, although she'd not recognized him until he'd gotten close to the edge of the platform. Picking up the photos of the corpse, she compared them. She was reasonably confident she was correct and the man in the photos and on the screen was the same individual. Though she couldn't be a hundred percent certain because of the camera angle, the time stamp worked: It was several minutes before the 911 call. Laurie carefully reversed the image and watched the man retreat up the stairs backward. Even watching it frame by frame, she sensed the man was running as he bumped into other people, who were obviously moving more slowly than he was. Checking the other side of the image, she could see that the track was still clear; the train had not yet arrived.

Laurie continued reversing the video frame by frame until the man disappeared from view. The only thing she'd learned was that the man was carrying a canvas bag of some sort. Sitting back in her seat, she allowed the video to run forward at normal speed. The man was indeed running. "He definitely doesn't want to miss the train," Laurie said to herself out loud as she watched the man collide into people. At normal speed the collisions appeared more jarring than when viewed frame by frame.

The man pressed into the crowds on the platform, clearly irritating people as he did so. One man even grabbed the Asian man's arm, but he yanked it from the stranger's grip and pressed on, continually glancing over his shoulder as if being chased.

"He is being chased!" Laurie blurted, leaning forward again. Two more Asian men had come down the stairs, and like the first one, they forced their way into the crowd with one of them holding an umbrella, the other empty-handed. As Laurie watched, the two pursuing men reached the other man just as the subway charged into the station. At that point, Laurie could just barely see the men of interest, as they were all shorter than the other commuters pressed up against them. For the next few moments there was little movement as the people exiting the train confronted those entering. Finally movement returned to the crowd, and when it did, Laurie could see that the man with the bag was seizing, or at least it looked like he was seizing while still standing upright, his head rapidly and rhythmically fully extending, then relaxing. As people began boarding the train and the crowd slowly thinned, Laurie watched the two men lay the stricken man down on the platform. By this time there was no convulsive activity, and the bag the first was carrying was now in the possession of one of the others. Laurie also recognized that the two men could easily have taken the man's wallet while they had been holding him upright, to explain why he did not have one when he arrived at the ER.

"My word," Laurie said out loud. "It was a robbery!" She continued to watch as people continued to pass around and over the supine body. She was amazed by the demonstration of how dispassionate New Yorkers could be. The only positive reaction was a man at the door to the train, who was placing his cell phone to his ear, making Laurie wonder if it was Robert Delacroix. She shifted her attention to the two Asian men as they calmly walked out of sight.

Laurie stopped the video. Running into the master

bedroom, she wanted to get Jack. She wanted him to see the video, even though she knew what he was going to say: "Okay, it was an apparent robbery, but maybe it wasn't. Maybe the bag belongs to one of the two who took it. The key thing is that the autopsy was negative."

Coming into the bedroom, Laurie pulled up short. As usual, when Jack said he was going to read in bed, he was already fast asleep. The heavy textbook he'd brought into the room was open and lying across his chest. Carefully, Laurie lifted it off and placed it on the side table. Then she turned off his bedside light. It was a ritual that occurred almost every night. Unlike Laurie, Jack had no difficulty whatsoever falling asleep or getting up in the morning, two activities that had always been difficult for her.

Back in the family room, Laurie took the disk from the DVD player and retreated into the study. There she put it back into the computer, went to camera five, and scanned through the file until she found the best frame of the second two men, then printed out a copy. Looking at the two thieves, she totally changed her mind about the case. Initially she'd been disappointed that her first case was an unidentified natural death, and totally pathology free to boot—hardly a case to challenge her competency. Now her perseverance was proving it to be much more interesting than anyone expected, especially herself.

Laurie began to feel the old excitement she used to feel when figuring out complicated and different cases, and she actually couldn't wait to get into the office in the morning and get the lab results and histology slides. The truth of the matter was that her intuition, which

she'd worried might have abandoned her during her
leave, was back and strongly suggesting that there were
surprises ahead. Her plan was not to reveal what she'd
learned from the security tapes until she figured out
what had killed the man. Laurie knew that by law,
perpetrators of crimes have to assume responsibility of
the health of the people they victimize: If a person has
a heart attack and dies while running from a thief, it
is considered a homicide, not a natural death, and the
thief will be tried and punished accordingly. Laurie
knew she was now dealing with a definite homicide,
changing the case from boring to engaging, at least
that's what she thought as she packed away the photos
and the disk in her bag she carried back and forth from
work.

The next job was to try to fall asleep—a trick for her,
given the new development she'd discovered with the
security tapes. On top of that was the realistic concern
about JJ possibly waking up. Sometimes Laurie wished
she did not need sleep, believing she'd be content to
read during the night. But every morning, no matter
what, she felt exhausted during the first hour or so and
recognized what the reality was.

After checking on JJ, who was fast asleep, Laurie got
herself ready for bed. When she at last climbed between
the sheets and turned out the light, she reflected on the
day. In hindsight it had not been entirely smooth. In
fact, it had been rather bumpy. She'd missed JJ, as all
her calls home reflected, and she'd been hurt when he'd
seemingly rejected her, suggesting a definite vulnerabil-
ity. On the work side, her case initially had not totally
reassured her of her sense of competency, but that
seemed to be changing with her evening's discoveries.

When all was said and done, she recognized she very much liked her job and felt reasonably sure she could be both a medical examiner and a mother, and do equal justice to both.

CHAPTER SIXTEEN

There they are!" Carlo said as Brennan turned onto 17th Street on the north side of Union Square. As usual the area was alive with people, including sidewalk musicians, panhandlers, and students of all ages and ethnicities. Despite the crowds, Susumu Nomura and Yoshiaki Eto still managed to stand out slightly because of their attire. Like the previous night, they were dressed in black sharkskin suits, white shirts, black ties, and dark glasses.

"Let's be clear on this," Carlo said. "We drive to the pier, supposedly to get the explosives for the supposed distraction, we all get out, saying we need everybody to help carry the explosives back to the SUV, and head inside. That's where we'll do the hit. Remember, these guys are going to be armed, and they don't hesitate to use their weapons."

There was a general grunt of acquiescence from all present. Brennan and Carlo were in the front seat, with Brennan again driving. Arthur and Ted were cramped back in the third row. The middle seats were left empty for Susumu and Yoshiaki.

Brennan pulled over to the curb in front of the Barnes & Noble store, which had closed some forty-five minutes earlier but whose interior lights were still on. Susumu and Yoshiaki were busy glancing in at the window display.

"Okay," Carlo said, twisting around in his seat and

looking back at Arthur and Ted. "You guys ready? You have your pieces handy?"

Both Arthur and Ted raised their hands to give Carlo a quick glance of their respective automatics and then lowered them out of sight. "Good," Carlo said. "We don't expect any trouble, but we might as well be prepared." Carlo then turned to Brennan. "Are you ready?"

"Obviously I'm ready," Brennan responded with a bored tone. Sometimes he thought Carlo was a bit too melodramatic.

Carlo lowered his window and whistled. Susumu and Yoshiaki both snapped around at the sound and quickly came to the car, bowing to Carlo as they did so. They lost no time climbing into the middle row, although they paused ever so briefly when they realized there were people in the backseat whose faces were dimly illuminated by the ambient streetlight.

"That's Arthur and Ted back there," Carlo called out in explanation.

The Japanese pair twisted in their seats to look at Arthur and Ted once they were settled and the door was closed. They bowed multiple times, repeating "Hai, hai" over and over. It was apparent to the others that they were significantly jazzed up, in anticipation of the planned burglary.

Brennan hooked a left around Union Square and traveled east on 14th Street all the way to the East River. There he headed north on the FDR Drive. For a while no one spoke. Everyone was juiced up but for different reasons. Arthur was the only one who was actually worried about what might happen, as he was by far the most reflective in the group and a firm believer in the adage: If something can go wrong, it will.

Brennan exited the FDR at 34th Street, got onto Third Avenue, and from there descended into the Queens-Midtown Tunnel. As Susumu and Yoshiaki had expected to head farther north on the FDR, they became restive at having entered the tunnel and immediately lapsed into an argument with each other in Japanese. It was obvious they were confused. It was Yoshiaki who spoke up.

"Excuse!" he said, leaning forward. "Why we go to Queens?"

Carlo turned in his seat, making eye contact with Yoshiaki. "Must get explosives," he said, mistakenly believing he had to use pidgin-like English. "We use explosives to make diversion while we break into iPS USA to get the lab books. Understand?"

"Where do we go in Queens?" Yoshiaki questioned.

"An old Vaccarro family warehouse on a pier at the river," Carlo said, still facing around. "We use it for storage. There's explosives there that we will use for tonight's explosion."

"What's a pier?"

"It's this long thing made out of wood that goes out into the water so ships can park next to it."

"*Futou?*" Yoshiaki questioned.

"Yeah, well, I wouldn't know."

"East River?"

"That's right. East River. The pier is on the East River."

For a few miles Yoshiaki and Susumu spoke loudly back and forth, to the point that Carlo became concerned they might refuse to go along and demand to be taken back to the city. But it didn't happen. Abruptly they fell quiet, and Carlo hoped they would stay that way for just a little longer.

Emerging from the tunnel, Brennan exited the expressway as soon as he could, crossed over Newtown Creek on McGuinness Boulevard, and turned right on Greenpoint Avenue. At first there were lots of bars and restaurants, but as they approached the river, the neighborhood deteriorated to a point best described as dilapidated-industrial. As Carlo looked out his window, the two things that stood out were the lack of lights and the lack of people. In sharp contrast to the vibrancy of Union Square, the area looked like a post-apocalyptic movie set. There seemed to be nothing alive until he saw a large rat whose eyes suddenly sparkled like diamonds as the rodent looked in the direction of the Denali's headlights.

Five minutes later Brennan pulled right up to the padlocked gate in the ten-foot-high chain-link fence, topped with coiled razor wire that surrounded the Vaccarro property. Carlo hopped out with the key, and in the glare of the headlights unlocked the gate to allow Brennan to drive in. Then, in the darkness, he relocked the gate before running forward and climbing back into the SUV.

The hulk of the concrete-block warehouse was on Brennan's left as he drove forward toward the base of the pier. About midway along the building's side, there was a small porch fronting a heavily padlocked entry door. Above the door was a wooden sign with peeling paint faintly bearing the name AMERICAN FRUIT COMPANY.

"Explosives here?" Yoshiaki questioned, staring out at the dark warehouse.

"This is it," Carlo said. He slipped his hand beneath the lapel of his jacket and unsnapped the strap that secured his Glock .22 in its shoulder holster. Then he opened the storage compartment between the two front seats and got out two flashlights, handing one to Brennan. When Brennan turned off the headlights, both he and Carlo switched on the flashlights. With no moon, it was black as pitch outside.

"Okay," Carlo said. "Everybody out to help carry the equipment." He and Brennan climbed from the car simultaneously. Carlo opened the rear passenger door for Yoshiaki, who was sitting behind him. Brennan did the same for Susumu. To emphasize that they were supposed to be carrying out material, Carlo continued to the back of the car and opened the tailgate. The plan was to go inside the office for the takedown.

Carlo continued on to the office door, pulling out the same ring of keys he'd used for the outer gate. With the flashlight under his arm he first unlocked the padlock and then the door itself. Just as he was about to open the door and get the interior light, on he became aware of commotion behind him. Turning, he witnessed Yoshiaki knocking away Brennan's hand. Brennan was merely trying to urge Yoshiaki forward. Both Yoshiaki and Susumu had stopped short of the porch in front of the entrance.

"We wait outside," he said. Behind him, Carlo could see Arthur and Ted emerging from the car. The problem was that they still had their guns in their hands as Carlo had ordered, in case there was some kind of emergency. The other problem was that Susumu happened to be looking in their direction while Yoshiaki was looking forward. Obviously, both Japanese enforcers had gotten suspicious about what was going down.

Susumu's reaction was to cry out *"Kaki,"* or guns, and draw his own weapon and pull off several shots, hitting Arthur in the right upper arm with the bullet exiting out the back. With his gun at the ready, Ted let fly a barrage of bullets of his own, several of which found their mark, one hitting Susumu directly in the chest, piercing his heart and killing him instantly.

Yoshiaki's reaction was to take off running. With no choice in the matter, he sprinted away in the direction of the pier, ducking and weaving as he did so, his reaction time catching everyone by surprise. Carlo and Brennan quickly directed their flashlights in the fleeing man's direction while struggling to get their own weapons from their shoulder holsters. Ted had to run a few steps forward to clear the car in order to get an open line of sight. He pulled off several more shots in quick succession but couldn't tell if he'd hit the fleeing man or not. Regardless, Yoshiaki kept running, ducking, and weaving, as he quickly disappeared from sight into the misty darkness hanging over the pier.

"Help Arthur," Carlo yelled to Ted. Arthur had fallen to his knees, holding his right arm with his left. He'd dropped his weapon after being struck. An expanding patch of red stained his shirt over his upper arm. "Shit, shit, shit! The fucker shot me!" he yelled, as if surprised. "Why did he have to shoot me?" he demanded. With Carlo's and Brennan's flashlight beams quickly receding as they ran after Yoshiaki, Ted and Arthur found themselves in complete blackness. Lucky for Arthur, there was little or no pain, just a heavy dullness.

Ted made his way back to the SUV, and opening the driver's door, he snapped on the headlights. Going from near perfect darkness to a bright illumination caused both men to squint. Wasting no time, Ted searched for something to use as a tourniquet, then pulled his belt free from his trousers. "Let's see the wound," he said as a warning before ripping Arthur's shirt from the cuff up to its armhole. On the front side of Arthur's arm midway between the shoulder and the elbow was a clean quarter-inch entrance wound. On the back side the exit wound looked like a disk of hamburger meat. Luckily for Arthur, it was not bleeding as much as oozing.

"You're going to live," Ted pronounced, realizing the tourniquet, for the moment, was not needed.

Brennan and Carlo had run the length of the warehouse and then pulled up short. Yoshiaki had run out to the end of the pier and stopped himself.

"We cannot allow him to escape," Carlo said, out of breath.

"You don't need to tell me that," Brennan said, equally out of breath.

"What is he doing?"

"It looks like he's taking off his shoes."

"Oh, shit!" Carlo said. "He's not going to try to swim, is he?"

"I think he is. He's taking off his damn clothes."

"Run out there and shoot him before he tries to get away."

"The hell I will," Brennan said. "He's sure to have a gun. You run out there!"

The two men stood there and watched. It appeared as if Yoshiaki was making a neat pile of his clothes. The next moment he was gone.

Without any talking, Carlo and Brennan, each holding a gun in one hand and a flashlight in the other, made a mad dash toward the end of the pier. As they neared, both slowed, fearful it might be some sort of trick to lure them in close. At a hesitant walk, they moved ahead, holding their guns directed ahead at the ready.

Brennan heard the splashing first, and he yelled, "He's in the water!" as he sprinted ahead, passing the tidy pile of clothes carefully placed on top of the pair of shoes. The shoes were oriented exactly parallel to the pier.

Brennan rushed to the very end of the pier. Yoshiaki could just be seen sloshing forward with an awkward head-out-of-the-water stroke, turning his face from side to side as he reached out with one hand and then the other. Brennan trained his flashlight beam on him as Carlo came up to Brennan's side. Both men trained their automatics on Yoshiaki and rapidly emptied their magazines. As the sound of the last shot faded away, along with its echoes from the dark neighboring buildings and piers, Brennan and Carlo stared at the spot where moments earlier Yoshiaki had been desperately thrashing about while attempting to swim to Manhattan. Now, like the rest of the river, it was as still as a pool of crude oil, reflecting the peaceful Manhattan skyline.

First for five minutes, then for ten, and finally for fifteen, Brennan and Carlo kept their flashlights trained on the spot, hoping it was the end of the embarrassing affair. At one time there was a sudden rapid swirl at the spot, suggesting the presence of some large creature, giving both men a scare, but Yoshiaki did not loom up for a sudden, desperate lungful of air. It was clear he was a goner.

"We must have hit him," Carlo said, breaking the silence.

"It seems that way. That was too close for comfort. If he'd gotten away, Louie would have had our heads."

"Now why don't you swim out there and retrieve the body?" Carlo said.

"Hell I will!" Brennan snapped with true emotion. Just the thought of entering the black, oily river with whatever it was hiding was enough to give Brennan gooseflesh.

"I was just kidding," Carlo said, slapping Brennan on the back hard enough to make the man step forward to prevent a fall.

Brennan grabbed Carlo's forearm before Carlo could retract it out of the way. "I have told you not to hit me," Brennan snarled, pushing his face in close to Carlo's. The tenseness of the preceding events made him overreact to this recurring provocation.

Carlo pushed him away roughly. "Oh, grow up. I was just kidding, for chrissake, about you swimming out there. You'd never find the body in a million years. With the currents here, the body's probably two hundred feet or so downriver." Carlo bent over to pick up Yoshiaki's clothes and shoes. "Let's get back and check on Arthur. We'll probably have to do an emergency run before we head out to the Narrows to get rid of Susumu."

The two men walked quickly back along the pier. Every so often the water beneath them emitted a swirling sound around the piles, attesting to the strength of the current.

"Louie is not going to be happy about Yoshiaki," Carlo said.

"Tell me about it," Brennan said, having cooled down a degree. "But the situation would have been ten times worse if the guy had made it to Manhattan."

"Maybe we shouldn't bring it up unless he asks. Hell, as strong as the current is, who knows where he'll end up. He might even make it to the ocean, where he was supposed to end up."

Brennan cast a quick glance in Carlo's direction. "It's your call. It's your job to communicate to the capo, but if you're asking if I would go behind your back and tell him, that wouldn't happen."

"Good," Carlo said. "Then I won't tell him unless he asks."

"How are you going to explain Arthur?"

"I'll tell him the truth. These Japanese guys are wild, which is why we wanted to get rid of them. They don't think twice about taking out their pieces and blasting away. Hell, Arthur's a good example."

Back at the car they found everything was okay. Ted had bandaged Arthur's wound with the arm of Arthur's shirt, and there was only slight bleeding. The main problem was that Arthur was in serious discomfort. Although initially it hadn't bothered him much, once the numbness wore off, he claimed the pain was terrible.

Stashing Susumu's body in a body bag and then into the rear storage area of the SUV, the men piled back into the vehicle and made their way out of the American Fruit Company's compound and headed back to Elmhurst. As soon as they were on the expressway, Carlo called Louie.

When Louie disconnected the phone line from talking to Carlo, he didn't know whether to be angry or relieved. From experience he knew that hits could go well or they could go bad. He was relieved to a degree that it was over but upset that Arthur had been wounded. Four against two seemed to have been more than adequate odds.

Without hanging up the handset, Louie pulled his address book out of his desk's center drawer and got the number for Dr. Louis Trevino. Doc, as he was known, had been the doctor for the Vaccarro family for many years. He'd been recruited from St. Mary's Hospital, where he'd done an internship and had handled most of the Vaccarro crime family's needs over the years, including a number of clandestine gunshot wounds.

The phone rang many times before a tired voice answered.

"Doc, it's Louie. We got a problem with Arthur."

"What is it?"

"A gunshot wound to the right upper arm, through and through."

"The bone involved?"

"I don't think so."

"That's a blessing. How about the major vessels?"

"Negative again, or so it seems so far."

"Where is he?"

"I told them to go straight to Saint Mary's. I'd guesstimate they'll be there in, say, a half-hour."

"I'll meet them in the ER," Trevino said, and hung up.

"Thanks, Doc," Louie said, even though he knew it was too late.

With the call to Doc out of the way, Louie sat at his desk and prepared for the next call. He knew what message he wanted to convey but wasn't sure of the words. As he pondered, he glanced out the window of his study off the living room of his grand waterside house in Whitestone, New York. With no leaves on the trees, he had a partial view across a neighbor's yard of the graceful Whitestone Bridge with its illuminated cables. Looking at the bridge reminded him of his much better view of the Throgs Neck Bridge from the living room, which faced in the opposite direction down his sweeping lawn to his dock. Thinking of his dock reminded him that it was soon going to be time to get his boat out of winter storage.

Pulling his mind back to the issue at hand, calling Hideki Shimoda to deflect any suspicion of Vaccarro involvement in Susumu's and Yoshiaki's disappearance as Paulie had cleverly suggested, Louie wanted to get it right. The key ingredient, he was aware, was that he had to act truly pissed off.

Galvanizing his courage, Louie made the call. To his surprise, the phone was picked up with a simple "Hai" after a single ring, as if Hideki had been sleeping with his hand on the receiver.

"All right, Hideki, what's the fucking story, and I don't want any bullshit," Louie roared. "I just got a call from my guys, who are still hanging around fucking Union Square waiting for your fucking guys to arrive. What's the fucking story?"

Louie rarely used profanity, but he had pulled out all the stops, thinking Hideki would expect it. The response was less than he hoped for. "Excuse me, I think you want to talk with my husband."

Louie rolled his eyes as a gruff Hideki came on the line. Louie tried to repeat the opening salvo but with significantly less profanity. After the mistake of not ascertaining who'd picked up the phone, it was the best he could do.

"Is this Barbera-san?" Hideki questioned.

"Who else do you think would be calling you at this hour?" Louie demanded, sounding as irritable as he could manage.

"You say Susumu and Yoshiaki not show up tonight?"

"That's exactly what I'm saying. And I want to remind you that this operation was being done for your benefit, not ours."

"That is true, Barbera-san," Hideki admitted. "Hold the phone for one moment. Let me call them to ask where they are. There must have been a misunderstanding. I am sorry. They are my most reliable aides."

Louie could hear Hideki speaking in Japanese to whoever was there with him. Then he came back on the line. "My wife is getting my mobile phone. I am most sorry about this. Is there still time to make the raid?"

"Let's see where your men are. If they are near Union Square, perhaps we could squeeze it in."

Louie could hear Hideki try to make two calls. Unsuccessful, he returned to Louie. "I cannot get them. This is very strange."

"So far as you know, they were aware the break-in was for tonight?"

"Absolutely for tonight."

"When was the last time you spoke to them?"

"Not since they drove me back to the office after visiting with you, Barbera-san. At that time they were eager to work with you again tonight. They said so specifically."

"Do you think there is any chance something could have happened to them?" Louie questioned.

"How do you mean?"

"Last evening my guys told me that your guys had expressed some fears about your rivals. Something about a threat they got if they went ahead and killed Satoshi."

"Which rivals?" Hideki asked warily.

"The Yamaguchi-gumi."

There was a pause. Louie let the idea germinate for a full minute before adding, "I could ask Carlo and Brennan if they remember exactly what was said."

CHAPTER SEVENTEEN

The taxi dropped Laurie off directly in front of OCME. She paid the fare and climbed from the vehicle. She was alone. Jack had half asked, half told her he wanted to get back to his beloved bike. Laurie didn't like the idea and feared for his life as she had from day one, but didn't stand in his way. Part of the reason she was disappointed he didn't accompany her was because if they traveled together it was easier for her to justify the expense of a cab, yet she'd taken one anyway because she was particularly eager to get to work as quickly as possible with what she had learned the evening before about her one and only case. She was brimming with confidence that it was going to be an interesting day. Little did she know.

The handoff that morning with JJ had been flawless and much easier than it had been the day before. Leticia had arrived earlier than scheduled. JJ had clearly recognized her and acted delighted to see her, so there were no tears. And Laurie, being less anxious than she had been the day before, had managed to have everything ready before Leticia appeared.

"Good morning, Dr. Laurie!" Marlene Wilson said in her usual lilting voice. Laurie returned the greeting and got buzzed into the ID room.

Sweeping into the room like an invading force, Laurie tossed her coat into one of the overstuffed vinyl chairs.

Then she stopped abruptly. It could have been the previous day! There were the same people in the same spots, doing the same things: Arnold Besserman was at the desk going through all the case folders of the bodies that had come in overnight; Vinnie Amendola was in the same chair he was in the previous morning and was equally absorbed in this newspaper; and most surprising of all, Lou Soldano was back again, fast asleep with his feet propped up on the radiator cover, the top button of his shirt undone, and his tie loosened.

Arnold was the only one who noticed her. He greeted her rather perfunctorily, without looking up from his work. After his greeting he went on to say, "I do want to thank you for taking over on the unidentified case yesterday morning."

"You're welcome," Laurie said, on her way to the coffee machine. "It's turning out to be quite a case."

"I'm glad," Arnold said with a tone and attitude that discouraged further discussion.

Suit yourself, Laurie thought silently. She would have explained a little more if Arnold had specifically asked, but she was glad he didn't, as she'd already decided not to talk about it with anyone, particularly with Jack, until she learned more about the cause of death. Overnight her creativity had hit on another idea, which was going to require redoing the external exam.

"Where's Jack?" Laurie inquired.

"Haven't seen him yet," Arnold said. "He didn't come with you?"

"He's back to his bike," Laurie said.

"The fool," Arnold pronounced.

Laurie did not respond. Although she agreed with Arnold about the bike riding, she did not think it was

Arnold's place to criticize Jack. To change the subject, she asked about Lou, wondering why he was there two days in a row.

"He came in with a real doozy, a floater, to be exact, and another unidentified individual."

"Oh?" Laurie questioned. She was immediately curious. A floater meant someone who'd been fished from the water. As there was a lot of water around New York because Manhattan was an island, there were frequent floaters. There were enough so that when one attracts the attention of a detective captain to stay up all night, it had to be unique in some way. As Laurie put sugar in her coffee, she decided to ask what the story was.

"There's not much of a story," Arnold said, finishing up with a case file and putting it on the to-do pile. "I mean, it was fished out of the water around Governors Island, which isn't all that unusual. What's unusual about it is that those who have seen the body claim it should be an exhibit in the Museum of Modern Art. The corpse's supposedly an unbelievable mass of tattoos from around his neck down to his ankles and wrists, and everything in between. I actually haven't seen it yet, but that's how it's been described. When I finish here, I'm going to take a peek."

"Can you tell the ethnicity?" Laurie questioned.

"Asian."

"What's the apparent cause of death? Drowning?"

"No. The description in the case file is multiple GSW. The MLI wrote that she thought someone had opened up with a machine gun from behind because there were as many as a dozen entrance wounds."

"Wow. Whoever killed him wanted him dead," Laurie commented as she recalled a similar case she'd seen in a pathology journal of a Japanese man with astounding tattoos who'd been shot multiple times and beheaded with a classical Japanese samurai sword called a *katana*. As described in the article, the man had been killed along with a number of others during a turf war between rival Yakuza families in Tokyo, Japan.

Laurie glanced over at Lou's sleeping form, becoming progressively curious why he would make the effort to come in for a floater. She doubted it was the tattoos. She imagined whatever it had been that had caught his attention must have been compelling since it required him to stay up all night two days in a row. "Why did Detective Captain Soldano come in with the body? Did he say?"

"I'm sure it's because he's interested in the autopsy. Why specifically, I have no idea. Why don't you ask him?"

Sipping her hot coffee, Laurie strolled over to Lou and gazed down at him. He looked equally as tired as he had the previous morning, if not a bit more. Again, he was not snoring but breathing very rhythmically and deeply. Remembering Jack's comment about Lou being better off the sooner he got into a real bed, she reached out and placed her hand on top of his. Lou had his hands resting on his chest, fingers intertwined.

"Lou!" Laurie called softly, trying to wake him as gently as possible.

"It's me, Laurie," she said, continuing to gently shake his hands. She watched as his eyes opened and went from confusion to recognition within a second or two. Then he pulled his feet from the radiator and sat up straight.

"Do you want a little coffee?" Laurie asked, straightening up.

"No, thanks," Lou managed. "Just give me a second."

"You don't need a doctor to tell you this habit of no sleep isn't good for you. Talk about burning the candle at both ends!"

Lou blinked his eyes a few times and then took a deep breath. "Okay," he said. "I'm firing on all cylinders. Where's Jack?"

"He's riding his bike this morning. I came by cab, and there was no traffic. God willing, he'll be here in a few minutes. I don't even want to think about the alternative. Can't you get him to stop?"

"I've tried," Lou said with frustration. "Hey, did you see what I came in with?"

"I assume you mean the floater. I haven't seen the body, but Arnold here described it."

"It's unbelievable."

"So I've been told. But I assume the tattoos are not what brought you in."

"Heavens, no," Lou said with a short laugh. "I'm in here with the concern that there might be some kind of underworld war in the making, particularly with some of these newer Asian and Russian gangs moving in and bumping up against each other. Business is not great for normal people these days, and when normal people suffer, so do the gangs, and they can get at each other's throats. It's standard policy to notify me if the Harbor Control Unit picks up any bodies that suggest a professional hit. The harbor is a key dumping spot December through March, when the ground up in Westchester or over in Jersey is too hard to dig."

"Okay," Laurie said. "Are you here to watch the autopsy, and if so, do you want me to do it, or do you want to wait for Jack?"

"It certainly doesn't matter to me. I'd be thrilled if you'd do it. The sooner, the better."

"Arnold!" Laurie called out. "Would it be all right with you if I do the detective's case?"

"Absolutely," Arnold said. "And that will be it for you. It's a light day, and besides, I owe you."

Laurie was about to complain that she wanted more cases until she stopped herself, remembering what she wanted to do vis-à-vis yesterday's case, especially since she found it rather coincidental that she was doing autopsies on two unidentified Asians back-to-back.

"Vinnie!" Laurie called. "How about lending me a hand? I know Marvin isn't in yet, but you are available. I also know you like working with Jack, but maybe he could survive for one day without your guidance. We need to start the autopsy on this floater right now to get Captain Soldano home as soon as possible."

Still hiding behind his newspaper, Vinnie closed his eyes and gritted his teeth at Laurie's request for his help. He felt like such a coward. Instead of coming forward to talk about the disturbing meeting he'd had with the Vaccarro henchmen, he'd followed their orders about the threatening letter. To avoid detection, he'd typed the letter on the mortuary tech's monitor but transferred it to a USB storage device on his key chain before deleting it. He printed it at a nearby Kinko's. To be safe rather than sorry he'd brought some latex rubber gloves so as not to leave any latent prints on the sheet or the envelope. Back at OCME, still wearing the latex gloves and avoiding being seen by the receptionist or anyone else, he slipped the envelope under the double doors into the foyer. To get back in, he'd run around the corner, entering through one of the receiving bays where the bodies were brought in.

"Vinnie!" he heard Laurie call again but much closer. Slowly he lowered his paper. Laurie was standing directly in front of him. "Didn't you hear me?" she questioned with mild irritation.

Vinnie shook his head.

Laurie repeated herself about starting the floater.

Resigned, Vinnie stood up and tossed his paper onto the chair behind him.

"Take Captain Soldano downstairs and get him set up. Then put up the floater. I'll be running up to my office but will be down shortly. Got it?"

Vinnie nodded, feeling like a traitor. He couldn't look Laurie in the eye. The problem was that he knew too much about the Vaccarro group, and he certainly did not put it past them when they had threatened to drive out to his house and watch his girls come home from school. He felt he was between a rock and a hard place.

As Vinnie led the way down to the morgue, he looked back at Lou and wondered what the detective was thinking. The last time Vinnie had been forced to do a favor for Paulie Cerino, Detective Soldano had been the one who found out about it. So Vinnie was appropriately terrified that he'd be the number-one suspect if Laurie ignored the threat and turned the letter over to the authorities, meaning the chief, Harold Bingham, something Vinnie expected she would do. All Vinnie could do was hope that the threatening letter would be considered an outside job, not an inside one.

Up in her office, Laurie closed the door, turned on her computer monitor, and proceeded to hang up her coat. Then she quickly changed into green scrubs before pulling on a Tyvek suit over them. As soon as the monitor came on, she got on the Net and looked up the article she'd remembered about the murdered Yakuza member. What she wanted to do was skim the autopsy finding, which she did rapidly. With that quickly accomplished, she left her office and descended down to the pit.

Having acclimated himself to the morgue environment by having watched so many autopsies, Lou had offered to help Vinnie get the body from the cooler and transfer it onto the autopsy table. By the time Laurie got down to the basement level and into the autopsy room, Vinnie and Lou had everything ready to start the case.

"Those are the most impressive tattoos I've ever seen," Laurie admitted. From the neck to the wrists to the ankles, everything was covered with intricate tattoos in a rainbow of colors, literally everything. "The problem is that it makes for a difficult external exam. But you can certainly tell he was a member of a Yakuza family."

"Really?" Lou questioned. "You mean because of the tattoos."

"More than that," Laurie said. She picked up the corpse's left hand. "He's missing the last joint of his left little finger, a common Yakuza self-inflicted injury. To show penance to a Yakuza leader if it's indicated, a Yakuza follower must cut it off at the joint and give the severed piece to his boss. It's a ritual way to weaken one's grip on a sword to make one more dependent on one's boss."

"Are you kidding me?" Lou questioned dubiously.

"I'm not," Laurie said. "And here's something else."

Laurie lifted the man's flaccid penis and pointed to a series of nodules. "This is another interesting Yakuza ritual. These are pearlings. They are actual pearls buried under the skin, one for each year in prison. The individual does it himself with no anesthesia."

"Ouch," Lou voiced. He and Vinnie exchanged an uncomfortable glance.

"How on earth do you know all this about Yakuza?" Lou questioned. He'd always been impressed with Laurie's general knowledge, but this seemed beyond the pale. Lou had some knowledge of the Yakuza organization and history from having spent six years in the organized crime unit with the NYPD before switching to homicide.

"I should just let you guys think I'm so smart," Laurie confessed, "but when I just went up to my office, I checked an article I'd remembered, involving an autopsy on a murdered Yakuza."

"I put up the X-rays on the viewer box," Vinnie said. He pointed.

"Excellent!" Laurie said, and clasping her gloved hands in front of her, she walked over to inspect them. There were multiple foreign bodies sprinkled around inside the chest and abdomen, and within several extremities. They all appeared to be either intact bullets or bullet fragments. The skull appeared to be foreign body–free.

"We'll be following all the bullet tracks," Laurie said to Lou. "Is there anything you'd specifically like to learn?"

"Whatever you think is appropriate for this kind of case," Lou said. "I'd like to get at least some of the bullet material, both cores and casings, to see if they are from the same gun or multiple guns. We've already photographed the tattoos to see if they will help make an identification."

"All the paperwork in order?" Laurie asked Vinnie.

"I think so. Obviously we've got the X-rays. The photos are in the folder, and I know the corpse has been fingerprinted. I think we're okay."

"Terrific," Laurie said. "Let's do it."

The group walked back to the table. "One thing I can see right away," Laurie said. "What we are looking at are exit wounds." Using her hands to smooth out the skin, especially around the multiple meaty exit wounds, Laurie tried vainly to find any hidden entrance wounds. She was unable to do so. "So this individual was apparently only fired upon from the rear. That's some information, wouldn't you say, Lou?"

"Most definitely," Lou responded, although he had no idea what it meant. "Maybe he was running away?"

"Could be," Laurie responded. "Or swimming away." Then to Vinnie she said, "Let's turn him over and look at the entrance wounds."

Vinnie followed Laurie's orders and helped turn the body, with Lou pitching in, but he did not respond verbally, which Laurie found odd. To Laurie, one of Vinnie's endearing characteristics was his wry, sarcastic humor, which often bested Jack's. But this morning it was absent. "Is something wrong, Vinnie?" Laurie asked when the now prone body was again properly aligned on the autopsy table. "You're so quiet this morning," she said.

"No, I'm fine," Vinnie said—too quickly, from Laurie's point of view. For a moment she briefly wondered if he was resentful that she had asked him to help her rather than allowing him to wait for Jack.

At that moment Jack came blasting through the autopsy-room doors in his regular clothes, merely holding a mask against his face, violating two rules simultaneously.

"Hey, what's going on in here? I'm ten minutes late and both a special NYPD case is snapped away and my personal mortuary tech has been kidnapped."

"You should have come with me in the taxi," Laurie lectured.

"Hello, Lou, and hello, Vinnie," Jack said, coming up to the table and ignoring Laurie's comment.

"Hello, Dr. Stapleton," Vinnie responded quietly.

Jack's head lifted, and he stared at Vinnie. "'Dr. Stapleton'? How formal, indeed. What's up with you? Are you sick?"

"I'm fine," Vinnie responded. The truth was that he experienced a sharp resurgence of his guilt with Jack's arrival. He wished he could leave and find someone else to take his place. In fact, the thought passed through his mind that maybe he should take a short leave of absence until whatever was going on with the Vaccarros and the subway case was over and done.

"My God, look at these tattoos!" Jack exclaimed, looking back at the corpse on the table. "That's fantastic. What's the story?"

"Floater," Lou explained. He told Jack the little that was known about the case so far.

"Interesting! I've never seen anything quite like it," Jack responded to Lou. Switching his attention to Laurie, he said, "You enjoy yourself! I'll catch you later. Hope histology and the lab turn up something on your case yesterday."

Jack started to leave but stopped. "Hey!" he added

when she didn't respond. Not only did she not respond, but she seemed hypnotized, staring at the Asian's profile with his head turned to the side. Jack snapped his fingers in front of her face, and she acted as if she'd suddenly awakened.

"This is incredible," she said. "I think I've seen this man."

"You mean you've seen this corpse, or do you mean you've seen the man alive?"

"Alive," Laurie said. "As incredible as it may seem."

"Where?" Jack demanded. "When?"

Both Lou and Vinnie responded to this exchange by staring at Laurie with an intensity equal to Jack's.

Laurie then shook her head. "It can't be!" she said, throwing up her hands. "It's too much of a coincidence."

"What kind of coincidence?" Jack asked as he stepped back to where he'd been, closer to Laurie. It was difficult to see her face through her plastic face shield.

Laurie again shook her head as if trying to dislodge a crazy thought. "Last night I made what might be a breakthrough on the case I autopsied yesterday—"

"I thought you didn't get a case yesterday," Lou interrupted.

"I got it after you'd gone home," Laurie explained. "Anyway, I suddenly think there might be a connection between yesterday's case and this case. Obviously I'm not sure at this early point, but I believe there's a possibility."

"What kind of connection?" Lou asked. "This could be important!"

"Now, don't get your hopes up," Laurie cautioned.

"At least tell me what you have in mind," Lou

pleaded. He was excited. This was exactly why he had become so interested in forensic pathology and took the time and effort to come to OCME. In a number of cases since meeting Laurie and then Jack, it had been the autopsy that had provided the critical facts to solve a homicide, he hoped just like the one currently lying on the table in front of him.

"I'd rather not," Laurie said. "Bear with me, please! Maybe this afternoon I'll have the facts that I need. I'm sorry I'm not being more forthcoming."

"This seems overly melodramatic," Lou complained. "If this case is a harbinger of growing tension in the organized-crime world, it's important we get the clue sooner rather than later, to limit fallout in the civilian sector. I don't mind the bad guys killing each other. In some ways, that makes the NYPD's job easier. It's when civilians get hurt that I get upset."

"I'm sorry," Laurie said. "It's all just jelling in my head at this point."

"Are you trying to prove something to yourself?" Jack questioned. "Is that the explanation, as Lou says, for this melodramatic approach? I mean, there is a possibility that Lou or I could add a thing or two to your thinking process."

"Maybe there's something like that involved," Laurie confessed. "I do want to do it myself."

"Well, just tell me one fact, then," Jack said. "Did you find out if your victim yesterday had a seizure?"

"Yes, I believe he did."

CHAPTER EIGHTEEN

The huge 747-400 banked gracefully on its approach into New York City's JFK airport. A few minutes later it touched down onto the tarmac on runway 13R with hardly a jolt, another perfect landing of Flight 853 from Tokyo to New York by way of the North Pole. Once the plane's momentum had been brought to the appropriate speed, the captain exited the runway and began the lengthy taxi to the terminal.

It had been a long flight for Hisayuki Ishii, and he stretched his arms and legs. Luckily, he had been able to sleep on and off for nearly eight hours and felt reasonably well despite having been incarcerated for more than half a day in an aluminum cylinder. Of course, having been in first class had helped. Vaguely he wondered if his two lieutenants, Chong Yong and Riki Watanabe, had fared as well a few rows back in business class.

The protracted flight had provided Hisayuki a rare opportunity to just think. His normal days were generally so full that it was a luxury to be able to concentrate. He hadn't come up with any particularly new ideas in relation to the current problems, just a clearer idea of what to do. Since Satoshi and family were now gone, it was the lab books he needed to get, which was what he'd thought at the beginning of the flight, and he was now more convinced. The lab books provided the legal basis of contesting the Kyoto University patents. Of course, the other issue of critical concern was the relationship with the Yamaguchi-gumi, the real reason he'd made the snap decision to fly to New York the morning after he'd met with the Yamaguchi-gumi *oyabun,* Hiroshi Fukazawa. He had to be certain that Saboru Fukuda did not suspect that Satoshi had been murdered, which would depend on whether Hideki Shimoda's men had carried out the hit the way Hisayuki had specified.

With those thoughts in mind, Hisayuki took out his cell phone and placed a call to Hideki. As the phone rang, he glanced out the plane's window. As high off the ground as he was, it seemed that the huge plane was crawling forward slowly, tempting him to complain to the staff, as he was impatient to arrive. Of course, he didn't, but the thought made him realize how tense he was concerning the situation and about learning what changes had occurred since he'd been in the air and out of touch: *Has the raid gone well at iPS USA? Were the lab books in their possession? Had there been anything in the media that might alert the Yamaguchi-gumi to the fact that Satoshi and his family had been murdered?* Hisayuki was eager to hear the answers to these questions and was understandably impatient for Hideki to answer.

When Hisayuki was about to give up, Hideki answered gruffly in English, suggesting he'd been asleep. He quickly changed his tone, his attitude, and his language when he recognized the voice of his *oyabun.*

"What has happened since we spoke last?" Hisayuki demanded, speaking quietly in Japanese. He'd learned during the flight that the Caucasian man sitting next to him spoke only English.

"Some things good, some things bad," Hideki said.

"Better to tell me the bad first," Hisayuki said nervously.

"My two most dependable men have disappeared since yesterday afternoon. You met them on your last visit: Susumu Nomura and Yoshiaki Eto."

"As I recall, they were supposed to go on the raid of iPS USA last night."

"That's correct, but they never appeared at the meeting place to hook up with Barbera's men. Barbera's men reportedly waited around an hour or so for them to show up, but they never did. When I tried to call both of them last night and earlier this morning, all I got was voicemail. I'm worried they are not going to reappear."

"What about the break-in?"

"It never happened, which is understandable. Barbera-san and his men were helping us, not vice versa."

Hisayuki paused and tried to think. This was very bad news indeed. Nervously, the only thing that came to mind was that the Yamaguchi-gumi had killed Hideki's men as revenge for Satoshi's murder. He asked Hideki if he thought likewise.

"I'm afraid I do," Hideki said regretfully. He then related what Louie Barbera had told him Susumu and Yoshiaki had said to Louie's men—namely, that they were afraid of the Yamaguchi-gumi because of a threat they'd gotten from them about killing Satoshi.

"Was this before or after the hit?" Hisayuki asked.

"It had to be before," Hideki said.

"That does not make sense to me," Hisayuki said, trying to understand. "From the Yamaguchi standpoint, there is little reason they would suspect we knew anything about Satoshi, especially his coming to America. And we

wouldn't have if it hadn't been for the government telling us. I truly do not understand what's going on, unless
the government is using this situation to sow discord
between us Yakuza and to excite a turf war." Hisayuki
thought about the government possibly being involved
in such a duplicitous scenario but quickly dismissed it.
The issue about the Kyoto patents was too important to
be mixed up with any secondary goals.

At that moment the plane arrived at the gate.

"We are going to be getting off here in a minute,"
Hisayuki said. "You've given me the bad news, but now
give me the good."

"So far there has been no mention in any of the local
or national media concerning Satoshi's or his family's
deaths."

"None?" Hisayuki questioned.

"None."

"But if that is the case, how would the Yamaguchi-
gumi know of Satoshi's death and know that Susumu
and Yoshiaki had done it or were about to do it?"

"I have no idea."

Hisayuki again questioned silently if the government,
for some unknown reason, might have informed the
Yamaguchi-gumi that the hit was going to take place,
but he again dismissed the idea. It did not make sense.
The government wanted Satoshi murdered, and they
also wanted the lab books. "I am confused," Hisayuki
admitted. "I have the feeling there is something else
involved in all this, but I fail to understand what it is."

"Perhaps Susumu and Yoshiaki will suddenly appear,"
Hideki said optimistically, "and have some reasonable
explanation of their whereabouts over the past twelve
hours."

"Wouldn't that be nice."

"Although there's been nothing in the media about Satoshi, there's a chance that may change."

"And why would that be?" Hisayuki questioned.

"When Barbera-san called me last night to let me know Susumu and Yoshiaki had failed to show up, he informed me about a problem."

"I'm listening," Hisayuki said.

At that moment Chong Yong, Japanese by birth but Korean by ancestry, and Riki Watanabe appeared at Hisayuki's row and began retrieving Hisayuki's hand luggage from the overhead bin. Most of the rest of the first-class passengers were already disembarking.

"I'm going to have to deplane in a moment," Hisayuki said to Hideki. "We can meet at the Four Seasons hotel on Fifty-seventh Street in an hour or so. Be there!"

"Certainly. But let me finish so you'll know what is happening. Barbera-san told me he has a contact at the city morgue who confirmed Satoshi's death was considered to be natural but that it is being investigated by a woman doctor who is apparently suspicious for some reason that it is not natural. What's scary is that she has a reputation for being correct and, in Barbera-san's words, solving difficult cases."

"That's not good," Hisayuki mumbled.

"I agreed, and so does Barbera-san. Last night he said that he's gotten a warning to her to drop her investigation."

"Has she done so?"

"I don't know yet. Barbera-san said he was going to check this morning."

One of the cabin attendants approached. "Mr. Ishii.

We are here in New York." Behind her came a crew of janitorial personnel with cleaning equipment.

Hisayuki stood but kept his phone against his ear. At the same time he nodded to Chong and Riki, who had his hand luggage, to follow him, and he headed for the door.

"Call Barbera-san and request a meeting this morning!" Hisayuki said. "Specifically, ask him if this woman doctor has heeded his warning, and if not, tell him that we would be interested in learning everything there is to know about her."

"I'll call him right away," Hideki said. "Will you be willing to drive out to Queens to meet him?"

"Only if he insists," Hisayuki said. "Maybe you could remind him that I've just flown in all the way from Tokyo. Perhaps he'll have mercy. But if he complains, tell him I'd be happy to accept his hospitality."

"I think he'll be willing to come into the city," Hideki suggested. "I think he likes it. Most all of our meetings are in Manhattan."

CHAPTER NINETEEN

Hello, Miss Bourse," Ben said brightly.

"Good morning, sir!" Clair said, pulling her eyes away from a novel she was surreptitiously reading behind her monitor. No one had come in during the previous half-hour, and she essentially had nothing to do.

"Is Carl in yet?" Ben asked as he walked by the receptionist, hardly slowing his rapid gait.

"Yes, he is!" Clair called after the CEO.

Poking his head into Carl's open office, Ben said, "Can I see you?" Without waiting for an answer, Ben continued down to his own office. He hung up his coat in his closet before sitting behind his desk. The late-March morning sunlight blazed into the room through the open door into Jacqueline's office that faced east. The back of his black leather desk chair was hot from its power. Ben called out hello to Jacqueline, whose desk was out of view, and she returned his greeting.

By the time Ben moved the latest batch of journals to the side and cleaned the center of his desk, Carl entered and took his usual seat front and center. With sun streaming though the open door into Jacqueline's office, he had to squint.

"Are you making any progress with a possible iPS RAPID deal?" Ben asked, forgoing any small talk. Ben had been thinking of little else to avoid obsessing about Satoshi presumably enjoying himself in Washington,

D.C., where Ben was now convinced he'd most likely gone.

"As much as can be expected in so little time. I sent them a number of e-mail inquiries last evening, a fraction of which they have already responded to. I think I'll hear back on most of them today. The remainder on Monday, for certain."

"Has anything so far changed your initial impressions?"

"No, not really," Carl responded. "I think they will respond favorably to an offer to purchase. What price range, I have no idea. My sense is that these guys are true researchers and not necessarily businessmen, and would like to cash out early in the game. Maybe they fear something else might come down the pike and best their patent."

"Could happen," Ben agreed. "But my intuition tells me the same thing. I think it's time to pounce, especially with our market value sure to go up, thanks to our licensing deal with Satoshi. Are you working on that as well?"

"I don't have time," Carl joked. "Of course I am. I'll be speaking with a number of analysts today to see where they think we are, valuewise."

"All right," Ben said, indicating that the short meeting was over. "Keep me informed. I want to move on this to take advantage of our angel investors drooling to get more equity."

Carl got up and stretched. "It's an enviable position to be in, I must say. As a CFO, I've never had the pleasure of this kind of situation with access to seemingly limitless capital."

Carl got almost to the door to the hall when Ben

called after him. "I have a ten-K training race tomorrow, so I'll be leaving early. I'll check in with you before I do."

Carl gave Ben a thumbs-up sign before turning back around to leave.

"Carl," Ben called out again. "I forgot to ask—have you seen Satoshi yet this morning?" Actually, Ben had not forgotten. Feeling superstitious yet again, he'd hoped that Carl would have brought it up. By having to ask, Ben was certain he was going to get a negative reply, and he did.

"Not yet. Did you ask Clair, in case he slipped by me?"

"I didn't," Ben admitted.

"He didn't come in yet," Jacqueline yelled out of sight from her office. "I asked Clair when I came in, and the answer was no, and he hasn't come in while I've been here."

"There you go," Carl said. "He's not here yet." Carl touched his forehead in a kind of salute, and disappeared down the hall.

Ben shook his head with disappointment and a touch of paranoia. Why was Satoshi doing this to him? Ben then glanced at the will and the other trust documents making him Satoshi's son's guardian as well as the trustee if something were to happen to the parents. Under normal circumstances, they would have provided him a modicum of reassurance. But they didn't. The problem was that they had not yet been signed by Yunie-chan, Satoshi's wife.

With sudden determination, Ben reached into his jacket pocket and pulled out his cell phone. With the same sense of superstition that had kept him from asking

Carl about Satoshi, he'd yet to try Satoshi's number that day. Ignoring the feeling, he dialed Satoshi's number. The moment he heard the beginning of the generic outgoing message, he voided the call. Instead, he dialed Michael Calabrese's office number. As usual, he didn't get the placement agent, and instead had to leave a message on the man's voicemail. As irritating as it was under the immediate circumstance, at least he was confident he'd get a call back, in contrast to the messages he had been leaving Satoshi.

Impulsively, Ben picked up the trustee document and turned to the signature page. There was Satoshi's signature, along with his *inkan* seal. The signature was nothing more than a wild scribble. Ben had learned that it was the reddish-orange *inkan* that was the important part, along with the two witnesses, who were both iPS USA employees. There was also Pauline Wilson's signature as the notary. The only thing missing was Yunie-chan's scribble and her *inkan* seal.

All of a sudden Ben felt a bit less anxious, even though the documents had not been signed by the wife. He thought there was a reasonably good chance Saboru Fukuda, with Vinnie Dominick's encouragement, could have the needed signature faked, as well as an inkan seal. He smiled at his paranoia. Next he looked at the wife's will. That could be faked as well, if needed, making Ben both trustee and guardian. With a comforting exhale, Ben realized if the worst-case scenario was to occur and something untoward was to happen to Satoshi with or without his wife, iPS USA would not find itself out in the cold vis-à-vis the license agreement. Shigeru would own them, and Ben would be the trustee.

Snatching up the legal papers, Ben passed from his

office into Jacqueline's. "I'd like you to put these papers in the safe," he said. "Put them with Satoshi's lab books."

"Will do!" Jacqueline responded while covering the telephone mouthpiece with her left hand.

"What's my schedule for today?" Ben asked. He'd been so preoccupied with working himself up over Satoshi and the new opportunity represented by iPS RAPID, he'd completely forgotten his planned schedule for the day. Of course, forgetting his agenda was hardly unusual for Ben.

"It's blank," Jacqueline said. "Do you remember telling me not to schedule today because of your race in the morning? You said you wanted to leave early. I took you at your word."

"I remember now," Ben said happily, like a teenager hearing that school had been canceled.

With a spring back in his step, Ben returned to his desk. He was looking forward to the race in the morning as the official beginning of his training for the Hawaiian Ironman event on the fifth of June. Picking up the top magazine from the newly constituted biomedical journal stack, Ben eased back and lifted his legs. He was just getting comfortable when the phone rang. It was Clair out at the reception desk with the message that Michael Calabrese was on the line.

With considerably less anxiousness than he'd felt when he'd put in the call, Ben answered.

"I know you called, but I have some possibly good news," Michael said eagerly. "Remember I mentioned that there was another potential angel investor for iPS USA."

"Of course," Ben said.

"Well, he's heard of the contract signing we had with Satoshi through Vinnie Dominick and he wants in. He already called me this morning and said he wants in to the same degree as Dominick and Fukuda. Since I didn't want to piss those guys off, I called and asked if they minded, since it will dilute them, but they don't mind. The reality is you guys are sitting on a lot more capital today than you were yesterday."

"It's coming at a good time, as we are actually considering making an offer for iPS RAPID in San Diego instead of just negotiating a licensing agreement. We think there's a good chance they might jump at an offer."

"Well, whatever you decide, the money will be there," Michael said. "Now, I know you called me, so what's up?"

"I was calling you about Satoshi," Ben said. "I haven't seen him since he signed the contract."

"Is that unusual?"

"I suppose not. One time he disappeared on a trip to Niagara Falls without telling me, and Carl said that he mentioned to him he was thinking of taking his family to Washington, D.C."

"Did you try to call him?"

"Of course. Many times."

"Did you try to call him when he went to Niagara Falls?"

"I did, and he didn't answer then, either."

"Then I wouldn't worry. He wants to get away once in a while and celebrate his liberation. He told me when he first arrived at the signing the day before yesterday that what he liked best about living in America is the freedom to do what he wanted rather than always doing what was expected of him."

"But I had specifically asked him the day of the signing to either come to the office or call me the following day, yesterday, because he had reminded me to find laboratory space for him, which I have now done. He was also to pick up some documents for his wife to sign, but he never showed up or called. He hasn't even shown up today, at least not so far."

"Well, it doesn't sound worrisome to me, if that's what you are asking."

"I suppose not," Ben agreed. "But it makes me uncomfortable. What I was going to ask you was to get in touch with Vinnie Dominick and ask where Vinnie and his guys had placed Satoshi and his family. You said it's probably one of their collection of safe houses."

"That was my understanding."

"Would you mind asking for me? I'd like the address and the phone number, if there is one. I'll feel better if I know how to get in touch with him if need be, and he's not answering his cell. I certainly would not tell anyone."

"They don't like to reveal any of their safe houses for obvious reasons, the main being because it's then no longer a safe house. I know Satoshi was told under no uncertain terms not to reveal where he was temporarily living. I know Fukuda-san is arranging more permanent housing. Anyway, I'll ask and explain your reasons. I mean, they are already entrusting you with a heck of a lot of their hard-earned money. I can't see why they wouldn't trust you with the address of one of their safe houses."

"It will let me sleep better," Ben confessed.

CHAPTER TWENTY

The floater had taken more time than Laurie had originally imagined, because the autopsy required tracing more than a dozen bullet tracks through the victim's body, the majority through the chest and abdomen. Most had hit against bone and were diverted, but some had pierced the body through and through.

About midway through the case, Lou had decided he'd learned all he was going to learn and left. So it was Laurie and Vinnie who had slogged through, painstakingly following each shot and gathering bullets and bullet fragments as they progressed.

At first Laurie had tried to bring Vinnie out of his apparent funk by actively attempting to get him to participate in the dissection, but she eventually gave up. Instead, with the part of her brain she didn't need to devote to the physical work, she tried to imagine how the previous day's case could be related to the case she was doing. Could it be some sort of vengeance killing? There was no way to know. Besides, Laurie was the first to question whether there was a relationship or not, and she found herself progressively eager to find out. What was going to make her more confident was to study the photo she'd made and view the security tape again, holding a photo of the current case to compare. Even then she knew she probably was not going to be one hundred percent certain but maybe certain enough to question its potential meaning. Laurie thought seriously that one of the pursuers in the security tapes she'd watched at home was the man she was autopsying at that very moment. But she was being realistic. It was never that easy to identify people, especially looking at a photo or a film of a live person as compared to a corpse that had been floating around in the river.

The one thing Laurie was particularly thankful for was Jack's sensitivity. She knew he knew that it had to be the security tapes where she'd seen the floater, but he didn't push her on the issue. Instead, he'd respected her wish to do the legwork on her own and gain professional confidence by going so.

"Thank you for helping me on this case," Laurie said to Vinnie, preparing to help him lift the body onto the gurney. "I'm sorry it was so long."

"No problem," Vinnie answered, but without emotion.

"Now I want to ask another favor."

Vinnie looked expectantly at Laurie without speaking.

"If there's a table available, I'd like you to bring out my unidentified case from yesterday. I want to repeat the external exam."

Vinnie didn't respond.

"Did you hear me?" Laurie questioned with a hint of pique. She was now certain he was not acting like himself. He was even avoiding eye contact.

"I heard you," Vinnie said. "When there's a table available, I'll bring it out."

"On three," Laurie said, holding the floater's ankles. She then counted, and together they shifted the corpse off the table and onto the gurney. She then walked away without another comment.

Laurie stopped by Jack's table on her way out. "It looks like you've got a child," Laurie said. She hung back and avoided looking directly at the preteen girl's face. Children, particularly infants, were always difficult for Laurie, despite her active attempt to be professional and to keep emotion from her work.

"Unfortunately, yes," Jack said. "And a rather heart-breaking case as well, so to speak. Do you want to hear?"

"I suppose," Laurie said, with a distinct lack of enthusiasm.

Jack picked up the child's heart from a tray and opened the edges of a slice he'd made to view a porcine aortic valve replacement. "A suture became loose after the initially successful replacement and got tangled in the valve. One suture out of a hundred! It's a tragedy for everybody: the surgeon, the parents, but of course, mostly for the child."

"I hope that surgeon can learn from his or her mistake."

"That's the hope," Jack said. "He's certainly going to hear about it. Are you off to work on yesterday's case?"

"I am," Laurie said.

"Good luck!"

"Thanks for not pushing me earlier to explain myself."

"You're welcome. But I'm getting awfully curious and want to hear about what you've got by the end of today. I'm assuming your watching the security tapes last night was a lot more fruitful than I had imagined."

"They were interesting," Laurie teased. "On another subject, Vinnie is not acting at all like himself today."

"Really? That sounds very unlike Vinnie. I did notice

he called me Dr. Stapleton when I stopped at your table. It's usually something a lot more derisive."

"Maybe it's me, as I did deliberately hijack him this morning. But I did give him the option to wait and work with you."

"Thanks for the tip," Jack said as Laurie moved on.

Laurie removed her Tyvek coveralls in the locker room and disposed of them before heading upstairs in her scrubs. The first stop was Sergeant Murphy's office, where she turned over the information she had involving the pickpocket episode seen on the security tape. Then she asked about John Doe.

"I haven't heard a damn thing about your case from yesterday," the sergeant confessed. "But I expect to hear something today. If I don't, I'll give Missing Persons a call myself. If they'd received any calls about a missing Asian male, they would have let me know."

Laurie thanked the sergeant before climbing a flight of stairs and dropping in on Hank Monroe, the director of identification in the anthropology department. Laurie knocked on the closed door. It seemed that Hank, in contrast to most everyone else, preferred his privacy.

Hank Monroe was no more help than Sergeant Murphy had been, saying that the Missing Persons Squad had admitted they had yet to run the victim's fingerprints on any local database, much less on the state or federal level. "As I believe I told you yesterday, they usually wait at least twenty-four hours or so, because the vast number of cases are solved by someone calling in within that time period. But as soon as I hear anything, you'll be the first to know."

From the director of identification's office, Laurie went up to toxicology and stopped in to see John

DeVries. "So far the screen for drugs, poisons, or toxins has shown absolutely nothing," John said with an apologetic tone. "I'm sorry. You did get the essentially negative blood alcohol, didn't you?"

"I did," Laurie said. "And I appreciate you making the effort to do it so quickly."

"We're happy to help," John said in his new persona. "But I want to emphasize that just because the toxicology screen is so far negative, it doesn't necessarily mean there is none present. With some of the more potent agents, so little is needed to kill someone that the only way to identify it is to look for it specifically. What I'm trying to suggest is that if you have any reason to suspect a specific agent, you have to tell us, and we'll specially look for it. Even then we can't guarantee success, even with the trick of running the sample through the mass spec twice."

"I understand," Laurie said, and she did. She had been involved in several poisonings over the years. One had involved finding the agent at the crime scene, the other by discovering evidence that the perpetrator had purchased the material. But in her current case, neither of those opportunities was available.

"We're not totally finished," John added. "If we find something, I'll be sure to give you a call."

Next Laurie went down to the fourth floor and entered the histology lab, bracing herself for Maureen O'Conner's invariable humor. She was not disappointed, nor was she disappointed about getting her slides overnight. As usual, Maureen came through with both.

Descending yet another floor, Laurie entered her office, eager to get to work. In order not to be bothered, she shut her door, which she rarely did. Next she deposited the tray of histology slides next to her microscope and turned on her monitor.

Her final act of preparing to get to work was to take out her cell phone and give Leticia a call. She actually felt proud of the fact that she'd resisted calling until almost ten. She thought it showed marked restraint, at least in comparison to the previous day. Leticia agreed.

"I'm surprised you didn't call earlier," Leticia said teasingly when she first answered.

"I'm surprised myself. How are things going?"

"Couldn't be better. We're staying in this morning, then going out to the park this afternoon. The sun is supposed to come out after noon."

"Sounds like a plan," Laurie said. While she had been talking to Leticia, she'd gotten out the photo she'd made from the security tapes and compared it to the photo in the new case file. It seemed that there was a definite resemblance between the man she'd just autopsied and one of the men in the photo. Actually, more than she expected.

After hanging up with Leticia, Laurie got the two security disks out of her bag and slipped the first into the DVD drawer. Then she put the photograph of the floater next to the monitor to make it easy to compare. With her mouse, she advanced the DVD to the appropriate time and pressed play.

The image was from camera five, and the timing was that of the victim rushing down the stairs to the subway platform. Within seconds, the two pursuing men appeared at the top of the stairs. At that point, Laurie stopped the action and then moved it forward frame by frame. As the action advanced and the men became larger and larger, Laurie alternately got a good view of first one and then the other. Although the two men resembled each other in terms of size and dress, one had a more or less full, oval face, while the other's was lean and narrow. Of course, the more obvious difference was that the thinner man was carrying an umbrella, while the full-faced one was not.

Laurie advanced the frames until she had the best view of the full-faced man, as it was clear the man she'd just autopsied also had a full, oval face. At that point, with the security tape halted, she picked up the photo of the tattooed gentleman in the cooler and put them side by side.

For several minutes Laurie stared alternately at the photo and the image on her monitor. In a sense, she was disappointed. From the initial comparison using the photo she'd made at home and the photo taken at OCME, she'd been optimistic and had counted on the identification being easy: It was going to be either a yes or a no. She hadn't expected a maybe, which seemed to be the situation. It was close. Alternately she looked at photos and then at the monitor image, again advancing the monitor image a frame at a time.

Still not certain, perhaps due to the dark glasses, Laurie quickly advanced the security tape to camera six and went to the same time sequence as she'd been on camera five. From that angle, something she'd not seen on camera five appeared. The man had a mole about the size of a dime on his right temple. It wasn't particularly obvious, but it was definitely there, no doubt about it. Checking the photograph of the right profile on the photo, there it was as well! Laurie was reasonably confident that the two people were one and the same!

She sat back in her chair, amazed at the coincidence. Then she sat forward again and continued watching the tape from the sixth camera to the point where the train pulled into the station. Although it was not easy to make out because of the crowd surging forward toward the arriving train, Laurie tried to see exactly what happened when the two pursuers reached the victim. She could not see any of their hands, but quickly the two men seemed to be supporting the victim while the victim appeared to be convulsing. It was very fast, only a couple of frames. What wasn't clear was whether the pursuers caused the victim to convulse or it was spontaneous, like a heart attack or stroke.

Laurie sat back in her chair again, watching the rapid denouement with the pursuers laying the now unconscious man onto the platform, having already stripped him of his bag and presumably his wallet. On this viewing, Laurie also saw something else she hadn't made note of the previous evening: how the oval-faced man, after relieving the victim of his belongings, carefully picked up the umbrella and opened it about halfway before closing it again. The impression was that it took some force to get it closed. The thought that immediately came to Laurie's mind was that the umbrella was being cocked like an air rifle.

Halting the security tape, Laurie was about to view the same sequence from the vantage point of some of the other cameras when a specific remembrance flashed through her mind. It was about a famous forensic case that she'd heard about in a lecture when she was a resident in forensic pathology. It involved the assassination in London of a diplomat from an Iron Curtain country she couldn't remember. It was carried out with the help of an air gun cleverly hidden by the KGB within an umbrella.

Putting down the photos that she was still holding, Laurie went online and did a quick search, and within seconds she was reading about Georgi Ivanov Markov, a rather famous Bulgarian at the time, who had indeed been murdered with a KGB-manufactured pellet gun hidden within the shaft of an umbrella. Most important, Laurie learned that the substance involved was ricin, a remarkably toxic protein derived from castor beans.

Going back to the Web, Laurie looked up ricin, particularly interested in the symptoms associated with ricin poisoning. Immediately she could tell that her case of the previous day could not have been a copycat of the Markov incident, at least not with ricin, as ricin caused gastrointestinal symptoms, and the symptoms developed over hours, not instantaneously, as with her case. As far as the delivery aspect, however, meaning a pellet gun in an umbrella, that was a definite possibility. Laurie was now eager to repeat the external exams.

Why she hadn't done a better external exam at the time, even if Southgate had supposedly done it and reputedly had called it negative, she didn't know. In fact, from her current vantage point she was embarrassed she hadn't done her own. Not long into the autopsy, her intuition was telling her it had not been a natural death, as there was no pathology at all: none! The challenge now was to prove her intuition was correct: whether there was a tiny entrance wound that he'd received through his clothing.

Laurie picked up the phone and called Vinnie's cell. She and most people at OCME had been finding that using personal cell phones was significantly more efficient than using the regular internal phone lines. She wondered if Vinnie's mood had improved. He answered after the first ring.

"How about my Asian John Doe?" Laurie asked. "Is he ready for another look?"

"A table is just opening up," Vinnie said. "It should be within a half-hour or so."

"Terrific! Should I just come down in a half-hour, or do you want to give me a call?"

"If you don't mind, I'll have Marvin give you a call," Vinnie said, continuing to suffer guilt about his very real fears of having been caught in an untenable situation where he was damned if he did and damned if he didn't. If he went to Laurie and took responsibility for sending her the threatening note and tried to convince her about what to do, he and/or his family, particularly his girls, would surely be harassed if not killed. If he didn't do anything and Laurie didn't heed the message, she could be killed. The situation was driving him to distraction. "He's available now, and I know you guys like to work together."

"Suit yourself!" Laurie said, finally truly irritated. It seemed to her that Vinnie had been trying to provoke her all morning, and now he'd succeeded.

Calming herself down, Laurie turned to the histology slides. Until she'd viewed all of them, particularly the sections involving the brain and the heart, and found nothing, there was still a slight chance yesterday's case was a natural death, despite her intuition to the contrary. Last night she'd become excited over the case. Now she was really excited with the added intrigue that she had both the victim and the killer, meaning the case might very well represent war between two organized-crime organizations just as Lou had feared, since at least one of the victims was most likely a Yakuza member.

CHAPTER TWENTY-ONE

There was no doubt in Vinnie's mind that Laurie knew he was acting out of character. Try as he might, he couldn't help it even though he tried. The problem, of course, was that he took the Vaccarros at their word since he'd heard all sorts of stories over the years, and Carlo and Brennan had threatened his daughters. Vinnie could not help but take such threats seriously. Being involved with such people was a lose-lose situation, and going to the police, unfortunately, was not an option.

Having begged off helping Laurie, he reflexively answered his phone when it rang only minutes later, thinking it was Laurie calling back for some change in the plans. Instead, to Vinnie's serious chagrin, it was Carlo, the Barbera hood.

"Good morning, Vinnie, buddy," Carlo said with a false sense of camaraderie. "It's me from yesterday. Do you remember?"

"I remember," Vinnie acknowledged, trying to sound normal but failing miserably. Carlo was the last person he wanted to talk to. If only he'd looked at the incoming number.

"I had some questions, if you have a minute."

Vinnie would have loved to say no, that he didn't have time, but he didn't dare. Instead he asked Carlo to hold on a minute until he could find a quiet spot. Quickly he ducked out of the mortuary office, where some of the other techs were gathered, drinking their first cups of coffee.

"Have you seen Dr. Laurie Montgomery yet this morning?" Carlo asked when Vinnie gave him the okay.

"I have," Vinnie said. "I've already done a case with her."

"Terrific," Carlo said. "And how was she acting?"

"She was acting quite normal. Not like me."

"I'm sorry to hear that. I hope your feeling out of sorts has nothing to do with us."

"It has everything to do with you," Vinnie said, vainly thinking that if he were up-front they might leave him alone. "Yesterday you said you just wanted to ask me some questions, and then, before you know it, you have me sending a threatening letter."

"What did the letter say again? I know you told me when you called me back, but I can't remember."

"I said what you told me to say, that if she didn't sign the case out as a natural death, she and her family would face serious consequences. I also said that if she went to the police about the warning, she and her family would suffer the same consquences."

"Good, good," Carlo repeated. "And you know she got your love letter?"

"As sure as I can be. I made it a point to check her office and saw it on her computer keyboard. It would have been hard for her to have missed it."

"And?"

"And what?"

"Do you know if she's read it?"

"I assume she has, but I wasn't hanging around to watch."

"Has her behavior changed?"

"Not in the way you want. In fact, like I suggested yesterday, the letter seems to have made her more intent on investigating the case. She even mentioned this morning that she'd learned something particularly interesting last night."

"Like what?" Carlo demanded, his tone changing from mockingly humorous to dead serious.

"I don't know," Vinnie said. "She said that she wanted to investigate a bit more. I think she believes she's made some progress, and my guess would be that's not in the direction of it being a natural death but rather a homicide."

Vinnie then heard muffled conversation, as if Carlo was trying to cover the mouthpiece of his phone. Fighting the urge to hang up, Vinnie waited, but while he waited he came to acknowledge that he was allowing himself to be drawn progressively into a situation that would not end well. Next Carlo could and probably would ask him to do something worse than compose a threatening letter, which already had been bad enough.

Vinnie hung up the phone, realizing as he did that he could be putting himself and his family in even greater jeopardy. So great was his panic that he made the sudden decision to leave town. It was his only choice. He had plenty of sick leave and vacation time available. Although he knew admin liked more warning, Vinnie was confident they'd make an exception, especially if he pleaded a family emergency.

With sudden resolve, Vinnie quickly put in a call to his wife, Charlene, who worked for her brother's moving company in Garden City, Long Island. He knew she'd be able to get the time off; their business had been slow. The real problem would be the girls and school, but such was life. As he waited for the call to go through, he ran up the rear stairs to head to the first floor, where the chief of staff had her office.

"Hastings Moving and Storage," Charlene said when she answered.

Vinnie didn't waste words. Charlene was aghast at first but was understanding when Vinnie explained that the situation involved Paulie Cerino and the Vaccarro organization. Having grown up with Vinnie in Rego Park, Charlene knew all about the Mob and the danger they represented. She also knew Vinnie was indebted to Paulie Cerino and what that meant.

"We've got to do this right away," Vinnie anxiously insisted, "like today! Get the girls and we'll be off. At least Florida is nice this time of year."

"I've got to pack some things," Charlene said, sensing Vinnie's panic.

"Of course, but don't make it your life's work," Vinnie urged. "And don't tell anyone we're leaving."

"What about my aunt Hazel? We can't just drop in on her in Fort Myers. And I have to tell my brother."

"Tell your brother, of course," Vinnie said, "but tell him not to let anyone else know. As far as your aunt is concerned, let's call her en route. We might be better off staying at one of those cheap motels near the beach."

"When will you be home?"

"As soon as possible, within the hour," Vinnie said. "At the moment I'm just outside the chief of staff's office. I have to get Twyla Robinson's blessing. I don't think there'll be a problem. It was just a week ago that she was reminding me how much vacation time I'm owed."

"I'll try to get some schoolwork to take for the kids."

"Good idea."

"Don't you think you should warn Dr. Montgomery?" Charlene questioned.

"I already did," Vinnie said. "That's why I have to leave. I don't want them asking me to do anything else. I know in my bones that's what they were about to do before I hung up on them."

"How long do you think we'll have to be in Florida?"

"Not long. Maybe a week or two. My sense is that all hell is going to break out here in the next day or so, and I want to be south of the Mason-Dixon Line."

CHAPTER TWENTY-TWO

Try him again!" Louie said to Carlo, referring to Vinnie Amendola. Louie, Carlo, and Brennan were in Carlo's car, heading into Manhattan to meet with Hisayuki Ishii. Brennan was driving, with Carlo in the front passenger seat and Louie in the back.

Although Louie had spoken to the *oyabun* on numerous occasions, he'd never met the man in person. After listening to Carlo's conversation with Vinnie, he was really looking forward to it. Obviously Laurie Montgomery-Stapleton was acting as Paulie Cerino had warned: uncooperative, dogged, and too smart for her own good. Something had to be done quickly if Satoshi's death was to remain an inconsequential natural death. Prior to learning this unpleasant exigency, Louie had assumed the conversation with the Yakuza leader was going to center on the lab books and how much money would be involved if they retrieved them. Now the conversation was going to be about Laurie Montgomery-Stapleton and how to get her to back off.

"The prick is not answering," Carlo said, flipping his phone closed. He was twisted around, facing Louie.

"Well, give it a break for now," Louie said. "I think we're going to need his cooperation. You guys might have to make a second visit to OCME if he doesn't answer over the next hour or so."

When they reached the Four Seasons, all three men piled out, turning the car over to valet parking.

With Louie in the lead, they went though the revolving door and up the half-flight of steps to the reception area. Skirting the desk, they passed the elevators and then up more steps to the bar and dining level. Since only Louie had ever been in the hotel before, both Carlo and Brennan were impressed with the stone walls and soaring spaces. To Brennan, it reminded him of an ancient Egyptian temple.

As it was mid-morning, the bar to the left was empty, and even the dining side to the right was sparsely occupied. It was easy to spot Hideki and his crew, especially given the man's sumo-wrestler proportions. He was hard to miss.

As Louie had dreaded, he had to go through the bowing and business-card ritual with Hisayuki Ishii while Hideki Shimoda made the introductions. Then they all sat down. Meanwhile, Carlo and Brennan wandered over to the left end of the bar. At the right end were Hisayuki's lieutenants, one as large as Hideki but with muscle, not fat. There were no introductions among the enforcers, but it didn't matter. They recognized one another other instinctively.

For a time Louie, Hideki, and Hisayuki engaged in mutually complimentary small talk, giving one another credit for the undeniable success of their business relationship, all admitting they had not imagined it was going to be so lucrative.

Then Hisayuki thanked Louie for his willingness to come to the hotel rather than making him travel to Queens. "It is a long flight from Tokyo to New York," he said.

"It is my pleasure," Louie said. He was favorably impressed with the *oyabun*. To Louie, Hisayuki made quite a statement in his expensive, fashionable clothes. But it was more than clothes and careful grooming that awed Louie. It was also the look in the man's eyes, his quiet intensity, and his apparent intellect. From experience, Louie could tell intuitively that the man was shrewd and a born negotiator who always had the best interests of himself and his organization in mind. Louie actually respected that, but it also made him take pause with the understanding he was facing a forbidable opponent.

"As I'm certain you are exhausted from your flight," Louie said, "perhaps we should get right down to business."

"That is most thoughtful of you," Hisayuki said, bowing yet again.

Louie found himself doing the same. It was the one thing he found trying when dealing with the Japanese. That and the fact that he felt he never quite knew what their agenda really was. "Let me be frank," Louie began. "Up until recently, we have been, I thought, reasonably open with each other—that is, until very recently. Is that your sense as well?"

Surprised and taken aback at such an open and direct question, Hisayuki hesitated, looking briefly at Hideki for support, as Hideki had been living in America for a decade or more. When support was not forthcoming, Hisayuki blurted, "Hai, hai," as if the Japanese word was a universal method of affirmation.

"But you guys, particularly my friend Hideki here," Louie said, nodding at Hideki, "were far from being up-front with us over the previous several days. Now, I don't want to beat a dead horse. . . ." Louie paused, questioning himself whether the two Japanese had any idea what the phrase "beating a dead horse" meant. "Do you understand 'beating a dead horse'?"

Both Japanese men nodded so quickly that Louie knew they had no idea.

"It means to talk about something too much, because Hideki and I already had this conversation. You see, the pickle we are now in has come from you people not telling us the truth—namely, that Satoshi was not a deadbeat and you weren't asking our help for a shake-down, but rather it was going to be a hit, which we never would have agreed to, because we try to avoid that kind of violence these days. It's an unspoken pact we've had with the police. We don't whack anybody, and they let us professionals alone, meaning they can concentrate on traffic issues and the real bad guys, like serial killers and terrorists.

"Am I making sense here, Ishii-san?" Louie asked, looking directly at Hisayuki. "Or should I call you Hisayuki? You can call me Louie."

"Hisayuki is fine," Hisayuki said, somewhat over-whelmed but recovering from Louie's forceful directness, making an effort to remember that Louie was not trying to be rude.

"Okay, Hisayuki, are you following me, or am I being a little too direct? From speaking with Hideki, I have a sense you guys are generally not quite so brusque. Is that fair to say?"

"Perhaps," Hisayuki said evasively. He wasn't exactly sure what *brusque* was but had an idea from the context.

"Well, here's the current situation as I see it," Louie continued. "From your side, there are the lab books that you guys are interested in obtaining. I'll be happy to talk to you about them, provided you're willing to let us have more information, because in retrospect, we feel that breaking into a firm on Fifth Avenue is more risky than we first believed. In order for us to be willing to help, we'd have to know more and be appropriately compensated. We'd also have to be convinced the books are actually there and available, if you know what I'm saying.

"From our perspective, we're interested in going back to the status quo before the mayhem your two guys, Susumu and Yoshiaki, created by whacking Satoshi on a crowded subway platform and blowing away his entire family in New Jersey. Are you still with me?" Louie paused, looking directly at Hisayuki, waiting for a response. To Louie, Hisayuki appeared slightly shell-shocked.

"Perhaps you could speak a little slower," Hideki suggested. "The *oyabun* speaks English well, but he doesn't get the opportunity very often."

"Sorry," Louie said. "I will speak more slowly, but I believe speed will be playing a role in what we do to avoid a deteriorating situation."

Hisayuki nodded but didn't speak. He felt off balance, as he was accustomed to being prepared and maintaining control of meetings. At present, he was neither. Susumu and Yoshiaki's disappearance had thrown him off balance. It was possible the Yamaguchi-gumi might already suspect that Satoshi and his family had been murdered by the Aizukotetsu-kai. If that were the case, then they were already involved in a very dangerous situation.

"Right now nobody seems to know what happened," Louie said, forcing himself to speak slower. "What I mean is that the family has not yet been discovered, since they were living in what I've been told is a deserted area."

Hisayuki assumed it was a location provided by the American Mafia partners with the Yamaguchi-gumi, but he said nothing.

"The family may or may not be discovered, which tells me that it's not an emergency today. At the same time, I want you to clean it up and get rid of the bodies, since you guys made the mess. We will help, because if and when it is discovered it's going to be just the kind of situation that I've been working to avoid. It will be recognized immediately for what it is, a gangland killing, and will make our communal professional lives miserable. So that's tomorrow. Sunday we can have a meeting about the lab books. How does this schedule sound so far?"

Hisayuki didn't move or speak.

Louie stayed quiet. He wanted some sort of response. He was beginning to think taking a meeting with Hisayuki was an exercise in talking to one's self. All the man did was blink. His reticence also made Louie think that Hisayuki might somehow suspect that Louie and the Vaccarro organization had something to do with the disappearance of Susumu and Yoshiaki.

After several minutes of uncomfortable silence, Hideki said, "You've mentioned tomorrow and the day after, but what about today? And what about this deteriorating situation you're referring to?"

"Thank you for asking," Louie said without sarcasm. "I've talked about the Machita family issue, but I haven't mentioned Satoshi. As you may remember, Hideki, last night we briefly discussed Dr. Laurie Montgomery-Stapleton."

"Ah, yes," Hideki said. "I mentioned what you said to the *oyabun*."

"That is true," Hisayuki said, suddenly breaking his silence. "This is something we are very concerned about. Has she responded appropriately to your warning?"

"Apparently not," Louie admitted, glad to be talking directly to the *oyabun*. Louie leaned back with one arm over the rail of his chair and called out to Carlo. Carlo stood immediately with a questioning look on his face. Louie beckoned him over. As he approached, the *oyabun*'s men slipped from their barstools and stood at tense attention until the *oyabun* gave them a wave to stand down.

"Try Vinnie again!" Louie said to Carlo. "If he answers, find out what the situation is at the moment!"

Carlo tried. He waited until voicemail came on, then hung up. He shook his head for Louie's benefit. Louie waved him away and turned to the others.

"We are having some difficulties with our contact," Louie explained. "But here's what we have learned. It seemed to our contact that our warning was not just ignored but might have acted as a catalyst toward greater effort on her part."

"But the death was considered natural?" Hisayuki questioned with particular interest.

"That's what we understand."

"Why would this woman then change her mind?" Hisayuki demanded.

"I don't know," Louie said. "Maybe it was the warning letter. The fact is, this woman is a very strong person, very determined."

"And she's just back from a yearlong maternity leave," Carlo added. He'd not moved despite Louie having waved him away. Carlo called over to Brennan. "Isn't that what he said?"

"Year and a half maternity leave," Brennan called back. He walked over to stand by Carlo. "And Satoshi was her first case, and only case, for that matter, so she was trying to prove something. At least that's what our contact said. It's kind of a worst-case scenario."

Louie turned back to Hisayuki and Hideki. "I had a conversation with my boss about this woman. When he talks about her, it is in almost mythical terms. He actually tried to kill her, as did another capo, without success. And adding to her mystique is that she's got connections with the New York City Police Department, which is not a good thing, as you can well imagine.

"Now with all this background," Louie continued, "we're also up against a specific time constraint. According to our contact, this doctor claims to have made some progress with the case that she will reveal later this afternoon, and it involves proving that the case is a homicide."

"How is she going to do that?" Hisayuki said with an air of disbelief.

"I think that's for you to tell us."

There was a silence.

"I think you owe us an explanation," Louie added.

"It involves a special toxin," Hisayuki said. "It is not something I am supposed to discuss."

"Fair enough," Louie said. "Do you think our Dr. Laurie Montgomery-Stapleton will figure it out?"

"It will be the first time, if she is able to do it. And we've used it before."

"Well, I don't think we should allow her to do that," Louie said. "We have to think of a way to discourage her."

"Perhaps we should kill her," Hisayuki said.

"That's not an option," Louie said. "When I spoke with my boss, he said killing her would unleash from the police a decade of harassment ten times worse than what we are trying to prevent. That doesn't make any sense."

"But if it were the same toxin, her death would be considered natural," Hisayuki proposed. "We have more of the toxin available."

Louie thought for a moment. Such an idea had not occurred to him. It was a possibility, and somehow satisfying. But the more he considered it, the less promising it seemed. It was taking a chance it wouldn't be discovered, yet Laurie seemed to be making progress. Louie didn't like taking chances. Besides, how could it be done so quickly? He wanted to do something that very morning. Unless he could be sure Laurie would leave OCME for lunch on her own, which was not something he could count on. Given how dogged she was, she probably didn't even eat lunch. The only other possibility was to get someone inside OCME and get the toxin to her that way. The only problem with that idea was that Louie's estimation of the possibility of it working was near zero, and that was being generous.

"I have an idea," Brennan said suddenly. "What about the kid? I mean, we threatened both her and her family with consequences."

"What kid?" Louie demanded, irritated that Brennan had the nerve to talk without being specifically addressed. It was embarrassing to have one's underlings thinking they could just speak out whenever they wanted. It gave the impression no one was in charge.

"The kid that caused the maternity leave," Brennan

said. "Why not snatch the child? I'm certain the doctor will drop whatever she is doing. If her child's gone, she's not going to care about whether some unknown person died naturally or unnaturally."

Louie's ire faded in a flash. *A kidnapping!* he thought. It was brilliant! It could be done right away. No one needed to die. And the police would have no reason to think organized crime was involved.

Louie turned to Hisayuki. "What do you think of kidnapping?"

"I think it is a very good idea," Hisayuki said. "We ask for a ransom so there will be no association with Satoshi. Satoshi's case will fade from significance."

"Exactly," Louie agreed.

"Will it be easy?" Hisayuki asked.

"I would think so. The hardest part will be taking care of the kid." Louie laughed. "Actually, snatching the kid will be easy if he is staying in his house with a nanny. It will be more difficult if he's in a childcare center. But with both parents being doctors, my guess is that it will be an in-house nanny situation."

"Can we help?" Hisayuki questioned. "It is very important for us that Satoshi's death continues to be considered natural and not a murder."

"And why exactly is that?" Louie questioned. "I mean, we've told you why we prefer Satoshi's death to be considered natural, but exactly why do you? If we are going to be working together, we have to be up-front with each other, as I mentioned in the beginning of our conversation."

"It was the Yamaguchi-gumi who brought Satoshi to America. If they find out he was murdered, there is a chance they might blame us. We want to avoid that."

Louie knew there were many more questions he could ask, but he was satisfied with the answer he got because it made sense to him, and he didn't care particularly about the relationship between the Aizukotetsu-kai and the Yamaguchi-gumi. As far as he was concerned, that was their business.

"Okay," Louie said suddenly. He looked up at Brennan. "Brennan, my boy," he said. "Since it was your idea, you are going to be in charge. Do you know much about kidnapping?"

"I'm in charge?" Brennan questioned with happy surprise. He briefly glanced over at Carlo, unsure of what that meant or how he should feel, but then quickly returned his attention to Louie. He liked the idea of being in charge. He liked it a lot. "The first thing I need to do is get my computer and learn as much about Laurie Montgomery-Stapleton as I can, starting with where she lives."

"We did a kidnapping over in Jersey a long time ago," Louie said for Hisayuki's benefit. "It went well, but it takes planning. There's two particularly dangerous times: the snatch and the pickup of the ransom. The rest can mostly be improvised. The snatch is first, but it should be easy in this situation, because it's an infant. There shouldn't be a struggle, depending on the nanny's reaction."

"You will let us know how we can help?" Hisayuki asked, interrupting.

"You can count on it," Louie said. He looked at his watch. "We have to move! I'd like to have the kid in our hands around noon, if it is at all possible."

"What will we do with the kid once we have him?"

"That's another issue," Louie said. "We have to find

a place. But let's not worry about that right away. We'll bring the kid to my house! My wife loves babies. Tomorrow we can find a place."

"What about the warehouse at the pier?" Carlo suggested. He didn't want to be left out in the cold completely.

"No heat," Louie said, standing up. "We don't want the kid getting sick. As I said, taking care of the kid might be the hardest part of this affair. We don't want to make it more difficult for ourselves, and he'll be no value to us dead. There's something called 'proof of life' involved in kidnapping episodes, which they will be demanding as we keep Laurie Montgomery-Stapleton busy with negotiations."

"Very nice to meet you, Ishii-san," Louie said while thrusting out his thick-fingered hand toward the *oyabun*. "We'd best get to work. Tonight, if you're up for it despite your jet lag, perhaps we could have dinner. Provided we get the kid, we can celebrate your arrival in our city and celebrate controlling our nemesis in OCME."

"That would be my pleasure," Hisayuki said, bowing and shaking Louie's hand simultaneously.

Louie self-consciously bowed as well. He then quickly repeated the gesture with Hideki, who had managed with some effort to get to his feet.

Louie began to herd Carlo and Brennan toward the stairs while calling over his shoulder to Hideki that he'd be in touch within the hour.

"I'll be waiting," Hideki called after them.

"Do you want me to try Vinnie Amendola again?" Carlo questioned. He felt he was still being sidelined, as his previous suggestion had been so quickly rebuffed.

"Absolutely not," Louie responded, heading down the stairs ahead of his two henchmen. "We'll only involve him as a last resort. He could easily be forced into becoming a double agent. Brennan, are you confident you'll be able to find out the woman's address from the Internet?"

"You'll be surprised at what I'll be able to find out about her in two minutes," Brennan bragged confidently. "Especially with being a public employee." Brennan was remarkably facile with computers. He had gone to a technical high school after having been thrown out of regular high school in his freshman year for truancy. At the technical school he'd specialized in computers and electronics. On his own, he'd learned how to pick locks with world-class agility to round out his résumé.

Rebuffed again, Carlo hung back and watched the upstart Brennan go through the revolving door. Carlo sensed he was being upstaged, and he did not like it.

The three men waited in silence while the valet service went for the car. Meanwhile, Louie was planning the details of the kidnapping and was enjoying himself. The previous kidnapping he'd done had been satisfying, and he had been dreaming of doing another someday. It was easy money, although still a challenge. Brennan was already mentally listing the websites he wanted to visit. He was sure he could get things as personal as Laurie's shoe size if he wanted. Carlo was watching Brennan, wondering how he was going to wipe the self-satisfied smile off his face.

When the car finally came, Carlo crowded out Brennan and got behind the wheel. Brennan allowed it to happen, as Carlo was officially higher in the pecking order, and it was, after all, Carlo's vehicle. Brennan settled for shotgun. Louie got into his usual place in one of the middle seats. Once they were under way, he said, "Okay, this is the way we are going to do it."

CHAPTER TWENTY-THREE

MARCH 26, 2010 — FRIDAY, 10:45 a.m.

Ben's phone shocked him with a ring that sounded much louder than usual, causing him to jump.

"Wow!" Michael said, genuinely impressed. "You picked up before the first ring had finished. You must be expecting a seriously important call."

"The phone scared the hell out of me," Ben confessed. "It's been tomb-like around here. I told my assistant not to schedule any meetings for me today, and she didn't. It's delightful."

"No meetings, no phone calls," Michael commented. "I'd be afraid I was dead."

"It's a great way to get some reading done. What's up?"

"I just heard back from Dominick. I'd called and left a message about you wanting the address and phone number where Satoshi's staying. You have a pen and something to write on?"

"Go ahead."

"The address is four seventeen Pleasant Lane, Fort Lee. Sounds charmingly suburban."

"If it's a safe house, it's not going to be charming in the slightest. Although Satoshi never complained, I imagine it's only a little bit north of being unlivable. How about a phone number?"

Writing down the phone number, Ben noticed that it was the same area code as his in Englewood Cliffs.

"Any news on the company you are considering buying?" Michael questioned.

"Nope," Ben said. "Carl is doing his due diligence. I don't think we'll have an answer yes or no for a couple of weeks."

"I'm glad you told me," Michael said. "I misunderstood. I thought it was days, not weeks. I'm going to have to call the prospective investor and tell him to hold his water. He thought it was only days away, as did I."

"How well do you know this dude?"

"I've known him for a long time and have done work with him before. He's an okay guy."

"Would it be fair to say he's in a similar business as the other angels?"

"That's fair to say," Michael answered. "He does well for himself, not in Vinnie Dominick's league but respectable."

After thanking the placement agent, Ben hung up and stared at Satoshi's home address and phone number. Ben wondered if he should call or just stop in on the way home. The address was only a few miles from his own abode, which would make stopping by an easy proposition, but it would also put off his knowing Satoshi was safe and sound.

"Oh, what the hell," Ben said to himself, picking up the phone. Although his paranoia was continuing to make him superstitious such that he now believed he'd be more likely to find someone home if he made the effort to drive, he'd decided to call. If the home was a Mafia safe house for a bunch of Mafia bums, it was going to be dirty and depressing at the very least.

Ben dialed the number, sat back, and smiled to himself. He was acting so juvenile. But after twenty rings and no response, Ben had to admit no one was home. It seemed that a visit was in order even though he was convinced it was going to be as in vain as calling Satoshi's cell. Obviously Satoshi and family were in Washington having a ball while he was stressing himself out.

CHAPTER TWENTY-FOUR

MARCH 26, 2010 – FRIDAY, 10:50 a.m.

When Laurie got involved in a task, she often became oblivious to the world around her. Such was the situation as she worked through the histology slides of the previous day's case. Instead of "John Doe," she'd begun calling the corpse Kenji, given his genealogical resemblance to a medical-school classmate. And giving the man a name seemed to narrow her focus even further.

The typical starting point when reviewing slides was where there was pathology, but in Kenji's case there hadn't been any. Instead, she started with the organ most closely associated with seizures, the brain. Knowing seizures could arise from very small lesions, or even from areas with no lesions at all, Laurie reviewed each slide methodically. Trusting Maureen and her careful supervision of the histology technicians, Laurie was confident she had representative sections from all sections of the brain. Beginning with the frontal cortex, Laurie worked backward into the temporal and parietal lobes. With each slide she'd start with low power, scan the entire slide, then move on to higher power. This took time and attention, so she was surprised when her phone rang, and further surprised it was Vinnie instead of Marvin, and that forty minutes had passed.

"You can come down now," Vinnie said. "The corpse is on the table." He spoke in the same perfunctory, emotionless tone that had irritated her earlier.

"Fine!" Laurie responded without sincerity. She was about to hang up when her curiosity got the better of her. "I was looking forward to Marvin calling. Why the change?"

"Marvin is busy on another case with the deputy chief," Vinnie said. "Besides, Twyla Robinson told me I couldn't leave until I was finished with you."

His response had caught her off guard. When the deputy chief was doing a case, it usually meant something interesting was going on; he rarely did autopsies unless there was a political aspect involved. She was also surprised that Twyla Robinson's name had come up. Twyla Robinson was a petite African-American woman as lithe as a fashion model with high cheekbones and glorious raven hair. As the chief of staff of OCME she was also a woman of steel. Laurie had always been impressed with her ability to run such a tight ship with such a varying mix of personalities.

"Need I ask why Twyla was involved in your helping me repeat an external exam?" Laurie questioned harshly. It was definitely not usual. "And what do you mean by you're leaving?"

"I'm going on leave for a family emergency," Vinnie said, now with some emotion.

"I'm so sorry," Laurie said after a pause. She suddenly felt guilty she'd been selfish in her response to Vinnie's unusual mood.

"Can I ask you to come down quickly? I really need to leave, and Marvin's tied up with an added case after the one he's doing."

"I'll be right down," Laurie said. "Why don't you just leave? I'm only going to repeat the external exam. I really don't need any help. I'll find someone to help me get the corpse on a gurney when I'm done. Really, it's okay—you should just go."

"Really?"

"Really," Laurie said. She was tempted to ask what the family emergency was about, but she didn't. Vinnie hadn't given her an in to ask such a question.

"What about Twyla?"

"Don't worry about her," Laurie said. "I'll talk to her if need be. You go and attend to your family emergency."

"Thanks, doctor," Vinnie said finally.

"You're welcome, Vinnie," Laurie said. For a moment she held the line open, hoping that Vinnie would be more forthcoming, but all she heard was a click. She hung up as well.

Laurie paused with her microscope in front of her, its light source still on. She shook her head. She knew it was human to view the world somewhat selfishly, but she was disappointed in herself for not having given Vinnie a bit of slack rather than immediately taking his behavior personally.

She clicked off her microscope light, leaped to her feet, grabbed a Tyvek coverall suit from the bottom drawer of her file cabinet, pulled it on, and was out the door.

As the aged elevator descended and she watched the numbers reducing, seemingly slower than usual, she banged lightly against the door as if it would speed it up. If she thought she was excited earlier, she was now a quantum leap more excited. The case was suddenly blossoming in unusual complexity, for which she could take credit, credit for persevering even in the face of Jack's attempt to quell her determination. Of course, she was not going to be critical of Jack, as she knew his motivation was her well-being.

Once on the basement level, Laurie ran, not walked, around to the locker room, quickly got herself appropriately attired, and pushed into the pit, which was in full swing.

Pausing just inside the door, she surveyed the scene. All tables were occupied with corpses surrounded by the personnel doing the cases, save for one, which Laurie presumed was her Kenji. Next she picked out Calvin Washington, mostly because of his intimidating size and because there were four people at his table rather than the customary two. The only other person Laurie could pick out from where she was standing was Jack, simply by the way he moved and laughed. Few other people found much to laugh about in the autopsy room, but Jack always seemed to find a way, particularly when he and Vinnie were on a case together.

Rather than going directly to Kenji, Laurie stepped over to Jack's table. He was working on a relatively young man, in his thirties or forties. Laurie could see that one leg was broken with a compound fracture. There was also a severe head wound and abrasions on his chest. It was clearly an accident of some sort.

"Quick, Eddie!" Jack called out, seeing Laurie approach. "Cover up Henry. Here comes my wife."

Laurie, with her gloved hands clasped in front of her like a surgeon maintaining sterility, said, "Hurry, Eddie, before I see anything." Eddie Prince was a relatively new mortuary tech whom she hadn't met before yesterday. "Well, well," Laurie continued. "It looks to me like a severe accident. Would it be appropriate to presume this was a bicyclist who'd had a disagreement with a taxicab?"

"Bus," Jack added.

All Laurie could do was nod. In point of fact, she did not like to joke about the issue. When she and Jack had first met, she'd thought there was something boyishly charming about Jack's insistence on riding his bike back and forth to work, but now, especially with a child, she thought it was selfishly foolish.

"How are things going?" Jack asked. "I see your case from yesterday is back. Is that a clue?"

"Could be," Laurie said, recognizing that Jack had immediately steered the conversation away from the bike-bus issue. Even doing cases like the one he was working on or having knowledge of the statistics, about thirty to forty bicycling deaths per year in New York City, did nothing to discourage Jack's behavior.

"Are we going to have a press conference this afternoon?" Jack inquired.

"It's not going to be that much of a revelation," Laurie said with a chuckle. "Although if it turns out to be what I suspect, I'm going to be pleased with myself, and you and Lou are going to be surprised at the very least."

"Then let's hope it is what you suspect."

Laurie moved on to Kenji. She put the papers that she'd brought from her office down on the writing surface. They were copies of outline drawings of the human body from both dorsal and ventral perspectives, where she could indicate any external findings of note. Then she went to get the only equipment she thought she would need: a scalpel, a digital camera, a handheld dissecting microscope, and a stainless-steel probe, which was nothing more than a thin metal stylus with a slightly nodular end used to probe puncture wounds, such as the tracks of bullets or pellets.

With the body supine, Laurie started with the head and face, poring over the scalp, the ears, the face, even the inside of Kenji's mouth, his ears, and his nose. Having recognized she'd done such a poor job on the external exam the day before, she meant to do an A-plus one today.

Moving on to the upper extremities, Laurie noted every irregularity, including cuts, bruises, moles, hemangiomas, and even calluses. Next were the chest, abdomen, and lower extremities. When she was finished with the ventral surface, she went to find someone to help her turn the corpse over. Jack had finished his case, and Eddie was available. He was happy to give Laurie a hand.

Laurie repeated herself on the dorsal surface. As she worked down the back, her pulse quickened. If there were to be a suspicious break in the skin, she assumed she would find it somewhere on the buttocks or the back or side of the legs. Just because she hadn't seen anything suspicious with her initial overall glance, Laurie maintained her careful, methodical scrutiny, and her systematic approach paid off. Within the gluteal fold where the buttocks join the leg, Laurie felt she'd found what she was looking for: a possible tiny puncture wound. It was a circular reddened area that required flattening the skin to truly appreciate. She took a digital photograph of the area, showing the puncture.

With the stylus in her right hand, Laurie flattened the skin with her left. Gently she applied the smaller end of the stylus to the reddened patch of skin, and with a slight pressure the nodular end popped inside. It was definitely a puncture wound.

Pressing a little harder but not so much as to create

an artifact, Laurie advanced the nodular end of the stylus until it hit the end of the track. Laurie took another photograph of the stylus in the track. Then, placing her fingers around the stylus where it disappeared into the skin, she drew it out and measured. The track was two and a half centimeters deep.

Laurie disposed of her gloves and left the autopsy room. Using the case's accession number, she found the X-rays, brought them back into the pit, and snapped them up onto the view box. Carefully she scanned the area in question on both the frontal and lateral views, in hopes of seeing a possible pellet of some sort, but there was nothing. That meant that either a pellet was used that was capable of being dissolved by the body or whatever toxin was used was injected directly. Either way, Laurie assumed the greatest concentration of the poisonous agent had to be at the end of the track.

Returning to Kenji with a new pair of gloves, Laurie picked up the scalpel and fell to work. What she wanted was the track itself, encased in a core of muscle tissue about the size of a wine cork. It sounded easy enough, but Laurie struggled. With the tissue being easily compressible, it was difficult to avoid cutting into the track. She wanted the sample to be en bloc. The hand-held dissecting microscope was a help, but it precluded the use of her left hand, and in the end, she didn't use it.

As Laurie worked with the scalpel, and having now ascertained that Kenji had been murdered, presumably with an umbrella air gun, her thoughts naturally drifted back to what agent might have been involved. She already knew it could not be ricin, as was used in the infamous Bulgarian's case. Although she did not know the specific poison, she did know some things about it. It had to be extraordinarily toxic, as the security tapes indicated. According to what she saw on the tapes, the poison had been almost instantly effectual. She also knew it had to be neurotoxic, because of the seizure, as a number of snake and fish venoms were. She eventually decided to go on the Net and check out seizure-inducing reptilian and aquatic neurotoxins.

Laurie struggled for almost half an hour, but the final sample approximately an inch and a half long and an inch thick looked very close to what she'd envisioned.

Laurie removed her gloves yet again and went into the supply room for a sample bottle and a sample custody tag. Back at the autopsy table, she put the sample in the bottle and completed the tag, which included the case's accession number, the date, and the location from the body where the sample had originated, and then signed it. She was being exquisitely careful: If there was to be a trial concerning the case, which she now considered a distinct possibility, the sample she was holding would be a key piece of evidence.

With her last chore finished, Laurie went looking for an available mortuary tech to lend a hand. With practiced ease she and the tech got Kenji off the autopsy table and onto a gurney. Wheeling the corpse herself out of the autopsy room, Laurie deposited him and his gurney back in the cooler, where the corpse would stay for the next several months, unless he was lucky enough to be identified and shipped off to his next of kin. "I know you're trying to tell me some things, Kenji," Laurie said out loud in the heavy stillness of the cooler, "and I'm trying to listen. We already have the person who killed you, but unfortunately we don't yet know who you both are. Be patient!" She stepped out of the cooler and closed its heavy insulated door, causing it to emit a final-sounding reverberant click.

Laurie had planned to take the sample directly up to toxicology on the fifth floor, but a glance at her watch changed her mind. She was aware that John DeVries was one of the most compulsive people she knew, and one of the ways he manifested his compulsiveness was to stop whatever he was doing at exactly noon, and take his old-fashioned lunch box with a thermos mounted in its vaulted top to OCME's sad excuse of a lunchroom on the second floor. The room was windowless, with cement-block walls. All that was in the room were a bank of vending machines filled with unhealthy food, plastic-topped tubular steel tables, and plastic chairs. Although Laurie could have stopped to say hello, she was reluctant to interrupt his lunch. It was also true that the room depressed her. Instead she went directly up to her office so as not to waste time. As punctual as John was about getting to the lunchroom at noon, he was just as punctual about returning to work at twelve-thirty, and Laurie planned to take the sample to him then.

CHAPTER TWENTY-FIVE

Louie was in seventh heaven. He'd not had such fun for a good decade. From the moment Brennan had suggested they kidnap Laurie Montgomery's kid to the moment he'd just slid into his favorite booth of his restaurant, he'd been totally engrossed in planning the operation. The kidnapping idea had been pure genius, and Louie gave Brennan full credit. First, it was a great way to kick the woman in the teeth for having been instrumental in putting Paulie in the slammer for more than a decade. Louie hadn't heard that story and had been surprised by it. He'd also been surprised by Paulie's prohibition of killing the woman. But in many respects, this was going to be better in that she'd suffer more. In Louie's mind, when a person got killed, they didn't suffer at all.

Second and foremost, the kidnapping would surely take the pesky woman's attention away from investigating Satoshi, which would be to everybody's relief.

And third, it could result in serious pocket change. Louie's last kidnapping, more than fifteen years ago, had netted for the Vaccarro group more than ten million dollars, making Louie eager to try another go-round. Unfortunately, Paulie wasn't of the same mind, and despite the success, nixed another. In Paulie's estimation, from hearing some horror stories, kidnappings were just too dangerous despite the potentially big payoff.

Louie shook his head and laughed. There was a certain irony about the fact that he was now about to mount his second kidnapping, partially based on retribution for Paulie, who had kept him from doing a repeat years earlier. This time he knew it wouldn't bring in quite the same money. The first one had been a Wall Street type whose net worth hovered around a hundred million. This time, the principals were a couple of salaried doctors, and he knew he couldn't count on more than a million or so, but worrying about that was premature and even secondary. The reason for taking the kid was to get Laurie Stapleton out of the picture.

"Hey, Benito!" Louie yelled at the top of his lungs, causing his own ears to ring. No one had come out of the kitchen, and Louie didn't know how long he had for lunch, since he was counting on getting a call any minute from Brennan. At that moment Brennan, Carlo, and two younger guys who had been working for Louie for close to four years, Duane Mackenzie and Tommaso Deluca, along with Hisayuki Ishii's two lieutenants, were sitting in a stolen white Dodge van outside Dr. Laurie Montgomery-Stapleton's house on 106th, waiting for their victim to appear.

Over the previous hour Brennan had more than fulfilled his promise to glean information about Laurie from the Net. Carlo had made himself useful by obtaining the stolen vehicle, which they planned to dump. All was ready for the snatch.

In response to Louie's sudden yell, which had rattled some of the glasses hanging over the bar, Benito came crashing out of the swinging door leading into the kitchen. He was full of apology, explaining that he'd heard nothing of Louie's arrival, as he usually did.

"I had no idea you were here, boss. Believe me!"

Louie reached out and gently laid fingers on Benito's forearm. He was, after all, in a gracious mood the way everything was going. "It's okay," he said, trying to calm the overexcited man. "It's okay," he repeated, before asking what was for lunch.

"Your favorite!" Benito said with alacrity, glad to have something on hand to make amends. "Penne Bolognese with fresh ground Parmesan."

Louie watched Benito retreat into the kitchen. Still thinking about the upcoming kidnapping, he'd come up with yet another one of its benefits. With Hisayuki's acquiescence and participation, he felt more certain that the *oyabun* would have no reason to suspect that Louie had any complicity in the disappearance and murder of Susumu and Yoshiaki.

Suddenly the phone at Louie's elbow jangled. Louie grabbed it as his heart skipped a beat. It was Brennan, as he expected.

CHAPTER TWENTY-SIX

There's a young woman coming out of the doctor's house right this second," Brennan blurted, sounding frantic. "She's carrying a kid in one hand and a stroller in the other. Do you think it's the kid we want or what?"

Louie felt his confidence falter. "Calm down!" he ordered sharply. All the talk he'd had with Brennan over the last hour about remaining calm and detached had apparently gone out the window. Louie had expected more from Brennan. Brennan obviously had allowed himself to get so wound up, he was not thinking clearly.

"How the hell are we going to be sure it's the right kid?" Brennan whined with a touch of desperation.

"You'll never be completely sure," Louie said, "but you can be pretty darn close to being sure. As a starter, do mother and child look alike?"

"No, the kid's white and the nanny's black."

"Well, I'd say that's pretty definitive."

"She's stuffing the kid into the stroller. She acts a little like she's impatient. You know what I'm saying? And the kid is bawling."

"That's not our worry. Now, is she ready to leave?"

"I'd say so," Brennan said. "Yes, they are! They're pushing off, heading for the park, just like you'd hoped."

"Sounds like it is going to be almost too easy," Louie said. Before he'd left them in front of Laurie's building, Louie had expressed the hope that the nanny would take

JJ to Central Park, as that section of the park was never as crowded as it was to the south, and usually rather deserted. Also, there were forested hills, which would provide near-perfect locations for a snatch.

With his hand motioning for Carlo to follow the stroller toward Central Park West, Brennan continued the phone conversation with Louie as if he wanted Louie to stay on the line and make all the decisions. But Louie, whether he sensed Brennan's intention or not, said, "Okay, you're on your own, and good luck. And also remember what I said earlier. Don't do anything silly. Use your head. Don't take any risks. There's no need, as there is always tomorrow, even if we lose some of the benefits of doing the kidnapping. You hear what I'm saying?"

"I hear you," Brennan assured.

"Let me hear from you when you have the child," Louie said before disconnecting.

Brennan flipped his phone shut and slipped it into his jacket pocket. "Don't get too close to make it look like we're following!" he said to Carlo, who was driving.

"I know what I'm freaking doing," Carlo snapped back. He wasn't happy at having to take orders from Brennan, especially with other people in the van. It had been a sudden, psychologically painful reversal of the status quo.

"Slow down and stop!" Brennan ordered, oblivious to Carlo's wounded ego. Ahead, the nanny was held up at the corner, waiting for the light to change on Central Park West. Just across the street, the park's pedestrian entrance was bounded by walls of dark-red sandstone blocks. There were a few buds on the otherwise leafless trees. There was also some yellow forsythia in bloom.

The van waited thirty yards from the corner for the

light to change. Carlo was drumming his fingers on the steering wheel. In the middle seats were Chong Yong and Riki Watanabe. Although they could speak passing English, they remained silent. In the far backseats sat Duane Mackenzie and Tommaso Deluca. They, too, were silent, intimidated by the two massively muscled men sitting in front of them.

"All right," Brennan said. "Let's review the plan now that we know for certain the woman and the kid are going into the park. Everyone except for Carlo will get out at the corner and follow them in, but not as a group. I'll go ahead, and you people string out behind me like we're all on our own. And make sure you've got your masks."

Brennan twisted in his seat so as to look at the people in the back as he talked. "It will be up to me to decide if it is a go or not, understand? I mean, the snatch might happen as soon as we're in the park, or later, or not at all, depending on what the nanny does. Worst case, she might be meeting up with someone. If that happens, we'll delay. Meanwhile, Carlo will be in the van nearby with the motor running. Once we have the kid, I want all of us to get into the van and get the hell out of here. Any questions?"

"What are we to do?" Riki asked.

"Good question," Brennan said without sarcasm after a slight pause. It had been Louie who'd ordered who was going to participate. Brennan had had the same question but chose not to ask Louie, fearing Louie might not think him capable of being in charge if the answer was obvious. "You're to be there in case something unexpected happens and we need more people," Brennan said, at least making a stab at an answer.

"The light is changing," Carlo called out.

Brennan turned back to face forward. "All right," he said commandingly. "Let's do it!" He leaped from the car, impatient to get the operation under way. As he watched the attractive black woman hustle into the park, he felt this was his opportunity to prove himself to Louie.

CHAPTER TWENTY-SEVEN

When Laurie got back to her office with the wine cork–sized en bloc tissue sample, she put it on her desk in full view so as not to delay getting it to John. Meanwhile, she fell back to examining the toxicology slides. Although she was now confident that Kenji had been murdered with a toxic agent, she still felt obliged to make sure there was no pathology in the brain to explain the seizure. After all, whatever toxin had killed him could also have been responsible for stimulating an existing pathological lesion, rather than causing the seizure inherently. It wasn't a serious issue, but it might influence her search for the toxin if she did find something. Besides, she wanted to be both complete and accurate for what she thought was going to be a triumphal presentation to Lou and Jack, and anyone else who might like to listen.

While she methodically searched the slides, she was able to multitask by trying to come up with what the specific toxin might have been. She assumed it was a neurotoxin, as she'd decided earlier, of which there were many different kinds in snakes, scorpions, aquatic mollusks, and even certain fish. With that thought in mind, she turned away from the brain slides temporarily to go online to review neurotoxins. Because she'd come to assume her two cases were people of Japanese ancestry, the one toxin that jumped into her mind was tetrodotoxin, possibly the most infamous toxin in Japan, since it was associated with multiple episodes of illnesses and deaths in unlucky sushi and sashimi lovers. The toxin came from bacteria associated with a number of creatures, including a particular puffer fish whose flesh was considered a delicacy in Japan. The problem was that the flesh could contain tetrodotoxin at particular times of the year, whereas it is usually confined to the fish's viscera, such as its liver and skin.

Laurie focused her search on tetrodotoxin, with the idea of seeing if it could cause convulsions when administered parenterally, meaning by injection. As she skimmed several of the articles, refreshing her general knowledge of tetrodotoxin, she recalled that it was a useful compound and was used rather extensively in medical research and even in clinical medicine. In clinical medicine it was used to treat cardiac arrhythmia and also as a pain reliever in extreme situations, such as in cases of terminal cancer and debilitating migraines. She thought this was an important issue in that it meant the drug was commercially manufactured, hence readily available. There were many other neurotoxins that were quite exotic and extremely difficult to obtain.

"Yes!" Laurie suddenly said, and snapped her fingers as she read that tetrodotoxin could, when injected, cause convulsions, which wasn't the case with the other classes of neurotoxins. Continuing on in the same article, she also was reminded of tetrodotoxin's impressive toxicity: Two hundred-thousandths of an ounce could kill a one-hundred-and-seventy-pound person. Laurie whistled at such a figure, realizing tetrodotoxin was one hundred times more poisonous than potassium cyanide.

While marveling over tetrodotoxin's lethality, Laurie's eyes wandered over to the institutional clock hanging on the wall over her file cabinet. It was nearly one p.m. Knowing John DeVries would surely be back to toxicology, she grabbed the sample bottle and headed to the elevator.

When Laurie walked into John's bright, spacious windowed corner office, which contrasted so sharply from his previous windowless cubbyhole, she could certainly understand how it could improve one's mood. John was just donning a fresh white lab coat as she appeared at the door. His secretary had yet to return from her lunch.

For a moment Laurie just stood there, transfixed by the man's metamorphosis. He was still tall and thin but no longer gaunt, and his former academic pallor had been replaced with a brush of color across his cheeks, making him look ten years younger.

"Ah, Miss Laurie," he said, catching sight of her. "I'm afraid there's been no change from this morning: no toxins or poisons or drugs."

"Did you run another sample?"

"Well, no," John admitted. "Not yet. We've been busy with a number of overdoses from last night."

"Well, I have some news that I'll clue you in on," Laurie said, dropping her voice in a playful fashion. "But you're not to tell anyone else until I have my mini–press conference later this afternoon."

"I promise," John said.

Laurie went on to tell John about her discovery from the security tapes that her case represented a robbery and that she had reason to believe he'd been murdered in the process with a toxin delivered with some sort of air gun. As she expected, John was immediately intrigued.

"You got all this from security tapes?" he asked. He was impressed.

"I did," Laurie said. "With a dollop of inference. By the way, do you recall a famous assassination that happened in London involving a Bulgarian diplomat? He was killed by a toxin that was shot into him by a pellet gun hidden in an umbrella."

"Absolutely," John said. "It was ricin. Are you suspecting your case was a copycat?"

Laurie nodded. She was impressed not only that John remembered the case but that he'd also remembered the specific agent involved. "I believe it was a copycat, to a degree."

"Are you then suggesting we should be looking for ricin?"

"No, I don't think ricin was involved, because the victim convulsed, and ricin does not cause seizures. But from watching security tapes, I know one of two perpetrators was carrying an umbrella. Because the subway station was so crowded, I wasn't able to actually see the umbrella used, but after the attack, when the victim was lying on the concrete, one of the attackers appeared to partially open the umbrella and cock it to get it to fully close. My sense is that the umbrella was some kind of air gun like the one involved in the case in London."

"What about an entrance wound?"

"Good question," Laurie commended. "I found one today when I redid the external exam. I'm embarrassed to tell you why I didn't find it yesterday. There's a small entrance wound on the back of the victim's leg at the juncture of the leg and the gluteal mass." Laurie held up her sample. "And this is an en bloc excision of the track, which seemed to be about an inch long."

"Perfect," John responded. He reached out for the bottle, held it up, and glanced in at its contents. "If the agent was not ricin, do you have any idea at all what it could have been?"

"Actually, I do," Laurie said. "I think it might have been tetrodotoxin."

John stopped looking in at the tissue sample and switched his attention to Laurie. "Do you have any specific reason to suspect tetrodotoxin?"

"First, I think whatever was used would have had to have been a neurotoxin," Laurie said. "Whatever it was, it definitely caused a convulsion. It was a short convulsion but a real one, both because it was seen by the nine-one-one caller and because I saw it on the security tape. Tetrodotoxin is known to be able to cause seizures when it is injected internally. This afternoon when I looked into neurotoxins, I didn't notice any others associated with convulsions. Second of all, the stuff is manufactured on a regular basis, so it's available. And third of all, and this is the least scientific, but I believe my patient is Japanese, and Japanese have a long history with the toxin, thanks to puffer fish."

"Sounds promising," John agreed with a laugh. "All except the last part."

"Now for the ninety-nine-dollar question," Laurie said. "When can we run it?"

"Why am I not surprised," John said, humorously throwing up his hands in mock despair. "I suppose you want it ASAP, like tomorrow, as if you are the only ME in this organization and we are sitting around up here, twiddling our fingers."

"I'd love to have it today," Laurie said with a smile. "It would be my coup de grace for this afternoon revelation."

John threw back his head and laughed. "I suppose I never can please you. You're always in such a hurry. But tell me, you used the pronoun 'we' when you asked when it could be run. Was that a literal *we* or a figurative *we*?"

"Literal," Laurie said without hesitation. "I was pretty handy around the lab in college and in biochem in medical school. If one of your techs or yourself could throw me some hints now and then, I believe I could muddle through it. As soon as I finish the rest of the case's histology slides, I have a free afternoon."

John regarded Laurie for a beat, wondering if it was a good idea to let an amateur loose in his lab or a recipe for disaster. In favor of allowing her to work there for the afternoon was that he liked her and respected her enthusiasm and dedication, and the fact that she had always appreciated his work and had frequently told him so.

"Have you ever used an HPLC/MS/MS, otherwise known as a high-performance liquid chromatography with tandem mass spectrometry unit, before?"

"I have," Laurie said. "During my residency training I spent some time in the lab as an elective."

"Also, we'll need some actual tetrodotoxin, which I don't have here, but they'll have next door at New York Hospital."

"I'll be happy to run next door to get it."

"All right, why not?" John said with sudden resolve. "I tell you what we'll do. I'll have one of my techs start by using a sonicator to turn some of this tissue sample into organic slurry. When you come back, I'll let you do the extraction with either n-butanol or acetic acid. I'm not sure which, but I'll decide by the time you get back. Sound okay?"

"Sounds perfect," Laurie said, flashing John a thumbs-up sign before spinning on her heels to head back to her office. She now had true motivation to finish up with the histology slides.

CHAPTER TWENTY-EIGHT

Ben Corey flipped closed the last journal from the stack on his desk and tossed it onto the pile that had been building on the floor next to him. It was the first time he'd had an opportunity to finish skimming all the current journals since he had started iPS USA, and it gave him a comforting sense of being under control, the exact opposite of what Satoshi's failure to check in was affording.

Taking out a Post-it note, he wrote "recycle" in large capital letters and stuck the note on the journal he'd just finished perusing. Then he stretched with his arms over his head, noticing it was getting close to one p.m. For a moment he toyed with the idea of asking Jacqueline to join him for lunch. They'd been lunching fairly regularly over the last month, and he wondered if it was time to take their relationship to the next level. From his perspective, he thought she'd been making some overtures in that regard, which he'd come to believe he ought to take advantage of, as his relationship with his relatively new wife, Stephanie, had taken a serious hit after the birth of their toddler, Jonathan. As hard as Ben had been working to get iPS USA off the ground, he felt he deserved some pleasurable diversion, which he wasn't getting at home.

"I'm going to be heading out now," Jacqueline said, standing in the open connecting doorway.

"Oh?" Ben questioned. Jacqueline had taken him completely by surprise.

"When you requested no meetings for today, I thought it would be a good day for me to take my mother for her annual checkup. Do you need anything before I go?"

Ben swallowed a laugh and said, "No, I'm fine. Take your mother to the doctor. I'll just sit here and pine away."

Jacqueline did a double take at the comment. Momentarily at a loss for words, she merely stared.

"The place has been so quiet," Ben explained. "Actually, I'll be leaving in a few minutes myself."

"Okay, fine," Jacqueline said quickly, willing to accept Ben's explanation even though it wasn't an explanation. "See you Monday."

"See you Monday," Ben echoed.

After Jacqueline had left, Ben sat at his desk for a few moments, wondering how much Jacqueline's attractiveness had influenced his decision to hire her, above and beyond her intelligence and superb résumé. With Stephanie it had been her body and her willingness to use it that had been key.

On his way out Ben stopped into Carl's office, where Carl revealed that iPS Rapid had sent him a flurry of e-mails that morning. "They seem to be very interested in an outright sale," the CFO said. "I don't know whether to be encouraged or to be more circumspect."

"I'm sure you'll figure it out," Ben said, confident in Carl's professional skills. "I'm heading home. Maybe you should do the same. Jacqueline has already left."

"I've too much to do. See you Monday."

Emerging into the sun on busy Fifth Avenue, Ben

enjoyed a mild surge of euphoria, having already adjusted to the disappointment concerning Jacqueline's unavailability. The weather was beautiful, with a strong smell of spring in the air. Things couldn't be better at iPS USA, save for Satoshi not calling, but in the face of the blue sky and sunshine, he was even optimistic about that. He liked the fact that the weekend had arrived. And last of all, he had the sense that he'd at least broken the ice with Jacqueline with his clever comment about pining away when she left.

With an enjoyable springiness to his step, he headed toward the garage but then stopped at 57th Street. Luckily, he remembered then and not later that he'd forgotten Satoshi's address. He could recall the street easily enough, but he couldn't remember the number. Happily, he went back up to his desk to get it.

Because of the upcoming weekend, other people were leaving early as well, and Ben had to wait at the garage for longer than he liked. But it wasn't all bad, and being in a good mood, he had the opportunity to flirt with several secretaries while he waited for his Range Rover to be brought up from the garage's depths. As a monthly customer, he did get some benefit in terms of getting his car sooner than day renters.

Once inside his car with the door closed, Ben promptly entered 417 Pleasant Lane in his GPS before turning on his CD player. Insulated from the noise of the city, he selected a Mozart CD and allowed himself to be surrounded by pure audio pleasure.

Traffic moved steadily uptown. As usual, he took the upper level of the George Washington Bridge to give him a stupendous unobstructed view of the sheer Palisade cliffs running along the New Jersey side of the river, accompanied by Mozart's piano concerto number twenty-one in C major.

On reaching the New Jersey side, Ben took the second exit as the GPS advised. The directions took him to a small run-down area with a number of abandoned two-story commercial brick buildings, reminding him of a fact that few people knew: Fort Lee had been the Hollywood of the country before Hollywood, California, took center stage in the movie business. Pleasant Lane turned out to be anything but. It was a relatively short three-block street. Interspersed between the abandoned commercial buildings were small cottage houses, all of approximately the same design. Most appeared to be also abandoned, with broken windows and front doors ajar. There was debris everywhere, including a few tireless, rusted vehicles resting on their axles and a number of mattresses with their coil springs poking up through the ticking.

"You have arrived," the GPS said in a pleasant baritone as Ben pulled over to the curb. "I certainly have arrived," Ben said mockingly. He studied the house. It looked slightly better than its neighbors in that the windows were intact and the front door was closed. What bothered Ben was that there was no indication whatsoever that the house was occupied. Then he noticed something else that was even more disturbing. Although the front door was closed, a central pane of glass was broken out, with just a few shards clinging desperately to the window's frame.

Certain that no one could be living in the house and beginning to wonder if he'd been deliberately sent to the wrong address as some kind of bizarre joke, Ben opened his driver's-side door and started to slide out of

his car. But he didn't get far. Blanketing the area was
the stink of putrefaction, strong enough for Ben to gag
before he managed to get back in the car and slam the
door. Even in the confines of the car he gagged a few
more times as if he was going to vomit.

Recovering to a degree, Ben looked at the house in
horror, frantically trying to envision what had happened
and what he should do. The house and the surrounding
area smelled overwhelmingly of death, a stench Ben had
rarely smelled, and only as a boy coming up on a dead
animal, such as a rabbit or a squirrel in the woods. But
Ben knew this was no rabbit or squirrel.

Ben grabbed a rag from the car and held it against
his nose. Preparing himself for the smell, he got out of
his SUV and started up the front walk.

Although he gagged several more times, he made it
to the front steps. He knew he should call 911, but he
wanted to make absolutely certain what he smelled was
not a dog or some other kind of large animal. Stepping
up on the porch, Ben could see shards of glass pepper-
ing the ground. To avoid leaving fingerprints, he used
the rag he had been holding against his nose to open
the door. It was unlocked.

He stepped from bright sunlight into relative darkness. He didn't have to go far. There in the living room
were the bloated remains of six people, all lying prone
with their hands on the back of their heads and their
faces resting in dried pools of blackened congealed
blood.

Ben nearly fainted at the sight and the markedly more
intense smell of death. He looked quickly at each corpse
to find Satoshi, only to be surprised when he realized
the scientist was not among the six. He knew he should

get out of the house, as the smell was truly overpowering, but the circumstances had him paralyzed. He told himself to move, but his body refused, leaving him frozen in time and space and utter silence. For a moment he didn't even breathe and in that instant he heard it. It was a high-pitched, soft keening. Unsure if it was a real sound or if it was a lamentation emanating from his own brain, Ben listened again. It was still there—and then it was gone.

"What the hell?" Ben questioned. He was still unsure if the sound had been real or imagined. Fighting an urge to flee the scene, Ben stepped over toward the staircase. At the base he stopped and stared up into the murkiness of the second floor. He was about to declare the disturbing sound a figment of his imagination when he heard it again. This time it sounded as if it was coming from the second floor.

With the hackles on the back of his neck standing straight up, Ben climbed the stairs, keeping his rag pressed against his nose and breathing through his mouth. By the time he got to the top, the sound had again disappeared. Ben stopped. There were two dormered bedrooms connected by a short hallway, with a small bathroom off the hallway. He could see that in each bedroom the bureaus had been searched, as the drawers were open and the contents strewn across the floors.

Ben checked both bedrooms. Each had a small closet whose contents were also pulled out and thrown onto the floor. The first bedroom had a small drop-down desk. Its contents and drawers were on the floor as well. It was apparent to Ben that someone had trashed the house, most likely searching for something. At that point

Ben heard the sound again, louder than it had been downstairs. At first it seemed to be coming from the bathroom, but when he checked it, he sensed that it was coming from a built-in bookcase directly across from the bathroom doorway. It was there in the hall that the sound was the loudest. Ben put his ear against the wall above the bookcase. To his surprise, the sound was the loudest, as if there might be a hidden room or closet occupying the equivalent space of the bathroom across the hall.

Ben quickly went back into each bedroom in turn. Each closet poked into the potential space, but there was no way in. Returning to the hallway, Ben grabbed the built-in bookcase and pulled. To his surprise, it slid out and the keening stopped. Now a new smell wafted out to join the stink of putrefaction. It was the smell of human waste. Suddenly, Ben remembered Shigeru, and that he was not among the victims down in the living room.

Ducking down, Ben entered a tiny room as black as pitch. Almost immediately he recoiled from something soft brushing his face. He swung his arm in front of him and grasped a string, tugging on a bare lightbulb.

Looking down, Ben found himself staring into Shigeru's pale, pleading face, his pupils the size of quarters.

"My God!" Ben said. "You poor, poor kid." Ben bent down to hoist the child into his arms but then changed his mind. Instead, he ducked back out of the hidden room to get a blanket. He could hear Shigeru immediately start his high-pitched crying again. "I'm coming," Ben yelled. Grabbing a blanket, Ben rushed back into the hidden room. Immediately, Shigeru stopped his unique wailing. The child was terrified to be left alone.

"Okay, big guy," Ben said, wrapping the flaccid child in the blanket. As he did so he noticed an empty baby bottle next to him. After he lifted Shigeru he glanced around the small, windowless room that had probably saved the child's life. If the house was a safe house, the room was probably used to hide drugs or weapons or both. In his mind's eye he could see Yunie-chan, Satoshi's wife, expecting the worst, desperately hiding the child.

Ducking out of the room again, Ben didn't bother with the light or the bookcase but rather tried to hold the child in one arm and the rag over his nose with the other. He carried the child downstairs into the kitchen to get him some water, knowing the child had to be seriously dehydrated. He also wanted to see if there were any more bodies, including that of Satoshi.

Holding Shigeru in one hand and the water in the other, he raced out of the front door and to his car, where he deposited Shigeru on the front passenger seat. Then he climbed in himself with the water. Aware the child desperately needed IV fluids, Ben let him have some water by mouth. Once he'd done that, he propped Shigeru on the passenger seat and dialed 911. He made sure the child was covered except his head, because he stank to high heaven.

CHAPTER TWENTY-NINE

Brennan had figured out at least one reason why Louie had sent six people instead of two, which he had assumed would have been adequate. The moment he and his four-man crew had entered Central Park, the nanny and the child had seemingly disappeared. What Brennan had not noticed in his excitement when he'd first seen the pair come out of the house was that the nanny was wearing running shoes.

Assuming that the nanny and her charge were just out of sight down the serpentine footpath, Brennan had insisted that everyone run, hoping to catch up to the pair. But Brennan and the others were seriously out of shape, and the footpath was surprisingly hilly. After only a little more than a hundred yards, Brennan and the others had stopped running. With his chest heaving and his hands resting on his knees, he managed to say, "This is not going to work. She must be a goddamn marathoner."

"All right, here's what we are going to do," Brennan continued, once he'd caught his breath. "We're going to split up to search for the nanny and the kid and stay connected by our cell phones."

"Most runners in the park run around the reservoir," Duane Mackenzie offered. "Why don't me and Tommaso head over there. It's east of here and a little south, if I remember correctly."

"Sounds like a plan," Brennan said. They quickly exchanged cell phone numbers. "You guys stay with me," Brennan said to the two Japanese men. "We don't want you getting lost in here. We'll head directly south."

The group started off together, with Duane and Tommaso looking for a pathway to branch off to the west.

As he walked, Brennan wasn't happy. He had never appreciated the park's size and its hilly topography, and had not imagined that they would lose the nanny and the kid so damn fast. He wondered what the hell he was going to say to Louie, especially with this being his first time in charge of an operation. As the group progressed, he began to believe they'd probably have to return to where the nanny and the kid had entered the park and just wait for them to return. The worry with that plan was whether they would be alone.

Then serendipity shined down on them. Off to the right they came across a playground with tire swings, a couple of tree houses, monkey bars, a brick pyramid, and a large sand area where the child had been deposited. The nanny was using the monkey bars to stretch her hamstrings.

"Bull's eye!" Brennan said to himself. Taking out his cell phone, he called Carlo.

"We've found the nanny and the kid," he said softly. "They are at the West One hundredth Street Playground. How about you drive down here, but I want you on the northbound side of the street. Just pull over to the curb and wait! Got that?"

"Of course I got that," Carlo responded without enthusiasm. He disconnected abruptly.

Brennan flipped his own phone closed. As wired as

he was, Carlo's acting out wasn't completely over his head. Brennan intently looked at the others with a devilish grin. "This is almost too good to be true. The playground is empty except for our target. How good is that?"

"How do we know for sure it's the kid we want?" Duane asked innocently, reawakening Brennan's major worry.

"We saw them come out of the house, didn't we?"

"Yeah, but what if there are apartments in the building? Or what if this lady was visiting whoever takes care of the doctor's kid? I mean, we could be making a lot of effort here and end up with the wrong kid. Shouldn't we make sure somehow?"

Brennan took a deep breath and looked back at the woman.

"Why not just ask her?" Duane suggested.

"Ask her what?"

"If the kid is whatever his parents' name is."

"She's not going to give me that information," Brennan said snidely.

"I bet you she will with this," Duane said as he pulled out a distressed leather wallet and flipped it open. Attached to one side was a shiny gold police badge. It said Montclair, New Jersey.

Taking the proffered badge, Brennan examined it. "Where did you get this?"

"On eBay. Ten bucks."

"Is it real?"

Duane shrugged. "They said it was real, but who knows. The point is that it looks real and it works. All you do is flash it like they do on TV. I've had fun with it. Everybody thinks I'm an undercover cop."

"Why not?" Brennan said at once. From his perspective, it was the one major concern that had been nagging him since the nanny and child had emerged from 494 106th Street.

"There's our ride," Tommaso said, pointing over to Central Park West. Carlo was just pulling up to the curb.

Holding the questionable police badge in his left hand, Brennan speed-dialed Carlo while watching the vehicle come to a halt. The call was answered immediately. "Are we clear?" he asked before Carlo had a chance to speak.

"No cops," Carlo said.

"We're on our way." Brennan hung up. He licked his dry lips, repositioned his holster so it was more comfortable, and switched the police badge to his right hand. Squaring his shoulders, he began walking toward the playground.

"You'd better be quick," someone said from behind. "Here comes a woman with a toddler."

Brennan quickly twisted to look. It had been Duane who'd sounded the alarm. Looking in the direction Duane was pointing off to the south, Brennan could see a woman had just rounded the bend in the footpath about a hundred yards away, pushing an empty stroller. The toddler was staggering along out in front by about ten feet.

Glancing back at the nanny, who was now no more than twenty or so feet ahead, Brennan made the snap decision to go ahead with the snatch. JJ was now off to Brennan's left, lying prone in the sand and making a kind of sand angel but in reality just kicking up a bunch of dust.

"Excuse me, ma'am," Brennan said, flashing open the

police badge and walking directly up to Leticia, who was still stretching. "Is this child from the Montgomery-Stapleton household?"

"Yes, he is," Leticia said, but as soon as the words left her mouth, her face clouded in sudden fear. Intuitively, she knew she should not have answered the stranger, especially when the badge disappeared and a gun came out in its place. Brennan had realized in the last seconds he'd forgotten his mask.

CHAPTER THIRTY

Laurie was having the time of her life, totally engrossed in her case. She'd finished with all of Kenji's histology slides, and as with the autopsy, she'd found nothing pathological. The man had been remarkably healthy, and had he not come up against tetrodotoxin or some other equivalent toxin, he'd probably have lived to be a hundred.

After finishing the histology slides, she had called both Jack and Lou about her proposed news conference. Jack was all for it and said he would be in Laurie's office at five sharp. Lou was the fly in the ointment, saying he wanted to be there but might be detained because there had been a double homicide in the Wall Street area of a couple of brokers who had not lived up to a customer's expectations. The last thing he'd said was that he would try his damnedest to be there.

With everything out of the way regarding her two cases, Laurie went back to the fifth floor, where John was waiting for her. He surprised her by saying he had taken the time to make another close inspection of the results of the toxicology screen on the plasma and urine of Laurie's case. "I got out some of our library matches for a number of neurotoxins, including tetrodotoxin, and compared them to your case."

"And?" Laurie questioned.

"It was interesting," John admitted. "There are some

little bumps where there would be peaks if tetrodotoxin were present."

"Are you suggesting tetrodotoxin is there, just not in sufficient concentration?"

"No, I'm not saying that. What I'm saying is that I cannot rule it in, but I can't rule it out, either. It's a subtle difference. Now I'm as curious as you are about what we'll find in the supposed pellet track. What about a pellet? Did you find anything like that, even a piece?"

"Nothing," Laurie said. "I probed around in the track's depths carefully. I also searched the X-rays. My guess is that the pellet could have been somehow digestible, such that once it was exposed to interstitial fluid, it slowly was digested. Well, it couldn't be that slowly, since it was gone when I went looking for an entrance wound around forty or so hours after the man's death."

"Certainly a subtle but effective way to kill someone. I have to give the perpetrators some credit. Unless the entrance wound is noticed, it will seem like a natural death."

"Which is exactly what happened in this case."

"Okay, let's get you set up in the lab," John said, getting up from his desk. "I've arranged some bench space for you upstairs on the sixth floor. It's actually in the same room with the liquid chromatography/mass spec/mass spec machines."

"Sounds delightful," Laurie said, following John into the stairwell and up to the sixth floor.

"I've also asked one of my techs, Teresa Chen, to be available for your questions. She's my in-house expert with the LC/MS/MS," he said as they headed into the lab.

It was a typical modern biological lab filled with

several large machines that automatically handled multiple specimens and needed very little attention once they were set up and running. The sound in the room was a general hum interspersed with mechanical clicking noises as individual specimens advanced on conveyors.

There was only one person in the lab tending the multiple machines. Teresa Chen's shiny dark hair was parted in the middle. She smiled graciously at Laurie and offered her hand when they were introduced.

"So here's your bench area," John said, indicating a stretch of countertop. "And I recommend using n-butanol for the extraction. I looked it up, and the butanol seems to be the most efficient. So are you ready?"

"I'm ready," Laurie declared. "Especially if Teresa is ready."

"I'm very ready," Teresa said with another smile.

"So I'll leave you to it," John said. "I'll pop in every so often to see how things are going."

After John had left, Teresa went to the refrigerator and brought back a small beaker. "Here's your slurry," she said, handing it over.

Laurie took the specimen. It was slight pink in color with the consistency of heavy soup. With fond memories of cozy afternoons spent in chemistry lab in college, Laurie looked forward to her afternoon in the OCME toxicology lab. There was something particularly rewarding about having the time and opportunity to be so closely involved in searching for the toxin on her own case. Luckily for her current peace of mind, she was totally unaware of the tragedy involving her child unfolding at that very moment elsewhere in the city.

CHAPTER THIRTY-ONE

Ben's day had gone from one extreme to another. It had started as one of his all-time best days. Save for the toothache-like concern of Satoshi's whereabouts and the question of why he had not checked in, Ben had rarely been quite so happy and optimistic. He'd taken a risk leaving his high-paying executive position at his old biotech firm. And there had been days of doubt, struggle, and difficult decisions. But that morning he'd felt as though it had all been worth it. His nascent company was in an enviable position of having signed an exclusive licensing agreement to control what he believed would be the key patent involving the commercialization of induced pluripotent stem cells. They were now starting the due diligence to purchase another start-up whose intellectual property included the current best patent for producing the stem cells. And they had access to seemingly limitless capital.

At a little after four in the afternoon of the same day, all that optimism had evaporated like a snowball on an August afternoon. Rather than feeling good, Ben was confused and anxious to the point of being fearful. Instead of being at home as he had planned, relaxing and looking forward to his 10K race in the morning, he was in his car, driving back across the George Washington Bridge, on his way to the medical examiner's office. His mission now was to view an unidentified corpse, whom he worried was going to be Satoshi Machita. The clerk he had spoken to, Rebecca Marshall, said the body had arrived at about six-thirty Wednesday night after the victim had collapsed on a subway platform. She had also described the victim as being somewhere between late thirties and middle forties, one hundred and forty pounds, five-foot-eight, with Asian features and closely cropped hair, all of which fit Satoshi's description.

As he drove down FDR Drive, surrounded by the Range Rover's luxuriously appointed leather interior, Ben tried his best to think. He usually found driving an aid to contemplation, with the hum of the engine and the road rushing mesmerizingly, blocking other thoughts. He needed to think while he still had some control over events. A lot had happened in the previous few hours.

The day had deteriorated the moment he'd smelled the putrefaction and subsequently discovered the bodies at the house in Fort Lee. It had been a horrific and shocking discovery. Except for rescuing little Shigeru, he wished he'd not gone to check on Satoshi. Maybe the bodies wouldn't have been discovered for months, and he would not be in the trouble he was in now, trouble that had started the moment the police had arrived.

By merely going into the house and contaminating the scene, Ben had vaguely worried he might be suspected of somehow being involved, but he was confident any such suspicions would be quickly put to rest. What Ben never imagined was that he'd been considered suspicious and a threat from the start.

After making the 911 call, Ben sat in his car, waiting

for the authorities to arrive while letting Shigeru take little sips of water. Ben had been totally engrossed in thinking about the fallout his discovery of Satoshi's family's mass murder was going to cause. There was no doubt in his mind that it would become a media event and spark a massive investigation. Even though he didn't find Satoshi's body among the others, he thought it might be in another part of the house. To Ben, the mass murder smacked of organized crime, possibly drug-related, and he believed the authorities would approach it as such.

For Ben, the idea of being involved in any major investigation was anathema, and the fact that he would be in this one was a given. Ben's connection to Satoshi as his employer would entangle both him and iPS USA. He had no idea what he could or should do.

Any serious investigation of iPS USA was terrifying. Today's economic reality had forced Ben into accepting dirty money. At first it had been relatively small amounts, which he made sure to pay off quickly. But as time passed and the economy remained flat, the temptation to borrow greater amounts grew. It was all timing. Like other victims of the recession, he had run into difficulty finding capital just at the time he'd needed it the most. It was then that he'd succumbed to Michael's constant pressure that the money was there for him and that it was completely safe to exchange the money for equity rather than taking it as a loan. Even Vinnie Dominick and Saboru Fukuda had assured him of its safety by explaining that their monies were untraceable through five or more shell companies located in all the usual less financially reputable counties in the world, where secrecy and baksheesh were king and whose governments were not signatories of the Mutual Legal Assistance Treaty.

While Ben had been sitting in his car with Shigeru, worrying about the upcoming investigation, the sound of approaching sirens had gradually penetrated his brain. At first the sounds were barely detectable, but their undulations rapidly increased in power until the flotilla of racing police cars with sirens screaming burst into view in Ben's rearview mirror. At first he was tempted to just get out to wait for their arrival, but he hesitated. The squad cars appeared to be approaching so fast that Ben was worried about his safety. And he was right. Amazed, he watched the cars gobble up the distance between him and them without slowing and then screech to a stop with one of the three vehicles spinning out in the process. Even before they were fully stopped, doors had burst open and uniformed Fort Lee police offers had leaped out with guns drawn. It was as if they thought the mass murder was in progress rather than days old, which Ben had been very clear about on the phone.

Ben was wide-eyed with sudden terror. He'd never experienced such a thing. All the guns were pointed at him, making him worry that a sudden move or noise might unleash a salvo. He tried to scrunch down in his seat but to no avail. Range Rovers were designed for maximum visibility.

"Out of the car!" one of the officers had yelled. "Hands free and point them toward the sky."

"Do it slowly!" another officer had shouted. "No sudden moves."

"There's a child in here with me," Ben had yelled. "He needs medical attention."

"Out of the car! Now!"

"I'm getting out," Ben had yelled. "I'm just the nine-one-one caller, for chrissake."

"To the ground! Spread-eagle!"

Ben had complied, pushing away a few empty beer cans and other debris.

In the next minute, several cops ran up behind him and patted him down. Satisfied he was unarmed, they cuffed him and then hoisted him to his feet. Ben watched as a number of the Fort Lee police ran up to the house with guns drawn and disappeared inside.

"Christ, what a smell!" one of the officers said, standing next to Ben and wrinkling his nose. To Ben he said, "Did you go in there?"

"I did. I didn't want to, but I heard a noise, which turned out to be this child," Ben said, using his head to point through the open driver's-side door of his Range Rover at Shigeru, whose face could barely be seen within the enfolding blanket. "Why the hell did you cuff me?" Ben pleaded. "Am I a suspect? From the smell, whatever happened here was days ago."

The officer didn't answer. The ambulance had arrived, its siren loud enough to cause Ben's ears to ring. Several EMTs leaped out, one going to the ambulance's rear to open the door, another rushing to where Ben was standing with his two guards.

"Where's the child?" the driver demanded. Ben had requested the ambulance when he'd made the 911 call.

"He's here in the car," Ben answered before the police could respond. "He's fine," Ben added quickly. "He's dehydrated, but mostly he's terrified. He'd been in a hidden room in the dark from whenever this disaster occurred. I'm a doctor. He needs an IV. He needs blood work. His kidney function has to be evaluated."

Ben turned to one of his captors, a uniformed officer identified on his nametag as Sergeant Higgins. "I'd like to go with the child. As I said, I'm a doctor. I can return here for questioning after the child is stabilized."

"Are you related to the kid somehow?" Sergeant Higgins questioned.

"No, I'm not," Ben said, "but . . ." It was at that moment Ben remembered the documents in the office safe: the two wills, one signed, one unsigned, and the trust agreement signed, making him the trustee of the trust that was going to own the key patents for iPS cells. For Ben, remembering the existence of the legal documents was like a sudden burst of sunshine in the middle of a terrible storm. Although he was no lawyer, the idea that he might have something to say about the patents' future couldn't be bad for the future of iPS USA and the necessary perpetuation of the licensing agreement.

"But what?" Sergeant Higgins said when Ben had paused.

"But I'm to be the child's guardian when the father's will is probated."

"Is the father in the house as one of the victims?"

"Not that I know of. I only saw the mother."

"Is the father dead?"

"That I don't know either," Ben admitted, making him realize his case for leaving the scene and going with the child was cellophane-thin, even if he was to produce the one signed will he had. Accepting reality, he turned back to the EMT. "Take the child, whose name, by the way, is Shigeru Machita, start an IV, but tell the hospital authorities that I will most likely soon be the guardian, and that I give permission to treat the child as I've already described. Also tell them I will be there as soon as I can."

"Okay," the EMT said simply, and then took off, rounding Ben's car to get to the front passenger door.

Ben watched the EMT lift the child, then quickly turn his head away as the smell of the child invaded his airspace. The EMT then ran Shigeru back to the ambulance's rear and handed him off to the other EMT, who'd gone back to the vehicle to prepare for receiving the child.

For a moment Ben found himself thinking about the legal issues that were sure to arise. Shigeru, like the rest of his family, was an illegal alien, without even a record of his entrance into the country. His Japanese citizenship would impact an American court's decision about his future. But where was Satoshi, and was he alive or dead? If he was alive, the legal issues were fewer. Could he have arrived home, seen the mayhem, and gone into hiding? It now seemed unlikely. Ben had an awful sinking feeling that Satoshi, like his family, was already dead.

As the ambulance made a three-point turn in the middle of Pleasant Lane, more police cars arrived, though without the same sense of urgency. Ben noticed these squad cars were from the Bergen County police.

A moment later an unmarked car and several white vans pulled behind the Bergen County police. On the side of the vans was stenciled: NEW JERSEY DEPARTMENT OF PUBLIC SAFETY, OFFICE OF MEDICAL EXAMINER. From one of the marked police cars emerged a plainclothes detective. He was of medium height and thickset, with a shock of brown hair going gray at the temples. It was clear he was a force to contend with. He was one of those people who radiated authority, determination, and intelligence all at once in a calm, unspoken way.

He walked directly up to Ben, who was instantly wary, and said, "I'm Detective Lieutenant Tom Janow of the Bergen County police." Without waiting for a response, he turned to Sergeant Higgins. "Is this the nine-one-one caller?"

"He is, sir!"

"Why is he in handcuffs?"

Sergeant Higgins paused, seemingly caught off guard by the question. "Lieutenant Brigs said to pat him and cuff him."

"For what reason?"

"Well . . . because the case was a mass murder."

"A mass murder that had apparently gone down a day or so ago, if I'm not mistaken," Tom said. His voice was even and matter-of-fact and without emotion or blame.

"Well, that's true," the sergeant admitted.

"Uncuff him!" Tom said calmly.

While Ben was being released he watched how efficiently the Bergen County police task force went to work. While the Fort Lee police continued to secure the area, the Bergen County contingent prepared to process the scene. Besides the plainclothes detective, there was a handful of uniformed officers, a number of crime scene investigators, and several medical legal investigators from the Bergen County medical examiner's office. The MLIs were busily suiting up in bioprotective clothing with some even donning closed circuit breathing apparatus like Aqua-Lungs to be ready to go into the building as soon as the local police declared it safe. There was even a representative from

the Bergen County district attorney's office, who'd
gotten out of his unmarked car and had walked over to
introduce himself to Detective Lieutenant Janow and
ask permission to listen in on the questioning of Ben,
which the detective agreed to instantly.

"Sorry about the cuffs," Tom said, once the shackles
had been removed. There had been a brief problem with
the key.

Ben acknowledged Tom's apology. Although he had
been worried about the situation when he'd first discovered
the bodies, the idea that he might be considered a suspect
had never dawned on him. "I'm not considered a suspect,
am I?" Ben asked while rubbing his wrists. He wanted to
be absolutely sure. He was already nervous enough.

"Not yet," Tom said. "Should we have our conversation in your vehicle? It might be more agreeable."

Not completely relieved of his concern about possibly
being a suspect, Ben agreed to the use of his car. Tom
got in on the front passenger side while Ben climbed in
behind the wheel. The investigator from the district
attorney's office seated himself in the passenger-side
backseat.

With his pad and pencil at the ready, Tom started
with the usual litany of questions, associated with Ben's
identity and history, rapidly writing as Ben spoke. As
they proceeded, Ben's evaluation of the man's pro-
fessionalism went up another notch. Tom's systematic,
experienced, and smooth approach to interviewing made
it clear he knew what he was doing while making it all
appear effortless. Within just a few minutes they had
progressed from Ben's identity to Ben's personal history
to the facts that led up to Ben's having stopped by the
Machitas' household on that particular day.

When Tom paused in his questioning, Ben could feel himself trembling and hoped it was not obvious. The feeling that Tom was almost too good at what he was doing made Ben progressively nervous that Tom might find out things that Ben didn't want him to learn. Ben seriously wanted to end the interview but hesitated to say anything, lest the wily detective take Ben's eagerness to cut things off as a sign that he had something to hide.

There was another reason Ben was nervous: He had not been totally truthful. In fact, he'd lied twice. The first deliberate lie had been when Ben said that Satoshi Machita had given him his home address, and the second had been that he had no idea how Satoshi had found the property.

At that point, one of the Bergen County police had come out of the building and rapped on Tom's passenger-side window. Tom had gotten out of the car, allowing Ben to turn and acknowledge the thin, bespectacled man sitting in his backseat. For a moment their eyes locked but no words were spoken. The situation did not encourage small talk. Five minutes later Tom climbed back into the car. As soon as he'd slammed the door shut, he went back to his questioning.

"Now, I've been told you did go into the house."

"I did," Ben admitted. "I can assure you that I would rather not have gone in, but I felt impelled because of the child. I had heard a high-pitched noise from the door. I didn't know at the time it was a child." Another lie, and Ben did not even know why he had told it.

"Did you bust the window in the door?"

"I did not. The door window was broken when I got here. The door was unlocked."

"Did you recognize any of the victims?"

"Just the wife."

"What about Satoshi?"

"He wasn't there, at least I didn't think he was, but I didn't go into the basement."

"He isn't there," Tom offered. "I've been told the bodies are all together in the same room, lined up on the floor: six of them."

"That's what I saw."

"Where is he?" Tom asked casually, as if he was inquiring about an acquaintance.

"I wish I knew," Ben said. "I had been trying to get in touch with him for several days. He'd been eager to get some lab space. I wanted to let him know it had been arranged. As I told you, the reason I stopped by here is to see him."

"When and where was the last time you saw him?"

"Wednesday afternoon. We'd had a small celebration in the office in the city after we'd signed a licensing agreement. He left early, saying he wanted to get home to share the good news with his wife."

"Was this licensing agreement going to be lucrative for him?"

"Immensely so!"

Tom paused for a moment, thinking, then took a moment to jot something down.

"Are you thinking that Satoshi might be the perpetrator, having killed his family except for the child?"

"If this had been domestic violence, he'd be my first choice," Tom said. "But I doubt this scene represents domestic violence. It's too smooth, too professional. This smacks of organized crime. I mean, I've been told the bodies are lined up like a production line. That wouldn't happen in a scene of domestic violence. This looks like a drug hit, but that doesn't mean we don't want to find Mr. Satoshi as a person of interest."

"Hmm," Ben voiced. Although he'd come to the same conclusion about the killing not representing domestic violence, he'd decided not to offer any more insight or information unless specifically asked.

"Did you know that the killer or killers made a specific point to remove all identification? If it hadn't been for you, we would have no idea who these people were."

"I didn't know," Ben said, progressively wishing he'd never come. "I did notice that the home had been ransacked." It was Ben's thought that the killer or killers had searched for something above and beyond identification. He had guessed it was Satoshi's lab books, but that idea he was unwilling to share.

"How much effort have you made looking for Satoshi?"

"I've called him repeatedly on his cell. Other than that and coming here today, I've done nothing specifically."

"As careful about removing identification as the intruders were, if they were to have caught Satoshi before coming here and killed him, they probably would have gotten rid of his identification as well. Did you contact Missing Persons in the city on the odd chance that there is an unclaimed Japanese corpse hanging out in the morgue?"

"I certainly did not," Ben responded.

Tom opened the door, stepped out, and yelled for one of the uniformed officers to kindly come over. When the officer did, Ben could hear Tom ordering him to go back to the car and call the Missing Persons Squad in

New York City and inquire about any unidentified Japanese corpse coming in over the last several days.

Tom returned and climbed back into the car. As he did so, he caught Ben glancing at his watch.

"Are we keeping you from something important?"

"Actually, yes," Ben said. "I'm worried about the child. Do you know where they've taken him?"

"The nearest hospital is in Englewood," Tom said. "You probably know that, since you live in Englewood Cliffs. How critical was the child, in your estimation?"

"Surprisingly enough, seemingly not critical at all. He was dehydrated for sure but probably not enough to cause internal organ damage."

"I'd guess that they probably took him to Hackensack University Medical Center. I can confirm that. Meanwhile, let me ask you a question. As far as you know, does your company, iPS USA, have anything to do with organized crime?"

Ben was stunned, and before he could help himself, he'd sucked in a tiny but audible gasp of air. The unexpected nature of the question had taken him completely off guard. Instantly recovering, he asked in the calmest voice he could muster, "Why would our biotech start-up, which is trying to cure degenerative disease for the sake of humanity, have anything at all to do with organized crime? Excuse me, even asking such a question is ridiculous."

Tom raised his eyebrows slightly and commented, "It's interesting your response to a question is a question, rather than a direct 'no.'"

"It is not surprising that I might be shocked by a question connecting my company to organized crime when we were talking about organized crime being related to this mass murder," Ben said, defending himself and his response. "Of course I would be taken aback. I think it is clear I came upon the scene totally unawares. I had absolutely no knowledge of this tragedy or anything possibly to do with it."

Tom took Ben's disclaimer in stride, and instead of responding, merely looked back at his notes. Ben felt his anxiety ratchet up another notch. He now had the feeling he was being played. He needed to get away; he needed time to think.

The officer dispatched to call Missing Persons rapped on Tom's window. Tom lowered it and looked at him expectantly.

"They do have a body that fits the description," the officer said. "It's at the New York OCME."

"Thank you, Brian," Tom said. He looked over at Ben and elevated a single eyebrow. "I think we are making progress." Turning back to the officer, he said, "Go back and find out where the boy from this disaster was taken."

The officer did a kind of half-salute before returning to his squad car.

"Maybe, just maybe," Tom commented, "we've solved the mystery of Satoshi, which I believe might ultimately provide key information for the death of the six people in this house."

"Possibly," Ben said without enthusiasm. A moment earlier he didn't think he could possibly get more nervous. But he had been wrong. He didn't see finding Satoshi as a positive step, at least not dead.

"I tell you what," Tom said, as if sensitive to Ben's mind-set. "I still have questions for you, but why don't I let you go and see the child. I have to go inside and

view a scene I don't want to see. But you have to promise me two things. After you've seen the child, I want
you to call and then go to the New York OCME over
in the city and identify or not identify, as the case may
be, the body they have in their cooler. Then I want you
to come back here, or if I'm gone, drive out to the
Bergen County police station, which is also in Hackensack. Is that a deal?"

"That's a deal," Ben said, eager to get away.

"Now, hold on for a minute! I'll find out for sure
where the kid was taken." Tom climbed out of the car.
Simultaneously, so did the investigator from the district
attorney's office, who had been listening in the backseat.

Good grief, Ben said to himself, once alone. There
had been nothing he'd liked about the conversation with
Tom. Ben shivered at some of the things that he'd said
and how he'd acted. From his perspective, it had been
an interrogation, plain and simple, in which he did not
shine. In a sudden burst of paranoia, Ben thought that
the only thing positive about the interview was that he'd
not been read his Miranda rights.

Ben straightened up and tried to calm himself. At
least the conversation, or whatever it was, was over for
now, and when it recommenced he'd have had time to
think.

Ben started the car when Tom returned to the
driver's-side window. "As I suspected, the child was
taken to Hackensack University Medical Center. I hope
all is well with him. And here, take my card." Tom
handed over his card. "It's got my mobile number. I
want to hear immediately, yes or no, on the ID in the
city."

"Wait a second," Ben said, just as Tom was about to

walk away. "I have a suggestion. I'm worried the child might be in danger. Obviously, whoever killed the entire family would probably have wanted to kill the child as well, and if and when they hear about his existence, they might want to finish the job."

"Good point," Tom admitted. "Thanks for the suggestion. I'll put a detail on him right away."

The route to the Hackensack University Medical Center had been quite direct, and even though it required going through several small towns, Ben arrived in short order. With his M.D. license plates, he used the doctors' parking lot near the emergency-room entrance even though he knew he shouldn't.

Although Ben's visit to the Machita residence was far more harrowing and unnerving, the hospital visit was not a whole lot better, given his mental status. But as troubling as the deaths at the residence were—if, in fact, Satoshi was dead—there was little risk involving a change in the status of the licensing agreement concerning the iPS key patents, a situation that would have been disastrous to iPS USA. Thanks to Satoshi's insistence on a bit of estate planning, Ben had an ace in the hole, even without the wife's signature on her will. He had Satoshi's will and the trust document, which didn't need the wife's signature, both fully signed and executed, with the will creating a trust for the key patents and the trust document appointing Ben trustee. What that all meant to Ben was that after probate he would control the trust for the benefit of Shigeru, meaning there would be no challenge to the licensing agreement.

Unfortunately after the hospital visit Ben's rosy

understanding of the legal issues would be sorely
undermined, and what had previously provided a modicum of comfort, the will and the trust document, he
now feared might be more paper tigers than solid
support for the status quo.

Ben had entered the emergency-room door and
presented himself as Dr. Benjamin Corey to command
more respect, as the ER was packed. Unfortunately, the
ruse did not work with the harried emergency-room
clerk, and Ben was forced to stand to the side and wait.

"I'm looking for a toddler who came in earlier," Ben
said authoritatively once he had the clerk's attention.
"He came in by ambulance. His name is Shigeru
Machita; he's about one and a half years old. Is he still
here in the emergency room, or has he been admitted?"

The clerk, dressed in scrubs, was being unmercifully
hounded by several of his coworkers, but to his credit
he stayed to finish with Ben. "There's been no Shigeru
Machita since noon," he said, looking up from the
screen.

"There has to be," Ben said. "The police told me he
was coming here."

"Could it be under another name?" Ben asked.

"If it is, you'll have to tell me," the clerk said.

"Of course," Ben said, hitting his head with the heel
of his palm. "How about a generic name, like Baby
Jack?"

"Yes, here's one!" the clerk said, before shouting
across the registration area to a coworker that he'd be
there in a second. "It's a baby John Doe," he said to
Ben. "Could that be it?"

"Maybe," Ben said. "What time did he come in?"

"Two-twenty-two this afternoon."

"That's about right," Ben said. "Where is he?"

"He's been taken up to pediatrics, room four-twenty-seven."

"Gotcha," Ben said. "How do I get there?"

The clerk gave rapid, complicated directions that concluded with the suggestion of following a blue line running on the floor. Ben forgot the directions and just followed the blue line on a labyrinthine route to a bank of elevators.

As he exited the elevator on the fourth floor and despite the chaos that reigned, one of the nurses from the nurses' desk caught sight of him and called out, "Excuse me. Can I help you?"

Ben angled over to the desk. The woman's nametag read SHEILA, RN.

"I'm Dr. Ben Corey. I'm here to see baby John Doe in room four-twenty-seven."

"That's nice," Sheila said sincerely. She was a boxy woman with dark skin and mid-length brown hair heavily streaked with blond. "I'm the charge nurse on the floor. We were hoping someone would be coming in. The little darling hasn't said a peep. The word is that his parents were killed in a mass murder."

"So far it appears only the mother was killed," Ben said, hoping it would remain true. "The father is missing. How is he doing?"

"Fine, considering what he's been through. He was dehydrated when he came into the ER, but that's been rectified. His electrolytes are now normal, and he's eating and drinking. But he's so quiet and hardly moves. He just stares at you with these huge, dark eyes. I'd like to have him say something, even cry."

"I want to take a peek at him."

"I'm afraid we can't allow that, but you can speak with the police officer who's here to guard him."

Ben did just that. After the guard looked at Ben's ID and looked at a list of doctors who had access, he was reluctant to let Ben in until Ben suggested Detective Janow be called. That was all it took, and Ben was escorted in by Sheila.

As Sheila described, Shigeru was lying motionlessly on his back in the crib with his eyes wide open. His eyes followed Ben as he came alongside the crib.

"Hey, big guy!" Ben said as he reached out and gently pinched the child's skin on his upper arm. After releasing it, Ben could see the skin immediately pop back into its original position, something that hadn't happened when Ben had gotten him out to the Range Rover. It was a crude but reliable test for dehydration. "Are they treating you okay here?" Ben twisted around the IV bottle to see what he was getting.

"*Okasan,*" Shigeru said suddenly.

Ben and Sheila looked at each other in surprise.

"What was that?" Ben questioned.

"I have no idea."

"It must be Japanese."

"I wouldn't know," Sheila said. "But hallelujah, he's said something. He must recognize you."

"Must be just from earlier today. Prior to today I'd seen him a couple of times, and then only briefly. But it's a good sign. If the father doesn't appear soon, apparently I'm going to be the guardian."

"Really?" Sheila questioned. "We had no idea."

"I told it to the EMT," Ben said. "I even told the EMT the kid's name. It's Shigeru Machita."

"I think you'd better talk with the social worker on the case."

"Of course," Ben said. He glanced at his watch. He didn't have a lot of time, since he'd committed himself to return to the city, but he thought it important to straighten out the identity and insurance issues.

While Sheila went to get the social worker, Ben stayed in Shigeru's room and tried to get the infant to say another word or respond to gentle tickling. Although he did not utter another word, he was physically responsive to the tickling.

Five minutes later Sheila returned with a tall, attractive Hispanic woman. She wore a blue silk dress beneath her long white coat. Her name, of course, was Maria, with a family name of Sanchez.

Sheila had done the introductions, and as soon as they'd been completed, Maria suggested that they talk in the nurses' lounge behind the nurses' desk. She had the demeanor of a savvy businesswoman who took her job seriously.

"Sheila mentioned that you had told the EMT the child's name and the fact that you were the guardian," Maria said as soon as they were seated and cut off from the bustle of the floor.

"I told him the name of the child and that after the father's will was probated I would possibly be the guardian. That is, of course, if the father is also dead, as feared. I'm really surprised there was such a lack of communication."

"The emergency room is a busy place."

I don't need a lecture about life in the ER, Ben thought but didn't say. He'd spent too much time in the ER as a surgical resident. To his assessment of

Maria's demeanor he added seemingly inappropriate animosity. Ben had begun to feel that he was being treated as a questionable character, trying to waltz in and steal an orphaned child.

"We're sorry your communication to the EMT did not get properly relayed. Be that as it may, what is your relationship to the child?"

With a somewhat hardened tone, Ben said, "I was or still am, again depending on the status of the father, his employer."

"Is there some question as to the status of the father? We were told the child's parents were both murdered."

"The mother was, but not the father. The father's whereabouts is not yet known, although there are some who believe he, too, is dead."

"Why do you believe you will be the guardian?"

For a moment Ben paused, wondering why he was bothering to answer all these questions. Maybe he should just go to the office and bring back Satoshi's will. But then he remembered it needed to be probated.

"Did you hear my question?"

"I did, but I'm beginning to feel this is akin to an interrogation, which I find inappropriate."

"Why didn't you come in with the child rather than showing up later?"

"It wasn't my choice. I was detained by the police after I had inadvertently stumbled on the murder victims. I found the child hidden in the house."

"Well, let me inform you what has gone on here at the hospital in your absence. With no name and no information, I contacted a social worker at DYFS, the Division of Youth and Family Services, here in New Jersey, which is under the Department of Children and

Families. She went immediately to one of the DYFS lawyers, who, in turn, went to family court and got DYFS appointed temporary guardian so we would be able to treat the child beyond emergency care. So far it hasn't been needed. But DYFS is now the guardian. That's a fact you'll have to live with."

"What if I produce the will and the DYFS lawyer can look at it."

"It wouldn't matter. The DYFS lawyer cannot change the ruling, only family court, and you couldn't take the will to family court because it is not probated. And since you don't know the father's whereabouts or state of health, you can't go to probate court. For now you are stuck with DYFS as the temporary guardian."

Ben was mildly overwhelmed.

"Let me ask you another question," Maria said when Ben failed to respond. "This child is obviously Japanese, or at least of Asian ancestry, and Sheila said he'd spoken when you arrived, but it wasn't English. Is he an American citizen?"

"No, he's Japanese," Ben said.

"Well, that makes it even more difficult, at least in my experience. In a case like this you cannot take anything for granted. A probate judge will decide the issues, not necessarily on what any documents say but on what he believes is in the best interest of the child."

"Oh," Ben said simply as a new wave of concern spread over him. Up until that very moment he still thought the licensing-agreement situation was safe and shielded from change. But now, suddenly, he was learning from a woman with experience in the arena of family law and probate that the licensing agreement's circumstance was not cast in stone but rather open to the interpretation of what was in the best interest of the child. Even Ben had to accept it would be difficult to justify his role as a trustee of the entity that owned the iPS patents when he was also CEO of iPS USA. It was a huge conflict of interest. And now Ben had to deal with the possibility of iPS USA losing its control of the Satoshi patents. Before visiting the hospital he'd been confident he was destined to be both guardian and trustee for Shigeru. Now there was the possibility he would be neither.

Ben exited FDR Drive at 34th Street and continued south on Second Avenue. The closer he got to OCME, the more unnerved he felt about everything: having to return for further questions from the Bergen County police detective, the chance that there might be changes in the key exclusive iPS licensing agreement, and that he was about to identify Satoshi's body. For a few blocks he considered the idea of not identifying Satoshi even if it was him but abandoned the idea as it would just postpone the inevitable—and direct significant suspicion in his direction. Ben realized his only hope was to avoid any suspicion of involvement at all, and to do that he had to remain cooperative.

He parked on a side street just a short distance from the OCME building. He paused a moment before entering but not out of fear of the sights he might be forced to confront within the morgue. Unlike laypeople, he had seen enough dead people to accept it as part of life. He'd even watched several autopsies as a student. He paused because his intuition was telling him loudly that Satoshi's death, even though he had had nothing to do with it, was going to have serious consequences.

To bolster his courage before entering, Ben reminded himself that there was a chance that the body he was about to see might not be Satoshi's. He also reminded himself that even if it turned out to be Satoshi's, there was no reason he couldn't appropriately and sagely deal with the problems and dangers that might arise. Knowledge was always best. It was ignorance that invariably engendered mistakes. If Satoshi was in fact dead, it was best if he knew it before anyone else, and if it was a natural death, it might not have any consequence whatsoever.

With a bit more confidence than he had had a few moments earlier, Ben pulled open one side of a double door and entered OCME. He checked his watch. It was almost quarter to five in the afternoon. Whatever was to happen, he didn't want it to take too long because of his commitment to stop either back at the scene or at the Bergen County police station and face Tom Janow for more questions before finally being allowed to head home.

The reception area was crowded with what seemed to be staff ready to leave after a long workday. He pushed through the people and approached the desk and asked for Rebecca Marshall, the clerk he'd spoken to earlier on the phone. He was told Rebecca would be down shortly.

Ben waited on an old vinyl couch, watching the people chatting in their dynamic little groups that formed and re-formed as people departed and new people joined. He wondered if they were aware of how unique their work was, and if they ever talked about it among themselves. They probably didn't—a good example of the adaptability of the human organism.

"Mr. Corey," a voice called out.

Ben looked up to his right. Somehow an African-American woman with a pleasant, kind face and tightly curled silver hair had managed to sneak right up to him. She clutched a manila case file and other papers to her chest. "I'm Rebecca Marshall. I believe we spoke earlier."

Rebecca let Ben through a door to Ben's right and closed it behind them. "This is called the family ID room," she explained. It was a modest-size space with a blue couch and a large round wooden table with eight wooden chairs. There were several framed posters with images involving the destruction that occurred on 9/11. Each had the caption NEVER FORGET in bold letters across the bottom. "Please," Rebecca said, gesturing toward one of the chairs at the table. Ben sat, and Rebecca did as well.

"As I mentioned on the phone, I am an identification clerk. As you can well imagine, identification of any body that is brought here is an extremely important part of our job. Usually we have family members who make the identification. If we have no family members, we rely on friends or coworkers. In other words, anyone who knows the victim. You understand, I assume?"

Ben nodded, and to himself thought, *I don't need a lecture; just show me the damn body, and I'm out of here!*

"Good," Rebecca said in response to Ben's nodding. "To start, I need to see your identification. Anything official with a photo. A driver's license is fine." Rebecca retrieved a blank identification form from the materials she had been carrying.

Ben took out his driver's license and handed it to her. When she was satisfied it was him, she wrote down the information on the form. Her tone and gestures were practiced and respectful, giving Ben the sense that she would be equally competent to handle the situation, whether he threw a fit of grief-evoked rage or, as he was doing, expressing apparent indifference.

With Ben's identification out of the way, Rebecca opened the case file, which was in the form of a large folder secured with an attached rubber band. Opening the folder, she reached in and pulled out more than a half-dozen digital photos. Very deliberately, she placed them in the proper alignment in front of Ben, who purposely kept his eyes glued to Rebecca's. When she was finished, they locked eyes for a moment before Ben looked down and focused.

The photos were a series of shots, face-on and profile. They were taken purely for identification purposes in that they were only of the face. Any portion of the body that would have been visible was covered with a towel.

Although Ben recognized Satoshi instantly, he purposefully kept his face neutral. He did not know why, but he did. Neither of them said anything, with Rebecca willing to let Ben take his time. In the stillness, an unintelligible murmur of the voices in the reception area could just be heard.

"His name is Satoshi Machita," Ben finally said, still glancing from one harshly lit photo to the next. He didn't realize how disappointed he sounded, which he assumed Rebecca reasonably took for grief. *Now it really starts,* Ben added silently to himself. Suddenly he decided it was not a good thing or, more realistic, totally inappropriate for him to be showing any emotion. He looked up at the clerk. "I thought I was going to have to look at a body like in the movies."

"No," Rebecca said simply. "We've been using photos for years. Before the digital camera, we used Polaroids. It is much better for most people than viewing the body, especially for family members or when the faces of the victims have been traumatized. But we have a way of letting people view the bodies if they insist. Would you prefer to see the body? Would it help your decision?"

"No," Ben said. "It is Satoshi Machita, I am sure. I don't need to see the body." Ben started to stand up, but Rebecca laid her hand on his forearm with the lightest touch he'd ever experienced from a person of authority.

"There's more, I'm afraid," she said. "But let me ask a question first. The doctor on this case is still here at OCME this evening. I told her you were coming in for a possible identification. She asked me if she might be able to meet you and ask a few questions if you'd been able to identify the body."

Ben's first reaction was no. The last thing he wanted to do was get hung up at OCME, since he'd already committed himself to more questions by Detective Janow. He wanted to get to Janow, get it over with, and get home around the time he had estimated when he had called his wife after leaving the hospital. But then he had a second thought. Maybe it might be a good thing to get hung up on an errand that the detective had sent him on. Maybe he could use getting caught at OCME as a way of begging off from seeing the detective again that night. He'd like to be more rested the next time he saw him. In addition, Ben was curious about Satoshi's death, and a meeting with the medical examiner handling his case was a promising way to find out the details.

"I can just call her and see if she's available right this

minute. We can take care of the rest of our business in the time it will take her to get down here. If you are willing, I want to make the call now to make sure I catch her before she leaves."

"All right," Ben said. "As long as it can happen now and not delay me too much longer. I have another meeting scheduled this evening out in New Jersey."

Worried that Ben might change his mind, Rebecca immediately called up to Laurie's office. When Laurie heard who it was, she tried to put Rebecca off, saying, "I'm in a meeting that's about to end. Can I get back to you in a few minutes?"

"That's not going to work. The gentleman I mentioned needs to leave for a meeting in New Jersey, and I've already taken up too much of his time. He came here out of his way to help us identify the victim, which he's done. We now know the identity of the case."

"Terrific!" Laurie said. "Hold on!"

Rebecca could hear Laurie talking but not the words.

Laurie came back on the line. "We'll be right down!" Then she abruptly disconnected.

Rebecca looked at the phone for a moment as if the phone would tell her who Laurie meant when she had said "we." Hanging up, Rebecca turned back to Ben. "She's on her way."

"So I heard," Ben said.

"So let's finish up quickly. I want you to write on several of these photos 'This is Satoshi Machita,' and then sign your name."

"Fine," Ben said.

"Do you know Satoshi's last address?"

"I do but not his phone number. I have that at the office."

"Do you know if Mr. Machita had any particular medical problems, old injuries, or identification marks?"

"I have no idea. He seemed healthy to me."

Rebecca was filling out the identification form as she was asking the questions. "What was your relationship with the deceased? That's the last question."

"Employer," Ben said.

CHAPTER THIRTY-TWO

Laurie got on the elevator first. She punched the button for the first floor but then pressed the door-open button and held it to keep the door from closing while Detective Lou Soldano and Jack boarded. Only then did she release the door, allowing it to close immediately.

Laurie was in a rare, self-congratulatory mood. Just before she'd gotten the call from Rebecca, she'd finished her mini–news conference—mini because it was attended only by Jack and Lou, concerning the only two cases she currently had: the two unidentified Japanese men, which according to Rebecca was now only one unidentified man.

In less than five minutes Laurie had been able to prove to Jack's and Lou's satisfaction that the second man, who was most likely a Yakuza hit man, as suggested by the extent of his tattoos, the pearling embedded in the shaft of his penis, and the fact that he was missing the last joint of his fifth finger, had killed the first individual during the commission of a robbery on a subway platform with an accomplice who was also of Japanese descent. She'd also been able to prove that the crime had most likely been carried out with an air-powered pellet gun hidden in an umbrella with a fatal dose of a toxin called tetrodotoxin.

The last point about the tetrodotoxin was not yet official, although Laurie was convinced. When Laurie had mentioned that final point in her presentation, she had admitted that the findings had yet to be certified by John DeVries. Although Laurie had come up with the correct peaks on the mass spec, John still wanted to certify the results by running the sample of known tetrodotoxin Laurie had gotten from the hospital next door.

"I cannot believe you've accomplished all this in two days," Lou said. "You're like an entire task force. You're supposed to be part of the support for us detectives. Instead, you've done our job and yours. It's unbelievable."

"Thank you," Laurie said. She knew she was blushing. Getting such a compliment from Lou truly meant a lot to her.

"On the security tapes there were two people involved in the killing," Laurie said, to divert attention away from herself. "I hope you are taking that into consideration."

"Don't worry, I remember. From what you've said, there's probably another body out there in the harbor, which I'll get right on. It's good that we'll be getting an ID on the first guy. It will provide a solid place to begin our investigation. As I said this morning, my biggest fear is that whatever is going on might be the harbinger of a nasty turf war."

"I don't think number one was a member of the Yakuza," Laurie said.

"We'll see," Lou said.

"And to think I tried to discourage you," Jack said, speaking up for the first time.

"You tried to discourage her?" Lou asked, looking at Jack with a questioning expression.

"I did," Jack confessed. "My sense was that her case

was a natural death, especially after a completely negative autopsy. I didn't want her to make a huge effort and then come up with nothing. Not on her first case."

"It's true," Laurie said. "He tried to talk me out of watching the security video, which did take quite a while. And then, of course, was the threatening letter. I have to say, Jack, that was a low blow. I suppose it bothered you when I failed to respond to your prank."

"What do you mean 'threatening letter'?" Lou blurted with immediate concern.

"We occasionally get letters or e-mails from paranoid people who somehow misinterpret our role," Laurie explained. "Usually we turn them in to the front office, who alerts security, and that's the end of it. The people are usually grieving and angry, having a problem dealing with the loss of a family member and want to put blame someplace. They used to upset me, but one gets accustomed to just about anything. No big deal."

The elevator door opened, and they all got out. Jack put a hand on Laurie's shoulder and spoke very deliberately. "I didn't write you a threatening letter! I'd never do that!"

Laurie tipped her head to the side. "You didn't write me a letter threatening me if I didn't stop my investigation into the first case?"

"Cross my heart and hope to die."

"Are you sure?" Laurie questioned. "I mean, doesn't it sound like your style of black humor? You were, after all, serious about trying to talk me out of continuing what I was doing."

"Maybe in some respects it sounds like me, but I assure you, I'd certainly never do it to you."

"What did the letter say?" Lou questioned

"I can't remember exactly, but it was short and to the point. Something like if I didn't stop working on the case there'd be consequences, and if I went to the police there'd be the same consequences. I mean, it was so over-the-top melodramatic. All the other letters I've ever gotten ran on and on with all sorts of ranting and raving. This one seemed like a joke in its brevity. Marlene had found it having been slipped under the front door. She put it on my computer keyboard."

"I'd like to see this letter," Lou said gravely.

"Fine," Laurie said with false indifference. She couldn't help feeling judged in the middle of a moment of glory, although she did feel a touch guilty. "Let's first meet the Good Samaritan who has identified my first case. Then we'll head back to my office and examine the letter."

CHAPTER THIRTY-THREE

On second thought, maybe I should leave," Ben said, pushing back his chair and standing up to stretch. Although he'd been waiting only a few minutes for the medical examiner, he'd begun to have second thoughts about agreeing to additional questions. It had occurred to him that although he wanted to appear cooperative, providing more information before obtaining counsel was probably not in his best interest. He had no idea if Satoshi's death had anything to do with the six deaths in New Jersey, but the chances were that it did. Having discovered the mass murder and identified Satoshi's body, he was going to be involved no matter what. It was best to limit any additional exposure and say no more. Ben was certain any defense lawyer he might hire would say exactly that.

Rebecca climbed out of her chair. "I wonder where Dr. Montgomery-Stapleton is? She said she was coming right down. Let me check." Rebecca opened the door, and as she did so she saw Laurie approaching across the expanse of the foyer registration area. Behind her were Dr. Jack Stapleton and another man whom she did not recognize.

"Here comes the doctor," Rebecca said, opening the door wider.

Laurie came in with a bit of attitude after the conversation about the threatening letter but quickly recovered when introduced to Ben.

Ben was immediately taken by Laurie's attractiveness and smile. For a brief moment his newly realized concerns about talking with the authorities moved to the back of his mind. A moment later, when he was introduced to Detective Captain Lou Soldano, they all came tumbling back. Meeting Dr. Jack Stapleton had no effect at all, not even the fact that he and Laurie shared the same last name. Ben was overwhelmingly concerned about meeting another detective. His paranoia spiked upward.

"First I want to thank you sincerely for taking your time to help us identify one of our cases," Laurie said. "I cannot tell you how important that is for us."

"I'm pleased to be of assistance," Ben said, hoping that his tenseness was not apparent. He noticed the detective pick up the identification form that contained his information and study it. "But I do have an important meeting in New Jersey that I'm already late for."

"We'll make it quick," Laurie said. "We have a second body, another Asian man, who came in last night. We would be very appreciative if you would take a look and see if you recognize him as well. We know there is some connection with him and the person you already identified. Would you mind?"

"I suppose not," Ben said without a lot of enthusiasm.

"It's the case I did this morning," Laurie said to Rebecca. "The case with the wild tattoos."

"Got it," Rebecca said, and slipped out of the room.

"Would you like to sit down?" Laurie said, gesturing at the table from which Ben had just arisen.

Laurie took the identification form from Lou and quickly glanced at it.

"How did Satoshi die?" Ben asked, trying to make the question sound like an unimportant afterthought.

"I'm sorry," Laurie said, placing the completed identification form on the table. "The case is still open, and
we cannot reveal anything to the general public until it
is signed out, and then only through our public-relations
department. If you were family it would be different.
I'm sorry."

"That's okay," Ben responded. "Just curious." He
was more than curious, but did not want it to show.

"So you were Mr. Machita's employer," Laurie said.
"Can you tell us about that?"

Ben repeated what he'd told Rebecca, emphasizing
that Satoshi was a very recent employee whom he did
not know particularly well. Ben also described his
company as being in the biotech field and that Satoshi
had been a little-recognized but talented researcher.

"I understand you called the Missing Persons Squad
this afternoon."

"I personally did not call," Ben said. "But I was
concerned. Mr. Machita did not come into the office
over the last two days, and he did not answer his cell
phone."

"When Mr. Machita collapsed on the subway platform, we have reason to believe a small piece of luggage
was taken from him," Laurie said, careful not to mention
the fact that he'd been murdered. "Would you have any
idea what could have been in the luggage? Could it have
been anything specific or particularly valuable?"

"I have no idea," Ben said, deliberately lying. If
someone had pursued Satoshi to rob him, Ben would
have guessed they had been looking for the man's lab
books, which were securely locked in the office safe.

Given the nature of Laurie's questions, Ben knew that
Satoshi's death was surely not a natural one and that he

had to have been murdered. Ben wanted to leave. He
didn't mind lying about something that could never be
proved, but he wasn't going to lie about something that
could. He didn't want to talk about what he'd been up
to in New Jersey that very afternoon, and he was terrified the next question might be about something
concerning Satoshi's family that would naturally lead up
to it.

A tentative sense of relief spread over Ben when
Rebecca returned with the case file of the unidentified
Yakuza hit man. She handed the file to Laurie, who
proceeded to take out the photos of the corpse. These
were not identification photos doctored to ease the
sensibilities of lay visitors. They were the stark-naked
full-body photos taken in the unremitting glare of sharp
fluorescent light specifically designed to emphasize every
defect and disfigurement. Although the tattoos reduced
the ghastliness to a degree, the stark alabaster color of
the exposed limbs and face from having been floating
around in the brackish river water couldn't be ignored.

Ben recoiled from the images, his response heightened by his general unease with a detective sitting right
in front of him. Once again his medical training and
experience came to his aid, and merely by sitting up
straighter he was able to recover his poise. "I've never
seen him," he said with a squeaky voice that even
surprised him. He cleared his throat. "Sorry, but I have
no idea who he is."

"Are you certain?" Laurie asked. "I know the tattoos
are a major distraction. Can you just look at the face
and imagine it in the full color of life?"

"I've never seen him," Ben repeated, "and I remember a face." Ben pushed back his chair and made a

performance about checking the time. "I'm sorry I can't help you with this case, but I hope I have with the first." He stood, and the others did as well.

"You have helped very much," Laurie said. "I want to thank you again."

Ben then reached out across the table to shake first Laurie's hand, then Jack's, who was sitting next to Laurie, and finally Lou's. Ben noticed that Lou deliberately held on to his hand longer than expected while drilling Ben with his dark eyes. "Interesting to meet you, Dr. Corey," Lou said, still clutching Ben's hand. When he let go he did so with a slight, final tightening before the release. Ben worried that it was like a message that they would be seeing each other again.

Lou's handshake had increased Ben's unease, a feeling he carried out to his SUV. *Was the detective really giving me a message?* Ben questioned silently. He hesitated before starting his car. "Good God," he said aloud. "I feel like I'm walking around in a goddamn minefield." Getting out his cell phone and Detective Tom Janow's card, he reluctantly made the call, vainly hoping, since it was now after six p.m., that the detective might beg off and reschedule for the morning. But such was not the case, particularly when the detective heard that the identification had been positive: The corpse was Satoshi Machita. To make matters worse, the detective was still at the scene, meaning Ben had to return to the worst stench he had ever had to suffer, which seemed, at the moment, uncomfortably symbolic in his current, anxiety-ridden state of mind.

CHAPTER THIRTY-FOUR

In the family ID room Laurie, Jack, and Lou had sat back down in their seats. Lou had been the only one who'd spoken. He had said he wanted a copy of Ben's full address and phone numbers. Laurie hadn't answered, but rather had tapped Satoshi's completed identification form with her middle finger, indicating that the contact information was there.

For several long minutes no one spoke. They looked at one another as if dazed. From outside in the foyer there was a sudden burst of voices that penetrated the closed door. No one moved, despite the apparent commotion. Laurie was the first to break the silence in the ID room. "What did you guys think?"

"An oddball," Jack suggested. "A very uncomfortable oddball. On the one hand, he seemed overly confident, on the other the proverbial banjo wire, ready to snap. He was actually shaking at one point."

"Could it have been because of identifying Satoshi Machita? Was it a kind of grief reaction, do you imagine? I saw the shake, too. I also got the message that being here, talking to us, was the absolute last place on earth he wanted to be."

"I should probably recuse myself from this discussion," Lou said. "I've seen him before."

"Really!" Laurie said, surprised. "Where have you seen him?"

"I don't mean I've seen him specifically. I mean I've seen his type. He's one of those snooty Ivy League guys. They act so entitled, like rules don't apply to them."

"Careful," Jack said. "You're hitting too close to home."

"I don't mean like you," Lou explained. "You question some rules from the angle of an enlightened philosophy, whether they make sense and serve everybody equally. This type of guy questions rules selfishly. It's about whether they make sense for him. As long as they make money, it's okay. He's a me, me, me kind of guy."

"I think he knows more than he's telling," Laurie said.

"For sure," Lou said. "I would have asked him a lot more pointed questions."

"I wanted to," Laurie said. "But I didn't think I could get away with it. He was here on his own accord and could have walked out whenever he wanted. Maybe you'll have a go at him someday when you're in charge."

"I suppose you are right," Lou said. "I can tell you this: During the investigation of these two homicides, I'm going to have Dr. Corey's company looked into with a fine-tooth comb. There has to be an interesting explanation why one of his employees was killed by several organized-crime hit men, especially with both hit men and the mark being Japanese."

"Sounds like a good idea to me," Laurie said. She reached out and put a hand on Jack's forearm and looked him in the eyes. "It's been enough of a day for me. What say you? Want to leave your bike here and ride home with me in a nice, safe, warm taxi?"

"No, thank you," Jack said. "I want my bike at home for the weekend." He stood up.

"Hey, what about the threatening letter?" Lou questioned.

"Fine!" Laurie said airily. But she was not looking forward to defending what had been, in retrospect, a bad decision. She realized she should not have dismissed it so cavalierly, even though at the time she was convinced it was an in-house prank of sorts by her husband. The wording had not been funny in any way or form, but it had been so different from all the other various and sundry threatening mail she had gotten that she'd immediately questioned its authenticity, and considered that it was not beyond Jack in one of his juvenile moods.

Laurie went through the door leading out into the reception area first, followed by Lou and then Jack. Jack was saying that he had all his stuff already downstairs at his bike. "I'll see you at home," he called to Laurie, and to Lou, "I'll see you when I see you."

Lou waved over his head to indicate he'd heard and then bumped into Laurie, who'd stopped abruptly. There was a flood of people in the foyer, some sitting, most standing. OCME employees had already left after finishing their good-byes to one another, and a new group of people had come in. With some of those new arrivals sobbing, it was obvious they had come to make an identification of a deceased family member. Another identification clerk was standing by the door to take over the ID room as Laurie, Lou, and Jack emerged. OCME had only one ID setup. Laurie apologized for holding things up.

Jack, who was still talking about heading directly

down to the morgue level rather than returning to his office, had to stop suddenly to avoid bumping up against Lou. He noticed Laurie was staring off to the left as if paralyzed. Following her line of sight, Jack saw an African-American woman sitting on the couch. She was in her mid-forties with heavy features on an otherwise narrow face completely overcome by grief. Grouped tightly about her were at least a half-dozen people. All were maintaining contact by touching her in an attempt to console her. Jack immediately found the woman familiar, but he couldn't recall where he'd seen her.

For Laurie it was another matter entirely. She knew the woman instantly, despite having met her only two or three times. It was Marilyn Wilson, Leticia Wilson's mother.

A sense of panic and fear spread through Laurie like a lightning bolt. With a kind of tunnel vision blocking out the periphery, Laurie started toward Marilyn, insinuating herself between other mourners. She was not to be detoured. With some effort and irritating a number of people, Laurie positioned herself in front of Marilyn. By squatting down Laurie got her face at the level of Marilyn's and asked the woman what had happened.

At first Marilyn stared back at Laurie with an expression of pure grief. Her eyes were awash with tears.

"It's Laurie," Laurie said, trying to break through the veil of anguish surrounding the woman. "What happened? Is it something about Leticia, or someone else?"

Mentioning her daughter's name had a profound effect. The moment it escaped Laurie's lips, the woman seemed to wake from a daze. The eyes that had been blankly staring into the middle distance now converged and the pupils constricted. When she finally recognized who Laurie was, her intense grief turned to intense anger. Shocking everyone, but particularly Laurie, Marilyn screamed, "You! You are the one to blame. If it weren't for you, my Leticia would still be alive!" Marilyn leaped up from the couch, causing Laurie to spring up and take a step back.

The people who'd been trying to comfort Marilyn had also been shocked and had recoiled. The next instant they tried to restrain her but were only partially successful. Marilyn, in a burst of tears, managed to get her hands on the sides of Laurie's neck, and when the women were pulled apart, Marilyn's nails dug into the skin below Laurie's chin, leaving a number of streaks of reddish abraded skin with a few tiny dots of blood.

Jack and Lou immediately went to Laurie's aid, wanting to check the extent of the damage. Also coming to Laurie's aid was Warren Wilson, Jack's regular basketball buddy. Jack, Laurie, Warren, and Warren's girlfriend, Natalie Adams, had been close friends for more than a decade.

Jack had no idea Warren had even been in the room until he'd appeared at Laurie's side seconds after the scuffle. He started to explain to Jack and Lou what was going on when Laurie bolted away without warning or explanation.

With a set, determined expression, she pushed her way through the crowd to the receptionist.

"Buzz me in!" Laurie demanded to the security man at the desk before dashing over to the main entrance door of OCME. She shook the doorknob impatiently until the guard hit the proper button.

"Laurie!" Jack yelled out over the tumult of voices.

He'd detached himself from Warren and Lou with a quick "I'll be back" the moment Laurie had darted away to the receptionist with no explanation. Reaching the door into the building, Jack managed to grab it before it had a chance to close behind Laurie. Pulling it open, he could see that Laurie was already far down the hall, nearing its end.

"Laurie!" Jack called out, with mild irritation that she was deliberately ignoring him. Picking up his speed, Jack pursued her. When he got to the end he could see the stairwell door was closing. Slapping it open, he could hear her footfalls descending below. In hot pursuit he reached the morgue level as the lower door was closing.

Laurie ran into the mortuary office. One of the techs was in the process of logging in a recently arrived body. "Where are you putting the bodies that have been coming in recently?" she demanded, out of breath.

"In the main cooler," the mortuary tech said. He tried to ask Laurie whom exactly she was looking for, but Laurie was already gone, racing down the morgue's composite-tiled corridor with her heels clicking loudly on its rock-like surface. Jack had joined up with her as she emerged from the mortuary office.

"What on earth are you doing?" Jack panted. "Why are we running?"

Laurie merely shook her hand to indicate she didn't want to talk; instead, she concentrated on making a sharp left-hand turn in the corridor in her slippery leather-soled shoes. By the time she was at the main cooler, she had to skid to a stop. Grasping the meat locker–style latch, she pulled open the heavy, insulated door. Stepping into the cold, misty interior, she snapped on the lights, which consisted of bare bulbs in metal cages that cast complicated crisscrossing shadows over the scraped and soiled white walls.

Jack entered as well and let the door click shut behind him. He shivered momentarily in the chill. Laurie was yanking down the sheets covering the bodies near the door, exposing the corpses' faces and upper chests. There were nearly twenty gurneys angled every which way, each with a shrouded body.

"Can I help?" Jack questioned. He was still in the dark as to what Laurie was doing, although having seen Warren upstairs, he was beginning to have a very disturbing idea.

Laurie didn't answer. She was intent on exposing each corpse's face and leaving it exposed as she went on to the next to avoid having to do it again. She had to move the gurneys around as she worked her way into the room.

Finally she hit pay dirt. As she flicked back a sheet, she caught her breath. It was definitely Leticia Wilson staring vacantly at the ceiling. Her pale, sallow face appeared nestled into a cumulus of dark, curly hair. The only defect other than the pallor was a small oval entrance wound in the center of her forehead, which to Laurie's practiced eye angled downward toward the base of the brain.

Laurie slapped her hand over her mouth and shuddered. Jack put his arm around her.

"Oh my God!" he said.

"Where's my baby?" Laurie questioned plaintively.

"Was that Leticia's mother upstairs?"

Laurie nodded as if in a daze. She had no idea what to think. Was this truly happening, or was it some kind of nightmare trick that her mind was playing on her?

"Come on!" Jack said. "Let's get Lou involved in this. We're lucky he's here."

Jack led Laurie out of the cooler and to the elevator. "I'll take you up to your office and then go down for Lou. Okay?"

Laurie nodded but didn't speak. She tried not to think about where JJ was at that moment or what he was doing or how he was feeling. She wasn't very religious, but she found herself bargaining with God for his safe return.

As if reading Laurie's mind, when they got to her office, Jack said, "Try not to think too much until we get advice." After taking JJ's photo from the top of her desk and stashing it in a drawer, he got her to sit.

As quickly as he could, Jack went back to the registration area, where there were significantly fewer people. Family members had gone into the identification room while some of the other visitors had left. Jack found Lou and Warren sitting together on the couch. They both stood when they caught sight of Jack.

"Sorry about all this," Lou said, as soon as Jack was in earshot. "Is Laurie holding up?"

Jack acknowledged Lou's concern and said Laurie was extremely upset but hanging in there.

"I checked up on the situation while you were away," Lou said. "JJ has been kidnapped. If it's any consolation, the police are taking this very seriously, declaring it a major case with all that entails. Even the commissioner has been apprised. The whole force is participating, and they've already put out an Amber Alert. The entire city is going to know about this. I just talked with the current head detective running the case as the case agent. His name is Bennett, Mark Bennett. He's out of the Major

Case Squad using help from detectives from the Manhattan North Borough. He's a good man, and you should be happy to have him on board. There are a number of other people involved as well, but Mark is the lead guy who will be pulling everything together."

"What about the FBI?"

"The FBI has been alerted, too. Everyone is taking this very seriously."

"So it's definitely considered a kidnapping?"

"Absolutely," Lou said. "A homicide and a kidnapping. Surprisingly, there was only one witness: a mother with her toddler. She was headed for the Hundredth Street playground when she glimpsed a gunman walk up to your nanny, shoot her, and with four accomplices calmly carry JJ and his stroller off to a waiting white van. The van's already been located, thanks to the Amber Alert. It was found abandoned in Garden City and hauled off to a crime scene lab to be thoroughly processed."

"Anything of interest obtained from the crime scene?"

"Crime scene unit is still working the crime scene. If there's anything to be found, they'll find it. I haven't seen this kind of mobilization in years. There's going to be enormous public interest."

"Any demands yet from the abductors?"

"Not a word, which I must say is somewhat disturbing. Demands are healthy, if you know what I'm saying."

"I can imagine," Jack agreed.

"We need to get into negotiation with the bastards."

"Why weren't we notified earlier?" Jack asked. He wasn't blaming, just questioning.

"Initially, the first responders had no identity on JJ,

nor did they have it on the nanny, for that matter. She was not carrying any ID. They figured out who she was from her cell phone, and even that was more difficult than usual."

"Let's get back up to Laurie," Jack said to Lou. "I don't want her to be alone too long. If I know her, she's probably going to blame herself for JJ's disappearance." He turned from Lou to say a fast good-bye to Warren, when Warren spoke up. "I know this is a difficult time, but I'd like to come with you. I want to assure Laurie that the family doesn't hold her in any way responsible for Leticia's death, despite what my aunt Marilyn said. She's obviously distraught out of her mind."

Although Jack was frantic and hardly thinking clearly, he tried to consider Warren's request in view of what he thought Laurie's best interests were. He almost immediately thought it would be good for her to hear what Warren wanted to say. Anything that could keep Laurie from falling into a self-critical despondency was going to help the situation. "Do you need to say anything to anybody before you leave here?"

"I don't," Warren said.

"Then come on up with us!"

As they ascended in the elevator, Warren told Jack what he knew while Lou called Mark Bennett back to say that the Stapletons were now aware of their child's disappearance. Lou tried to keep his voice as quiet as possible.

"Where are they at the moment?" Detective Bennett asked.

"They are still here at OCME."

"Ask them to get home ASAP," Mark said. "We

haven't heard from the kidnappers, which worries me. I'm hoping they'll initiate contact through the Stapletons' home phone, and I want to get the phone wired up so we can listen in on it and also track the incoming calls. As you probably know, in child kidnap cases with no demands, seventy or so percent of them are dead in the first three hours."

"Thanks for the information," Lou said, making sure Jack was not listening in on his conversation and thinking that he would not pass on that particular statistic to Laurie and Jack.

"I just wanted you to know, since you said you'd be hanging around with them," Mark added.

"I'll get them home right away," Lou promised. "And if you want to talk with me before then, you have my mobile number."

"I have it, but I'm coming over to the Stapletons' myself to make sure everything is done right."

"Will you be willing to talk to the couple and explain everything that is being done on their behalf to retrieve their son?"

"Absolutely. Maybe I'll call Henry Fulsome and have him drop by as well. Do you know Henry?"

"Can't say that I do."

"In my book he's the best crisis negotiator the NYPD has. He has a hundred percent record of resolving hostage situations without the loss of a single life."

"That sounds like something they'd love to hear. Of course, it means getting to the point of having a hostage situation to negotiate."

"You're right in that regard. We have our investigative work cut out for us. There's no time to waste."

Up in Laurie's office the three men found her sitting

at her desk, looking blank and pale, as the enormity of her situation had fully set in. She was holding the threatening letter, which she wordlessly passed on to Lou. Having reread it herself, she was even more embarrassed that she'd not taken it seriously. Lou read it quickly, shaking his head.

Warren stepped up to Laurie as she stood. They hugged for a moment, and then Warren apologized for his aunt's behavior. Laurie managed to thank him and said she understood.

"I'm going to hang on to this letter," Lou explained. "And now let's head on to your house. I'll explain what's happening on the way."

CHAPTER THIRTY-FIVE

When Laurie, Jack, Warren, and Lou pulled up in front of Laurie and Jack's town house they were surprised by the throng waiting for them. Cops were everywhere, standing on the stoop and the sidewalk, or waiting in their vehicles. Vans, police cars, and FBI vehicles filled the street.

Laurie braced herself for what was ahead. Since leaving OCME, her emotions had careened from one extreme to the other. One minute she'd felt victimized and despondent, and in the next she felt a kind of fierce anger. She was not going to allow kidnappers to take her child away.

As Laurie and the others climbed out of Lou's car, Laurie forced herself to center on the fighting stance. Although feeling overwhelmed and powerless earlier, she was now eager to meet the case agent, whom Lou had described to her as he'd filled her in on the situation during the drive.

The initial introductions were carried out on the stoop. Mark Bennett had been first, a bear of a man who had come forward with his hand extended as Laurie came up the front steps. "I'm Detective Mark Bennett," he said, shaking Laurie's hand vigorously. "I'm a detective from the Major Case Squad, and I'm here to get your child back as soon as possible." He then went on to introduce a number of other people, including crisis negotiator

Henry Fulsome and a host of other people, other detectives, crime scene specialists, technicians, and even a special agent of the FBI. Laurie found herself impressed with the detective, who seemed to her a walking, talking crime deterrent who spoke of the perpetrators as cowards who needed to be rounded up and thrown into prison for the rest of their lives.

"I'm sorry we have to invade your home for a few days, ma'am," Mark continued as they all entered the brownstone. "But we have to get to work to get your boy back, and time is of the essence. I'm particularly interested in getting our technicians to work on your phone line to wire it up and make both tracking incoming calls and listening in easy. We're also going to put in our own entirely new additional phone line."

"Please," Laurie said, gesturing that the house was theirs. "We appreciate all of you being here. Do whatever is necessary." She and Jack began taking coats and hanging them up in the closet when the phone suddenly rang. Instantly, all conversation stopped. Everyone turned to stare at the phone perched on its little mahogany console table.

"Mrs. Stapleton," Mark said. "Answer it!"

With some hesitation, Laurie approached the phone. She grabbed onto it and looked at the detective for encouragement. Mark nodded and motioned for her to pick it up. When she did, she said a faltering hello.

"Is this Laurie Montgomery-Stapleton?" Brennan questioned. He tried to sound angry and impatient, as Louie had ordered. To his chagrin, his voice quavered. He was nervous.

"Yes," Laurie said, requiring her to clear her throat. She was suddenly terrified and needed to reach out and

lean against the wall to maintain her balance. She instinctively knew it was JJ's abductor.

"We have your kid."

"Who is this?" Laurie asked, struggling to sound
authoritative but failing miserably.

"It doesn't matter who it is," Brennan said. He was
now more successful in modulating his tone. "What's
important is that we have your kid. Would you like to
talk with him?"

Laurie tried to respond but couldn't, not with the
force of tears that had suddenly threatened to burst
forth.

"Are you still there, Mrs. Stapleton? I need you to
speak. I cannot be on the line for more than a moment."

"I'm still here," Laurie managed. "I want my child
back. Why did you take my child?"

"I want you to start to mobilize some cash, and I
want you to do it quickly. Do you understand?"

"I understand."

"Do you want to talk to your child? I'm trying to be
patient."

"Yes, I do." Laurie wiped tears from her eyes.

"Okay, you little brat," Brennan said off-line. "Say
hello to your mommy."

There was silence.

"Maybe you'd better say hello to him," Brennan said,
coming back on the line. "I'll put him on again."

"Hello, sweetheart," Laurie said, assuming the phone
was being pressed against his ear. She was desperately trying
to avoid crying. "It's Mommy here. Are you all right?"

"Well, he's smiling," Brennan reported. "Whatever
you said, he's smiling. Should I shake him up a bit and
get him to cry?"

"I want my child back immediately," Laurie demanded. "Don't shake him!"

"Getting your child back isn't going to happen immediately, Mrs. Stapleton, but it could happen soon. It will be up to you if you are to get him back at all. You have to mobilize cash. Am I clear on that? We're not going to require cash, but you'll need cash to get what we'll be demanding. You'll be needing a lot of cash."

"Yes," Laurie managed with a shiver.

"And another thing. We don't want you to work with the police. We know they are there at your home right this minute. Get rid of them. We will know if you don't listen to us, and it will be your son who'll suffer. We'll send him to you a piece at a time."

There was a pause. "I hope you're taking this all in," Brennan said, not waiting for Laurie to respond, "because I'm going to have to hang up. But there's one more demand. I'll be calling you back tomorrow, so I want you to be available at any time, day or night. Until then, have a nice evening."

There was a final click. For a moment Laurie continued to hold the phone to her ear as she tried to get herself under control. She was afraid if she did anything, even move, she would break out in tears.

Mark stepped over, took the phone from her hand, and placed it back on its base. "I'm sure you don't feel it this minute, but hearing from the abductors is a very positive development. We are truly relieved. It confirms what we had hoped: that this case is about kidnapping for ransom and not something else. When the kidnapping is for ransom, it is in the kidnappers' best interest that the victim stays alive and healthy."

CHAPTER THIRTY-SIX

As the hour closed in on eleven o'clock, Laurie and Jack accompanied Detective Mark Bennett down the stairs to say good-bye when the detective declared that everything they needed to do had been accomplished. The most important thing was the Stapleton phone. It was now being monitored twenty-four-seven, and incoming calls could be traced from a bank of equipment in a small makeshift office set up in a guest room on the first floor.

"I'll be checking in by phone in the morning," Mark said, pausing at the front door. Except for the officer manning the communications equipment, who was going to stay all night, Mark was the last person from the NYPD to leave.

"Thank you for all you've done," Laurie said. Not only had he supervised everyone else's work, he'd taken the time to explain to Laurie and Jack everything that had been done up to that point. It started with the 911 dispatch of the first responders from Central Park Precinct Twenty-two, and the Manhattan North Patrol Borough, who had secured the crime scene, interviewed the only witness, initiated the process of declaring the Amber Alert, prepared the BOLO (Be On the LOokout) for a white van with six adult men and one infant, and established a leads-management folder at the NYPD's Real Time Crime Center.

Mark had gone on to explain that after the first responders' work had been done, an initial supervisory officer had dispatched an evidence collection unit as well as a crime scene unit while also reviewing the sex offenders registry in the area of the kidnapping and entering the case into the National Crime Information Center's Missing Person File.

"It had been then that I got involved," Mark had explained. "After both the police commissioner and the mayor's office were briefed, the case was referred by the chief of detectives to the Major Case Squad, as well as the FBI, and Team Adam. As I'm part of the Major Case Squad and was available, I was assigned to run it. What I've managed to do with my staff so far is to debrief the first responders and the only witness, and review all the information that's currently in the leads-management system at the Real Time Crime Center at One Police Plaza."

Jack opened the front door. A cool nighttime breeze wafted in off the street. A few yells from an intense basketball game on the neighborhood court were borne on the wind. "Looks like a real neighborhood around here," Mark noted. "It's almost eleven and the kids are still playing hoops. I'm glad to see it, and not just because it helps keep them out of trouble. I like it because it means it is a community."

"It is a great neighborhood. Warren, whom you met upstairs, is one of the local leaders. He and I play hoops all the time, particularly on Friday nights. We'd be out there now if it weren't for this ongoing tragedy."

"Earlier I told you what had been accomplished so far in this case. All that pales to your cooperation and having a name and a description to apply to the victim.

I'm sorry you are having to go through this, but you and your wife are, by necessity, key players. We need your help. In return, I give you my word that I, and everyone I command, will do everything in our power to get your boy back healthy."

"Thank you," Laurie and Jack said in unison.

With a quick parting salute, Mark bounded down the steps and entered a waiting unmarked official car. Both Jack and Laurie silently watched the vehicle head up to Central Park West and turn right on West Side Drive.

"I have a lot of confidence in him," Laurie said, in an attempt to buoy up her spirits. "I'm exhausted, but I know I'm not going to be able to sleep." She crossed in front of Jack and re-entered the house.

Before Jack went in, he looked over to watch the basketball game sweep up and down the court. Although he'd been actively avoiding thinking about consequences, he suddenly found himself hoping beyond hope that JJ would be found soon and not be harmed so as to be able to grow up and experience the multitudinous joys of life.

Back upstairs, Jack looked for Laurie. With all the excitement suddenly over, he was worried how she was going to cope, just as he worried about himself. He was surprised not to find her in the kitchen. Neither of them had taken the time to eat anything, as Detective Bennett had kept them busy answering questions about JJ and his complicated medical history. Bennett had also quizzed them about the kinds of service people who regularly visited the house and if any had their own keys. Next he'd had them gather objects likely to contain JJ's DNA, find current photos of the child, and even try to figure out what he had been wearing when he'd been abducted.

Jack paused when he heard voices coming from the family room. He'd almost forgotten that Lou and Warren were still there. He was doubly surprised to find two additional men in the room. Both were talking to Laurie, who was listening intently.

"Ah, Jack," Lou said. "Please come in! There are some people I want you to meet."

"Yes, dear," Laurie said. "Come in!"

Everyone stood as Jack advanced into the room, making Jack wonder about the apparent formality. He looked at the two strangers, neither of whom he had seen until that moment. Both stood ramrod-straight with shoulders back, with closely cropped hair and dressed in snug, carefully tailored navy-blue suits, crisp white shirts, and regimental ties. They both were slightly taller than Jack's six feet and looked to be in their early forties. Particularly because of their svelte figures and hard, taut faces, they appeared to be in superb physical shape. Jack's impression was that they were military, possibly Special Forces in civvies.

"This is Grover Collins," Lou said, pointing to the stockier of the two men.

Jack shook hands, peering questioningly into the individual's glacially blue eyes. The grip was strong but not too strong, more confident than anything else.

"Terrific to meet you," Grover said, with a hint of an English accent.

"And this is Colt Thomas," Lou said, gesturing toward Grover's African-American partner.

"My pleasure," Colt said with a handshake the mirror image of Grover's. Jack hardly thought of himself as an expert in accents, but if he'd been forced to guess, he would have described Colt's as Texan.

"Now, first let me apologize," Lou said to Jack. "I have taken it upon myself to invite Grover and Colt here tonight because I think you and Laurie ought to hire them."

Jack's eyes went from Laurie and then back to the guests. "Hire as what?" he asked.

"I think time is of the essence," Lou continued, ignoring Jack's question, "and these gentlemen happen to agree with me. Is that fair to say, gentlemen?"

"Indeed," Grover confirmed without hesitation. Colt merely nodded.

"Please, sit down!" Jack said, realizing he was the de facto host at this impromptu meeting.

Everyone returned to their seats. Jack brought over a straight-backed chair and sat down himself.

"I had the pleasure of working with these gentle-men a few years ago," Lou continued, "and I was very impressed, which is the reason I called them tonight. They're a relatively new breed. They're kidnap consult-ants."

"'Kidnap consultants'?" Jack questioned. "I didn't even know there was such a thing."

"Actually, there are now quite a few of us," Grover said. "We refer to ourselves as risk managers as we prefer to stay more or less in the shadows."

"I was not aware of them, either," Lou admitted. "Not until I had the pleasure of working with them on a kidnapping case—for a very successful outcome, I must add."

"We've been born by demand," Grover explained. "Kidnapping flourishes in circumstances of disorder and confusion, which the world has seen rather enough of these days, such that there has been a serious uptick in incidence of kidnapping the world over, but mainly in the Americas and Russia."

"I was not aware of it," Jack said, "but it does make sense."

"There are thousands of cases each year in hot spots like Colombia, Venezuela, Mexico, and Brazil. We have about forty field operatives in our firm, CRT Risk Management. We're active all around the world, and the only thing we handle is kidnapping. I'm just back from Rio, and Colt returned yesterday from Mexico City."

"Are you ex-military?" Jack asked.

"How could you tell?" Grover smiled. "I'm ex-SAS, and Colt is ex–Navy SEAL. Returning to civilian life after military service has been difficult for us Special Forces fellows, and this kind of work seems to have been tailor-made. Sitting in a La-Z-Boy smoking a pipe and watching reruns of game shows is not a possibility for any of us. We love our work."

"Tell them what you told me," Lou said. "Why you could particularly help in their situation."

"Having been briefed about your case, several things jump out at us. First of all, the NYPD, like all police departments in the USA, have had limited experience running a kidnapping. It's just the opposite with us. It's all we do, and as kidnapping has grown worldwide, it's become more sophisticated, both in terms of how the abductors work and how we professionals respond.

"Second of all, our motivation is different from that of the authorities. The authorities actually have conflicting goals. They, of course, want to rescue your child, but that's only one of their objectives. They also want to catch the perpetrators, and I say 'perpetrators' specifically, because modern kidnapping is a team sport, and often they want to catch the perpetrators with about equal zeal as they want to free the abductee. In other words, there are political ramifications for the police and the FBI. Also, what else is occasionally troubling is that the authorities often are competitive with each other, which is hardly the kind of situation that is the most successful.

"None of that is applicable to us. Bringing your child home safe is our one and only goal and concern. We don't care about the perpetrators. We don't care if they get arrested; we don't care if they get convicted. If they do, all the better, but it is not our goal, whereas with the police or FBI it most certainly is. As far as your son is concerned, we then have a step on the police or FBI. We don't worry about warrants for searches or listening devices; we don't concern ourselves with Miranda rights, and we can and are, on occasion, heavy-handed with suspects. When we need information, we get it. Let's put it that way."

"Do you consider yourselves vigilantes of sorts?" Laurie asked.

"Not in the slightest," Collins said. "Our sole goal is the safe recovery of your child as soon as possible. That's the mission. If an abductor gets hurt, that's their problem, not ours, but we're not about to punish anyone."

"You're only talking in generalities, Grover," Lou complained. "Tell them what you told me about specifics. Tell them why you would be good for this case in particular."

"Detective Soldano has been very open with us," Grover continued, "and he has shared with us the file from the Real Time Crime Center. He's also let us read the threatening letter which you had received and ignored."

"There were reasons," Laurie said, embarrassed anew.

"I can understand why you might have ignored it," Grover said. "So don't be hard on yourself. It only mentioned you, not your son. But the combination of your son's abduction and the letter tells us that this case needs to move forward quickly to minimize the threat to your child, and that's the way we will approach the case if you decide to employ us. Knowing the police and how they work, my strong sense is they will be conservative and wait for the abductors to communicate here and begin a negotiation, as they already have done. The passive approach, which is a tried-and-true method, isn't appropriate in this situation. We believe the approach should be more proactive by anticipating consequences. Although it's generally difficult to discover where a victim is being held, the opposite is true in this case for a number of reasons. We think these kidnappers are not experienced. The snatch was poorly planned and executed. Experienced kidnappers don't start the game off with a homicide, as Lou can tell you."

"It's true," Lou offered. "On the last and only kidnapping case I was involved in, the snatch was the most carefully planned part of the whole deal."

"Second," Grover continued, "there was no apparent research as to the extent of personal wealth. If I'm not mistaken, there is no huge payday here, like a huge family fortune that can be tapped."

"Hardly," Jack responded. "All of our savings are tied up in this renovated house.

"Let me tell you, in a kidnap-for-ransom case these days, it is extraordinarily rare for the perpetrator not to have done extensive research into the victim's finances. It suggests that the kidnapping was done not for monetary gain but for something else entirely. The talk about money is probably a distraction at best."

"If the threatening letter is associated with the kidnapping, as we believe it is, the real issue is for you to stop investigating the case mentioned in the letter, at least in the short run. What can you tell us about it?"

"It's a case I'm taking over," Lou said, speaking up before Laurie. "It was initially thought to be a natural death, but Laurie has proved otherwise. We also have a name: Satoshi Machita. Just this afternoon Laurie has established quite believably that it was an organized crime–sponsored assassination. Beyond that I cannot say."

"Interesting," Grover said, pausing while he pondered this new information. "The possible involvement of organized crime is an important new wrinkle."

"It's certainly going to quickly influence my homicide investigation," Lou added.

"I'm also curious about the tone of the letter," Grover said. "It's as if a third party was involved, making me think there might have been an element of extortion playing a role. I mean, why this anonymity?"

"My thought exactly," Lou said. "And there was a situation of such extortion in OCME about fifteen years ago. Remember, Laurie?"

"Of course I do," Laurie said. "Vinnie Amendola had been indebted to the Cerino Mob for saving his father way back when. And today Vinnie was acting very out of character. In fact, he took an emergency leave, supposedly for a family emergency."

"Did he say where?" Lou questioned.

"He didn't," Laurie said.

"Well, I know what I'll be doing first thing in the morning," Lou said.

"That could be helpful," Grover said, "but I don't think we should wait until this Vinnie is located and questioned. I'm concerned about the child's safety. Whoever the abductors are, they surely don't mind killing, as evidenced by how they did the snatch, and I'm worried what they will do with the child once they believe they have achieved their goal of getting Laurie out of the morgue to keep her from discovering what she's already discovered, which I'm assuming they don't know as of yet."

"What exactly would you do?" Jack asked. He did not see anything else that could be done other than wait for the abductors to call and then trace the call. "All I can see is what the police are doing, trying to get the bad guys into a negotiation. JJ could be anywhere, anywhere at all in the whole state or neighboring states."

"I think your child is nearby," Grover said. "Considering the way the case has gone so far in terms of a near total lack of planning, your son is probably at one of the participants' homes. In many respects, handling and housing an infant is logistically easier than an adult. With an adult, all sorts of precautions have to be taken for them not to know where they are secreted away and a method for housing them such that they never see their captors, unless, of course, the abductors never plan to release them. But killing the victim makes getting anything in return impossible because of elaborate proof-of-life mechanisms developed for the exchange process."

"Okay," Jack said. "I understand all that, but how

do you propose to find out where our child is being held? That seems impossible to me."

"It is often difficult, if not impossible," Grover agreed. "But there are unique situations that can help, as I believe there are in this circumstance. First, there is the strong possibility Vinnie Amendola may be able to help by providing information about who the kidnappers are. But we shouldn't wait for that possibility, although we will encourage it. No, the unique circumstance is the fact that you are living in a city with true neighborhoods. People who are not New Yorkers probably would not understand, as they see New York as a massive, impersonal city. While we've been here waiting to speak to you and your wife, I've had the pleasure to talk with your friend here, Warren Wilson, who is very concerned about your child and eager to help."

Grover gestured toward Warren, who nodded in confirmation.

"He's told me," Grover continued, "that you and your wife are respected and universally liked members of this neighborhood, which is close-knit, and have been so for almost twenty years. He also mentioned your generosity, in respect to the playground across the street, and about young men who have stayed in school and gone off to college because of you. It's a wonderful story, which is now going to come back and reward you."

"How so?" Jack asked.

"One thing that CRT has learned over the years in handling hundreds and hundreds of kidnapping cases is that the kidnappers often watch over their victim's families, mainly to ensure that the families comply with their demands. One demand, which is always a part of the kidnapping scenario, is to keep authorities away from the action. The only way they can do that is by watching that there isn't police or FBI traffic in and out of the family's residence. If they see that happening, they bring it up on the next call and make another distant threat that such and such will be done to the victim.

"And if we are correct in assuming this particular kidnapping is not primarily a kidnap for ransom but rather a way to keep your wife from her work, there is even more reason to suspect they will have a watcher on duty, at least during the daylight hours."

"So you intend to catch this watcher? Is that the idea?"

"It is indeed. The reason that it works, which we've been able to use maybe a half-dozen times before, twice in São Paulo, Brazil, is that these are stable, tight neighborhoods where the residents quickly recognize people hanging around who don't belong. Warren has offered to do that for you, starting early tomorrow morning. He assures us this is a very tight community with experience picking out strangers to keep gang violence to a minimum."

Jack looked at Warren, who again nodded in confirmation.

"Once you catch the so-called 'watcher,' what do you do?" Jack questioned.

"Best not to ask," Grover said. "First we make certain the individual is a watcher on the case in question. Then we ask him or her where the victim is being held. As I said earlier, in contrast to the police or FBI, our hands are not tied by legal niceties. Our interest and concern are finding and rescuing the victim. Sometimes it takes more persuasion than others."

"And once you have the location, what then?"

"It depends to an extent on how concerned we are about the victim's plight. If the risk is low, we'll try to determine before a raid where and under what conditions the victim is being held. Sometimes, like with your son, we would move on a rescue immediately. But that's when Colt here comes into play. He is CRT's major rescuer. His talents are legendary. He's capable of entering a home and taking pierced earrings out of people's ears without waking them."

"If we hire you," Jack questioned, "how will the police react? Do you or we tell them or keep it a secret?"

"We tell them. Actually, we try to work with them, even to the point of giving suggestions when appropriate. We never tell them what to do, just what we've done in the past that seemed to work. Plus, we're all for the police to have the credit when the victim is rescued or exchanged. We truly do not want the credit in the media, because we do our job better with anonymity."

"Can I ask the cost?"

"By all means. Colt and I as a team will be two thousand dollars a day plus expenses. Obviously, with no travel the expenses will be minimal."

"Excuse me for a moment," Jack said, rising to his feet. He motioned for Laurie to step out into the hallway. Once there, he asked, sotto voce, "Well, what do you think?"

"I was impressed by Detective Bennett and how the police have responded, but I'm also impressed by these two men. They have enormous experience. I'm just so upset I don't know if I can make a rational decision, although the idea of being proactive appeals to me."

"Well said," Jack responded. "I can't claim to be clear-thinking, either. Let's get Lou's and Warren's opinions."

"Good idea," Laurie said.

Jack stuck his head back into the room. He motioned to Lou and Warren that he'd like to speak with them, and they responded immediately. When they were all in the kitchen and out of earshot of the men from CRT, Jack said, "Laurie and I realize we're not in the best condition to be thinking rationally, and frankly are a bit overwhelmed. What do you people think we should do?"

"I think you should hire these guys," Lou said. "That's why I called them. I think it is a lucky break they are available."

"What about you, Warren?"

"I'd hire them. What can you lose? And I'm more than happy to help for JJ's and for Leticia's sake. And all the guys will be happy to pitch in. It's not a problem."

"Terrific!" Jack said decisively, trying to find a way to lift his spirits as the nightmare continued to unfold around him.

CHAPTER THIRTY-SEVEN

It had not been a good night for Laurie or Jack. Once the house was empty, save for the single detective hidden away manning the telephone equipment, the horrors of their experience set in with a vengeance. Knowing their child was in harm's way in the company of terrible strangers who might be mistreating him, and being powerless to do anything about it, was a kind of torture they had never experienced. They also spoke of Leticia and the tragedy she represented, and how her death would be a source of guilt for them for the rest of their lives.

Laurie finally fell asleep around seven, after a particularly long binge of tears, but Jack had not slept at all. By seven-thirty he'd given up, made himself a pot of tea, and sat in the family room. He was breathing, but that was about all, his mind an exhausted blank.

It was in that state that the phone rang. Jack answered it in a panic, not because of who he thought might be calling but rather to try to keep it from awakening Laurie.

"Hello," Jack blurted.

"I want to speak to Laurie Montgomery-Stapleton," Brennan ordered, again trying to sound angry and demanding, as if he'd had reason to feel slighted.

"She's asleep," Jack answered. Although he'd not heard the man's voice the evening before, Jack knew instantly with whom he was speaking, which filled him with boundless fury and resentment. He had to restrain himself from verbally attacking the man.

"She'll speak to me if she knows what is good for her son."

"You can speak with me," Jack ordered. "I'm the father and the husband."

"I need to speak to her, not you but her," Brennan insisted. "Don't argue with me. Otherwise, I'll go out to the car, drag the bloody bastard kid back in here, and make you regret giving me a hard time."

"Okay," Jack offered, obviously not pleased but unwilling to put JJ at any additional risk. Jack laid the phone onto the side table and rushed back to the bedroom. When he pushed open the door, Laurie was sitting on the side of the bed. She was leaning forward, head in her hands, elbows on her knees.

"I'm sorry. It's him, and he insists on speaking with you."

Laurie nodded, reached over, and put her hand on the phone, but she didn't answer immediately. Rather, she took a deep breath to try to prepare herself. She had a wicked bi-temporal headache as if she had drunk herself into a stupor the evening before.

"Hello," Laurie said with a voice as tired as she felt.

"Tell your husband that when I call in the future, I want to speak to you and no one else. Is that clear? He tried to insist that I talk to him. Tell him if that happens in the future, something will happen to the tyke. Your kid will lose something, like I said last night, such as an ear or a finger, which I'll be happy to send to you to make sure you know we are serious."

"Is my child there with you now?"

"No, not this time. He's out in the car. But later this afternoon, when I call again, I'll bring him to the phone. Now I'm ready to give you our demands. Remember, no police or the kid gets hurt. We want a million dollars, but not in cash. Cash is too bulky, and it can be marked. We want a million dollars in D perfect diamonds. We don't care about the size, but the diamonds have to have a combined wholesale value of a million dollars. They are easy to get in New York City. Any questions?"

"What do we do if we don't have a million dollars?" Laurie asked in a matter-of-fact fashion.

"You and your husband are doctors," Brennan said. "You can get a million dollars."

"All our money is tied up in our house."

"Whatever," Brennan said, and then hung up.

Laurie replaced the receiver slowly and looked up at Jack. "Could you hear his side of the conversation?"

"Pretty much." Jack said.

"It sounds like he's role-playing to me."

"I think Grover was right about these people being novices and that the ransom is of secondary importance," Jack said. "Otherwise, why would he be so insistent about talking with you? He wants to make sure you are here and not back at OCME."

"Maybe so," Laurie said. The fact that these goons, whoever they were, had her son and were threatening to harm him was the only issue she was at all concerned about, and she desperately wanted him home.

"Can I bring you anything?" Jack asked.

"No," Laurie said, a flood of despondency washing over her.

"Why don't you come and take a shower? Then

maybe you might want to eat some breakfast. Remember, we didn't eat at all last night."

"I'm not hungry."

"That's the point. Why not shower? Maybe a shower will make you hungry."

"Leave me alone," Laurie snapped. "I don't want to shower or eat. I just want to lie here."

"Okay," Jack said. "Meanwhile, I'm going downstairs to see how the police guy did with that call. Do you remember his name?"

"I never learned it in the first place," Laurie commented, sounding like a true depressive, falling back onto the pillow. She would have loved to have slept, but she knew it was out of the question. She felt exhausted, depressed, and hopped-up all at the same time.

Jack went down the stairs to the first floor and knocked on the guest-room door. It was quickly opened. The plainclothes officer staying in the room immediately introduced himself. His name was Sergeant Edwin D. Gunner.

"It just dawned on me," Jack said guiltily. "You haven't had anything to eat. Would you like some breakfast?"

"Some coffee would be nice," Edwin said. "I'm not much of a breakfast guy."

"Did you catch that recent phone call? It was the kidnapper."

"I did catch it," Edwin said, following Jack back up the stairs.

"Could you trace it?" Jack asked.

"Absolutely," Edwin said.

"To where?"

"To one of the remaining thousand or so public
phones in the city. This one is in a twenty-four-hour
Laundromat on the Lower East Side. Of course a squad
car was dispatched as soon as the trace was completed,
but don't be optimistic. The kidnapper would have been
long gone."

"No doubt," Jack answered. He quelled a fantasy
about being there clutching something like a crowbar
the moment the goon hung up the phone.

CHAPTER THIRTY-EIGHT

Warren Wilson lived on the same block as Laurie and Jack but at the Columbus Avenue end. He'd taken the very first shift, starting at six a.m., to look for strangers watching Laurie and Jack's building. Jack and Laurie's building was several hundred yards in the direction of Central Park and stood out as one of the classiest buildings in the neighborhood, with neatly tended window boxes and a shiny brass knocker. At that time the window boxes were still filled with winter foliage.

To give himself a bit of cover, Warren had borrowed his downstairs neighbor's dog. It was a pleasant little white thing that barked at everything, including cars. His name was Killer. Since there were so few people in the street at six a.m. on a Saturday, Warren had wanted some reason to be strolling up and down the block, and Killer was happy to oblige, as long as he was permitted to smell every tree and fire hydrant he and Warren encountered.

After Warren had left Laurie and Jack's the previous night, he'd gone home and called five of his oldest friends, all of whom had lived in the neighborhood from birth. They all played basketball regularly and had gone to high school together. All were African-American like Warren. All worked and lived in the neighborhood and knew most residents by their first names.

Since it was Saturday they were more than willing to

help. With good weather in the forecast, they'd already planned to spend the afternoon on the basketball court almost directly across the street from Laurie and Jack's house.

Exactly a half-hour late for his stint, which was supposed to have started at ten a.m., Flash showed up. "Hey, man," Warren said as Flash approached, slouched over, wearing dark glasses and hip-hop clothes. "You look a little worse for wear."

"Don't give me shit," Flash said. "I don't know why I agreed to this torture. Who am I looking for again, and why?"

Warren explained the situation as he'd done the night before. "Now don't go to sleep on me," Warren advised. "Because if you do, I'm going to kick your ass."

"You and who else?" Flash joked.

For the four hours and thirty minutes Warren had stalked the neighborhood, he'd seen nothing at all suspicious. There had been surprisingly few pedestrians, and those he did see had expressed no interest in Laurie and Jack's house. Nor had any particular vehicle driven up and down the block. In every way it had seemed like a normal early-spring Saturday morning on 106th Street, with chirping birds, a few dog walkers, and not much else.

As soon as he'd been relieved and had returned Killer to his owner, Warren went back to Columbus Avenue, picked up a *Daily News* at the Korean sundries store, and ducked into one of the many local coffee shops for a coffee and a bagel. He'd barely been able to read the headlines before his cell phone went off. Checking the screen, he could see that it was Flash.

Feeling annoyed that Flash was already bothering

him, Warren answered the phone with his emotions apparent. All he said was "Yeah!"

"Pay dirt!" Flash said simply.

"What do you mean 'pay dirt'?" Warren questioned with growing irritation. "You've only been there for fifteen minutes."

"I don't know how long it's been, but I got a bozo here who's looking might suspicious!"

"Really?" Warren questioned dubiously. "There's no way you can tell if someone is a watcher in fifteen minutes."

"This guy is acting awfully suspicious, acting like he's here for the day, and I've never seen him before."

"Yeah, well, you watch him! If he's still acting suspicious after a period of time, then call me back." Warren rolled his eyes and broke the connection. "Jesus Christ Almighty," he said under his breath, tossing his phone aside as if it had been its fault for bothering him.

Fifteen minutes later, after Warren had eaten half his bagel, drunk half his coffee, and had breezed through an uninteresting sports section, his phone rang again. Again, it was Flash.

"Okay," Warren said, still highly suspicious. "What's happening?"

"He's still acting weird. He's a Jersey guy, or at least he's got Jersey plates on the black Caddy Escalade he's driving. It's like he's advertising he's a watcher. At one point he suddenly climbed out, went through a routine of calisthenics."

"Don't get too close. People who are acting as watchers are hypersensitive to being watched themselves. In fact, how far away are you now?"

"Fifty feet or so. I'm across the street."

"That's too close. Move away and don't look at him! I tell you what—go over to the basketball court. I'll meet you there with a ball. We can pretend we're practicing."

"What if he moves his car? Do I follow?"

"No, if he moves just try to get the plate number without being obvious."

"Got it."

With a gulp Warren downed the rest of his coffee. Snapping up his paper, he ran out of the coffee shop. When he reached 106th Street, he purposely slowed to a walk. As he headed for his house, he could see Flash entering the playground. He could also see a black SUV parked on the playground side of the street.

"Where have you been?" his girlfriend Natalie questioned casually when Warren came through the apartment's front door.

"Out!" Warren said, opening the hall closet to get one of his several outdoor basketballs.

"This early?" Natalie questioned. Saturday morning was the morning of the week that she and Warren generally lazed around. "What time did you go out?"

"Around six," Warren said, coming into the living room and giving Natalie a peck on the cheek.

"Six? What on earth were you doing outside at six?"

"Walking Killer. But look, I'll explain it later. Flash is out on the court. We're going to practice a bit."

"Okay," Natalie said indifferently. If Warren wanted to be enigmatic about his Saturday-morning activities, she could not have cared less. "Have fun!"

Warren descended back to street level and headed toward the playground. There were now many more people around, including a bunch of toddlers in the

sandbox and preteens on the swings. As he got closer
to the black SUV, he could see that it had heavily tinted
windows that precluded any view into its interior. He
stayed on the right-hand side of the street until he was
abreast of the car in question, then crossed directly in
front of the Escalade. Although he could tell there was
someone sitting behind the wheel, he couldn't see any
features at all, partly because he avoided looking directly.

Reaching the sidewalk, he waved and called out
Flash's name. Flash responded in kind. Warren made a
point of not turning around as he continued on into
the playground.

"Has he moved?" Warren asked, coming up to Flash.

"Are you asking about the guy or the car? I can't see
the guy, and the car hasn't moved."

Warren tossed the basketball to Flash. "Let's do a quick
game of one-on-one. Don't look at the car, but keep an
eye on it just the same.

Warren was by far the better player and won easily,
but Flash won the trash talk. Both were out of breath.
Even though when they started they'd told each other
they were just going to play easy, once the game started,
their natural competitiveness had taken over.

"Let's take a rest," Warren said. He went over to the
bench seat, sat down, and took out his mobile phone.

"Oh, yeah!" Flash teased. "He wins one lucky game
and wants to retire."

"Give me a sec and I'll give you another chance to
lose," Warren teased back. "I want to call the big guys.
As much as I hate to admit it, I think you found yourself the watcher."

While Flash used the opportunity to practice his jump
shot, Warren called Grover Collins. Warren told Grover

that he believed they'd already identified a watcher at Laurie and Jack's house.

"How long have you been keeping tabs on the individual?" Grover asked, acting as if he was not surprised in the slightest at Warren's rapid success.

"Not long—fifteen to twenty minutes. He's parked just across the street from Laurie and Jack's house, and he's not being subtle. I've been told he's already gotten out and done calisthenics."

Grover laughed. "Bloody confident, I'd say."

"Bloody stupid, I'd say," Warren countered humorously, trying to mimic an English accent.

"Try to keep an eye on him, but be subtle."

"Will do. Actually, it's very easy. We're here using the basketball court as we do every Saturday."

"If he drives away, don't try to follow him. He'll either return or someone else will undoubtedly come to take his place. I'll pick up my partner. Are you armed?"

"Of course not!" Warren said, with a tone reflecting how crazy he thought the question was.

"Well, perhaps it would be better if you were. If both I and Colt would somehow mess up, which we never have, I wouldn't want you to be vulnerable. I presume you have access to a weapon of some sort."

"I have something," Warren admitted vaguely.

"We'll be there as soon as possible. Remember, be subtle!"

"What's the plan, if I may ask?"

"The plan is simply that we are going to come over and invite this gentleman to come with us for a short party and ask him what we need to know. Luckily, we just rented a convenient spot for the party. When we know what we need to know—namely, the address where the Stapleton child is being held—we will bring our friend back to his car, where we would appreciate getting a hand putting him back so he can sleep off his medication."

"Will you need help getting him from his car into your car?"

"Heavens, no!" Grover said. "But thank you for the offer. The main reason we don't want your help is because it is a felony, of course, to take someone elsewhere against their will, which we justify as an eye for an eye, a tooth for a tooth. As for the practical legal aspects, we have our own in-house defense attorney. Anyway, the answer is no. We do the kidnapping."

CHAPTER THIRTY-NINE

I think we can give ourselves a compliment," Colt said to Grover. Colt was driving, and Grover was studying the MapQuest directions. "That little event was carried out extraordinarily well."

The event he was referring to was their surprising the watcher and transferring him from his car to the back of a rented black Ford van. At the moment they'd burst into his SUV, which he'd failed to lock, the man, whom they later learned was Duane Mackenzie, had not been doing much watching, except for watching the ongoing neighborhood basketball game. As a consequence, Grover and Colt had been able to get their hands on the SUV's front door handles and the doors open before Duane could react. By that time, he had two suppressed Smith & Wesson automatic pistols pressed against his neck while he was being relieved of his own weapon.

"Now, here's what you are going to do," Colt had said to the shocked and terrified Duane. "We're going to get out of the SUV and walk directly across the street and climb into the back of that black Ford van without making any fuss. If you do, you are going to get blown away. Am I understood?"

"Who are you?" Duane tried to demand, but his voice quavered in terror.

"Shut up!" Colt had snapped. Then to Grover:

"How clear does the neighborhood look?" He wasn't about to take his eyes off Duane.

"It looks good," Grover had said, avoiding using Colt's name. "No pedestrians except two heading away, and no oncoming cars."

Colt, who had been on the driver's side, had yanked Duane out of the SUV and had marched him quickly down the street. Colt had lowered the gun temporarily to his side. Grover had caught up to the other two at the back of the van and had opened the back doors.

Once the doors were wide open, Colt had forced Duane inside in a smooth and practiced fashion. Inside the van was an open, domestic oriental rug, onto which Duane was forced to lie prone. Grover had climbed in as well, and as Colt kept the barrel of his gun pressed against Duane's neck, Grover had bound the man's arms with duct tape, gagged him with a small rag secured with duct tape, and then rolled him up in the rug. The whole episode, from entering Duane's vehicle to his being bound inside the rug, had taken less than a minute, and the only person to have been a witness was Jack. Thanks to the discussion the previous evening, he had noticed the SUV and had been watching it continuously.

"Where should I turn east?" Colt asked, as he headed south on Central Park West.

"Either at Fifty-ninth or Fifty-seventh," Grover responded. "Fifty-ninth will be fine."

They were on their way to Woodside, Queens, where they had rented a small two-story house. It was brick, with a garage entered from a back alleyway. The garage had been key. They wanted to avoid any curiosity when unloading their guest.

"Do you think he is adequately terrified?" Colt asked. Part of the technique was to scare the hell out of the victim to loosen his tongue.

"I think so," Grover said. "I certainly would be." He checked his watch. "I hope this doesn't take too long. We've a lot to do today."

They crossed over the Queensboro Bridge and onto Northern Boulevard, then onto 54th Street. The house they had rented was in the middle of the block. Colt turned into the alleyway. The garage door had an automatic opener, one of whose buttons Grover pressed as they approached. The garage door rattled upward, and Colt expertly pulled the van in and killed the engine.

"Let's get our tools in first, get set up, and then come back for our guest."

"Sounds good to me, but let's not make this our life's work," Grover said.

CHAPTER FORTY

The phone again jolted both Laurie and Jack, causing their pulses to speed up. A half-hour earlier it had been Warren apologizing for disturbing them but telling Jack that a handful of the boys were already out at the court and thinking they might start earlier than usual that afternoon. He wanted to know if Jack would like to join them to take his mind off what was going on. Jack had given the idea a brief thought, but after looking at Laurie had decided not to do it. He reasoned that they needed to be with each other even though they had run out of things to say. For both, the hardest part was feeling helpless while flipping back and forth between despondency and anger.

Before he'd hung up, Warren did have something at least interesting if not hopeful to say. He'd said that he and Flash had found a possible watcher, and Grover and Colt had come and hauled the man away.

"I actually saw the abduction," Jack had admitted. "Do you know where they took him?"

"No idea," Warren had said. "But we're supposed to wait around for when they bring the guy back. That's why we decided to start playing early."

The second time the phone rang, neither of them wanted to pick it up. Laurie sat in a club chair, Jack on the couch next to the corner table where the phone lived. At that moment he was in the depressed side of his cycling emotions and was not sure he could interact with anyone. Nonetheless, after a few more rings he picked up the handset. He expected it was Warren trying to put more pressure on him to play ball, but it wasn't. It was Captain Detective Mark Bennett.

"How are you people doing?" Mark asked. "Did you get any sleep?"

"Sleep is not in the cards today," Jack said. "Is anything happening? You know we got another call?"

"Absolutely," Mark said. "I listened to the recording a number of times and have even visited the Laundromat from where the call was made in hopes of talking to an employee who might have remembered the incident, but no go. At least we know the way they are going to communicate with us, which is important in and of itself."

"Is that going to help?"

"Yes and no. There's still a lot of public phones in the city, so we cannot stake out all of them. But it is something we'll keep in mind as things progress. The important thing is that they came up with a specific demand, which means the negotiation will be starting. That's an important milestone."

"And reminded us of a previous demand," Jack said. "They said no police. They threatened to physically hurt JJ if we don't respect it."

"That's a demand kidnappers generally make," Mark said, "and for obvious reasons, we are sensitive to the issue. We will certainly not broadcast our involvement in any way or form. Whether you tell the media or not is up to you, although we strongly recommend you don't."

"What about your coming in and out of here?" Jack questioned. "And what about the officer downstairs?"

"The officer downstairs will remain for now but will not be going in and out your door. We will be appreciative if you temporarily provide him with food and drink. Today or tomorrow we will figure out a way for him to get in and out and to be replaced without it being obvious to anyone watching the building. It is one of the benefits of living in a row house with multiple entrances into the rear common area."

"No one is going to be coming in and out of the front door?" Jack questioned, just to be certain.

"Absolutely not," Mark said.

"Anything else on your end?" Jack questioned.

"Yes," Mark said. "I got a call from the people going over the white van that was used for the snatch. As we suspected, it was stolen, and as we suspected, it had been carefully wiped down. Still, we were able to pick up some partial and a few full prints, and all of them have been sent for evaluation. Something like that could be a big breakthrough. Also, we have put out an APB on your coworker, Vinnie Amendola. So far he's evaded it; I mean, I'm not trying to suggest he's doing it purposefully, just that we've had no responses.

"Now I have a suggestion for you," Mark continued. "As you know, they have indicated they want the ransom to be in D perfect diamonds, which is clever on their part. Diamonds worth a million dollars will be easy to get but not without money. I'm afraid you should begin to see what kind of money you will be able to raise and how you are going to do it."

"All our savings are completely tied up in our house.

It has no property mortgage and no construction mortgage, either."

"I encourage you to talk to your bank and see what kind of cash you might be able to expect on a financing deal. What about life insurance?"

"I have some but not much," Jack said.

"Well, give it a go. When we get to that point of the negotiation, we have to have an idea of what's the top amount we'll have to work with. Now, do you have any questions? We are putting all our efforts into your case. I just spoke with the commissioner. He is extremely interested in having the case resolved yesterday."

"I do have a question," Jack said. "What do you think about finding out where these people are holding my kid?"

"It happens, but it is very rare. It also, in our opinion, puts the kidnapped individual at heightened risk. Our experience is to get the kidnappers to the bargaining table and negotiate the best terms possible for the release."

CHAPTER FORTY-ONE

We're ready," Grover announced after he positioned the IV pole he'd assembled next to the bed. They were in the smaller of the two bedrooms in the Woodside row house. On the bed was a piece of three-quarter-inch plywood about six feet long and two feet wide with a two-foot arm board sticking off one side. A black bag containing an assortment of medication and syringes was on the night table, along with a fresh roll of silver duct tape.

"Time to bring in the guest," Colt said. He and Grover were wearing latex gloves both for protection and also to avoid leaving any fingerprints around the house, which had been rented under an assumed name with cash up front. The CRT motto was: One could never be too safe.

Returning to the van downstairs, they unrolled Duane, who looked as terrified as they had assumed he would be.

"Come on," Colt said, pulling the man up to a sitting position. "Let's head inside to party."

At first Duane tried to refuse getting out of the van, until Colt produced his gun from under his jacket. Duane immediately changed his mind about resisting, and climbed awkwardly out. With Grover leading and Colt following, they marched the tremulous man out of the oil-scented garage, up the stairs, and into the small bedroom. When Duane saw the board on the bed and the IV, he tried again to hold back.

"No more fighting," Grover said, giving Duane a push toward the bed. "We're going to do what we are going to do, whether you fight or not, unless you want to tell us what we need to know."

Duane made an effort to speak.

"Are you trying to say you're willing to talk with us?" Grover questioned. Grover looked into the man's dark eyes as Duane nodded assent.

Grover looked at Colt questioningly. "Give it a try," Colt said.

Grover reached out, and taking the end of the duct tape plastered across Duane's mouth, gave it a sudden forceful yank, pulling out a handful of Duane's whiskers in the process as well as the rag. Duane yelped and gritted his teeth.

"Who are you guys?" he said when he'd recovered.

"I'm afraid that's not the issue," Grover said, his English accent suddenly more apparent. "You have two seconds to be cooperative."

"What does it mean to be cooperative?"

"It means telling us where the child is whom you and your accomplices kidnapped. Tell us where the child is or we'll make you tell. It's your call."

"I have no idea what you are talking about."

"What were you doing sitting in your car on One hundred and sixth Street?"

"I was watching a basketball game in the local park."

Unhappy with the answer and the accompanying attitude, Grover unleashed a lightning karate chop to the side of Duane's neck. Initially the man's knees buckled, and he would have fallen to the floor if Grover had not caught him under the arms. Anticipating each other's moves, Colt reacted by snatching up Duane's legs, and together they heaved him onto the board on the bed. Next came the duct tape, which Grover grabbed from the bedside table. While Duane was still in a limp daze from the karate blow, Grover and Colt had succeeded in duct-taping him to the board.

"All right!" Duane said in desperation as soon as he could talk. "I'm sorry. I didn't mean to be a wise guy. I was watching a house to make sure the woman didn't go out. I swear. That's all I was doing—making sure someone didn't come out of her house."

"Too late," Grover snapped. "We don't have time to fool with you."

With deftness that came with practice, Colt started an IV.

"What the hell are you doing?" Duane cried, struggling vainly against the duct tape. "What are you going to give me?"

"Check my math," Grover said. "It's point-seven milligrams per kilogram. What do you say, he weighs about eighty kilograms?"

"That would be my guess."

"Okay, that means fifty-six milligrams," Grover continued. "Let's make it sixty." Quickly he drew up the medication into a syringe, tapping it to eliminate the bubbles, then handed the syringe to Colt across Duane's body.

"What the hell are you giving me?" Duane demanded. His eyes were open to their fullest, watching. Colt, unhappy with the fact that there still was some air in the syringe, was holding the syringe upright and tapping the side as Grover had done.

"No, don't!" Duane pleaded. "What is it? What does it do?"

"It's called Versed, if you really want to know," Grover said. "But it's a waste of time to tell you, because you're not going to remember any of this. Among other characteristics, the drug is a wonderful retrograde amnestic."

"What the hell is an amnestic?" Duane clamored.

Both Grover and Colt ignored Duane. Colt used the IV port and injected the drug.

"Jesus Christ in heaven," Duane yelled, watching Colt resheath the needle with it plastic cover. "What did you . . ." Duane had tried to ask another question, but his voice trailed off. He was already asleep.

"It amazes me everytime we use this stuff," Colt said, handing the now empty syringe back to Grover.

"It's a wonderful drug," Grover agreed. He took the empty syringe after finishing filling a second syringe with ten milligrams of valium to be used later. "Check and see how easy he is to arouse."

"Hey, Duane!" Colt called, slapping the side of Duane's face. "Come on, wake up!" He slapped a little harder before grabbing Duane's chin and shaking it. "Come on, big guy! Come back to earth."

Duane's eyes fluttered open with a befuddled faraway look. "Wow," he said with a smile lighting up his face. "What . . ." he began to ask but then forgot what he had been thinking.

For a few minutes Colt asked innocuous questions, which Duane answered with some humor. The only problem was that he had to be awakened repeatedly.

"So what's going on with this kidnapping?" Grover asked out of the blue. The previous questions Colt had been asking were of a more personal nature.

"Not much," Duane answered. "We're all just sitting around waiting for the fun to start."

"What kind of fun?"

"Trying to figure out how to exchange the kid for the diamonds without getting caught."

"You sure don't want to get caught," Grover agreed. "Where is the kid being held?"

"At Louie's place."

"Louie who?"

"Louie Barbera."

"Where's Louie's place?"

"In Whitestone."

"What's the address?"

Duane didn't respond. Colt slapped him several times, and his eyes reluctantly fluttered back open.

"I asked you for Louie's address," Grover said. "Louie Barbera."

"Three-seven-four-six Powells Cove Boulevard."

Grover quickly wrote the address down.

"Who's taking care of the kid?" Grover asked.

"Louie's wife. She's loving the kid. She wants to adopt him and is giving Louie a hard time about it. Louie wants to move the kid."

"To where?"

"I don't know. Someplace on the river. They're trying to get some heat into an old warehouse."

Grover and Colt exchanged a knowing look across Duane's motionless body. "Another reason we have to make a rescue tonight," Grover said. "We don't want to do a raid and come up empty-handed."

"I like to have at least a day to check the place out," Colt complained.

"We're going tonight!" Grover said. "We cannot risk

losing the opportunity. Now that we have an address, it's a go. This afternoon will be a chance to do a drive-by."

"A drive-by is practically worthless," Colt complained again.

"It's a problem we'll have to live with. Do you have any additional questions for our guest?"

"Duane," Colt called out, slapping the man's face harder than he had earlier, as if it was his fault Colt was not going to have a full day and evening to reconnoiter. "Does Louie have any dogs?"

"He has two," Duane said. "Two really nasty Dober-man pinschers that run around the grounds."

"Shit," Colt said. "I had a feeling this was too good to be true."

"Look on the bright side. If someone has big guard dogs on the property, the chances are they've become lax with their alarm systems."

"Good point," Colt admitted reluctantly. "Now let's wind up here and get out to look the place over."

They got their equipment and Duane back into the van. Grover made one last sweep around the house to make sure nothing had been left before leaving the keys on the kitchen table.

Heading back to West 106th Street, Grover made it a point to call the office. The line was picked up immediately, as CRT had people available twenty-four-seven, three hundred and sixty-five and a quarter days a year.

"Is this Beverly?" Grover asked. Over the years he'd gotten to know most of the receptionists by the sound of their voices.

"It is," Beverly said cheerfully.

"Are any of the researchers around this morning?"

"Yes, I saw Robert Lyon just a few moments ago."

"Could you page him and ask him to give me a call on my mobile?"

"Not a problem. I'll do it right away."

When Robert returned the call, Grover said, "I need some help today."

"What do you need?"

"I have an address for a house in Whitestone, New York. I need you to find out all you can about it. Get on the city assessor's office website and see if they have a floor plan available. Find out who owns it as well, and call me back on this line as soon as you get any details. We'll be breaking into the house tonight, so we need as much information as possible." He gave Robert the address and disconnected.

His next call was to Warren.

"We are on our way back," Grover said when Warren answered, out of breath. "We are definitely going to need some help getting the watcher back into his vehicle. After all the excitement, he's sleeping rather soundly."

"No problem," Warren said. "We're all here playing basketball as usual. Did you get what you needed?"

"I believe we did," Grover said. "He was very accommodating."

"Good," Warren said. "How long before you'll be back here?"

"I'd say thirty to forty minutes. Saturday traffic is a relative breeze. We're coming in from Woodside."

"See you then," Warren said and hung up.

Twenty minutes later Colt turned onto Laurie and Jack's street. He pulled up directly behind Duane's van to limit the exposure of the group carrying Duane and putting him back in his vehicle. Grover jumped out as soon as Colt came to a halt. To avoid attracting too much attention, Grover jogged over to the basketball court instead of shouting from across the street. He waited for a play to be over before calmly calling through the chain-link fence to get Warren's attention.

"Flash and I will be right there," Warren said once he saw Grover waving at him.

With four people involved, there was no problem moving Duane from where he'd been rolled up in the carpet in the back of the van to his vehicle. At Grover's insistence, he was put in the driver's seat and draped over the steering wheel.

"He's really out," Warren commented. "What did you give him?"

"A drug called Versed," Grover explained. "And he's about to get some intramuscular Valium. We want him to sleep for a good long time but make it look like he's drunk himself into a stupor." Grover produced a bottle of vodka from the van, and with Colt rousing him, Grover forced the man to take a mouthful of liquor, most of which dripped down the front of Duane's shirt. "Perfect," Grover said. He replaced the bottle's cap and then tossed the half-full bottle onto the front passenger seat. "If his accomplices come looking for him, they'll find him acting drunk but never guess he'd been dragged off and treated with a tongue-loosening drug."

"But he'll remember himself."

"No, he won't," Grover said with assurance as he gave Duane the Valium in his upper arm cavalierly, injecting it directly through his shirt. "Not only does Versed make one particularly talkative, it causes retrograde amnesia. He'll be lucky to remember getting up this morning."

"Very slick," Warren said.

"Could you guys keep your eyes on this vehicle? I'd like to know if his accomplices do show up. I'd also like to get any license plates if it could be done without arousing any suspicions. I don't want them to know we know they've been here."

"Until when do you want us to watch it?"

"At least until two or three a.m., but I know that's asking a lot. Yet I'd appreciate it, as long as you guys have the manpower and inclination to do it."

"Not a problem," Warren said. "Those bastards killed my cousin and have Laurie and Jack's toddler. I'd stay up all night myself. We'll be using the court until early evening. After that, I'll have the guys who'd been scheduled for today, but weren't used, watch tonight."

"With the proviso they don't let themselves be seen. This point is truly important. If kidnappers feel they are being watched or followed, they get very antsy, which invariably puts the victims in extreme jeopardy. If they start feeling the authorities are closing in, the kidnappers kill their victims and dispose of the bodies, never to be found."

"Understood," Warren said simply, and he did.

After leaving the neighborhood and before heading out to Whitestone, Grover and Colt drove down to Midtown to visit the home office. CRT occupied an entire floor on East 54th Street. It was usually a beehive of activity, but since it was a Saturday and since ten of the thirty-nine partners were currently away running ten active cases in eight countries, the place was mausoleum-like.

"Robert told me to say he would be in the lunchroom," Beverly had said when Grover and Colt first appeared. The so-called lunchroom was a windowless affair more suited for storing cleaning supplies than for serving as a snack room. There were several vending machines and a space for the communal coffee machine. Robert was alone, nursing a coffee while working on his laptop.

"Did you have any luck?" Grover asked.

"Not a lot but some. First, I did have luck with the assessor's office, which, I might add, was a great idea on your part. They had a rudimentary site plan and better floor plans, as the estate went through a major renovation and reassessment after the current owner bought it about a decade ago."

"Are you using the word *estate* literally or figuratively?"

"Literally. There's over an acre, which is big for the area, with a pool, a tennis court, and a pier."

"So it's waterfront property?"

"Yes. It has four hundred feet of frontage on the East River. The house is almost ten thousand square feet, and pretty much covers the site except for the pool and tennis court. In my mind, that's an estate."

"I agree," Grover said. "Let's see the plans."

Robert had printed out the plans from the assessor's office on eight-and-a-half-by-eleven-inch paper. Colt kept the site plan but immediately handed the floor plan back. "Double the size of the copy. I might have to search for the child, and I need to know the house like the back of my hand."

"I also have a street map of the town," Robert said, handing that over as well before running off to enlarge the floor plans.

"Uh-oh," Grover said after a brief look at the map. Robert had the location of the house marked with a red cross. "It's on a dead-end street."

"That's not a problem," Colt said. "We'll approach from the water. We certainly don't want to be hemmed in by a dead-end street."

"Approach in what? You are not going to get me in the water again, no way." About ten years previously, Colt had insisted on using scuba gear to approach another waterfront property in Cartagena, Colombia.

"We'll rent something like a Zodiac and pull in under the pier. There has to be a marina out there in the area."

"How did you do researching the owner?" Grover asked Robert when he came back with the blow-ups.

"Not good. It's listed as being owned by a Panamanian financial company who pays the taxes and utilities. But when I tried researching the Panamanian company, I found it was owned by a Brazilian company, et cetera. You know the story."

"Shell companies," Grover said with a nod. "Another sign that this kidnapping involves organized crime."

Colt checked his watch. "Grover, it's after two! We have to get our butts out to Whitestone, especially now that we need to locate a boat. And I'm going to need time to put together an operational kit for tonight."

"All right, let's do it," Grover said. "Robert, if you learn anything more about the house or its owner, give me a call on my mobile. This exercise has to go down tonight, so do what you can!"

"Will do," Robert said.

"Also, Robert," Colt said, "have you seen anybody from logistics this morning?" Logistics at CRT really meant one man. His name was Curt Cohen, and he was a master of the procurement and maintenance of just about anything in the world, particularly in the arena of electronics and weapons: anything and everything a risk management, ex–Special Forces agent would need to carry out his or her mission as a kidnap consultant.

"Curt himself was here this morning looking for something special for Roger Hagarty, who is in Mexico running a case."

"How convenient," Colt said happily. "Could you find him for me and have him call? I'm going to need some special things myself."

"I'll be happy to," Robert said cheerfully.

"Let's go," Grover said, grabbing Colt's upper arm and giving him a shove in the general direction of the elevators. "You're the one's been growling about the time."

On this second trip to Queens, they chose to use the Queens-Midtown Tunnel. As Grover drove, Colt used the time to study the floor plans and commit them to memory.

"I don't think you'll have any trouble finding JJ," Grover said, aware of what Colt was doing.

"I'm glad you are optimistic. But I don't want to get in there and be figuratively stumbling around in the dark."

"It's always better to be safe than sorry—pardon the overused expression. But if the wife is so fond of the child, I'll bet you the kid will be smack-dab in the middle of the master bedroom."

As they emerged back into the daylight from the tunnel, Colt went back to the floor plans, but his cell phone interrupted him.

"It's Curt," his caller announced. "Robert said you were in need of some special equipment."

"I need a gas-based dart pistol loaded with enough ketamine to stop an adult water buffalo in heat. One that has the green laser aiming devices. To be truthful, chances are I'll be facing a couple of Dobermans."

"Very funny," Curt said, "but a humongous dose is not going to help. With ketamine darts, the animal doesn't instantly fall over, even if I err on the high-dose side. That's public folklore. The dog is going to stumble around for a few minutes and might still be dangerous. Keep that in mind."

"So a dog might be able to chew on me for several minutes after I hit him with a ketamine-filled dart?"

"I'm afraid so. It can happen, unless you want to kill the dog."

"Thanks for the good news. In addition to the dart pistol, I'm going to need my usual climbing kit with several fifty-foot lengths of rope. Also, one window anchor for a fast escape."

"No problem. What else?"

"Some sort of an over-the-shoulder bag capable of supporting up to forty pounds."

"How big?"

"About a yard long, twelve to fourteen inches high. Big enough to hold a one-and-a-half-year-old child. And, oh, yeah, an eyedropper."

"What about any special weapons?"

"Give me something small and light but makes a lot of noise and I don't have to aim."

"You mean like an Uzi?

"That's fine."

"What else?"

"The usual breaking-and-entering tools, like lock picks, glass suction cups, and glass cutters."

"Is that it?"

"I believe so," Colt said. "If I think of anything else, I'll give you a quick call."

"When do you want to pick everything up?" Curt asked. "I'll have it all at the front desk with your name on it. What about night-vision goggles?"

"Thanks for reminding us," Colt said. "Let me ask Grover."

"Of course I want night-vision goggles," Grover said, hearing both sides of Colt's conversation.

"Tonight's forecast is calling for clear skies and a gibbous moon," Curt said. "Just in case you haven't checked."

"I still want the night-vision goggles," Grover said.

"Same with me," Colt added.

"And I want a sniper rifle with a night-vision scope in case Colt is being chased when he comes out of the house with the kid."

"Don't even suggest it," Colt said.

"It's better to be . . ."

"Yeah, I know, 'safe than sorry.' Let's abandon the clichés, will you please!" Colt pleaded.

"What time?" Curt said, interrupting the two agents. "What time do you want this stuff available by?"

"We don't need it until around eleven. I don't want to do this break-in until after one a.m., or even later."

"It will be waiting for you by nine p.m. If you suddenly think of anything else, call me and I'll do my very best."

"Thanks, Curt," Grover and Colt echoed into Colt's cell phone.

CHAPTER FORTY-TWO

MARCH 28, 2010 – SUNDAY, 12:31 a.m.
WHITESTONE, QUEENS, NEW YORK

After picking up all the equipment that Curt had rounded up for them, Grover and Colt had retraced the route that they had used that afternoon traveling from CRT's main office out to Whitestone, Queens, a trip that had been very worthwhile indeed. The first thing they had learned that afternoon was that the group that had kidnapped JJ were not quite the amateurs Grover and Colt had earlier suspected. The perpetrators were cleverly and covertly watching the location where they were holding the child, 3746 Powells Cove Boulevard. It had only been over the last fifty or so years that professional kidnappers had realized that surveillance was a smart move, so that if the authorities, by one mechanism or another, were closing in on the hideout, the people holding the victim could be alerted to move on if there was time or kill the victim and hide the remains in a previously prepared location. Without the victim or the victim's remains, prosecution of the case was always difficult at best. The only reason Grover and Colt had discovered these watchers was because they had specifically looked for them. It was two guys in a black SUV tucked into a neighbor's driveway.

The second important thing they'd been able to achieve on their afternoon reconnaissance was to locate a good-size marina in the town just beyond Whitestone.

Although the marina was technically not yet open for the season, they had been able to rent a Zodiac and a boat slip. They had to rent the boat for a week to justify the marina to get the outboard out of winter storage.

Trying the boat out, they had motored back to 3746 Powells Cove Boulevard. Seeing no one, particularly no guards, as they had from the land side, they'd allowed themselves to approach under the pier exactly the way they would that night. Sitting there under the wooden pier, Colt had used his laptop to scan the usual wireless alarm frequencies and write them down, while Grover had kept vigilance. At one point Grover thought he'd heard a baby wail. Looking at his partner to see if he'd heard, Colt lifted his eyes from the computer screen, smiled, and gave a thumbs-up sign.

The three-story house itself was appreciated much better from the water side. It was constructed of reinforced cement in a faux-Mediterranean style. Half buried in the top of the surrounding retaining wall were pieces of broken glass, and above it coils of razor wire. Despite this formidable defense on the land side, the waterfront was completely open, with the house set back about a hundred feet from the water's edge. Immediately in front of the house was the pool. Along the side was a tennis court. They had seen the dogs, but only from a distance when they had left.

Now, just after midnight, pulling back into the marina where they had rented the boat that afternoon, Grover doused the headlights. With only the light from the moon, he drove around to the water side of the building and backed up to the pier where the slip they had rented was located. The marina itself was mostly dark, except for dim lights in a display window on the roadside, containing gleaming marine hardware, such as stainless-steel cleats and mahogany blocks. On the water side the only lights were positioned out on the pier complex on the top of long poles and directed downward to provide cones of light at various locations. The weather could not have been more perfect, without a visible cloud. There was no wind to speak of and the surface of the water was placid.

With little talk, the men unloaded the gear at the base of the pier. Then while Grover moved the SUV back to the parking area, where it would be less conspicuous, Colt carried the equipment out to the Zodiac and quickly stored it aboard. They worked quickly and silently. Only two cars went by on the road, and neither stopped or even slowed.

With a hand on one of the pier's big cleats for mooring yachts, Colt steadied the boat while Grover jumped on. Immediately he started the engine before Colt boarded. Keeping the power low, Grover guided the boat out of the slip and then out of the pier complex. He had access to the night-vision scopes but didn't need them for this phase of the operation. He did not turn on the running lights.

Not before motoring a thousand yards or so out into Little Neck Bay did Grover significantly up the speed. Like most outboards, the motor was noisy, and he kept the power limited to what was needed to get the boat planing and then to maintain it.

Moving progressively away from the shore, where there was significant artificial illumination, it became gradually darker except for the area immediately around the moon, and thousands more stars blinked on in the rest of the inverted bowl of the darkened sky. With the water temperature in the forties, the wind created by the Zodiac's forward motion was bitingly cold, and both men hunkered down as best they could.

Rounding Willets Point, Colt and Grover suddenly had the illuminated span of the Throgs Neck Bridge in sight with the Whitestone Bridge beyond, both soaring over the water from Queens over to the Bronx. Ten minutes later they passed under the Throgs Neck Bridge.

As the Throgs Neck Bridge dropped behind them and the Whitestone loomed ahead, Colt steered the Zodiac to the left and headed for shore at approximately the location of 3746 Powells Cove Boulevard. About five hundred yards out, Colt cut the power. At one hundred yards, Colt turned off the motor. The two men picked up paddles and paddled the rest of the way.

Most of the homes lining the shore were completely dark. A few had one or two lights on, either on their elaborate seaside terraces or within their homes. One home off to the far left was ablaze with lights. From where Grover and Colt were, they guessed it was a party because there were both indoor and outdoor lights and people could be seen on various terraces and balconies. Despite the distance, the faint sound of voices and music occasionally drifted across the water and reached their ears.

Although Grover and Colt had conversed in low tones earlier, confirming their plans, once the motor had been turned off and they were approaching the tip of the Barbera pier, they were completely silent. They were even careful with their paddles as they drew them through the water, lifted them out, and slipped them back in unison, pushing the boat forward silently, closing in on the pier.

Except for a slight incandescent glow from one of the second-story windows, the house was dark. Looking down the sides of the building, there was a much larger glow emanating from the street side of the house, where the garage was located. The only sounds were the intermittent distant sounds of the party and the continuous lapping of the waves against the shore.

The tide was in so that the distance between the water surface and the underside of the pier had narrowed to only about four feet. Still, the Zodiac's prow easily slipped in under the wooden deck. Grover remained in the boat while Colt jumped up on the pier to accept the equipment that Grover handed him. When everything was out of the boat, Grover climbed out as well.

Colt was already dressed in what he called his custom assault pants suit, with specifically designed pockets and clips for all his gear. The benefit of such an outfit was that he had instant access to each implement, such as the ketamine-dart pistol hooked to a clip on his left, and the Uzi hanging on a similar one to his right. Grover had a similar outfit and helped Colt prepare for the current strike. After he'd loaded a particular pocket, he'd pat the pocket and whisper out loud the name of the object it held so Colt could mentally check it off. It could be a disaster to be in the middle of a task and be missing a specific tool. Another benefit of having a separate pocket or clip for everything was that Colt could move silently without tools or other devices hitting up against one another.

"Ready?" Grover whispered.

"Ready," Colt replied. Quickly he tested his small radio clipped on the point of his right shoulder. A similar device on the point of Grover's right shoulder came to life. "Testing: one, two, three. Testing." The stock phrase popped into his own microphone positioned in his right ear.

Now completely outfitted and with a shoulder bag hanging off his right shoulder, Colt silently ran the length of the pier and slipped into the shadows of the stairs that rose up to the level of the pool.

Meanwhile, Grover quickly rearranged some deck furniture to serve as a rest for using the sniper rifle. He also moved the Zodiac around to the best position for a rapid getaway. With that accomplished, he returned to the deck furniture, climbed in among it, and sighted through the night scope of the sniper rifle.

Thanks to the scope, Grover was able to see the problem before Colt. It was the sudden movement that caught his eye. It was the dogs coming along the left side of the building from the street side of the compound. Quickly, using the radio to warn Colt, Grover drew a bead with his laser on the front dog and squeezed off a single shot. He could tell instantly he'd hit the dog as it tucked its head and tumbled head-on into the pool. The second dog, ignoring the plight of the first, rounded the edge of the building, missing the pool and dashing laterally across Grover's line of sight.

With Grover's warning, Colt had dashed up the steps, snatching the gas-powered dart pistol from his belt in the process. Worried about the two dogs, he'd bolted for the tennis enclosure. Although he'd not heard any barking, he'd heard the dogs' snarls and heard their feet thundering against the ground. It was at that moment that he'd detected the suppressed sound of the sniper's rifle. Reaching the door to the tennis court, he snatched it open, rolled around its edge, but had not gotten it fully closed when one of the Doberman pinschers collided with it at a full run. Had Colt not been holding fast to the door, he might have been bowled over by the animal's momentum.

The dog scrambled to its feet, and with fangs exposed, lunged at Colt, who responded by firing the dart pistol. The sound was more of a thudding hiss than pistol shot. The dart embedded itself in the dog's chest but didn't stop the dog from trying to bite Colt through the string-like mesh that composed the bulk of the door. Worrying as much about the noise the animal was making as getting bit, Colt reloaded and shot him again, this time in the hip. Despite the second dose of ketamine, the dog was still on his feet, trying to get at Colt through the netting. His wobble became progressively more intense until he keeled over.

Colt used the time to contact Grover.

"Thanks for getting one of the dogs," Colt said quickly.

"You're welcome."

"Where is he?"

"In the pool."

"Any change with the house?"

"Not that I can see. Since the glow in the second-story window hasn't changed, my guess is it's a night-light. Anyway, no other lights have come on, so you're clear to go."

"I'm on my way," Colt said, switching off the radio.

After pushing against the door to move the now anesthetized dog out of the way, Colt made his way out of the tennis court and along the side of the house to reach the illuminated pool. The other dog was floating on the surface but with the head submerged and bleeding into the water. At that moment the pool lights went out, causing Colt's heart to skip a beat. Glancing at his watch by lifting its blackout cover, he breathed out with relief. It was exactly two a.m., strongly suggesting that the pool light was on a timer. Without any more delay, Colt went to one of the sliding glass doors leading into a sun porch. Taking out a suction device, he applied it to the glass next to the door's locking mechanism. He then ran around the device with a glass cutter, snapping out a perfectly circular hole. He repeated the mechanism with a slightly smaller suction device, snapping off a hole in the inner layer of thermopane. With that gone, he could reach in and unlock the slider.

Colt paused for a moment. In some respects the first step inside the house was the most nerve-racking. Using his computer earlier, he'd turned off the various wireless alarms in the house, although he couldn't be one hundred percent sure he hadn't turned them on instead. It depended what state the alarms had been in before Colt had interfered. Taking a breath, he stepped through the door. Even before the alarm sounded, Colt could tell he'd tripped an infrared motion detector, because a red light blinked near the crown molding. Just as the alarm began to sound throughout the house, Colt hit his computer's enter button. The alarm system was now off, but it had begun to sound.

Flattening himself against the wall, Colt strained to listen, holding his breath. He thought he heard distant voices, but then realized the voices were accompanied by music and that the noise was coming in through the open door and was the party on the other side of the cove. Then there was another deep, low rumbling sound that caused Colt to hold his breath again while he tried to identify it. It was a refrigerator compressor.

"Moving out," Colt whispered into his radio after closing the door to the pool deck and donning his night-vision goggles.

"All clear," came back in his earphone.

Colt moved quickly and catlike from the sun porch into the kitchen. Thanks to the night-vision equipment, he could see well enough to avoid obstacles. From studying the floor plans, he knew exactly how to get to the master bedroom suite, which was positioned directly over the first-floor kitchen, facing out over the water view.

Unfortunately, the back stairs were as old as the main part of the house, built in the 1920s, and not built particularly robustly. As Colt quickly mounted them, they let off a series of creaks and groans, enough to cause Colt to pause once he reached the second floor. Besides the Sub-Zero compressor, all he could hear was reassuring snoring coming from the master bedroom.

Colt remained motionless for a full minute. There was no change in the snoring, nor any additional sounds. He was about to advance toward the open master bedroom door when his earpiece crackled to life. "Houston, we have a problem": Grover's code that the mission might have to be aborted.

"Ten-four," Colt responded, meaning he'd gotten the message but could not have a conversation.

"Intruder coming down right side of building. Must be a normal check. He is not hurrying. I have him clearly in sight. Will worry about his seeing dogs or me."

"Proceeding," Colt responded. He then moved

ahead, and reaching the door to the master bedroom, he carefully scanned progressively more and more of the room. The first thing he saw of interest was a crib. Moving on, he saw the bed. It was king-size with a niche above its head containing a statue of the Virgin Mary clutching the Christ child. The niche was illuminated with a dimmed light to serve as a night-light. There were two people in the bed, presumably Louie Barbera and his wife. After another brief pause to make certain both people were asleep, Colt moved across the thick carpet to the crib and got his first look at JJ. In the darkness and using his night-vision goggles, the boy's hair color appeared greenish-gray rather than blond as it had been described, but his face was just as cherubic as reported. He was on his back with arms out to the side and fists next to his head.

"Past the tennis enclosure without problem," Grover said. "Now lighting up a cigarette. So far, so good."

Colt glanced back at the people in the bed less than ten feet away. Although the chances of them hearing anything at all were very low, he couldn't help but be concerned, as close as he was. Yet he didn't want to have to abort now, so he turned back to the child. Taking out the eyedropper he'd previously filled with the appropriate amount of Versed, he pulled off the syringe cap he'd used to cover the dropper. Reaching into the crib, he inserted the end of the dropper into the child's mouth.

"Heading for the pool end of the building," Grover said, hesitating. "Now continuing on. Thank goodness the pool lights are off. He seems satisfied all in order. He's now walking down the left side toward the street side of the compound."

Slowly Colt compressed the eyedropper bulb, pushing the solution of Versed into JJ's mouth. Almost immediately JJ responded by reflexively sucking on the eyedropper. *Yes, little guy,* Colt said silently, knowing he was taking full advantage of JJ's nursing reflex. Then, after ten seconds of making room in the shoulder bag, Colt lifted the child out of the crib and slipped him feetfirst into the bag. As expected and hoped, the child did not complain or make a sound. Standing back up, Colt was about to hoist the bag up on his shoulder when Louie Barbera coughed loudly, waking himself and his wife in the process.

"Are you all right, dear?" Mrs. Barbera questioned.

"I'll live," Louie said. He pulled his legs from under the covers, sat up on the side of the bed, and put his feet on the floor.

Colt froze except for his left hand, which silently pulled the veterinary gas-powered dart gun from its belt clip.

"Are you getting up?" Mrs. Barbera asked while settling herself back under the covers.

"For a moment," Louie admitted.

"Check the boy. Make sure he's covered."

Grumbling something about the kid getting more attention than he did, Louie raised his bulk to an unsteady standing position, then launched himself toward the crib.

Amazed he'd not been seen, Colt took a step back as Louie lurched toward him. He debated what to do. Should he just wait it out with the unlikely chance there would be no confrontation, or should he be proactive? The question was answered when Louie reached the crib, bent over, and stuck in his hand. Clearly he was confused, as his hand searched in progressively desperate sweeps around the crib's interior and found nothing.

Colt shot him in his sizable ass with a ketamine dart.

"Shit!" Louie yelled as he stood up, yanking the dart out of his left buttock and trying to look at it in the darkness.

"What in heaven's sake is the matter?" Mrs. Barbera demanded, as Louie's scream had jolted her upright in bed.

"I got stuck with something." Louie yelled with a mildly garbled voice. He extended the dart toward his wife despite there being no chance of her seeing it in the darkness. He then let go of the crib with the intention of walking over to her. He didn't get far. After a few tottering steps, he fell over onto his side.

Frantically, Mrs. Barbera scrambled off the end of the bed in a swirl of chiffon. As she bent over her husband, Colt let loose with the third ketamine dart. The woman let out a scream that eclipsed her husband's.

"Houston, we have another problem. Two men are approaching on the run on the right side of the house. Perhaps a silent alarm has been tripped."

Colt hauled the bag's strap over his shoulder and zipped the bag closed. Thankfully, JJ had not made a sound.

"Second dog has been discovered," Grover said urgently in Colt's ear. "Men with weapons drawn now running toward terrace. Do not try to leave same way you went in. Abort, abort!"

With his night-vision goggles still in place, Colt ran from the bedroom and into the dressing room, and from the dressing room out into the second-floor hallway. At the moment he reached the hallway, lights went on in the kitchen downstairs.

"Only one man went into house," Grover said. "Second man on terrace standing guard."

Colt ran down the second-floor hallway, entering a bedroom on the right. He locked the door behind him but knew it was a flimsy lock that would not slow a determined pursuer but for a second. "Exiting second-story bedroom right. Take out perp on terrace. Arrange boat for quick getaway. Have target."

Dashing to the window, Colt took out the window anchor and extended its arms. He reached the window and threw up the sash. He then raised the storm window. Grabbing a length of rope clipped to his side, he threw the bulk out the window before attaching the end to the anchor, which merely bridged the window opening. Putting the shoulder bag around to his front, he pushed it out the window and then stepped out himself with one leg, keeping tension on the rope attached to the anchor. Pulling out his other leg, he then rappelled down the side of the building.

Once on the ground, Colt unhooked the Uzi from his belt and started for the water side of the house. Passing the tennis enclosure, he could see the anesthetized dog. Reaching the edge of the house, he slowed, positioned the Uzi at his waist, ready to fire, then leaped out into the open. The ploy was not necessary. Grover had taken his suggestion. The perp was spread-eagle on the terrace with a clean hole mid-forehead—undoubtedly more work for their legal defense team if the hoodlums were crazy enough to call in the police.

In the open, Colt did not dally but rather ran down the steps from the pool level, across the small intervening patch of lawn and then the length of the pier. Grover had the boat out in the clear. By the time Colt arrived the engine was running. Pulling the shoulder bag around in front of him, Colt jumped into the boat while Grover put the engine in gear and hit the throttle. Again, he purposefully left off the running lights.

Mildly out of breath, Colt unzipped the shoulder bag. JJ was nestled in against some towels, sleeping, like a baby totally unaware he'd changed hands again. "You've been wonderfully cooperative," Colt yelled to the child over the roar of the outboard.

Looking back at the house, Colt saw a series of flashes. "Incoming fire," he shouted to Grover, who instituted some evasive steering, but neither he nor Colt thought it necessary as far as they were out on the river. Their plan was to head north for the opposite shore until the black, low-lying boat was no longer visible from shore before turning east, the way they'd come.

It was a quarter to four a.m. when Colt pulled up to Laurie and Jack's house. The neighborhood was completely quiet, without a pedestrian or a dog in sight. If it were not for the streetlights, it would have been totally black, as the moon had set. The house was dark as well, except for a single light recessed into the front door's lintel.

Grover got out and opened the rear door. He leaned in, and after checking JJ, who was still sound asleep in the shoulder bag, he hefted the bag out of the vehicle. When Colt came around, he handed JJ to Colt. "You deserve the honors tonight. Compared with you, I was a mere spectator."

"You had your moments," Colt argued. "Taking out that first dog and the perp on the terrace was what made it possible."

"You're being too generous," Grover said. "But thank you."

They did not rush as they reached the stone steps and started up. Once at the front door, they positioned themselves with the bag containing JJ between them.

Grover leaned on the bell and kept it depressed for a full minute. After he let go, he descended back down the stairs and craned his neck, looking up. A single window was now illuminated. Grover climbed back up the stoop and positioned himself where he'd been earlier. Finally the door was pulled open and Jack and Laurie filled the doorway.

"Mr. Collins and Mr. Thomas," Jack said, surprised and not surprised at the same time. "You are either awfully early or awfully late. What can we do for you?" He was not willing to guess.

"I believe we've found something that belongs to you," Colt said. He lifted the shoulder bag, put it in Jack's outstretched hands. Since the zipper was already open, he merely gently pulled apart the bag's sides to reveal its angelic occupant.

Reining in her hopes for fear of disappointment, Laurie let herself emerge from around Jack and peer into the bag. Although she squealed with unbridled delight, she momentarily was not willing to snatch out her child for fear that she was seeing a figment of her imagination. But her reluctance rapidly faded, and her confidence rapidly grew such that she reached into the bag, pulled out the sleeping toddler, and clutched him to her bosom.

Half laughing and half crying, Laurie bombarded Grover and Colt with a hundred questions while JJ continued his slumber in her arms.

"Tomorrow or the next day or the next will be time enough for your questions. For now let us say that he had been treated extraordinarily well by a woman who apparently loved him dearly."

With a huge smile on his face thanks to this sudden, happy turn of events, Jack asked the two kidnapping consultants if they'd like to come into the house. But Grover and Colt gracefully declined, saying that they had to return their equipment to CRT before rousing their legal defense team and paying a visit to the police. "We have to confess the sins we committed in rescuing JJ sooner rather than later, although we won't be admitting to them all," Grover said with a wink. "And thanks for allowing us the opportunity to get your son back."

"You're thanking us?" Jack questioned with disbelief.

EPILOGUE

Detective Captain Lou Soldano surprised himself by finding a legal parking place on Laurie and Jack's street just two doors away from their house. Both had taken an indefinite leave of absence from OCME after the trauma of John Junior's short but emotionally traumatic kidnapping. Although Lou had not seen them face-to-face since that fateful Friday, he had spoken with them on the phone on several occasions, the last time being the previous evening when Lou had set up the current meeting for today. Until now, he had felt they needed their privacy.

After climbing the five steps to the stoop and ringing the bell, Lou checked his watch. It was now ten minutes before the onset of the raids, which were going to occur simultaneously at their three separate locations. The knowledge that they were about to take place gave Lou a great sense of satisfaction as well as excitement. At the same time, he felt a bit badly about not participating, but since there was no way he could be at all three locations at once, he'd decided to be at none and celebrate their occurrence with Laurie, since she was most responsible for the raids taking place. It had been a combination of her intuition, doggedness, and investigative forensic intelligence that had made her see a homicide where others saw a natural death. She had been the one to connect the homicide to organized crime—specifically, the working relationship existing between the Mafia and the Japanese Yakuza.

The door opened, and Jack and Lou greeted each other warmly. "You don't have to schedule a formal visit," Jack admonished as they climbed the stairs. "You can always just drop in."

"Under the circumstances, I thought it best to call," Lou explained. "Kidnappings are rather unique emotional events, to say the least. How is everybody doing?"

"Everybody is doing fine, except for me," Jack joked. "JJ seemed entirely normal as soon as he woke up from his anesthetic, and has been normal ever since, provided you believe the behavior of a normal one-and-a-half-year-old is normal."

"I vaguely remember," Lou said. Both his kids were out of college.

"The only problem is that Laurie continues to blame herself for the kidnapping episode, no matter what anyone says. And now she's having this internal battle about whether she wants to be a full-time mom or a mom who also happens to be a world-class medical examiner. Please talk to her. I can't, because I'm happy either way. I want her to do what she wants to do."

They passed the kitchen and walked into the family room. Laurie got up from the couch and gave Lou a sustained hug, thanking him profusely for suggesting that they use Grover and Colt of CRT.

"It made all the difference in the world," Laurie said, tears coming to her eyes and embarrassing Lou in the process.

"I just thought they could get JJ back faster," Lou mumbled, trying to downplay his role in the affair.

"Faster!" Laurie blurted. "They got him back the very next day. It was like a miracle. If they'd not helped us, I'm convinced JJ would still be in the hands of the kidnappers."

"No doubt," Lou said. "Did Grover and Colt confirm to you why JJ was snatched?"

"No, we only spoke to them once, and that was on Monday. They called briefly, just to check in on JJ. We haven't spoken to them since, because they told us they were off on a case in Venezuela that very evening."

"Just as they had guessed, the kidnapping was done as a late, desperate effort to deter you from working on the Satoshi Machita case. Any ransom demand was going to be mere icing on the cake. They were afraid of you, Laurie, not OCME in general, just you."

"That's hard to believe," Laurie said.

"And it doesn't speak very well for the rest of us at OCME," Jack said, trying to inject an element of humor. Jack bent down and picked up JJ, who felt ignored by the grown-ups and was letting everyone know.

"It might seem hard to believe to you, Laurie," Lou said, "but not to those in the NYPD, the FBI, CIA, and Secret Service. Your recent work with the Satoshi Machita case combined with JJ's kidnapping resulted in the formation of the most efficient task force I've ever been part of. Since Sunday, this task force has accomplished months' worth of highly successful investigation, such that . . ."

Lou paused to look at his watch. It was three minutes before eleven.

"Such that what?" Laurie questioned.

"This is super-secret," Lou said, lowering his voice for effect, "but in two minutes at three locations,

representatives of the four agencies I just mentioned will
be raiding three private companies: iPS USA, headed by
Benjamin Corey; Dominick's Financial Services, headed
by Vincent Dominick; and Pacific Rim Wealth Management, headed by Saboru Fukuda. All computers, storage
devices, and documents will be confiscated, and all the
principals will be arrested, including CEOs, CFOs,
COOs. This is going to be a big deal. I can feel it in
my bones. It's going to have a big effect on Mob cooperation with the Japanese Yakuza, if it doesn't sever it
completely. It'll seriously reduce the ballooning crystal
meth problem here in the Big Apple. Thank you, Laurie.
You are an asset to the city, so when you consider
whether you want to be just a mom or a mom with a
career, please keep in mind that you will be sorely missed
if you choose the former."

Laurie glared at Jack, feigning anger. "Have you been
talking about me?"

"I always talk about you," Jack confessed, holding
up his hands in mock surrender. "But I assure you I
had zero input into Lou's assessment."

FBI Special Agent Gene Stackhouse had been selected
as the overall leader of the task force comprising representatives of the Federal Bureau of Investigation, the
Central Intelligence Agency, the Secret Service, and the
New York City Police Department. He, like the other
agents except for the group from the NYPD, was dressed
in a dark blue uniform with black lettering indicating
his agency. Most carried weapons, either Glocks or MI5
rifles. The NYPD agents, all SWAT team members, were
dressed in the usual black and carried a wider variety of

firepower. Everyone wore helmets and bulletproof vests. Everyone had been fully briefed and were impatient for the word "go!"

Special Agent Stackhouse was particularly wired and ready to explode into the highly choreographed activity he'd planned the moment the second hand of his chronograph reached twelve. The start time was to be exactly eleven o'clock a.m. at all three sites to eliminate any chance of one company calling another to hide evidence.

"Masks on!" he yelled, as the second hand of his watch passed three. A small microphone clipped to his shoulder epaulet flap conveyed his voice to all nine unmarked vans: three at each location, with six people in each van, for a total of fifty-four law-enforcement officers.

Gene Stackhouse was in the passenger seat of the first van at his location, which was on the left side of Fifth Avenue just north of 57th Street. The two other vans were directly behind. When the second hand swept past the number eleven, he counted: "ten, nine, eight . . ." He unsnapped his holstered Glock pistol. "Four, three, two, one. Go!" All four doors of the three vans sprang open, shocking the various pedestrians on Fifth Avenue. The team dashed across the wide sidewalk, threw open the doors of the building where iPS USA was quartered, and swarmed the security desk. The guards were ordered not to communicate with any of the building's tenants, particularly iPS USA.

"What's going on?" one of the building security guards demanded, trying to sound authoritative. He'd been impressed and terrified at seeing the intruders' firepower but relieved when he saw FBI, SECRET SERVICE, CIA, and NYPD on the backs of jackets.

"We are executing a number of warrants." Stackhouse

yelled, directing his men toward a waiting elevator. "Remain seated! No talking! No phoning!" Snapping his fingers toward a CIA agent, Stackhouse directed him to stay with the building's security people to make sure the orders were followed.

Once all the remaining agents were in the elevator, its doors closed and it shot up to the iPS USA floor. When it arrived, it was as if the elevator belched out the eager agents, who dashed past the shocked Clair Bourse and fanned out in the iPS USA office in predetermined directions. Clair would have screamed if she hadn't been so immobilized by one of the initial agents running directly up to her, pointing his gun at her, and commanding, "Freeze!" The idea of the rapid, assault-like entrance was to deny anyone the opportunity to do anything at all to any evidence. Jacqueline, hearing the freeze command out in reception, had reached behind her to try to close the safe but had been specifically commanded not to do so by the two agents who had charged into her office.

Having studied the floor plan in advance, everyone knew exactly where to go. Stackhouse and another FBI agent, Tony Gualario, had run directly to Benjamin Corey's corner office. They caught the CEO and the CFO, Carl Harris, having a meeting.

As Stackhouse and Gualario swept into the room with their pistols drawn, Ben started to leap to his feet.

"Remain seated!" Stackhouse commanded. He leveled his gun at Ben, who immediately sank back into his leather desk chair. The same thing transpired with Gualario, who was aiming his weapon at Carl.

"Are you Benjamin Corey of five-ninety-one Edgewood Road in Englewood Cliffs, New Jersey?" Stackhouse demanded.

"I am," Ben said with shock that quickly changed to fear. Suddenly he knew exactly what was happening.

"I am Special Agent Gene Stackhouse of the FBI. I am here to execute a number of warrants, including the search of iPS USA and seizure of all evidence pertaining to money laundering, wire fraud, mail fraud, conspiracy to defraud the U.S. government, and tax evasion. I also have a warrant for your arrest for violation of the same federal statutes."

Stackhouse paused, cleared his throat, and pulled out a single sheet of paper from his pocket. "I have yet another warrant for your arrest, but I better read it, since I've never personally served such a warrant." He cleared his throat again. "Interpol arrest warrant: IP10067892431. Benjamin G. Corey of Five-ninety-one Edgewood Road, Englewood Cliffs, New Jersey, USA. Interpol requests the arrest and extradition from the USA to Japan of the above named individual, pursuant to treaty arrangements between the two countries to stand trial for first-degree murder on or about February twenty-eighth, 2010, in the Prefecture of Kyoto, Japan."

"What?" Ben demanded. "I never—"

"Hold up!" Stackhouse ordered. "Don't say anything until I Mirandize you."

"I found the missing lab books," one of the FBI agents said, coming in through the connecting door from Jacqueline's office and presenting them to Stackhouse.

"That's great, George," Stackhouse said, seeing the two blue books and recognizing George by his voice. "The Japanese government will be pleased. But let me finish up here reading the Miranda rights. If you want to do something else useful, call the other two teams and make sure their raids have gone down as planned."

Stackhouse cleared his throat again. He'd taken out a three-by-five card, on which he'd written the Miranda rights, to be sure he got them right.

"I already know my Miranda rights," Ben groused. He was incensed that the Japanese government would charge him with a crime that he'd gone out of his way to try to prevent.

"I still have to read them," Stackhouse insisted, and he proceeded to do so, as did Tony with Carl.

After Ben and Carl had been handcuffed, George came back into Ben's office. "Both the other raids went flawlessly," he said. "All the principals have been arrested, and a ton of evidence has been collected."

"Perfect," Stackhouse said. "Let's get on with collecting all the evidence in this office. Remember! We're to get everything: every computer, storage device, fax machine, and cell phone. Plus every document, letter, or memorandum. Let's do it!"

APRIL 18, 2010
SUNDAY, 1:45 P.M. – NEW YORK CITY

Here he comes," Laurie said, spotting Lou Soldano walking north on Columbus Avenue. Laurie, Jack, and JJ were sitting at an outside table at one of their favorite haunts, Espresso Et. Al., which was located just south of the Museum of Natural History. Actually, only Laurie and Jack were sitting, because JJ was, at the moment, sleeping in his reclined stroller. Thanks to the café's location on the east side of the avenue, it was catching all the sunshine available on a beautiful, warm spring day.

Laurie scraped back her metal chair and waved her hands above her head to get Lou's attention. Lou waved back and adjusted his trajectory so as not to have to wade through the long line at the café's main entrance. Instead, he simply stepped over the low chain stretched between potted plants that defined the café's outdoor terrace.

After a quick hug with Laurie and a high five with Jack, Lou sat down in the chair saved for him. He looked like he'd just gotten out of bed, with his hair brushed haphazardly and his eyelids still heavy with sleep. He had, however, taken the time to shave, and there was still a bit of shaving cream clinging to his right earlobe.

"Thanks for coming to see us," Laurie said.

"Thanks for inviting me," Lou said. "I'm glad you got me out. It's such a beautiful day. It would have been a shame to have wasted it vegetating on my couch, which is probably what I would have had you not called. So tell me, what's this good news you have to share? Is it what I'm hoping it is?"

"That I don't know." Laurie laughed. "Anyway, I'm going back to OCME!"

"Terrific!" Lou said sincerely. He raised his hand and high-fived Laurie. "I was hoping that was what you'd say. Visiting OCME is just not the same if the only person I get to see is boring old Jack. Congratulations! When is it going to happen?"

"A week from tomorrow," Laurie said. "The chief has been so good about it, I can't tell you."

"He's not being good, he's being smart," Lou responded.

"Hear, hear!" Jack said, raising his wineglass for a

toast. Then, remembering that Lou was "wineless," he sat up in his chair, looking for their waitress.

"I couldn't be happier for you," Lou said, leaning over toward Laurie. "Of course, that's at least partially a selfish response. I've been missing you at OCME since your maternity leave started. But beyond being selfish, I think it is the best decision for you and JJ. You are so good at being a forensic pathologist, and you seem to get a lot of secondary gain out of it. I thought you'd go back, but to be truthful, I thought it would take more time for you to realize you could and still be a great mom. If you don't mind me asking, can you tell me what made you decide so quickly?"

"It certainly wasn't one thing, but rather a host of things. First of all, there was the tragedy of Leticia's death, which I don't want to be entirely in vain. Maybe that sounds a bit strange, but not to me. She died because she was taking care of JJ so I could go back to work. Somehow I think I owe it to her memory to do it."

"That doesn't sound strange to me at all."

"I also recognized that kidnapping JJ to get me off a case was a one-in-a-million phenomenon. It's not going to happen again. But the most important realization is that there are people out there who are absolutely superb nannies and love being nannies, and have made it a true goal of being the best nannies they can be. For me to be comfortable working, I need someone who truly wants to be with JJ full-time and who is also willing to be my partner so I can remain as involved as possible. Do you know what I mean?"

"I do," Lou said. "You need someone who will be as good a mom and as attentive to JJ as you would be if you weren't going to have a career as well as be a mom. If push comes to shove, JJ's needs trump any career ambitions—"

Jack interrupted Lou, having gotten the attention of the waitress. "We're having a Vermentino. Do you want to try it, or do you want something else? We're also having Caesar salads with chicken. What do you say?"

"Whatever," Lou said with a wave. He was a meatloaf-and-gravy sort of guy, except when he was with Jack and Laurie. Besides, at the moment, he was more interested in the conversation with Laurie than what kind of wine and food he wanted. "I suppose the fact that you are coming back so quickly means you have already found someone whom you believe fits the bill?"

"I believe I have," Laurie admitted. "I put out a feeler about a week ago to all my friends, particularly my college friends, and found an Irish woman who had been the nanny for a woman I knew in college whose two children are now teenagers. My friend had actually been trying to find a placement for the nanny, since she'd been so loved she'd practically become part of the family. When I met the woman, I knew she was perfect from the very first words out of her mouth. And she's willing to live in. I mean, being a nanny is her life's mission."

"All right! Let's try that toast again!" Jack said when the waitress brought Lou's glass of Vermentino. Jack held up his own glass of wine, and the others followed suit. "To Laurie's return to OCME; to JJ's resilience, since he's been acting entirely normal; and to Leticia's memory and scholarship fund!"

The three friends clicked glasses and then took healthy swallows of their wine.

"What's this about a scholarship fund?" Lou asked after putting down his wineglass.

"We tried to think of something to honor Leticia's memory," Jack said. "A neighborhood college-scholarship fund was what we came up with. Laurie has been in contact with Columbia University, and they seem to like the idea as a nice addition to their efforts of neighborhood outreach. Laurie and I have already started the funding by setting up a yearly stipend and inviting others to do the same. Plus, we've also started planning various neighborhood fund-raisers. We think it will be good for the community."

"I couldn't think of anything more appropriate," Lou said. "Great idea!"

"What's been going on in the legal arena?" Laurie asked. "I've been curious ever since you stopped by the house and told us about the corporate raids."

"It's been a mixed bag, as usual," Lou said. "All the big honchos have been bonded from all three companies except for Benjamin Corey. They are all to be arraigned this week and, of course, all will plead not guilty, including Corey. What the prosecution is doing now is putting serious rollover pressure on the lesser officers to cop a plea in exchange for testimony on the big guys. It's going to work, for sure, thanks to all the evidence obtained during the raids in unlocking the secrets involving all the organized-crime shell companies. More important, the comfortable relationship between the Long Island Mafia and the Japanese Yakuza is a thing of the past, at least in the short run, and I hope in the long run as well. Thanks to you, we are going to see a lot less crystal meth around town."

"Why wasn't Benjamin Corey bonded?"

"Because of the international warrant for his arrest on the murder charge for the security guard in Kyoto, Japan. He would have been bonded if it had been just the white-collar crime. If anybody is a flight risk, it's him. Right now his biggest effort is in trying to fight extradition. I tell you, I wouldn't want to be in his shoes. Even if he prevails on the extradition issue, he's still got to face the money-laundering charges. I mean, I just can't understand it. A guy with that kind of background and education: it was as if he was trying to see just how much he could get away with."

"I see it more like a Greek tragedy," Laurie said. "The fatal flaw of greed evidencing itself in an individual who most likely started out with an altruistic desire to help people, just like ninety-nine percent of other medical students."

"But how could that happen? I don't understand it."

"It's the unfortunate marriage of medicine and business. In the mid–twentieth century you could do well in medicine, but you really couldn't become truly wealthy. All that changed when medicine in this country did not emerge as a responsibility of government, like education or defense, as it did in most every other industrialized country. Add to that the U.S. government's inadvertently contributing to medical inflation by passing Medicare without effective cost controls, by generously subsidizing biomedical research without maintaining ownership of the resultant discoveries for the American public, and by its patent office awarding medical process patents, like for human gene sequences, which it's not supposed to do by law. I tell you, the medical patent situation in this country is a total mess, which is already starting to haunt the biomedical industry, but that's another issue.

"Unfortunately," Laurie continued, "today if a doctor wants to become truly wealthy, and a lot of them do, it is reasonably within their grasp by choosing the right specialty, getting involved in the pharmaceutical industry, the health-insurance industry, the specialty-hospital industry, or the biotech industry. All these industries say they exist to help people, which they can, but it is more of a by-product, not the goal. The goal is to make money, and do they ever."

For a few beats Lou merely stared at Laurie. Then he chuckled in a mocking manner. "Do you expect me to understand what you just said?"

"Not really," Laurie agreed. "Just take from it that I am not surprised that someone like Ben Corey could be enticed from being an individual with true interests in becoming a caring doctor to an individual whose main goal is to become a billionaire. Most, if not all, medical students are altruistic to begin with, but they are also competitive. They have to be, to get into the best college, to get into medical school, and to do the best to get the most coveted residencies to get into the best medical specialty, meaning, most likely, the one that pays the most so they can pay down their student loans the fastest. What they don't realize is that the profession in this country has drastically changed over the years, mostly because of economics."

"What about the new healthcare legislation? Isn't that going to help?"

"In a generous moment I might say it is a start. At its core, there is the goal of some sense of social equality in regard to medical care as a resource and a responsibility of government. But in this country medical care is a competitive stakeholder industry, and the new legislation doesn't change that; it just re-sorts the relative power of the stakeholders. I'm afraid the ultimate effect is going to be more pressure for costs to rise, since, like Medicare, there aren't enough specific cost controls."

"Jack, do you feel as negative as Laurie does?" Lou asked.

"Absolutely," Jack said without hesitation. "Don't get me started!"

"Let's change the subject," Laurie suggested. "What about JJ's kidnapping issue? What have you learned?"

"Well, as I mentioned when I first got here, we now know for certain it was staged specifically to get you, Laurie, off Satoshi Machita's case. Ransom demands were actually a cover for the plan. I'm also happy to report that we now have in custody the triggerman who killed Leticia. His name is Brennan Monaghan, but the person really behind the event we've now learned is one of the capos of the Vaccarro family named Louie Barbera, with whom I have had run-ins in the past. I'd be ecstatic if this episode was going to put him away, but that's not going to be the case. Once again, he's going to walk."

"How can that be?" Laurie demanded.

"From the police's perspective, it's the trouble with using the likes of CRT. As we discussed that fateful night when I introduced you to two of their principals, their primary goal is to resolve the kidnapping to the benefit of the victim and the victim's family. Their methods don't take into account that any evidence obtained illegally is unusable in a court of law, as is the situation in JJ's case. CRT found out where he was being held essentially by kidnapping and drugging a Vaccarro underling, a hardly kosher strategy from a legal perspective. It's a good thing they have such good defense attorneys; otherwise, they wouldn't still be in business."

"I'd rather have JJ back than have adhered to the niceties of the law," Laurie admitted.

"Of course you would," Lou agreed. "That's why I suggested you employ them. That advice was from me as a friend, not as a policeman. As a policeman, I wouldn't have done it, since their methods often trample constitutional rights, and such behavior is certainly not good for society as a whole over the long haul."

"What about Vinnie Amendola?" Laurie asked. "Is he still on the lam?"

"He's been back for over a week," Jack said. "We've been so caught up in the scholarship and nanny business, I forgot to tell you."

"Thanks a lot," Laurie said mockingly. "Well, what's the scoop? Is he in any kind of trouble? Did he write the threatening letter?"

"He did," Lou explained. "Ultimately, he'd been found by the authories in south Florida and brought back here to New York on a warrant. He was extremely cooperative, and no charges have been filed even though he was an accomplice of sorts. Everyone recognizes he was being extorted and in a difficult situation, fearing for the lives of his daughters and wife. On top of that, he did, after all, warn you with his letter. You're not interested in filing any charges, are you, Laurie?"

"Heavens, no," Laurie said, with an expression suggesting it was the last thing in the world she would want to do. "I'm looking forward to thanking him for trying to warn me."

At that point the waitress came with their Caesar

salads. Everyone pitched in to try to make room on the
small glass-topped wrought-iron table. When the waitress withdrew, Lou raised his wineglass.

"Let me make a short toast. To forensics and what
it can do for law enforcement! It's the one thing we
have that the bad guys don't have!"

With nods and laughter from the three friends, they
all clicked glasses for the second time.

extracts reading groups
competitions books new
books discounts extracts extracts discounts
competitions extracts reading groups discounts
books new events
reading groups new events reading groups
events books extracts discounts
new books titles reading groups
reading groups interviews
events extracts extracts events
books discounts interviews books
new books events events interviews new books extracts
reading groups books extracts events new
discounts extracts discounts books
www.panmacmillan.com
extracts events reading groups
competitions books extracts new